first
Bride
to fall

first *Bride* to fall

NEW YORK TIMES BESTSELLING AUTHOR
GINNY BAIRD

Entangled Publishing, LLC
644 Shrewsbury Commons Ave., STE 181
Shrewsbury, PA 17361
Visit our website at www.entangledpublishing.com.

Amara is an imprint of Entangled Publishing, LLC.

Edited by Heather Howland
Cover design by Bree Archer
Cover art by LightFieldStudios/Gettyimages
Interior design by Toni Kerr

Print ISBN 978-1-64937-210-9
ebook ISBN 978-1-64937-223-9

Manufactured in the United States of America

First Edition July 2022

AMARA

ALSO BY GINNY BAIRD

To my awesome girls,
Sally, Kelly, and Kaitlin,
for teaching me about daughters,

My adventuresome son,
Gordon,
for broadening my horizons,

My dear children by marriage,
Karen and Andrew,
for enriching my life,

My kids' wonderful partners,
Tom, Zach, and Brian,
for enhancing our family,

And to my amazing husband,
John,
for being there.

I love you all!

CHAPTER ONE

Nell's mom strode into the coffee shop like a woman on a mission, her boots clacking against the worn oak floor. Bearberry Brews was not yet open for business, but already, sunlight streamed through its street-facing windows and door. Exposed wood beams hung overhead, and whitewashed walls held black-and-white photos of beachy scenes. The ocean lay just beneath Majestic, Maine's cliffside perch, and its music filled the town.

"Girls, I've got great news!"

Nell stopped studying the spreadsheet on her laptop to stare at her mom. Silvery strands laced through her fawn-colored hair. She seemed to be graying more lately. Maybe the financial troubles their café had been dealing with were stressing her out more than Nell thought?

"Oh yeah?" she asked, but her sisters were oblivious. Misty was supposed to be opening the register, but she was playing on her phone. Probably texting one of the many guys in the Misty Fan Club. Charlotte, their marketing guru, sat at a table, sketching in her notebook.

Their mom cleared her throat, startling Misty into attention. "Oh hi, Mom." She stole one last peek at her phone and slid it in her hip pocket.

Nell's mom walked over to Charlotte's table and plunked her purse down beside the notebook, but Charlotte kept drawing, her hair catching the light like a raven's wing. She had her earbuds in, lost in her own world. Until her mom reached forward and plucked both of them out.

Charlotte's chin jerked up. "Uh," she said with wide blue eyes. "Is something going on?"

"Yes. There *is*."

Nell's pulse raced because she'd seen that funny look on her mom's face before. Her too-bright smile made those creases surrounding her mouth and eyes extra visible. Nell adjusted her knitted circle scarf, sweeping her long curls off of her frilly ivory collar, and privately issued a plea.

Please don't let it be about a guy. Please, please, please. Please.

During the past few months, Grace Delaney had begun prodding Nell and her sisters about settling down. She'd even tried fixing all of them up a time or two. It wasn't like any of them were *that* old—or desperate.

Their mom pursed her lips, bursting at the seams. Okay, what kind of news *was* this? Had their folks won the lottery? Or come into a windfall? That would be amazing for their struggling coffee shop and might take their mom's mind off of weddings for a while—

"One of you is getting married!"

Or not.

Nell's nerves stood on end. From her sisters' slack-jawed expressions, they were just as shocked.

"Married?" Charlotte's voice cracked. Prodding them about dating was one thing. Jumping straight into holy matrimony was something else.

Misty's pink-tinted ponytail swung sideways.

"You're joking, right?"

But wait. If this was a joke, then why wasn't her mom's mouth twitching, and where was that sparkle in her light brown eyes?

Nell's gut clenched.

"I'm not joking." Their mom scooted out a chair and sat at Charlotte's table. "My visit with Jane went better than I expected."

Misty scowled. It had been nearly two decades ago, but John Strong's betrayal still stung. By default, his wife, Jane, was equally in the sisters' bad graces.

"The fallout between our two families was John's doing," their mom cautioned, "not Jane's. And anyway, John's gone now, and Jane feels terrible about what happened. We all agree that he took advantage of your dad."

"Yeah," Charlotte grumbled. "All Dad's work made the Strongs their fortune." The man had sneakily cheated their trusting dad out of the company's lucrative international distribution rights in exchange for full ownership of this standalone café.

Their mom nodded. "Which is why Jane wants to repair things by bringing the family businesses back together again. Just as was intended when your dad and John first founded Bearberry Brews." She placed her hands on the table, displaying knuckles aged by years of kitchen work, and her meager wedding band. Their dad had never been able to afford giving her a diamond ring. "There's one small catch."

Sweat beaded Nell's hairline. Catches of any kind made her nervous.

Their mom removed her thin leather jacket and draped it over the back of her chair. "You recall Aidan?"

Ugh, yeah. Vaguely.

Charlotte grimaced. "Geeky Aidan?"

Misty pulled a face. "Ew. Him?"

Her mom rolled her eyes. "There's nothing 'geeky' about Aidan anymore. He's all grown up and a real catch, according to Jane."

Nell smirked. Nothing like a mother's love.

Misty was already running a search on her phone. "If he's so hot, why isn't he on social media? Hot, rich guys love to show that kind of thing off."

"Jane says he's very private."

"He's a *bajillionaire*." Charlotte took out her phone, and Nell used her computer. "He's got to be *somewhere*." They all typed with rapid-fire fingers, each in a race to find Aidan first.

Nell located him on the Bearberry Coffee corporate page. There was contact information for him as CEO but no photo. "You didn't get a picture of him?"

Their mom's smile wavered as she settled into the seat across from Charlotte. "He never technically stopped by, but Jane assured me he's very handsome," she quickly added. "That's why he keeps a low profile and pays techies to keep it that way. The women are all after him."

"Uh-huh," Charlotte said, sounding just as doubtful as Nell felt. Adult Aidan was likely as awkward as his kid self.

Misty rubbed the side of her nose that wasn't pierced with a silver stud. "Why are we talking about Aidan anyway?"

Nell was wondering the same thing. Her mom had walked in here bragging about great news and marriage, then suddenly switched to—

Oh noooo.

Her mom shifted in her chair. "Actually…quite a lot."

The sisters exchanged freaked-out glances.

"When John died and left his business interests to Aidan, he created a provision in his will that Bearberry Coffee has to stay in the family. It can't be sold or subdivided for a period of time."

Misty braced herself against the counter. "What if Aidan doesn't want it?"

"Oh, but he does. And he's eager to share." She motioned to the table where Nell was. "Misty," she said. "Why don't you sit with your sister?"

Misty's big hazel eyes grew larger. Rimmed with her heavy eyeliner, they looked enormous. She clearly wanted to bolt. Instead, she obeyed her mom, stepping around the counter and inching her way across the room in tiny baby steps.

Charlotte leaned back in her chair and crossed one of her cowgirl boots over the other beneath the flouncy hem of her short peasant skirt. She had great legs and was proud to show them off. Unlike Nell, who lived in stretch pants. Which was okay with her. Comfort was key.

"So," Nell asked warily. "Who exactly does Aidan plan to *share* with?"

Her mom's face lit up. "One of you! Only…" She winced. "There has to be a wedding first. Without that, the merger can't go through."

Misty groaned up at the ceiling. "I *knew* I shouldn't have come in today."

Nell gawked at her mom. "You're talking a marriage of convenience?"

"There's no reason it can't lead to love."

"And every reason that it won't!" Charlotte challenged. She anxiously stroked the crystal that dangled from a leather strap around her neck. Its calming properties didn't appear to be working at the moment. "*Mom*. What were you and Mrs. Strong thinking?"

Nell blew out a breath. "Don't forget about Aidan. He signed on for this, too."

"Yeah," Charlotte said. "Why *is* that?"

"He wants to make amends. Between the two families and the businesses. Instead of being off on its own, Bearberry Brews would assume its rightful place in the Bearberry Coffee universe." She gestured to the chalkboard on the wall behind the register displaying their cute company logo and the list of berry-infused coffees that were signatures of their brand. "We'd be secure again, all of us, and your dad…" Her voice trailed off. "Your dad might become like his old self again."

The room grew quiet at the mention of their father, the ocean's sounds penetrating through the thick stucco walls. The roiling surf and seagulls' calls cemented Nell's sorrow. Bob Delaney had never fully recovered from being conned by John Strong. He'd had trouble acknowledging the betrayal at first, but once the truth had become inescapable, he'd fallen into a funk. He lost the spring in his step and his lighthearted smile. He still was a loving dad, though. He'd do anything for his girls. Just like they would for him.

Anything, except for maybe this.

Their mom backpedaled. "Nobody's forcing anyone into this, girls. Jane and I are simply presenting
an opportunity to you kids, and Aidan's taken it.
He's not focused on romance right now anyway. He's
got corporate concerns on his plate, and other things
to keep him distracted."

"So, the marriage doesn't have to be"—Charlotte
gritted her teeth—"consummated?"

Their mom shook her head. "Nothing like that. I
mean, it's not like anyone's going to be suing anyone
in court over noncompliance. Jane said Aidan's indif-
ferent to the arrangements. His bride can lead her
life, and he'll live his. There will be some travel, of
course, and cooperation on business matters. We're
talking more of a professional partnership than a
standard marriage."

That sounded dismal to Nell. Not like the story-
book ending each of them deserved.

"How long does this 'marriage' have to last?"
Misty asked.

"At least five years," their mom said. "After that,
if there's a split, the equity in the joint businesses
will be divided evenly between the two families as
communal property."

Charlotte frowned. "Five years is a long time."

"Time that we'd be wasting," Misty said. "Where
is all this coming from? This is pretty drastic."

Their mom fidgeted with her wedding band, turning it around on her finger. "Bearberry Brews is in
worse shape than you know. Your dad and I took
out a loan to get through the rough patch last winter,
and now it's coming due."

"What?" There'd been no loan cited in Nell's

accounting data, and she kept the books. "So those cash reserves we were relying on?"

Their mom sighed and stopped messing with her ring. It had grown looser lately. She seemed to have dropped a few pounds. "Weren't actually ours at all. They were on credit from the bank."

"When do you have to pay everything back?"

"By October first."

Nell's pulse pounded in her ears. That was only a month away. "Oh Mom," she said. "I wish you'd told us sooner."

Their mom's shoulders sank. "There was nothing any of you could have done."

"But your trip to London," Charlotte said. "How did you—?"

"Jane paid for it. The ticket was her way of extending an olive branch. She didn't know how badly our shop was suffering. And it's not just the shop, I'm afraid. The loan we took out was a home equity loan. So if we can't pay it back, we might lose the house, too."

Nell's head reeled. That would be worse than just losing the business. Her parents were approaching sixty. Where else would they live, and what else could they do? If their dad's spirits were low now, it would devastate him to lose Bearberry Brews *and* their house.

This was bad. No. Terrible. Her mom normally wasn't like this. Desperation had set in. Even if the three sisters pooled their small savings and whatever personal loans they could get, it wouldn't be enough to cover the entirety of a home equity loan. They could cobble a few payments together, sure, but beyond that? The numbers didn't add up.

"I'm sorry. I realize how outlandish this sounds now. It seemed so much more logical and even exciting when I was with Jane." Their mom let out a defeated sigh. "But you're right. No matter how much Jane and I want to heal the rift between our families, you girls deserve the lives you want, not a marriage that'll go nowhere just to get rid of some loans. Please forget I even asked. Here." She extracted a business card from her purse and handed it to Charlotte.

Charlotte flipped it over, scanning some handwriting. "What's this?"

"Aidan's card. His cell number's on the back." She gave a wan smile. "I thought you might want it in case—"

"Hello, loves," their dad called out, ambling into the room from the kitchen. Bob Delaney had thick gray hair, cobalt blue eyes, and a round face that stayed permanently ruddy. "Having a little confab out here?"

Their mom sat up straighter in her chair. "Just talking. About…things."

Charlotte slid the business card into her notebook.

He studied them curiously. "Things?"

"*Dad*," Misty whined. "Why didn't you and Mom tell us about the bank loan?"

Their dad rubbed the back of his neck. "I was hoping you wouldn't have to know." He glanced at his wife. "That your mom and I would find a solution."

"Hopefully a better solution than *this*," Charlotte muttered.

Her mother glanced away, pink rising in her cheeks.

"Wait." Their dad set his hands on his hips. When he spoke, his disappointment was clear. "Please tell me you didn't pitch that cockamamie idea about Aidan?"

When she didn't answer, he shook his head. "You listen to me, girls." He glanced at each of them in turn. "I won't have it. Won't have any of it. We Delaneys have done okay for ourselves for a number of years. Through thick and through thin, we've stood by each other, and we'll find a way to survive this. A house is just a house, and this building"—his gaze swept the room—"is nothing but stucco and stone. Whereas you…" He brought a hand to his heart. "You are my flesh and blood. My *life's* blood. And not one of my precious daughters is going to marry *anyone* for anything other than love."

CHAPTER TWO

"One of us has to marry Aidan."

It had taken ten minutes for their father to stop giving the group of them suspicious looks and head back into the kitchen, taking their mom with him. Nell wouldn't want to be a fly on the wall for *that* conversation. Instead, she and her sisters hurried into the storeroom—which was actually the large walk-in pantry behind the coffee roaster—for privacy.

Nell gaped at Misty. "We most definitely do not!" she whispered. "A marriage of convenience? Are you serious?"

Charlotte tugged at her crystal. "This is bad."

"I know." Nell stepped closer, tightening their circle. Charlotte was the tallest, and Misty the short, petite one. Height-wise, Nell fell somewhere in the middle. "What are we going to do?"

"What *can* we do?" Charlotte said. "None of us wants to marry Aidan."

Misty sighed. "But what about Dad? You saw his face."

Charlotte frowned. "Do you think this is why Mom's been working so hard to fix us up?"

That registered with Nell. "Yeah, bet so. She was worried about what might happen to us if Bearberry Brews went under. We'd all be out of work then."

"We can't let them lose the business," Charlotte said.

Nell set her chin. "We can't let them lose their *house*."

The three of them stared at the hardwood floor, the tips of Misty's and Charlotte's boots pointing toward the toes of Nell's red ballerina flats. The seconds ticked by. Really, short of winning the lottery or finding buried treasure somewhere on the beach out back, there was nothing any of them could do to bring in the kind of money the bank would demand.

Charlotte was the first to look up. "Misty's right. One of us should do it."

Misty's mouth dropped open. "I— What?"

Was Charlotte volunteering? "You?"

"Not *me*. I just meant…someone."

Misty shook her head. "Not me. Nuh-uh. No way."

The two sisters looked at her.

Nell squawked. "You've *got* to be kidding me." Just because she didn't have a boyfriend or a social life and hadn't dated in forever, that didn't mean *she* should be stuck with Aidan. She wanted to see if there could be something there with Grant. Sure, she hadn't mustered up the courage to approach him yet, but she would never get a chance to if she hopped on a plane and moved to England. Even if an arranged marriage *could* help her dad and save their family business. Not to mention their family home. All of which made her feel about a billion times worse.

Charlotte shook her head. "Nell couldn't handle it. All that travel. An international lifestyle." She appeared dreamy a moment, then snapped herself out of it. "With Aidan. Right," she said, as if remembering. "In any case, it's only five years," she said. "I'm twenty-eight. So."

"You'd be out by thirty-three," Misty told her. "Still young. Ish."

Charlotte smirked. "Since you're the baby, you'd be the youngest of all."

And Nell would be the oldest. But even with that, even absolutely hating the idea, she couldn't ignore the tug on her heartstrings to take care of her sisters. That's what she'd always done. She kept track of appointments, helped balance their budgets, and had been known to grocery shop for one or the other sister a time or ten.

She'd even made both of them bagged lunches before coming into work today, something she'd done many times as a child because her parents had to get over to their coffee shop early. Neither had noticed the bags in the refrigerator yet, but when they did, they would tell her for the millionth time she didn't need to still do this—all the while devouring the food. They ran such full schedules they might not otherwise pause to eat during the workday, and Nell knew it.

Still. A girl had to draw the line somewhere.

"I've got an idea," Nell said, wanting to be fair about it. "We'll draw straws."

"Too random," Charlotte told her.

Misty crossed her arms. "That hardly gives anyone a chance."

"For what?" Nell asked her.

"For finding alternatives."

A light bulb went off in Nell's brain. "Misty," she said. "You're a genius!"

"Yeah?" Misty appeared pleased. She scrunched up her lips. "Why?"

"What if we each give ourselves a chance to find someone better?" Nell asked, her excitement growing. "Our fated match. You know, true love."

Grant was the only man she wanted. He seemed kind and intelligent and accomplished, owning a camping store right here in town. And boy, was he sexy. All she had to do was get him to notice her and then move things along from there. Assuming he was interested.

Her stomach knotted as she acknowledged the risk. What if she braved it and went after him, and then he sent her packing? At least then she'd know for sure that a relationship with Grant was off the table. She'd been too scared to learn the truth until now, but that was before this clock started ticking.

Misty clucked her tongue. "Yes! If any of us can do better than Aidan, we will."

"That's a very tight timeline," Charlotte warned. "We'd each have to find ourselves a guy before October first. That's thirty days."

"Not just *find* him," Nell said. "Pin him down." Her mind took a flirty road trip that involved her pinning Grant to the ground, after they'd been play-wrestling or something. Their hearts would be beating…she'd look in his eyes…then maybe he'd make the first move and kiss her. Her pulse hummed.

Nell shook off the heated thoughts and scanned their faces. "I'm talking an engagement, and I don't mean any kind of fakey one, either. It has to be authentic for any of us to get out of marrying Aidan."

"Right," Charlotte said. She glanced at Nell, then at Misty. "We'll need accountability, so we know an actual marriage is planned."

Nell spied a stack of old newspapers that they sometimes used as packing material when stowing things away. "How about an announcement in the Seaside Daily?"

Charlotte's face lit up. "That's perfect, Nell. Once it's announced in there, there's no turning back."

Misty nodded. "Everyone in town will know. So."

"So. There's your accountability," Nell concluded.

"Okay then," Charlotte said. "How about we make a deal? Whichever one of us has *not* found true love by September thirtieth—"

"*And* become publicly engaged," Misty put in.

Charlotte nodded. "And become publicly engaged—"

"Then *she'll* be the one to bite the bullet and marry Aidan." This all sounded reasoned out enough to Nell, but a small issue niggled at her. "But...what if we all find alternate husbands by then?"

Misty shrugged. "I say after the first two of us get engaged, it's game over."

"Yeah," Charlotte said. "The last sister standing is who'll get to be Aidan's bride. For the sake of the business."

"And the family," Misty added. "We're doing this for Dad—and Mom."

Nell held her breath, hoping they were doing the right thing. Then she recalled the distressed look on her mom's face and the sadness in her dad's eyes, and she was certain they were. Five years wasn't an eternity. Not even for her, at thirty and the oldest.

But losing their business and their home would destroy both of her parents indefinitely.

"Okay," Nell said. "Then, we're all agreed?" Her sisters viewed her askance, and Nell knew what they were thinking. Charlotte and Misty were counting on the fact that Nell would be the one to marry Aidan in the end. But all was fair in love and war, and she didn't intend to go down without a fight. Her Prince Charming was out there, and while the odds of him being Aidan Strong were incredibly slim, the likelihood of him owning an outdoorsy store in Majestic was somewhat better.

She hoped.

"Agreed," Charlotte said.

Misty's eyes shone. "Agreed."

She whipped out her phone and stared at Charlotte, who was ready. She slid Aidan's card out from between the pages of the notebook she'd set on a shelf and read the number aloud while Misty typed it in.

Nell frowned. "Wait. What are you doing?"

She pressed send, and her phone whooshed. "It's already done!" She turned her phone around and showed them her text.

Heard about the deal. We're in!
Will let you know who in 30 days.
50-50 share after five years.
No fringe benefits.
Misty, Charlotte, and Nell

Nell gulped. "He's going to think we're money-hungry just like the women he's avoiding online."

"No," Charlotte said. "He's going to see this as an opportunity for him to do the right thing, just like his mom promised ours."

Misty's cell dinged, and she stared down at it.

Nell's heart hammered.

"Well?" Charlotte asked.

"We have our answer." Misty shot them a cock-eyed grin.

Brilliant. Yes and yes.

Charlotte blinked. "Wait. Thirty days? That won't be soon enough. Not in time to get Mom and Dad that loan payment by October first."

"It will be if we can get Aidan to wire some of the money," Misty suggested.

"Right," Nell said. "Like a bridge loan until the actual merger? There's usually a grace period for loan payments. So if he's able to send the money quickly, Mom and Dad could still avoid default."

Charlotte thought on this. "Yeah, but he'd have to agree."

Misty was already typing. "I'll ask him."

A couple of minutes later, he answered.

Just say how much and when.

Nell and her sisters gawked at each other, the seriousness of their situation sinking in.

OMG. We're really going to do this.

Nell broke a sweat.

One of us is going to marry Aidan Strong.

And it's not going to be me.

The storeroom door popped open, and dark-haired, gray-eyed Lucas Reyes appeared taken aback. Their nice-looking café manager had started working at Bearberry Brews as a teen and was almost like a part of their family.

"Uh. Hello, ladies? Just coming in to grab

some…filters."

"Hey, Lucas," Charlotte said.

Misty shared a little wave and scooted along behind Charlotte. "Morning!"

Lucas met Nell's eyes. "Everything okay in here?"

"Ah. Yep. Just, um…planning our September." She smiled at his handsome face with that three-day beard, wondering if things would be simpler if he was her type.

But he wasn't. And she doubted that she was his.

Her mind was already whirling with ideas about someone else, anyway. While she'd put off pursuing Grant Williams for years, she no longer had the luxury of waiting another second. If she wanted to turn her secret dream of being with him into a reality, she had to wake up and smell the coffee—and get busy doing something about that. *Now*.

CHAPTER THREE

After the café closed at six, Nell grabbed her laptop and a corner table to do some online snooping. Ever since her private chat with her sisters, she'd been thinking about that bet. By lunchtime, she'd made up her mind. She was going to reach out to Grant by signing up for one of those outdoorsy adventures he led.

Lucas was the first to leave after cleaning out the coffee roaster. It was Friday and his weekly job. "Catch ya later!" Nell looked up to find his gaze lingering on Misty, but Misty was turning chairs upside down and setting them on tables, focused on her work.

"Bye, Lucas," Nell said. "See you Monday." She was grateful to have tomorrow off. That fit perfectly with her plan of getting to know Grant better in person.

"Nite, Lucas!" Charlotte called, wielding the handle of a wide-angled broom.

Their barista, Mei-Lin, picked up her purse from behind the counter, her coal-black hair grazing her shoulders. "I'm out of here, too."

Mei-Lin Chen and Misty had been best friends since middle school. When they were kids, Mei-Lin had spent so much time at the Delaneys', their dad had joked he had four daughters, not three. Only-child Mei-Lin hadn't minded. She'd loved being a part of their household.

She shot Misty a look through her frameless glasses and wiggled her eyebrows like she knew something. "Save you a stool at Mariner's?" she asked, mentioning the nearby bar belonging to the fancy seafood restaurant.

"Yep!" Misty answered. "See you there."

Charlotte stopped sweeping. "Misty?" she gasped once Mei-Lin had gone. "You *didn't*."

"We said we wouldn't tell Mom and Dad, not friends."

Nell sighed. Their bet would be all over Majestic if they weren't more careful about it. Then again, she couldn't really blame Misty. She and Mei-Lin were super close.

"Just be sure she doesn't tell anyone else," Nell advised.

Misty folded her arms in front of her. "She won't."

Charlotte glanced at Nell's computer. "What are you doing over there, anyway?"

She'd located Grant on various social media platforms, but the only one he seemed to update regularly was his Instagram. It was more of a professional account for his store, Blue Sky Adventures, but still. There were some new photos of him scattered among the others of impressive wilderness scenes. He looked as gorgeous as ever with that wavy blond hair and a solid build, fine-tuned from all that mountain climbing and whatnot he did.

Nell clicked the link to his camping store, trying to pick out her adventure. The sooner she saw him the better, and signing up for one of his outings was a great excuse. It was also a super way to prove to him that she was his kind of back-to-nature girl.

Although it was true she didn't spend huge amounts of time outdoors doing adventuresome stuff, she'd always admired those who did. She was also very good at being green.

Hey. She recycled.

She browsed through various excursion options, but some looked too daunting. She wasn't up for risking life or limb. She just wanted a chance to catch Grant's eye and get a little conversation going about the future. The very *immediate* future.

She clicked on a photo of a campfire. Camping might be fun. But there weren't any more camping trips scheduled until the end of the month, and she couldn't wait until then. Rappelling seemed too dicey for someone who hadn't trained for it. Whoa. Whitewater rafting, too. Seeing as how she got seasick on ferries, that was definitely out.

But wait. Hiking seemed easy. It couldn't be that different from walking, and Nell walked everywhere in Majestic. All she needed were some sporty clothes. She could buy those tonight. She registered for the next hiking trip, which started bright and early in the morning, and a confirmation bubble popped up before she got redirected to the homepage. A large colorful photo of Grant wearing a big grin and sunglasses greeted her. He was in a T-shirt and a life vest and held a paddle, looking amazingly handsome.

"You're going kayaking?" Misty asked over her shoulder, causing Nell to jump.

"No." Nell shut her laptop, but Charlotte set a restocked napkin holder on the table and pried the screen right back open. Where had the two of them come from? They must have sneaked up on her while she'd been filling out forms.

"That's Grant Williams," Charlotte said, drooling over his photo. "*Nice*."

"Hey!" Even though it was true, she didn't need her sister ogling Grant. That was *her* job.

Misty's eyes danced as she sashayed toward the kitchen. "Still mooning over Grant? Gee, Nell, you'd think after *all this time* you'd have finally done something about him."

This got Nell's dander up. "Who says I haven't?"

Misty tossed her dirty rag into a bussing bucket, then spun on her heel. "What?"

Charlotte, who'd begun walking away, turned as well. "You and Grant? Seriously?"

Nell's pulse fluttered nervously. "Well, we *are* meeting up tomorrow," she said. "Truth is, if things go as well as I think they will, I might no longer be a part of this bet."

Misty rolled her eyes. "It's about time. You've knitted him all that stuff every year for his birthday."

"But never gave any of it to him." Charlotte frowned. "You sold it all on Etsy."

Misty smirked. "Because you chickened out."

Accurate. "Did not."

"Did *so*." Charlotte made an irritating clucking sound and flapped her elbows like wings, acting like a big old momma hen scolding her young.

Nell huffed and started packing up her stuff. Maybe her secret crush hadn't been quite so secret. And maybe she *had* been too scared to follow her heart before. But all of that went out the window the second her mom walked into the café this morning.

"Okay, well, who's to say I won't give Grant his birthday present *this* year?" She slid on her plush purple jacket, sensing her sisters' doubt, and that irked her no end. "Neither of you thinks I can do it, do you?"

"I believe you can do anything you set your mind to, Nell." Charlotte patted her shoulder and then said, "But that doesn't mean I won't do something that'll win me this bet first."

Misty squared her small shoulders. "I think you ladies are in for a contest. Nell might have hidden her connection to Grant, but I've got my connections, too. Really hot ones."

Charlotte slipped into her long cardigan sweater, cinching its belt. "And I've got a guy or two up my sleeve." She shook out her arms and winked. "Maybe more."

"You two go right on ahead," Nell said, her irritation building. "Because I'm pretty sure that I'm going to land Grant first."

"Okay," Charlotte said, "but that's going to take more than one date."

Nell bristled. "Who says it's only one date?"

Misty set a hand on her hip. "You did. You said you're seeing him tomorrow."

"Yes, I am. That doesn't mean I haven't seen him before. Or that I won't also be seeing him the day after, and the one after that. You have no idea how long things have been going on or how close Grant and I have gotten."

Charlotte gave a teasing scoff. "Uh-huh. Well, you're going to have to find a way to wrap things up—quickly—if you're going to beat the two of us."

Nell bit her tongue.

Her sisters' skepticism only inspired her to want to try harder.

Extra hard. Harder than extra hard, even.

Why oh why had she suggested this plan?

Because she deserved every bit as much happiness as Charlotte and Misty, that's why. She'd never had half their luck with guys. Charlotte was always on a new boyfriend, and Misty went through men like candy. Whereas Nell had had one—count it: *one*—serious relationship. That had ended in disaster because it had only been serious on her side.

"I suppose we'll see," Nell finally said.

"Yeah," Charlotte replied coyly. "I guess we will."

Charlotte switched off the lights, and they were just about to leave when Nell's phone dinged. She stared down at the two incoming text messages from Grant. One provided directions to the hiking site, and the other delivered a liability form for her to e-sign and return.

"Who's that?" asked Misty.

"Grant." Nell lifted her chin. "Confirming for tomorrow."

Charlotte blinked at Misty. "She's actually going out with him."

"*Yeah, she is*," Nell said, speaking for herself.

Misty's eyebrows knitted together like she couldn't quite believe it. "So, you and Grant are what now? Dating?"

Nell was so annoyed, she couldn't resist embellishing. "We're practically exclusive!" They'd have to be *at least* that shortly if they were going to be engaged by month's end. Nell's stomach did a queasy flip-flop. She really had her work cut out for her.

Charlotte's jaw dropped. "You. Exclusive? With Grant?"

She hadn't *totally* lied. She'd inserted that "practically" in there.

Meaning almost. Not quite.

New attraction coming soon!

She hoped.

Because there was nothing she wanted more than Grant actually falling in love with her. In a real way. With his whole heart. Not pretend.

Nell licked her dry lips. Pretty hard to walk back that dating thing now. What's more, she didn't want to. How dare Charlotte and Misty be so judgy, assuming that naturally Nell would fail and they would win their bet. "I said *practically*. Meaning things are looking good."

She flashed Grant's first text in their direction.

"See?" Nell grinned. "He's all-in."

Looking forward to it!

G.

Misty scanned the message. "Looks like he's all-in for something." She stared up at Nell. "What's the link?"

"Directions," Nell said calmly, even though her heart was beating a million times a minute. She dumped her cell back in her purse. "We're meeting up at a *very romantic* spot." She decided not to mention they'd have nine other hikers tagging along as chaperones.

Charlotte's eyes widened. "Wow, Nell. Way to go."

"Yeah," Misty said. "Nice going."

Nell swallowed past the lump in her throat.

Operation First Bride, here I come.

CHAPTER FOUR

Grant took a head count by the trailhead in the parking lot.

Only nine so far, and ten had signed up for this hike.

His buddy Jordan Caldwell leaned toward him. "How much longer should we wait?" Jordan was Grant's assistant manager at his camping store. He also occasionally tagged along on adventures to lend support, like he was doing today.

Grant checked his watch. "Let's give Eleanor D. five more minutes." Then they'd need to get things moving, with or without her. It was already fifteen minutes past their designated meet time, and the others were getting impatient.

The two younger couples were staying at the Majestic B&B. Big-city people out for a fun adventure, who were obviously growing chilly in the cold coastal air. The Gomez family had their RV registered at the nearby campground. Both of their teenage daughters appeared bored, standing close together and several feet away from their parents.

The only Zen one in the bunch was the young guy in a bucket hat and with the mega-beard. He wore hiking boots with shorts and a tie-dye shirt under his jacket. He kept his eyes closed, steadying himself on his trekking poles. Either he was very at home in nature or way hungover from partying the night before.

Grant scanned the partly cloudy sky, then checked the weather app on his phone. There was only a slight chance of rain later, and they should be up and back from their circuit hike in plenty of time. He'd asked people to bring rain gear just in case it started drizzling, but a few raindrops shouldn't really affect their short hike.

A faded red sedan screeched into the parking lot, scattering gravel.

"Uhhh," Jordan said under his breath. "What's *that*?"

The car was a foreign make with several dings and dents in its doors and one end of its front bumper drooping. The driver pulled into a parking place, and the driver's side door popped open. A bundle of hot pink emerged. The person slammed shut the car door and searched the area, locating the group.

"A woman." Grant blinked. "I think."

She wore bubblegum pink running leggings and neon pink ankle boots that didn't look like they were made for hiking. A pompom bounced on her pink flamingo hat, her long brown curls tumbling past—what? A dead pheasant attached to her ski jacket? The jacket was also pink. Of course.

"That collar has got to be fake," Jordan whispered.

Given that it was fuchsia and feathery, probably so.

"Sorry I'm late!" she called, trudging in their direction. "Got turned around."

She huffed and puffed, her ragged breath clouding the morning air.

If crossing the parking lot left her winded, Grant

worried about her capacity for taking this hike. It was only a moderate one. But still.

Gauging by her outfit, she'd never been hiking before.

At least not in any serious way.

The closer she got, though, the more familiar she seemed. "Eleanor D.?"

"Yeah, I—"

"Wait." He knew in a flash of her big brown eyes. Brownish eyes with hints of gold around the irises. She also had really long eyelashes. Somehow those caught his attention. "You're Nell Delaney, right?" She was the one he'd been in high school with? Also the one who worked at her folks' shop, Bearberry Brews?

A rosy hue swept her cheeks and the bridge of her nose, which was lightly freckled. Her freckles matched the cinnamon highlights in her hair. "That's me!"

Grant scratched the side of his head, and then he got it. So, Nell was her nickname. He'd never thought much about it one way or another. Or her. Until now. That she was here. Looking so much like a fish out of water, but also—a little weirdly—amazingly adorable. His neck warmed because he didn't typically weigh the cuteness of women in his adventure groups. That would be unprofessional. Which was why he wasn't doing it now. Absolutely. Not.

She waved at Jordan and then the others. "Hi, everyone! I'm sorry I held things up."

"No worries." Jordan nodded. "Jordan Caldwell."

"He's helping lead the hike," Grant explained. "And I'm—"

"Grant, I know." She gave him a sly smile, and his stomach did a little twirl. What? Seriously? "I mean, it's pretty obvious. Your photos are all over your website."

He cleared his throat, reminding himself of his role. Polite. Professional. *Not at all interested in her.* "Weren't you and I in school together?"

Her cheeks turned pink. "Yeah. I didn't think you'd remember."

He did all right. He'd seen her in the halls, but she'd not been in his class. She was maybe a year or two younger. She looked different now, like she'd come into her own as a confident woman. They'd never really spoken when he'd gone into her parents' shop to pick up some baked goods or maybe a hot tea, but she'd seemed really poised in her job. She'd been a bit awkward as a teen but had grown out of that. Obviously. As evidenced by her confident smile. And her very direct gaze.

His heart hammered.

"Um, yeah. Sure do." He raked a hand through his hair. "You started some kind of knitting club, right?"

Her face brightened. "I did."

"Still at it?"

She laughed and pointed to the scarf wrapped around her neck. "Yep."

Adorable and talented. Nope. He was *not* going there. Especially not with all the others around. "Well, good work," he quipped. "Keep at it."

"That's my goal!" She grinned, and his neck burned extra hot. He turned to Jordan, who raised his eyebrows. Jordan always picked up on things and would give him a hard time about this later. Women sometimes hit on Grant. Sure. He was used to it. But he never thought of returning the favor. Until about five seconds ago. But he wouldn't. No way.

Nell caught them exchanging a look, and her color deepened. Maybe Grant had it wrong and it was Jordan she was into, not him? Not surprising, really, since ladies always liked Jordan with his deep brown skin and warm, always smiling eyes. Which was fine, of course. It wasn't like Grant was in the market for a relationship, especially not one with Nell. Even as cute and talented as she was. He was perfectly happy dating once in a while but otherwise keeping to himself. Girlfriends and him? Bad mix.

He rubbed his hands together and glanced around. "We'll get started in a minute," he told the group. "Last call for facilities and all that." He thumbed toward the rustic restroom building beyond a split-rail fence.

One of the teenagers held up her hand. "How long is the hike?"

"Round trip, about two to two and a half hours, depending on how long we stay to admire the views." He grinned. "Coming down will take half as long as going up. The incline's kind of steep."

The teen tugged at her sister's arm, and they departed for the bathroom. A few of the others did, too.

The Zen guy opened his eyes and leaned into his trekking poles. "We're leaving?"

"Not yet," Jordan told him. "In a sec."

"Cool." He slid on his sunglasses and waited.

Grant turned toward Nell.

"Thanks, I'm fine." Her smile alarmed him because it was…warming. He tried to shake off the feeling, but it clung to him like the heat from a campfire after an icy rain. He'd thought for a minute she was interested in Jordan, but her gaze was glued on him. For whatever reason, that pleased him. Not that he was normally in competition with Jordan.

He studied Nell's outfit and its mixed-sporty vibe. It looked like she hadn't been able to decide if she was going running or skiing this morning. And those flashy moon boots were definitely not meant for mountain trails. "I didn't know you were a hiker."

"Oh. Um." She nervously fiddled with a lock of her hair. "Yes. Yeah, I'm really into it."

He suppressed a chuckle. If she'd been on a hike a day in her life, he'd be shocked. He glanced down at her boots. "Those got tread?"

Her forehead wrinkled. "You mean this?" She lifted one foot behind her to show him, and it was pretty much what he'd guessed. Those boots were all for fashion and not about serious work. The sole also had a price sticker on it from a local discount store.

At least the ground was dry.

"These *are* okay, right?" She fretfully scanned his eyes. "They're new."

"I'm sure they'll be fine," he said kindly. "The terrain's pretty forgiving, except for that scramble near the top."

She swallowed hard. "Scramble?"

"I'll grab the rope." Jordan headed to the boulder where they'd left their gear. He picked up the coil of rope and slung it over his shoulder, tossing the daypack to Grant, who caught it.

Nell's eyes widened as she watched their exchange. "There's a *rope*?"

This time, Grant couldn't help but laugh. She seemed fairly freaked about the particulars of this trip. Definitely not a regular hiker. Far from it. He slid the straps of his daypack over his shoulders and winked at her. "We're taking it just in case we need it for the summit. Most should be fine without it, though."

"But I thought this was a moderate hike?"

"Moderate enough." Grant cocked his head at Nell, unable to resist teasing her. She seemed to be putting on a big act, and he had no clue why. He was kind of intrigued to find out. "You did sign the waiver?"

"Yeah." She bit her bottom lip.

"Then we're golden."

Trepidation was written in her eyes, but Nell had nothing to be concerned about. Both he and Jordan were experts at leading hikes, and this was a very basic one.

Why had she signed up for this outing to begin with? None of the Delaneys were adventuresome, as far as he knew. But hey—who was he to argue with someone's newfound interest in the great outdoors? Apart from the sticker on her boot, she had a price tag dangling from the back of her ski jacket, but he decided not to mention that part. Jordan saw it, though, and sent him the side-eye. In response, Grant held in another chuckle and shook his head.

He detected a faint mossy scent in the air, a smell that he'd learned often portended rain, which was odd, since every weather app he'd checked had said any precipitation would hold off until later. Worst-case scenario, if things got wet, they could always skip the scramble at the top. "We'd best get going," he announced once everyone had returned.

Grant took the lead and headed up the trail first. Jordan would bring up the rear, corralling any stragglers so they wouldn't be left behind. Judging by her uneasy gait in those obviously not-yet-broken-in boots, Grant suspected that their principal straggler would be Nell.

"Should I follow them? Or?" he could hear Nell ask Jordan.

"Yeah," his friend said. "I'll be right behind you."

Grant smiled to himself. She was cute and quirky in those very pink clothes of hers, and he couldn't wait to find out what she was really doing here. Maybe she had challenged herself to try something new? He certainly couldn't fault her for that. In fact, he kind of admired her for stepping out of her comfort zone. If more people did that, this world would be a much more interesting place.

• • •

Nell peered over the ledge of the precipice in horror as rain came down in droves. Her clothing was soaked, and her boots were muddy. Plus, she suspected her mascara was rushing like rivers down both sides of her face.

How had this happened?

One minute, the group was up on the perfectly dry summit, admiring the amazing far-off ocean views. A split-second later, thunder boomed and the heavens opened up in a startling downpour. Everyone had been surprised, including Grant, apparently, who'd grumbled under his breath to Jordan something about weather apps being unreliable.

This entire hike had been a fiasco. She hadn't had a second alone with Grant, much less the opportunity for a private conversation. She'd tried to catch up with him on the trail, but he'd kept moving so briskly, like a trailblazer in an adventure film, jovially leading the way. Meanwhile, she'd hobbled along in her too-tight and pinching boots, which only seemed to fit worse when she was going uphill, rubbing uncomfortably at her toes and ankles.

When they'd finally gotten to the rocky stretch of the trail on a steep incline, she'd hoped Grant would at least be the one to give her a boost in getting over some of the larger boulders. But no. He'd scrambled to the top of the summit first, leaving Jordan at the bottom to give people a leg up. Jordan was extremely nice-looking and kind. He just wasn't Grant. He had been very encouraging, though, and Nell had surprised herself by making it to the top along with the others. It wasn't a huge climb. Only ten feet or so.

It looked a lot more daunting from up here looking down.

"Nell," Grant said from beside her. "Nell, can you hear me?"

She stared at him numbly and nodded. The other hikers had already descended and were huddled by a thicket of pines. As a safety measure, since things were slick, Jordan had secured the rope to a sturdy tree on the summit while Grant instructed the group on doing what he called an arm rappel. The idea was to align the rope behind your back and tuck it under both armpits before wrapping your arms around it and latching on with both hands.

You then were supposed to descend gradually while keeping a grip on the rope, and it was strictly one-at-a-time. Jordan coached people down from the bottom, and Grant stayed at the top, lending his encouragement, too. Everyone seemed to get this easily except for Nell, who hadn't been able to stop trembling since she first peered over the edge.

The teenagers shivered, and everyone looked miserable standing in the rain. The temperature had dropped by at least ten degrees, and Nell was freezing, too.

The only thing was her legs wouldn't move. Neither would her mouth.

This clearly wasn't an intro-to-romance moment.

It was more like a "Survivor" one.

Grant checked his sports watch and then the sky. "You need to lead the others back," he told Jordan. "If you're going to beat the bridge."

She gaped at Grant. "What's wrong with the bridge?"

"It tends to wash out in heavy rains."

Nell's heart pounded. That did not sound good.

Jordan sent Grant a worried look.

"We'll be right behind you," Grant said to Jordan. He glanced at Nell, and she involuntarily backed up a step. It wasn't like she was trying to be difficult. She'd never been one for heights, and the climb down looked a lot steeper than it had going up, especially with all that rainwater rushing down across those boulders and making them slippery.

Lightning crackled across the sky, and the Gomez dad eyed the path. He sent his wife a pointed look, then glanced at their girls. Everyone else was obviously eager to move on, and she didn't blame them. The situation was dicey here and getting worse by the minute.

"Nell." Grant's husky voice was a whisper. "You can do this, and I'm going to help you."

"Help me where? Into a nosedive? I've never been great with heights. Never ever ever."

"Nobody's nosediving here," he said calmly. "It's a short descent. Easy-peasy."

"Easy-peasy for you to say! You've done this a billion times!"

"You can do it, too. It's not that far. I'll go first and spot you."

A lump lodged in her throat. His soothing tones were doing very little to calm her. Okay. Maybe they were helping somewhat.

"Nell. Look at me."

She didn't want to, but she did.

Grant shared a confident smile. "You've got this."

She locked on his dreamy brown gaze, seriously wanting to believe it. This was so not the fun adventure she'd anticipated. If she didn't risk the climb down, though, she'd wind up dying up here anyway. Single and unloved. Romantically unloved, that was. At least she wouldn't have to marry Aidan then. That would mean she wouldn't get a chance with Grant, either, and she needed for that to happen. After the brave front she'd put on for her sisters, she couldn't shy away from this challenge now.

Operation First Bride was in full play.

Only it wasn't exactly working out swimmingly.

It was more like she was drowning in it.

"I'll send you a text when we make it down," Grant called down to Jordan. "If you don't hear from me shortly, call the park rangers."

The *park rangers*? If she wasn't so cold, she'd have flushed with embarrassment. She was making such a mess of things. Still, she couldn't move. Her heart pounded, and her palms felt damp. But of course they were. She was standing in the pouring rain. Maybe she was having a panic attack.

The group peeled away with Jordan in the lead, and Nell experienced a sudden shock of abandonment. But it was okay. Things were okay. Grant was still with her.

He ran a hand through his damp hair. The man was hotness personified from his wet jacket to his saturated khaki-colorcd hiking pants, his plastered-to-his-body clothing hugging his rock-hard frame. Oof. If she wasn't so terrified, she'd be drooling.

One of the coupled-up women waved enthusiastically to Grant. So did her friend. The Gomez mom shared an equally smitten-looking wave. Oh well. Nell couldn't fault them for their taste. She also couldn't help but notice that Grant hadn't picked up on any of the fan-girl adoration. Well, good. Because the only person's adoration Grant needed to pay attention to was hers. Once she figured out how to appeal to him.

She was obviously failing at that now with her freak-out-in-nature moment. But it wasn't her fault about the heights. She knew she had her limitations around lighthouses and such, but she'd never scaled a mountain. So this element of fear was brand new. Still. She was *not* giving up. Charlotte's annoying hen imitation came back to her. Or, chickening out.

Thunder clapped again, and the group hastily retreated, disappearing down the rocky trail. Rainwater rushed in rivulets, their footsteps kicking up mud splatter as they went.

Nell's panic spiked.

She was going to be trapped up here indefinitely. With Grant. Which meant, when she ultimately died of hypothermia, she'd be bringing him down with her. Not an ideal way to begin—or end—a happy relationship, with both of them drenched and shivering. He might never even want to talk to her again after this. Assuming they made it down alive.

"Here's what we're going to do," Grant said, bending enough to meet her eyes, his hands on her shoulders. Likely to keep her steady. "I'll go down first, and you follow. If you slip or anything, I'll be there to catch you, and hey, it's not even that big of a drop."

Nell nodded. That didn't sound too bad. She could do this.

Maybe.

If they went really, really slowly.

Grant nodded, then released her. As she watched, he wrapped the rope around his back, bent his knees, and eased himself over the rocky ledge, stabilizing himself with the rope.

"Now, you come next," he instructed once he'd reached the bottom. "Get the rope around your back like I showed you. Good." When she had it positioned the right way, he nodded. "Get down low first when you're coming off the summit."

She inched toward the ledge, and her knees shook. "My dad always says, just because someone *tells you* to jump off a cliff—"

He full-on chuckled. "You're not jumping."

"Feels like!"

She bent her knees, and moisture seeped through her running pants, chilling her. She never would have picked them out for the hike if she'd had any idea how uncomfortable they were. She'd kind of assumed they be like leggings. But no, they were tighter—everywhere. And not at all waterproof. Cold rain prickled her cheeks as she scooted backward toward the ledge, peering over her shoulder.

"You're doing great. Keep going."

She did, but her movement must have been imperceptible, because Grant said, "Nell?"

"I'm trying!"

He inhaled deeply below her. "Okay. It's okay. You're doing fine," he said kindly. "Like I said, it's a very short way down."

She swallowed hard and inched along.

"Great," he said. "Now, keep coming. Little by little easing your grip on the rope."

She accomplished that, too, but her whole body shook. He'd said he'd catch her, but what if she slipped right through his arms and landed on her head?

"Nice going," he said. "You're almost there."

She followed his instructions, her pulse thudding in her ears. She felt dizzy but fought it.

Grant was there. Right there beneath her. Things

would be fine.

Nooo. Things were *slippery* and *wet.*

One of her boots lost its grip on a rock; then the other did, too.

Her legs shot out from under her, and Nell spun sideways, clinging to the rope. It burned through her grip, stinging her palms—

She yelped and let go.

"Nell!"

But it was too late to stop it.

She was falling.

CHAPTER FIVE

Grant seized Nell around her middle with one strong arm, and her back slammed into his chest, taking the backward tumble.

Oomph!

They hit the ground with a *thud* in a curtain of rain.

Pain spread across his back and shoulders as her body weight crushed into him. Since she was barely half his size, he could take it. He'd still pay for it later with some bruising.

It was good they'd landed on soft earth versus rock, which is why he and Jordan had positioned the rope where they had as a safety measure. The ground was even softer now thanks to the rain, with huge puddles spreading everywhere.

"Hey," he asked hoarsely. "Are you all right?"

"Yeah. I'm…fine." She squirmed in his embrace, flipping around, and suddenly they were face to face, her chest bearing down on his.

A blush swept her cheeks, and his heart stuttered.

"Good," Grant rasped. "That's good. I'm glad you're not hurt."

Her breathing went rough and ragged, pulsing through her kissable lips, and he nearly lost his mind. She was so soft and smelled like…heaven. All sweet and summery like a honeysuckle vine. And she was tangled around him.

Heat coursed through his veins, despite the

drowning rain. He hadn't been with a woman in a while, and everything about Nell was hitting him hard. Who knew what had possessed her to come on this hike, but even laying in a puddle and covered in mud, he was grateful for it. He wanted to kiss her.

Which, considering their circumstances, meant he needed to get a grip. *Immediately.* He came to his senses with a jolt. "Should we, uh…?"

Apparently so did she. "Ah, yep!" Right. You couldn't get more awkward than that.

She blinked and scrambled off him, standing too fast. Her right foot slid, and her knee buckled. "Argh! *Oooh.* Oh nooo."

Grant sat bolt upright, regaining his focus. Raindrops raced down his face and streaked from his hair. He frowned. "What happened?"

She placed her right foot on the ground, then picked it up again. She moaned. "My ankle. I think I did something to it."

"Hang on, I'll take a look."

"What?"

"I'm a certified Wilderness First Responder."

A thunderclap boomed, startling her, and she accidentally put too much pressure on her right foot again. She cried out, and Grant's stomach sank. "Don't move." He pulled himself upright, and the ground gave a nasty sucking sound as he broke free from the mud.

His clothes were drenched, and his whole back was caked in muck.

He shook himself off and strode over to her, nabbing his waterproof daypack as he went. Every inch of him smarted. He motioned to a nearby rock under an outcropping. They needed that shelter from the rain so he could examine her and tend to any injuries. He led her by the elbow, and she hopped along on her left foot, trying not to slip again. "Just take it easy," he cautioned. "We'll get there."

Nell sat on the rock looking pitifully drenched, and his soul ached for her. He hated that this had happened on his watch. He was always so careful, and he was grateful he'd broken her fall. He couldn't have predicted what came afterward…or her reaction to him.

Had she felt the same chemistry? Is that why she bolted up so quickly? Regardless, on account of him, she'd made a misstep and gotten hurt. He was hoping not too seriously.

"How's your head feeling?"

She rubbed the back of her head, the part that had rammed into his chin. Her pompom hat had softened some of the blow, but not enough of it. "A little sore back here."

"Anything else hurting?"

She scanned her wet jacket, extending her arms. "No. It's just the ankle."

"Okay. I'm going to need to take a look at it." He pinched her boot's toe box. "That hurt?"

She shook her head. He then gingerly rotated her ankle by manipulating her boot, tilting it ever so slightly upward, downward, then side to side.

"Ow! *Ow*. Ow—ow, ow, Grant! *Stop*."

"Sorry." He undid her Velcro bootstraps and slid it off. He had to check for localized sensitivity and discoloration. "I'm going to need to remove this sock. Okay?"

She grimaced. "Okay."

He examined her bare foot and ankle for any visual signs of trauma, noting the adorable bright yellow polish on her toes. The cheerful little splashes of color were unexpectedly endearing. He grinned up at her. "Nothing's broken."

"You sure?"

"Ninety percent."

"Ninety?"

"Does it hurt now?"

"Yeah, it's throbbing."

"But worse when you step on it?" She nodded, and he produced some athletic tape from his kit. "I think you've just rolled it. Did it hurt before you, um, stood up?"

"No, not till then." She shrugged sheepishly, looking so adorable in a sopping wet way. He needed to get her out of here and to shelter fast.

"Which side hurts more?" He pressed lightly at her ankle bones, and when he touched the outer one she sucked air through her teeth.

"Got it." He gently straightened her foot at ninety degrees. "Can you keep your foot still like that?" She nodded, and he wrapped her ankle with the athletic tape using three stirrups, three Js, and three figure eights, covering her ankle bones and instep to provide stability. "You're doing great," he said, finishing up. "Can you wiggle your toes for me?"

She moved them just fine, her nail polish flashing like small rays of sunshine in the gloomy rain. He checked his tape job to ensure there were no gaps.

"You'll need to stay off this for a day or so, and ice it. If it starts getting worse instead of better, I'd check in with a doctor." He eased her boot back on, securing the Velcro loosely. "I'd better drive you home. You got someone who can come back for your car?"

"Yeah, my sisters."

He'd seen them before. Not in school, since they were younger than Nell, but around town. Both also worked at the coffee shop and were very attractive women. Neither one exactly had Nell's charm, though. "Charlotte and Missy, right?"

"Misty," she corrected with a smile. "For Michelle."

He chuckled. "Your folks were big on nicknames, huh?"

"Not too big. Charlotte's still Charlotte."

"That's a good name. Solid."

Her lips twitched. "And Nell is…?"

"Musical," he finished, surprising himself when he said it, because it rang true.

"Well, I like Grant. It's rugged." She swung a fist through the air, and he laughed.

"Thanks. I think." He glanced at the rope, knowing he needed to retrieve it. "This will only take a sec." He untied one of the end knots and tugged at a section of the rope until the rest of it fell free, tumbling off the overhang.

She blanched. "Just like that?"

He chuckled at her worried look. "Takes practice."

"I guess you've practiced a lot."

He coiled the rope in his hands before slinging it

over his shoulder. "Yeah."

Her eyes sparkled appreciatively, and he puffed out his chest. Totally without meaning to. Just happened. Wow. She was a beautiful woman. Mysterious in her own way. He didn't know why he'd been bowled over by her toenail polish, but he had. She was full of little surprises.

He cleared his throat. "Why don't you try standing?"

She did, but her legs buckled. "Oh!" She sank back down on the rock.

"Hang on." He slid the daypack over his shoulders, then slipped his arm around her waist, helping her up. "Loop your arm around my neck."

She looked up, but he was a good five inches taller than she was, just over six feet. Grant grinned at their predicament. "Okay, my back."

She latched onto him, and even though his back was sore, his body warmed at her touch. He *liked* being close to her, liked knowing he could protect her from anything else just waiting to happen. But they still weren't moving very fast.

She loped forward in baby bunny hops, and each one caused a gasp of discomfort.

Winds roared through the trees, pelted by the heavy rain. They'd never make it back to the parking lot at this pace. "Tell you what," he said. "I've got a better idea."

She stared up at him with those pretty brown eyes, makeup running down her face, and for the love of him she looked just like a sweet baby racoon. "Yeah?"

In one swift move, he grabbed her behind her

knees, the rain and wind swallowing her little shriek. The next instant, she was gathered in his arms like a dripping wet mermaid who'd just emerged from the sea. The image did nothing to douse the simmering heat inside him. She definitely had a siren's appeal with that long curly hair and that sweet freckled face of hers. He could imagine her capturing some sailor's attention and the hapless guy losing his bearings.

Not that he was going off course himself. He was taking this descent very carefully.

"You're sure you're okay?" she asked self-consciously. "I'm not too heavy?"

He chuckled. "Honey, you're a lightweight to me."

"Thanks." She blushed liked he'd embarrassed her, or maybe she'd just been pleased by his hint at her tiny size. And she was a little-bitty thing compared to him.

One of his hiking boots slid on the slope, but he righted himself quickly, tightening his hold on Nell. She clung onto his shoulder with her other arm wrapped around his neck.

He grinned down at her. "Strangely, I could get used to this. Minus you being in pain, of course."

She laughed. "Equally strangely, I agree," she said. "I've always kind of liked you." She bit her lip like maybe she regretted sounding flirty.

He didn't mind her saying that, though. Nice to know they were on the same page. "Yeah? I've always liked you, too."

Her eyebrows knitted together. "Really?"

"Well, I would have if I'd known you better. We

never had any classes together."

"I was—am—two years younger."

"Ah. A fair young maiden of thirty," he teased.

She laughed, and his body warmed further, despite the rain. He'd never paid too much attention to a woman's laugh before. But he liked Nell's. It seemed all sunshiny, like those brightly painted toes of hers.

"Grant?" she asked a little shyly. "Are you seeing anyone?"

"No. Are you?"

"Not at the moment."

Nice. He snuggled her in a bit closer. "That's probably good, then. Your boyfriend might get jealous of me carrying you down the trail."

"Well. This *is* a medical emergency."

He studied her playful expression, glad she could joke. That had to mean she was feeling okay. "Even so."

She locked on his gaze, and there was a look in her eyes like she wanted to say something more. Then the rain picked up, drumming the earth and the leaves all around them.

They were almost to the parking lot. On one hand, he regretted that she'd no longer be in his arms. On the other, he'd much rather continue getting to know her somewhere warm and dry. The storm seemed determined to make that impossible. "This has to be the front of that nor'easter coming through."

Worry furrowed her brow. "Do you think we'll make the bridge?"

"Don't know." He'd find out when they got to the

SUV so he could text Jordan to update him on their situation and make sure the others had gotten out safely.

"Is that the only way?"

"There is one other." Of course, that road could be flooded out, too. Fortunately, though, he had a backup plan and a decent place for them to stay if it came to that. Tending to Nell overnight would be a welcome distraction from the weather. He enjoyed her company, and she seemed to enjoy his. He could take care of that injured ankle of hers and make sure she was all right. And maybe he'd get to the bottom of why she signed up for his hike.

• • •

We're stranded.

Okay, yes, she was stranded with Grant, but she might have preferred better circumstances. Circumstances that didn't include a washed-out bridge. Something planned would have been so much better. That way she'd have known to bring some nice clothes and makeup along, beyond the basic lip gloss she kept in her purse. She'd used the bathroom near the trailhead before they left, and her reflection was horrific. She'd had to scrub her face clean with industrial hand soap and paper towels to cure her weeping mascara.

Now, she felt like crying for real. She was cold and achy. Getting hungry, too. She'd only had time to grab toast and coffee for breakfast, and that had worn off somewhere between the scramble up the hill and her meltdown at the top.

"Well, there goes that," Grant said as rushing rapids swept by, carrying pieces of the bridge's pilings with them.

Nell stared out the rain-streaked windshield. She had her hurt ankle propped up on Grant's dashboard in the boot. Her foot felt like it was swelling, too.

"Didn't you say that there's another way?"

"Yeah but..." He grimaced. "Maybe if we'd started earlier? That road is low-lying near a stream. It tends to flood over."

"Maybe it hasn't yet?"

"Yeah. But no." He shook his head. "I'm pretty sure that it has."

"We won't know until we check, will we?" He had the defrost on and the heat cranked up, but she still had goose bumps. She shivered, and he seemed to take pity on her.

"All right," he said, relenting. "We can go and check." He gave an exaggerated groan but didn't sound seriously grumpy. It was more like he was indulging her and was resigned about that. "If it will make you feel better."

"Yeah." She smiled. "It would."

They only made it halfway down the road of their alternate route before they had to stop because of a tree that had fallen across the road, blocking it. Through its spindly branches dotted with gold and brown leaves, Nell spied the low spot in the road that was in fact heavily flooded. Even if the tree hadn't been in the way, they couldn't have made it through.

Argh. He was right. The road was impassable.

"Eeep. My bad." She slunk down in her seat, and her eyebrows arched. "Sorry?"

"No worries." He began backing up his SUV to turn them around. "I've got some place we can go to wait this out."

She stared at him in surprise. "What? You do?"

"I keep a cabin up here. Fishing cabin. It will do just fine for tonight."

"Overnight?" She swallowed hard. "You mean, there's no hope of us getting back down the mountain today?"

"Might have been earlier," he teased lightly. "If someone hadn't created a huge fuss about coming down off the summit."

"I didn't create a fuss!" she said. Her face warmed. Okay, maybe she had. "Not a *huge* one anyway," she amended with some humility.

"No, you're right." His eyes danced. "Your tantrum was teeny tiny."

"Tantrum?" She huffed. "I came down. Eventually."

He smirked and shook his head. "Yeah. Very hard."

"Oh no." She gasped, wondering if she'd hurt him more than he'd let on. "You're not…? I mean, not hurt anywhere?"

He read her worried look, and his expression softened. "Honestly, I'm fine. I'll probably have bruises, but those will heal." Next, he shot a look at her ankle. "So will your ankle. But we need to get some ice on it pronto."

Ice. That sounded good. Maybe his cabin wasn't as rustic as she feared. When he first mentioned it, she worried it was a real backwoods affair with an outhouse or something. If he had ice, he at least had electricity. Maybe his cabin was even posh? With a jacuzzi! Ooh, a nice soak in a hot tub would be great about now. "So, how far away is this cabin?"

"Not very. We'll be there in about ten more minutes."

That was handy and maybe for the best. The weather didn't seem to be improving, so getting off the road seemed wise. "How long have you had it?"

"About five years."

"Five? Nice."

"Yeah, and I love it." He gave her a cockeyed grin, and her heart pitter-pattered. "I hope you'll like it, too."

If Grant would be there with her, she was certain she would. When it came to Operation First Bride, this could actually work out fantastically. She and he would have more time to get to know each other, just the two of them alone—without any outside distractions around. Her stomach rumbled. With all the excitement, she'd gotten really hungry.

"Is there food at the cabin?"

"Yeah, some. In the pantry and the freezer."

She considered his profile, heartened to be playing house with him. "Do you cook?"

"Just a bit." He turned to her. "You?"

"Yeah. Some."

"Well, no worries about that," he said. "Today, the meal prep is all on me."

Nell sank back in her seat, feeling happy despite her injury. This wasn't so bad. In fact, other than her ankle and embarrassing herself in front of a group of strangers, things were going great. While

the turn in the weather had caught them off guard,
she'd get to make lemonade out of lemons by
spending time alone with Grant. They'd have the
whole rest of the day and evening to get to know
each other better.

They drove down a long gravel road and pulled
up to a ramshackle house with a tin roof. It didn't
look posh at all. Instead, it was ultra-basic, with a
pair of old wooden rockers on its front porch that
looked like they'd seen better days. In a way, she
was shocked the building had withstood these
winds.

"That's it?"

"Home sweet home." He grinned at her. "Or,
my home away from home. This is where I go to get
away from it all."

"That sounds nice." Nell pasted a smile on her
face. It was pretty far away, all right. Basically in
the middle of nowhere. But that was okay. That
was good. She glanced down at her phone in her
purse, hoping she could still get a cell signal. She
needed to text her sisters and let them know
where she was so they wouldn't worry when she
didn't show up at work in the morning. And hinting that she was sleeping over at Grant's ought to
keep their pesky doubts about where she stood
with the bet at bay.

Even if it wasn't entirely true. But maybe a night
at his cabin would be the start of something amazing. Stuck together in a cabin—that was a romance
novel trope, wasn't it? And she loved romance
novels. Nell devoured them by the dozens.

She grinned brightly. "This place is great! I'm

sure it's even more awesome inside."

"It is." He hopped out of the SUV and then went around to her door. "Now," he said, helping her down from the vehicle and onto his gravel driveway. "Let's get you inside and out of this rain."

CHAPTER SIX

Grant inserted his key in the lock and pressed open the dingy front door. "After you."

"Thanks," she said, holding onto her purse strap with one hand and hopping over the threshold. He switched on some lights and steadied her elbow, leading her into the cabin. It was not nearly as bad as it had appeared from the outside. It was bare-bones furnished, though, and she didn't spot a TV. But maybe it had all he needed for his fishing get-aways.

They reached the small living area with a hooked rug, a ratty sofa with a coffee table, a threadbare armchair, and not a whole lot else. Oh yeah—there was a small table in a teeny kitchen and another room that was the bedroom, judging by the foot of a bed she saw through the open doorway. Everything was knotty pine, including the low ceiling and walls.

"It's chilly in here," she said, bracing herself against the back of the sofa.

"Won't be for long." Grant shut the front door and walked to a stack of logs beside a woodstove. "We've got this."

He frowned down at her boot, and she saw she'd left a trail of mud tracks behind her on the hardwood floor. "Oops!" she said, and he glanced behind him, seeing he'd left tracks, too.

"Looks like a three-footed something lumbered in here."

She giggled at the face he made, imitating a Sasquatch with his fingers held in front of his mouth like fangs. "Horrifying!" she said, and then she laughed again. She glanced toward the kitchen. "Got some paper towels or maybe a rag?"

"Don't you dare." His dark eyes twinkled. "I'll clean it up." He studied her saturated clothing. "We should probably both get changed first," he said. "The hot water works. You want a shower?"

A hot shower sounded like heaven. Her whole body ached from the long hike, her fall, and her trials in the rain, but her ankle was seriously throbbing.

He noted her gaze on her boot. "We'll cover the athletic tape in plastic, and you can try to keep it out of the water. It's a small walk-in shower. You should be fine."

That all sounded great, but what would she wear after that? Her clothes were totaled. "Don't suppose you've got a washer and a dryer?"

He shook his head. "Not up here." He read her worried look. "But I do keep some spare clothing around. We can probably find something that works."

He strolled into the bedroom and rummaged through the dresser, returning with a pair of sweatpants and a sweatshirt. He had a pair of boxers folded on top. They had colorful fishing lures on them. Grant shifted on his feet. "Um. Not sure if you need…?"

"Thanks!" Her face burned hot as she took the stack. "Er. Maybe?"

"I mostly sleep in those. If you prefer briefs—"

"No, no." She wanted to melt through the floor.

She'd not expected one of their first civil in-person conversations to be about his underwear. "These are great."

"Why don't you give me your jacket?" he said. "I'll hang it here by the fire to dry."

She nodded and backed into the bathroom, setting the fresh clothing on the sink rim. The bathroom was tiny, so not a lot of extra space. Not even a closet. She could barely fit in it.

She unzipped her jacket, and it dripped on the floor as she handed it over.

Nooo. It still had the price tag attached. The price sticker part was so wet, it was hard to read it. So maybe he wouldn't know she'd gotten it at a rock-bottom price? And only yesterday?

He held up her jacket, admiring its fuchsia feather collar. "Designer, huh?"

Nell grinned tightly. "Yeah."

"Nice." He nodded behind her. "Fresh towels and body wash under the sink. Shampoo, too. A few new toothbrushes and such if you're interested. Help yourself." He started to shut the door, but she pushed it back open.

"Let me grab my purse. I've got a brush and… stuff in there." Like her phone, so she could privately text her sisters. Come to think about it, she had more than one use for those boxers. She giggled at her sly idea. There'd be no doubting her dating prowess after that.

She'd partly shut the door when he shoved his hands in his jeans pockets. "Nell."

"Huh?"

He hung his head and then looked up. "I'm really

sorry about your fall. You getting hurt and everything. When I teased you about the tantrum, I didn't
really mean it." He frowned. "I probably shouldn't
have said that."

Her heart fluttered because he looked so adorably sincere. She couldn't believe he was guilting out
over that. "No, you were right," she said. "I'm sorry
about freaking out like that. I didn't mean to, and I
know it was bad for the group—having to split up
like that. I'm sorry about falling on you, too."

His lips twisted wryly. "That part wasn't so bad."
He held a little glimmer in his eyes that looked almost—predatory.

Nell caught her breath. "No. Uh." She licked her
lips, thinking about when she'd landed on top of him
and about how he'd almost kissed her. At least, he'd
looked like he'd wanted to, and she'd wanted him to
as well. A lot.

She backed up a step and stumbled, accidentally
setting down her right foot. "Ow!" She stared down
at her wrapped ankle, remembering. "Er. You got
that plastic?"

"I've got some trash bags," he said. "Why don't
you get undressed, and I'll wrap you up?"

"What?" Her heart hammered. Yeah, she wanted
him to fall for her, but no, she wasn't ready to get
naked with him yet. In an old-fashioned way, she'd
been kind of hoping to save that for their eventual
honeymoon. Assuming they had one.

She planned to paint a slightly more adventuresome picture for Charlotte and Misty, though. Why
not? They were always bragging on their boy toys,
and now Nell finally had one of her own. At least

she could make it look that way to them. She eyed the boxers again. Besides that, she intended to fake it until she could make it with Grant.

Which would hopefully be sometime within the next twenty-nine days.

He chuckled. "You can wrap yourself in a towel or something."

"Uh…okay." She shut the door, her heart hammering. Then she stripped off her very icky clothing. She had to tug off the boots first, and the right one was snug. But she finally worked it free, one inch at a time.

She slid the tight running pants down past her wrapped ankle and moaned, wincing at the jolt of pain. Next, she examined her panties—back and front. When she'd slipped in the mud, she'd landed on her butt, and the damage had seeped through the legging-like material. Maybe she could wash them out in the sink and dry them overnight?

At least then, she wouldn't be stuck wearing Grant's boxers indefinitely. Her face heated again, and she remembered he was waiting on her, so she hurried in removing her long-sleeve top. That was still clean, thanks to the waterproof jacket. Her bra was safe, too. So there were small mercies in this wardrobe disaster.

A moment later, he knocked at the door. "Ready?"

She opened the door the tiniest crack. She had the towel wrapped around her, but her bra and panties were still on. He couldn't tell that, though, because the only part that she stuck out of the slightly opened door was the bottom half of her right leg—up to the knee.

"O-kay," he said calmly. "Let's get to this."

She heard plastic crinkling and peered out the door.

Grant had crouched near the ground with a cut section of a black trash bag and a roll of medical tape. His focus was on her leg, so he didn't see her spying on him.

"I'm going to slip this over your foot," he called without looking up, "and start taping now. I'll try to be careful with the pressure."

She leaned back a bit and said, "Thanks."

She peeked at him again and caught him grumbling to himself about bad luck and rotten timing. Something also about women at his cabin? It was indistinct, so not totally clear.

His chin jerked up, and he saw her watching him. "Oh hey!"

She bit her lip. "Hey."

He stood and shook out his shoulders. "You're all set. But try to keep it out of the water anyway. The heat will be no good for it."

"Got it, thanks!" she said and quickly shut the door.

• • •

Grant heaved a breath. When he'd started out this morning, he'd never expected to wind up here with Nell Delaney. He hadn't had a woman up at his cabin since Susan. After that, he'd vowed to keep this place as his man cave and never let a woman set foot in here again. But today with Nell was different. This wasn't about romance. They'd had an emergency. Besides that, Nell clearly wasn't Susan.

Susan was all about spiffing things up and wanting to change things. Paint these authentic knotty pine walls white and hang up art prints. She also wanted to toss out his very comfortable furniture and start over with a mid-century modern ensemble. It was only when he understood that she also wanted to make-over him that he'd decided he wanted out.

Grant shook his head, thinking of Nell. He'd always figured her for the quiet, shy type. But she'd exhibited a different—mildly flirty—spark today when he'd carried her down that mountain. She wasn't really forward, though. Definitely not the type to want to hop right into bed together and snuggle up. Not that he was entertaining those thoughts, either. That wouldn't be right under the circumstances. She'd gotten hurt on his watch, and he still kicked himself for it. The least he could do now was look after her, while doing his best to be a gentleman.

He glanced at his small kitchen, getting an idea. It was after one o'clock, and Nell was bound to be starving. He knew that he was. While he wasn't any kind of gourmet cook, he was pretty skilled at opening cans. He'd make them something to eat, maybe something hot to warm them both up. But first, he'd light a fire and change out of these sopping wet clothes of his. Oh yeah—and clean up that muddy mess on the floor. He could wait to shower later.

• • •

Nell giggled and snapped her pic.

This really is so embarrassing. But those fishing lures are awfully cute.

She took care to not place her wrapped ankle in the frame. Or the top of her body, which was decently clothed in her long-sleeve T. She'd already stripped away the plastic covering on her leg, and it had managed to do its trick by keeping her ankle dry. She'd toweled off her hair and run her brush through it, too, and applied a touch of lip gloss for good measure.

The boxers sagged a little, settling on her hips, and her photo revealed a flash of her super pale belly. The text that accompanied it read:

Spending the night at Grant's cabin.

There. That was that. She'd let Misty and Charlotte draw their own conclusions.

She giggled again, feeling more than a little duplicitous, which wasn't her usual jam. But honestly, she was so tired of being good all the time. Besides that, she'd had a bad time with twisting her ankle. Might as well make the best of it.

And there was every indication the day would get better.

Her stomach rumbled. Hopefully the better part of the day began with something to eat. She was famished.

Nell tugged on the sweatpants, taking care with her right ankle, and then slipped the sweatshirt over her head. Both items of clothing swallowed her up, with the legs of the sweatpants bunching up by the floor. She cuffed the legs and the arms of her sweatshirt, too, then took a quick look in the mirror. It was fogged, so she wiped it clean with a towel.

Her eyebrows arched at the pretty picture.

For no makeup and injured, she looked pretty good.

She stared down at her baggy clothing, understanding she'd have to make do.

She grabbed her cell phone from where she'd set it on the sink and dropped it back into her purse. The phone wedged deep in a hollow of her extra-large corduroy shoulder bag, nesting between her knitting needles. She took her current projects with her everywhere. Who knew when she'd be stuck waiting during a doctor's appointment, or get held up at the pharmacy while picking up her dad's heart meds?

She still did that on a routine basis, since the small cottage where she lived was on the other end of town from Bearberry Brews but not far from the pharmacy. Her parents lived closer to the coffee shop, so it made perfect sense for Nell to pick up her dad's prescriptions. Her mom's dry cleaning, too. She'd never minded doing those things anyway, just like she didn't mind packing her sisters' lunches. By now, taking care of everyone else had become second nature to Nell.

Which made her pursuit of Grant slightly unnerving, because she was finally looking out for herself. Her current project was, awkwardly, something for him. His birthday was September seventh, but he didn't know that she knew it. It might actually seem kind of stalkerish if he did.

But Nell had known about his birthday since high school. Grant's girlfriend had decorated his locker with all sorts of streamers and balloons and a big heart-shaped, homemade birthday card, which had made Nell extremely jealous at the time.

She'd had her braces then and had not been nearly as eye-catching as Grant's cute cheerleader girlfriend. Nell was actually surprised at Grant's comment today about remembering her from high school. He'd been great at sports and all things popular, and she'd been the mousy sophomore. Until today, she hadn't known that he'd known she was alive back then.

She'd decided on the spot, on Grant's eighteenth birthday, that she was going to let him in on her existence someday. And she was going to make him the best birthday gift ever. Something much better than a homemade card. So, she began knitting with love.

She'd made scarves, not-so-great mittens, a throw blanket once, and even a few ties.

Some sweaters were better than others, but the cardigan was a major fail.

This year's endeavor was a hat, and she liked it! It was in fall colors: golds, browns, and oranges, which reminded her of Grant. Since he was outdoorsy. And intelligent. And born in almost-autumn. And about the best-looking, sweetest guy she'd ever met. He even started a club in support of animal rescue in high school, and members volunteered at the local animal shelter.

Nell had joined, too. Unfortunately, her volunteer days had almost never matched up with Grant's.

She sighed.

Basically, he was perfect.

And now, he was probably growing impatient, wondering how long it took one woman to wash her hair. She laid her hand on the doorknob, and her cell phone dinged.

She bit her lip, thinking it might be one of her sisters.

But no.

Instead of that, it was a notification.

Message failed.

That was just her luck. Maybe there was no cell service up here?

Nell pressed open the door and walked out into the small living room.

Grant turned from where he'd been working at the stove. "Good shower?"

"Uh-huh, the best."

He studied her outfit, and his eyes twinkled. "A little large on you, huh?"

She shrugged. "Just a bit."

Nell skip-hopped over to the sofa and set down her purse. She'd left her muddy boots in the bathroom along with her soiled clothing and was barefoot. A fire blazed in the woodstove, which had its door open, casting a cheery glow over the room as heavy rain pounded the tin roof. Heat radiated in her direction, and the scent of something cooking, too.

"I made us some lunch," he announced.

She stared at him in surprise. "How sweet."

"It's pretty basic. Tomato soup and PB&Js."

"That sounds fantastic," she said, because it did. "Thank you."

"Hop on over here and prop your leg up. I've got some frozen veggies in the freezer that we can use to ice it. Also…" He nodded at a bottle of ibuprofen by

a full glass of water on the table. "You should probably take two of those. That will help with the pain
and the swelling."

Nell took a fresh look at the cabin, which she'd at
first assessed as dreary. With a fire blazing and lunch
about to be served, it looked homey instead.

She glanced back at the shower. "I left my clothes
and boots in the bathroom."

"That's fine," he said. "We can deal with those
later."

He pulled out a kitchen chair, and she sat at the
table. "No cell service up here?"

His eyebrows rose.

"I tried to text my sisters. I didn't want anyone to
worry if I don't make it back for work in the morning."

"It's doubtful you'll be going in to work tomorrow," he said. "One way or another." He situated her
leg on another chair after propping it on a sofa pillow.
"With so much other damage in the area, clearing the
roads up here won't be a priority. You shouldn't be on
your feet anyway. You'll need to rest this for at least
twenty-four hours." He placed a bag of frozen vegetables on her ankle, using it as an ice pack.

She laughed, seeing the vegetables were frozen
peas. "My arch nemesis."

"What? You don't like peas?"

"Never could stand them."

She pulled a face, and he laughed.

"They go really great with soup and sandwiches."

She grinned. "I don't know about that."

"Hey, give them a chance. As for cell service," he
said. "We're too far away from any towers, but I do

get a cell connection through my internet. It's satellite, though, so not really great in bad weather. When the storm lifts, things should reconnect. I'll get you the login info later."

He served them both a cup of soup, then carried those and their plates, which were already loaded with sandwiches, to the table.

"What kind of jelly?" she asked him.

"Grape. Is that all right?"

Nell chuckled. "Any kind would be all right. I'm starving."

He nodded and pulled out his chair, sitting as well.

"I appreciate your making lunch," she said. "You didn't have to."

"I know. But I was hungry, too."

She took a bite of sandwich, noticing he'd used creamy peanut butter. She preferred crunchy, but it honestly didn't matter. "What do you not like?"

"What do I *not*…like?" His mouth twitched. "As in, food-wise?"

"Yeah."

He took a bite of his sandwich. "Crunchy peanut butter."

She laughed and had to cover her mouth because she was chewing.

"Wait. What's so funny?"

"I love crunchy peanut butter."

"Oh." He stared down at her plate. "Sorry."

"No, no," she said quickly. "It's all good! This sandwich is delicious." She took a sip of tomato soup, which was hot and warming. "This too."

"What do *you* not like? Other than peas?"

"Chocolate."

He blinked. "Okay, I know that's a lie. That's genetically impossible."

"What?" She giggled. "Why?"

"I've never met a woman who hates chocolate."

"I didn't say I hate it. I said that I don't like it. There's a difference."

"Oh yeah?"

"Yeah." She dabbed her mouth with her napkin. "For instance. If there's a dessert that's not all chocolate but that has chocolate in it, like yellow cake with chocolate icing, I'll eat it."

"Brownies?"

"No."

"Chocolate fudge?"

"Nuh-uh."

"Hot cocoa?"

"Not going there."

He arched one eyebrow, and electric tingles raced down her spine. "You are one peculiar woman."

"I'm not peculiar." She grinned. "I'm just particular. I know what I like."

His eyes danced. "Noted."

"What else is on your list?" she asked him.

"What else is on yours?"

She laughed. "Not too, too much. Except for Brussels sprouts."

"What?" He feigned shock. "But those are delicious. Especially roasted. Yum."

She wrinkled up her nose and teased. "Way to smell up a house."

"You probably don't like cabbage, either."

"Are you kidding? I have to like that. I come from good Irish stock."

He chuckled at her proud expression. "I like it too. It's a great Saint Patrick's Day staple."

"At Mariner's?" she asked.

"Yeah. They also make a superb lamb stew."

"That's what I hear."

"You mean you've never tried it?"

"Not yet."

"Then get it next time."

She wished she could get it with Grant, with a side dish of a romantic view. "I'll keep that in mind."

"What's more," he said with a grin, "how about I take you?"

Her heart stuttered. Was he asking her on a date? "Ser-seriously?"

"Sure. If you'd like."

Oh boy would I like. I'd like a lot.

"Unless," he continued with a flirty twinkle in his eye, "you've started seeing someone between now and an hour ago on the trail?"

"I…no! Not at all." She blushed. "I would love to go to Mariner's with you."

Grant leaned back in his chair, seemingly pleased with her answer. Nell could barely contain her excitement. A date. With Grant. And *he* asked.

It was so much more than she hoped for on the first day. Even her propped-up ankle didn't hurt so much anymore. She was finally doing it—taking ownership of her dreams and her life. If Grant eventually fell for her as hard as she hoped, that would be terrific. But, even if he didn't, exchanging fun banter with a really attractive guy felt good. She was new at this but getting better. Hopefully she'd be a pro by the time they went on that date.

"So," she asked casually, drinking from her water. "Anything else on your 'don't like' list?"

"Not much. I'm pretty easy." He frowned. "Only coffee."

"What?" Nell grew wide-eyed. Peanut butter was one thing, but it was hard to imagine the guy she spent forever with not liking a cup of joe. All of her fantasies about them being cozy and drinking morning coffee together in bed went up in one big poof, like a frothy cappuccino cloud.

"I'm sorry if that's harsh." He grimaced. "Seeing as how that's your family's business and all."

Nell reined in her shock. Not liking coffee was okay. She could keep having her wake-up coffee, and he could enjoy his hot tea or whatever.

"No, no. It's fine." She viewed him curiously. "When did this aversion start?"

"Oh…" He scratched his chin. "Sometime in college. I'd been out partying with some friends, and later on they decided I needed coffee. Lots of coffee. Too much coffee…" He looked like he wanted to retch. "If you know what I mean."

"Oh no, don't say it."

"Yeah. That coffee didn't like me much, either."

She could only imagine. "So what do you drink now?"

"Tea. And I go light on the booze now, too, for a lot of reasons."

She suspected one of those reasons had to do with his dad, who'd had a drinking problem that all of Majestic knew about. He'd been kicked out of the bar at Mariner's several times for surpassing his limit, even during daylight hours. An occasional caring soul had walked him into Bearberry Brews for coffee, where Nell's folks had sternly instructed their staff to always treat the man with compassion. So she didn't fault Grant in the least for his teetotalism. She wasn't a huge drinker herself. One glass of wine on occasion nearly did her in.

Her mind tripped back over his comment about coffee.

"Wait." She experienced a mild moment of panic. She hadn't started a day without coffee in years. "There's no coffee here, is there?"

"Ahhh. Sorry, no. I've got tea, though. And..." He winced. "Cocoa."

She belly laughed at his expression. "I like tea, too. It's just not—"

"Coffee," he said deadpan, and she laughed again.

"You're very funny."

"Yeah? So are you." He smiled and finished his lunch. So did she.

"Bearberry Brews is big on coffee, huh? So many specialties." When Nell reflected on it now, the few times he'd come in, he'd ordered tea. She should have recalled that. "Do you have a favorite?"

"I do." Nell giggled because it was one of their most decadent flavors. "Blueberry Cheesecake Pralines and Cream."

"Wow. That sounds rich."

"It is. And it's worth every calorie."

Grant smiled at her. "Any other favorites?"

"Coffees?"

"I mean in general, like...snack foods?"

"Easy. Popcorn. You?"

"Trail mix."

"Figures." Next, she asked, "Color?"

"Blue."

"Green," she replied.

"Holiday?" he asked.

"Thanksgiving!"

He shook his head. "Hands down, Fourth of July."

"The Fourth of July?" she asked. "Why?"

Grant turned up his palms and grinned. "Everybody loves a parade."

Nell chuckled at this because Majestic held a pretty special one each year.

"Wait," he said. "Do you hear that?"

She set down her water glass and listened.

She heard nothing but the lapping flames from the fire.

Grant glanced out the kitchen window. "The rain. It's stopped." Nell looked around the cabin and out its modest windows facing the gravel driveway, seeing the same thing. A heavy mist rose off the earth like steam, but the sun peeked through a hazy sky.

He stood and walked to the front door, throwing it open.

Birds chirped outside, and something tumbled like a rushing river.

"What's that?"

He peered over his shoulder. "The waterfall."

"Waterfall?" Nell's heart took a happy leap because she'd never seen one before. "How cool. It sounds so close."

"It is close. A half mile or so behind the cabin. Dumps into the stream where I do my fishing."

He must have read her eyes, because he grinned. "Want to see it?"

CHAPTER SEVEN

Grant would do anything to capture the grin on Nell's face. She looked just like a kid on Christmas morning. So excited about something as basic as a waterfall. It wasn't a huge one, but it was pretty awesome.

"I'd love to see it," she said from where she sat at the table. "Only." She frowned, staring at her ankle.

Grant shut the front door. "I carried you before. I can do it again."

"Yeah?" Her smile lit up like a sunrise, and making her happy felt good.

"Sure." He shrugged and patted his back. "I'll carry you piggyback."

"Okay." She scooted out of her chair, and he checked out her feet.

"Piggyback or not, though, you can't go barefoot."

She grimaced, probably imagining wrangling her achy ankle into that boot again.

His gaze darted toward the bedroom. "Tell you what," he said. "You wear a boot on your left foot, and we'll layer up the other one with a couple of my thick hiking socks. That should keep your feet warm."

"Yeah, thanks. My piggies will be grateful."

He laughed. "I haven't thought of them as 'piggies' in a long time."

"Our dad used to play that game with us, me and my sisters."

"This little piggy went to market… This little piggy stayed home…?" he joked.

"Your dad too?"

His cheeks sagged. He wished he'd had a fun-loving dad. But his father had been far from it. He'd been more like argumentative and ornery, especially after drinking too much. Which he unfortunately did often. "Not my dad, no. My mom when I was really little. She's gone now."

She viewed him sadly, and he suspected she was remembering what the rest of Majestic knew. That, when Grant moved to town, it was the last stop in a string of relocations orchestrated by his father, who'd had trouble holding down a job. He'd died two years ago in May, and Grant still missed him, oddly. Even though he hadn't been the greatest dad, Grant got that he'd loved him in his own way. He just hadn't corralled enough strength to pull his life together.

"I'm sorry about your dad," she said. "I heard."

He didn't ask what she'd heard, fearing it was negative. Grant wasn't sure how many folks were aware that his dad had died from liver cancer, but he figured a fair number of them guessed. By the time Grant and his dad moved to Majestic, Grant was a senior in high school and his mom had already been gone for five years.

"When did you lose your mom?" she asked softly.

"When I was twelve." He swallowed hard. "She was great when she was around, though." His voice went scratchy, and he cleared his throat. "A really great mom."

Nell got up from the table and tossed the frozen

peas back into the freezer. Then she hobbled over to him.

"Grant." She placed her hand on his arm and looked up into his eyes. "I'm sorry."

Somehow, that small comfort meant a lot. Grant didn't often talk about his family. He hadn't even told Susan certain things. Particularly about his mom.

He stared into Nell's pretty brown eyes, and they glimmered with understanding. Compassion, too, and maybe something else. "Thanks."

"You know," she said. "You still have her with you in here." She motioned to her heart, and he knew it was true. But there'd been so many times when he'd wished he'd had her around in reality instead of in his imagination. Like when he'd graduated high school, and then college. And when he'd started Blue Sky Adventures.

She'd been outdoorsy, too, and her love of nature had inspired Grant's. She would have loved his store. His dad had barely acknowledged its opening and hadn't bothered showing up for it after promising that he would.

"I bet she would have been very proud of you," Nell said kindly.

"You think so?"

"You own your own business, Grant. That's a big deal."

"Yeah, well. My dad kind of thought it was a waste of time. Creating a career out of recreation." He regretted the bitterness in his tone, thinking he should change the subject. "In any case." He drew in a deep breath, then released it. "Time's moved on."

"And you're very successful." She held an admiring twinkle in her eye, and he was warmed by it.

"Thanks, Nell. Bearberry Brews seems to be doing fantastic, too."

She pursed her lips at his mention of her family business. "Um, yeah. They…are? But they've also seen better times. Honestly."

"Oof. I'm sorry to hear it. The economy's been a little rough as of late."

"Yeah. Last winter was especially hard."

"What do you do there?" he asked lightly. "Besides making highly caloric coffees?"

She laughed. "I keep the books."

"You're the accountant?"

"Yeah."

"That's a big job."

"It's what I trained for. Before that, my mom handled things, but she was burning out."

"Understood."

"Misty runs the register," she volunteered. "And Charlotte handles publicity. Apart from that, we all chip in. Lucas, too. He's sort of like the general manager."

"Oh yeah, I've seen Lucas around. He was in my class at school."

"That's right!" she said. "He's great, honestly."

He gave her a scrutinizing look, wondering if there was any interest there. For whatever reason, he hoped there wasn't. Okay, all right. He knew the reason. The reason was because *he* was developing an interest in Nell. It was hard not to be attracted to her with her pretty smile and her incredible brown-and-gold eyes. On top of that, she had a softness about her, something sweet and wonderful. She'd been so kind about his mom.

She laughed at his expression. "Lucas has never been the guy for me, if that's what you're thinking so hard about over there."

Was he that obvious? "No?"

"I'm into another type." She rolled her eyes. "Adventuresome. Outdoorsy."

He couldn't help but grin at her come-on. "Well, that's good to hear."

"What's your type?"

He locked on her gaze, unabashed by his interest. "I think I'm looking at her."

Color bloomed across her face, sweeping the bridge of her nose and those adorable freckles. For a moment, she appeared tongue-tied. But he could tell she was pleased by his comment. He was glad, because if she was going to dish it out, she was going to have to take it. Flirting went both ways.

She fiddled with her hair, seeming to collect herself. "How about we see that waterfall?" she asked after a pause.

He cracked a grin. "All righty. Let's get going."

He walked over to the coatrack near the woodstove where he'd hung their jackets. Both were drier than he'd expected, which was nice. Each also felt toasty inside.

She hopped over to the sofa and picked up her purse. "I want to take my phone so I can document this."

But, somehow, she held it wrong, and a bunch of items cascaded out onto a sofa cushion: a wallet, a brush, a tube of lip gloss… Her phone landed on some knitted object. Knitting needles sat beside it, protruding out of a multicolored skein of yarn.

Her cheeks turned pink. "I like to keep my projects with me. Just in case."

He chuckled, but he admired that. She obviously valued her time and didn't like wasting it. "Some folks carry a book."

"Or an e-reader," she said. "Yeah, I sometimes do that, too."

He cocked his chin. "So. What's that you're knitting?"

She had the look of a deer caught in somebody's headlights, but he had no clue why. "It's a, uh…hat."

He strode over to the sofa and picked it up. It was about three quarters of the way done. He got an impish impulse, and he tugged it onto his head. It didn't quite cover his ears in its partially completed state.

"Nice." He wiggled his eyebrows. "Is it for me?"

The color drained from her face.

"Hey, whoa. I'm sorry." He took the hat off. "I was just fooling around."

"No, it's fine. Really. It's just not finished."

He turned it over in his hands. "Looks good though. Like the colors. Very fall-like."

She bit her lip. "Thanks."

He studied the hat some more, then met her eyes. "Who's it for, then? Not you?"

She shook her head.

"A friend?"

Her color deepened. "Somebody special."

He dropped the hat back on the sofa. She'd said she wasn't dating, but she might be interested in someone. In that case, he wasn't so sure he wanted to hear about it, so he decided to change the subject. "What else have you made?"

Her phone dinged, then dinged again.

Then it started going crazy.

Ding, ding, ding, ding, ding!

"Guess the WiFi's back on." He shot a glance at the ceiling, figuring the satellite had reconnected.

She snatched up her phone, holding it toward her.

He glanced at her phone. "Who's that?"

"Just my sisters."

Ding.

"I told them I was safe."

Ding. Ding.

"And up here with you."

Ding, ding, ding, ding, ding, ding!

"They, uh…" She frantically scanned the incoming messages, then grinned. "Said to tell you hi."

"Oh. Well." He shifted on his feet. "Tell them hi back."

She nodded and sent a quick reply. "Sorry about that." She silenced her phone. "I let them know I won't be in tomorrow."

"Good idea."

He handed her jacket, and she put it on. She slipped her phone into one of its pockets.

"I'll grab your left boot from the bathroom," he said, "and those socks." He looked forward to their outing and to holding her close again. Even if it was by piggyback. "Then we'll take a little nature hike."

• • •

Nell giggled when Grant carried her down the front steps of his cabin. She had her arms around his neck, and he'd latched onto her legs as they wrapped around his big strong back.

"Giddyup," she said, lightly pumping her heels, but she immediately regretted digging in so hard with the right one. Her ankle pinged. "Ow!"

Grant chuckled. "Whoa there, partner," he teased. "The ground's still slick, so we won't be moving that fast."

The back of his neck smelled like manly body wash or cologne, and Nell breathed him in. She almost had to pinch herself to believe this wasn't a dream. While she might have seen Grant's fishing place as run-down at first, his rustic cabin had morphed into a romantic getaway for two. And she was spending the whole night there. With him.

She stifled a happy sigh. This was better than the first date she'd imagined over coffee at her place. They'd have much more time to get to know each other. One-on-one. Without anyone around to distract them. She was already getting to know him better, and he was getting to know her. Apart from being handsome and amazing, Grant was kind and funny, too. And, when he'd made that flirty comment about her being his type, her heart had sprouted wings.

Sunlight streamed through the trees, their branches teeming with colorful fall leaves, all golds, reds, and browns. Tiny droplets clung to their surfaces like glistening autumn tears. An aftermath of the rain. The crisp air nipped at her cheeks, but she was warm enough in her toasty jacket and the dry hat Grant had loaned her.

Grant traipsed across the gravel drive and around the cabin to a path that led through the woods and then down a hill. The more he walked along, the louder the sound from the falls grew, roaring like a majestic lion. Nell's heart pitter-pattered because this felt straight out of a daydream—well, minus her ankle. He was taking her to see a waterfall, and carrying her there had been his sweet idea.

"You doing okay?" he asked her.

"Yeah, great. You?"

"Never better."

Her heart warmed at the sound of that. It was like all her wildest fantasy-dreams were coming true. She held her breath and made a wish that things would continue to go well between them. If the past hour was any indication, they were in for a wonderful rest of the day and hopefully a stellar night.

She didn't quite have the nerve to tell him about Aidan, but she planned to as soon as she could. She couldn't smash any hope of a future they had with such a heavy-handed truth. That would feel like a weird overshare this early in their friendship, and she hoped their budding friendship would develop into something more.

No. She and Grant needed to give each other a chance, without Aidan getting in the way. Then if Grant really began to like her, she could ease into the avoiding-marrying-Aidan conversation. She wasn't entirely sure how, but she was hoping an answer would come to her. Sooner rather than later.

"So, you're a big hiker, huh?" he asked as he walked along.

"Um. Only recently. I've been more into other outdoor activities in the past."

"Oh yeah? Like what?"

Somehow she didn't think reading on the beach after applying massive amounts of SPF 50 sunscreen and while wearing a big floppy hat was what he had in mind. She knew she'd need to choose carefully, though. What if she claimed she could do something as dangerous as whitewater rafting, and he suggested they do that together?

Her mind raced back through the options listed on his website. "Camping!" she announced because that sounded safe. It was also pretty easy. *I mean, how hard can it be to set up a tent?* "A girl's got to love a good campfire."

He chuckled. "Yeah. What's your favorite camp-fire meal?"

Think. Think. Think. "Hot dogs! Fun toasting marshmallows afterward, too." She'd seen plenty of people do that in movies.

"Something tells me you skip the s'mores."

"Ha-ha." She was curious as to what he meant. "Why's that?"

"Because, um." He glanced over his shoulder, his eyebrows arched, and her pulse spiked. "S'mores are made with chocolate?"

"Oh, right! Chocolate and—"

"Graham crackers," he finished.

She'd been about to say peanut butter, but of course s'mores were made that other way. She'd heard about the weird gooey treat, but up until now had kind of forgotten about it. She didn't even know real campers ate them. Wasn't that more like Girl Scouts?

He kept trudging along. Now they were on an incline, headed uphill.

"What's your favorite campfire meal?" she asked him.

"Fresh trout, when I catch it." He called behind him because the noise from the falls was growing louder. "I hope you like fish?"

The truth was she didn't, but she didn't want to be rude. "Um. Why?"

They rounded a turn. "Because that's what we're having for dinner."

"I'm sure it will be delicious."

He side-stepped the mossy pebbles scattered along the path. "What kind of pack have you got?"

"Pack?" What was he talking about? Batteries? Beer? No. Wait. A backpack? "A really big one," she said. "But not too big. Light enough for me to carry, but large enough for all my important"—she scrambled for the word he'd used on their hike—"gear."

"Brand?"

She took a stab at it. "L.L.Bean?"

"You can't go wrong there."

He sounded approving, and she felt like she'd dodged that bullet.

Then he fired another round.

"Tent?"

What was this? A test? Nell bit her lip, fearing that's exactly what this was. "Huh?"

"I was just wondering what kind of tent you use."

"L.L.Bean," she said, thinking that had worked the first time.

"I was actually asking about the type."

Nell sensed they were treading into dangerous

territory. It was like he was laying down landmines everywhere. "Oh. It's very basic. Super basic. You know." She reached out her arms and made a triangle shape with her fingers in front of his face. "Like this."

"Really?"

Her mind searched furtively for answers, but all she could picture was a green canvas house with an apex and a zipper flap. "Usually, Misty puts it up. So she'd know more about the details."

"Misty?"

"Yeah. I go camping with my sisters. Always have. Every year. It's like a tradition." Now she'd have to text them and tell them about that. Just in case Grant mentioned camping to them.

"But you sleep in it, too? This tent?"

"Sure."

"So. Is it a single- or a double-wall?" Now he was being facetious. Either that, or he was trying to trip her up.

"Single or double. Ha." She chuckled at the question, then furrowed her brow. "Just what…are you asking?"

"How many walls?"

"*Four*," she said with confidence. "Definitely four."

"Wow," he said. "That must be something new."

Wait. *How* had she gotten that wrong?

"So it's freestanding?"

"Sorry?"

"Your tent, Nell. The one you and your sisters use. It doesn't require rope or cord, and metal stakes—"

"No, no." Her forehead felt hot beneath her hat. "It's nothing like that. It's one of those." He had her so rattled, she tried to recall what he'd said. "Standalones!"

"Standalones?" He tested out the word like he'd never said it before. "Right."

She hadn't expected this to be so complicated. At the same time, she wasn't ready to admit she'd never done any of the things he probably liked to do. Now was not the right time to highlight their differences. This was the moment to cement what they had in common. Or what they could have in common. She'd be more than happy to go camping with Grant in the future.

"And it's a really, really nice one," she added. "Super roomy and comfortable."

"Must be, for all three of you. How much does it weigh?"

"Weigh?" Who on earth weighs tents? She guessed people like Grant did. She tried to arrive at a good number.

"Um. I think around fifteen pounds?"

Grant whistled. "Must be a palace!"

Wait. What?

They crested a ridge, then headed downhill toward the splashing water sounds below them. Good. She hoped they'd get there soon so they could end this conversation.

"So, this fancy four-walled tent of yours—"

Nooo. Not that again.

"Does it have a rain fly?"

She gulped. "Really, I'd have to ask Misty."

"Do you sleep in it blindfolded?"

She faked a laugh. "Of course not. But I do wear one of those eye-patchy things. To be honest, I'm usually so exhausted from all our hard camping work that by the time we head to bed I barely notice."

"O-kay."

He shook his head and kept going, but she could tell he was thinking about everything she'd said. If this was a test, she was probably getting a D minus right about now. Maybe there were some camping magazines around the cabin? If she could find them, she could sneakily read up. Or check on her phone. Only, the battery was low, so it would be going dead soon. She didn't have her charger with her, either.

"So. What does Charlotte do, all this time while Misty's putting up the tent?"

Seriously? She was so sure they'd dropped this.

"She builds the campfire."

"That's nice. And you?" He peered back at her, and her heart hammered, because it was kind of sounding like he didn't believe her. At the same time, he wasn't challenging her directly. So maybe in some strange way he did.

"I'm gathering kindling," she said, because who was he to argue with that? Nell wiped her sweaty forehead beneath the rim of her hat. That entire interrogation had been excruciating. She probably could have put up and taken down two or three four-walled standalone tents in the time it took to explain all that.

The roaring of the falls grew louder, threatening to drown out their chitchat, and she wished they would. That way, she could stop talking about camping and screwing things up.

Grant rounded another bend, and they continued their descent, the splashing-water sounds growing closer. The waterfall's pounding was so loud it had to be just beyond that curtain of trees, and Nell couldn't wait to get there. She'd love to talk about *anything* but tents.

They reached a clearing by a gurgling stream, and Nell gasped.

Cascades tumbled off a high ridge, hitting ledge after rocky ledge as they funneled down, down, down into a swirling eddy. A fine mist kicked off the falling water, dusting her face with icy cold sprinkles that felt like tiny pinpricks. Fall foliage fluttered around them, and holly bushes hugged the mountainside, their deep red berries glistening in the blazing sun.

"It's amazing."

"Yeah." He adjusted his hold on her. "It is."

"I don't think I've ever seen anything so beautiful." She caught her breath and paused as a burst of colors lit up the western sky, high above the crest of the waterfall.

They arched through the clouds in a stunning display.

Red. Orange. Yellow. Green. Blue. Indigo. Violet.

Nell's heart fluttered. "Grant," she said breathily. "It's a rainbow."

He followed her gaze. "Oh wow."

She hugged his neck, setting her chin on his shoulder. "Thank you for this."

His voice rumbled warmly. "You're welcome."

They stood there in silence, enjoying the

spectacular sight as well as the nature sounds. Though she'd never been much of a nature girl before, Nell was starting to get the appeal of it. It was special to appreciate the gifts the earth gives us. It was extra special to appreciate them with Grant.

"I'm glad that I saw this with you," he said, his voice husky.

"Yeah." She sighed. "Me too."

Her phone buzzed in her jacket pocket, and she remembered.

He had the same thought at the same time. "Want to snap a pic?"

"Yeah."

He turned them around, jostling her on his back, and she chuckled.

"What are you doing?"

He grinned back at her. "Selfie time."

"Ooh, good idea." How cool to have the waterfall in the background with her in front. Even cooler if he could be in the picture with her. She opened her camera app and handed him her phone. "Do you mind?"

"You want me in it?"

"Yeah, I want you in it." She playfully shoved his shoulder. "It's on account of you that I saw it."

He extended his arm, holding it high above them so they were nicely framed against a backdrop of the falls.

"Say…chocolate!" he said as a joke, since she'd told him she didn't eat it.

She started to protest his ribbing, then grinned. "Oooh—chocolate!"

Her phone buzzed with a text.

He glanced at it, and she snatched it back from him.

"Er...thanks!" Just in time, too. It was Charlotte again, sending a slew of love-y emojis. Misty was right behind her with kissy-face emojis and GIFs in reference to Nell's pic of her in Grant's boxers. Nell giggled and sent them the photo of her and Grant by the waterfall, which really was the cutest.

Charlotte and Misty immediately loved the pic.

Charlotte wrote: *Sweet!*

Misty said: *Aww, congrats!*

Nell remembered the camping story, figuring she'd better warn them.

If Grant asks about it, say that we go camping every year.

This time, Charlotte answered first.

Who?

The three of us.

Then, Misty chimed in.

In a tent? No thanks.

Nell frowned. She needed their help and not their judgment, which it seemed like she was getting anyway. They never thought she could do this, but yeah, she was. Misty claimed hot options, and Charlotte had men up her sleeve, but Nell had a beautiful rainbow and her rugged mountain man. She replied quickly, typing behind Grant's head, intending to end this exchange on a high note, albeit an exaggerated one.

Maybe Grant and I can take you sometime. You know, after we're MARRIED.

Sorry girls, guess who's going to be the First Bride?

Meeeeee!!!!

Okay, she was definitely getting way ahead of herself, and there were one too many "e"s and exclamation marks.

Whatever. She pushed *send*. That ought to get her sisters thinking. Let them imagine whatever they wanted to. She and Grant might not be engaged, but things were going very smoothly. So maybe by the month's end…

Misty: *Wait. No WAY. Nell???*

Charlotte annoyingly added: *I'll believe it when I see it.*

She added an emoji of a ring.

Before Nell could reply, Grant asked her, "Your sisters again?"

"Ah, yeah." She tucked away her phone. "Just checking in."

He laughed. "You've got a very involved family."

"Yeah."

"They must love you a lot."

"They do. And I…" Her heart seized up. What was she doing to Misty and Charlotte by focusing on her own happily ever after? Essentially relegating one of them to five cold years of misery with Aidan Strong. "I love them, too," she finished, guilty thoughts consuming her. She shook them off, reminding herself that this was a fair contest between the three of them, and they were likely working just as hard to beat her as she was them.

But this was her moment to shine and emerge victorious.

Operation First Bride might have stalled a bit on that summit in the rain, but it was fully back on track now. Had been coming back on track ever since Grant carried her down the mountain and took her to his cabin for shelter during the storm. Now that storm had lifted and they were experiencing an incredible rainbow together, just like the happy ribbon of light that was glowing ever brighter in her soul.

She was liking Grant so much, and he was liking her for the things in common that they shared and because of how well they got along with each other. A few minor differences didn't matter so much, like them enjoying different types of foods—or him not drinking coffee. And even if she'd never been camping, she'd be more than happy to go and learn something new. That would be fun, but she'd probably better let him pick out the tent.

"You'll have to text me that photo," he said.

She recalled she had his number from when they coordinated about the hike. "All right," she said, giddily retrieving her phone again and sending the image on. "There!"

"Thanks."

A slew of freaked-out text messages from her sisters popped up on her phone.

Then the screen went black, and her cell died.

Oh, well. At least she'd sent Grant that photo!

He spun them back toward the falls, and they admired the view for a bit longer. This was probably one of the most special moments Nell had ever experienced in her lifetime. And, wonderfully, she was experiencing it with Grant.

After a while, he peered over his shoulder. "Ready to head back now?"

But it was so breathtaking here she couldn't bear

to leave. More clouds lifted, and the sky burned bright blue as the spectacular rainbow began fading.

"Just another minute."

He nodded and gazed up at the waning rainbow, lost in his own thoughts.

She could only hope that those thoughts were positive ones about her. Because there was no question about it. She was definitely seeing Grant as someone special—and not just in an abstract fantasy way anymore; in a real flesh-and-blood way. The more she learned about him, the more surprised she was by her attraction to him, which only kept growing stronger.

She gazed up at the rainbow's brilliant arch, and her heart beat faster.

Miracles happened every day.

Maybe it was finally time for a miracle to happen for her.

CHAPTER EIGHT

Grant carried Nell back into the cabin and deposited her on the sofa.

He'd never forget that rainbow or the excited glow on her face when he'd snapped that selfie. He was glad he'd asked her to send him a copy. That was an adventure worth remembering. This whole day was worth remembering. He still felt bad about Nell twisting her ankle, though.

"Thanks for the nature hike," she said, shucking her jacket. She smiled, and he felt all warm and tingly inside. Nell definitely had an effect on him, even when she was inventing wild stories about made-up camping trips. He chuckled to himself over her very obvious lack of knowledge regarding the basics. Tents were essentially either single- or double-walled these days, though all of them had four sides, of course.

She lacked knowledge in the hiking department, too.

If she'd told the camping fib to make him like her better, he was inclined to give her a pass. He just wasn't sure why she'd signed up for this morning's hike to begin with. She'd clearly been in over her head.

"Nell?"

"Hmm?"

"About this morning's hike…"

"What about it?"

"Is there a reason you signed up for it?"

"Yes! I wanted to…commune with nature."

"You'd never done that before, had you?"

"What? Commune?" She blinked. "Of course I have. I spend lots of time on the beach, for example—working out."

He scrutinized her for a moment. "You don't have to do the Ironman to impress me, you know."

"Whew! That's good. Ha-ha." Her forehead creased, and then she asked, "What's that?"

"A triathlon. It's like running a marathon combined with intense biking and swimming."

"Then double whew!" She giggled nervously, then added, "Triple!"

She looked so adorably trapped, he couldn't help teasing her further. "I can help you start training if you'd like?"

"Um. Sure. But, you know." She glanced at her ankle. "It might be a while."

"Gotcha." He winked, and her cheeks colored, making her look cuter than ever. "Maybe you should just stick with camping for now?"

"Yeah, that's my thinking, too."

"When's your next trip with your sisters?"

"Um. Not until next summer, actually."

"Well, if you decide to go sooner, maybe I can tag along?"

Her eyebrows knitted together, and she looked like she'd been backed into a corner. "Oh, sure. That would be cool."

"I could even help put up your tent." He strolled over to the short table beside his armchair and picked up a bunch of magazines, bringing her the stack. All were about camping, backpacking, and other types of outdoor adventures. "Maybe if you look through these, you'll spot that high-end model you use. That fancy, four-walled deal."

She grinned tightly. "Right."

He chuckled to himself, deciding to stop teasing her. "Want some hot tea?"

She laid the magazines on the coffee table and removed her boot. "Maybe in a bit."

"Okay, I'll make us some shortly. In the meantime, I think I'll grab that shower." He walked to the woodstove and stoked it. "Need to use the facilities first?"

She shook her head. "No, thanks."

She dug her phone out of her jacket pocket and frowned.

"What's wrong?"

"It's dead." She made a pouty face. "And I don't have my charger." She glanced around the room. "Maybe you've got one up here that I can borrow?"

"Sorry." He frowned. "That looks like an Apple. I've got an Android."

"So the chargers?"

He shook his head. "Don't match up. You can use my phone if you'd like, though?" He didn't see the harm in that. It wasn't like he kept state secrets on it or anything.

"That would be great, thanks. I want to tell my sisters my phone's out of commission so they don't worry." When he nodded, she asked, "Do you think we'll be out of here by tomorrow?"

"Hard to say about the bridge, but the road could clear. We can check in the morning." Inwardly, though, he hated the idea of leaving the cabin. "Why don't you prop your foot on a pillow on the coffee table, and I'll go grab your favorite vegetable cold pack."

"Thanks, Grant." She propped up her foot like he instructed and stared around the room. "So, what do you do up here when you're not fishing?"

He returned with the frozen peas and also handed her his phone, which he'd grabbed off the kitchen counter. He entered his password and gave it to Nell.

"I don't know. Relax. Read." He eyed the selection of dog-eared paperbacks he kept on a bookshelf in the corner, then the stack of magazines he'd given her. "Play solitaire."

She wrinkled up her nose. "Sounds a little lonely."

He hadn't exactly felt lonely in the past. After having Nell here, though, he might think about things differently in the future. Grant was used to spending a lot of time alone. While he enjoyed leading his adventure groups, he found it a little taxing to be socially "on" all the time, so he liked having his down time. "It's all right." He shrugged. "I'm used to being on my own."

She grimaced. "Sorry to intrude on your solitude."

He laughed and set his hand on the doorframe. "No worries. I like having you here."

Her eyes sparkled. "Maybe we can play cards later?"

"I've got other games, too."

"Oh yeah?"

He pointed to the coffee table, which was actually an old wooden blanket chest that had belonged to his grandfather. "Everything's in there if you want to take a look."

• • •

Grant shut the bathroom door, and Nell glanced down at his phone. She should probably send her text message first, then browse through some of his magazines so she could bone up on her vocabulary. Grant was asking a lot of questions about her camping expertise, and she was failing every one of them. He'd already suspected she wasn't a hiker. The price stickers on her jacket and boots hadn't helped, either. If she could at least cling to the camping illusion, he'd have some respect for her as an outdoorsy sort of woman.

Even though he claimed that didn't matter, maybe it did. His past girlfriends were probably all super athletic with healthy natural glows from spending so much time outdoors. Like swimsuit models or movie stars—the kind who starred in action films. Just because Nell wore a one-piece swimsuit and had a cushy bum, that didn't mean she wasn't attractive. She liked her body very much and owned every minor curve. Okay, some of the slightly more major ones, too. And her cellulite. Each thigh dimple was very special to her, almost like a child. She'd even named a few of them. Not that she'd ever tell Grant that.

She glanced down at his baggy sweat clothes, thinking they didn't do her figure any favors. When she dressed well, she looked great, and she knew exactly how to dress for her body type. Which was why the hot pink Lycra running pants hadn't exactly worked. They'd pinched her tummy, waist, and thighs, and other uncomfortable places. It had been a huge relief to take them off. If Grant wound up taking her to Mariner's, she'd pull together her prettiest outfit ever.

She couldn't wait for that date. But for the moment, she had to.

She needed to text her sisters. She knew their numbers by heart because their parents had gotten them all cell phones at the same time, and the ending of each phone number was just one digit off from the others. Nell had started driving, so she'd clearly needed her own phone. Charlotte only got one because she'd argued that her sports coaches required one for contact purposes. *Like, honestly? They couldn't have texted Mom or Dad, or called the house?*

Misty had basically whined and cajoled her way into getting her own phone, declaring it was necessary for her personal safety. *Yeah, from her cool tween friends, who'd razzed her for lagging behind technologically.* She'd only been twelve. And so she'd received her first cell phone four years earlier than Nell, who'd had to wait until her sixteenth birthday like it was this huge deal. And it had been, but Charlotte and Misty had benefited, too. It was always that way with her sisters, but this time, Nell was racing out ahead of them. She was determined to find happiness first.

She sighed, recalling Charlotte's and Misty's

precious kiddie faces: They'd been so adorable as babies, and she'd been really protective of them growing up, defending them from bullies and showing them how to tie their shoes. She'd also taught Charlotte to read and Misty how to bake cookies. Later, she'd helped them with their homework and had served as an advisor when they'd begun dating boys. It was sweet that they trusted her judgment, despite her lack of experience.

She'd been their leader. Their mentor. Their shepherd.

And they her cute little lambs.

Her heart seized up.

And now I'm throwing them to the wolves.

Factually, it was more like a lone wolf named Aidan Strong.

This didn't make Nell feel any less guilty, though.

She rolled back her shoulders, redirecting her energy.

Misty and Charlotte would be okay. Besides that, neither of them were children any longer. Everybody here was a grown-up, and all three of them had agreed about the anti-Aidan plan. Nobody had been forced into anything. It was just like their mom had said—they'd each made a free choice. And Nell's choice had been to enact Operation First Bride, which was right on track.

For all she knew, Charlotte and Misty were already in a race to find husbands for themselves. Misty probably had guys lining up around the block, and Charlotte had plenty of exes to choose from. The one in the toughest predicament was obviously her. Which was why she had to work twice as hard to win.

Or, *not lose*, and have to marry the son of her dad's late archenemy.

She opened Grant's text app, and the first thing that popped up was the photo she'd sent him of the two of them together by the waterfall. She left that one alone for him to look at later, and she created a group text to Charlotte and Misty. Nell's number ended in zero, Charlotte's in one, and Misty's in two.

Hi, it's Nell. Phone died. Texting from Grant's. Will catch you up when I get home!

Misty sent an emoji thumbs-up a few seconds later.

After a lag, Charlotte did, too.

She was glad for the acknowledgment of her message, and also glad that neither of her sisters had tried to respond with any sort of annoying or nosy correspondence that could have embarrassed her in front of Grant. It was his phone, after all.

That task done, she became curious about the other numbers on his recently texted list.

It wasn't like she had to look too hard to learn who he'd been communicating with. The trail of messages was right there in his history, pretty much in plain view.

Okay. Wait.

She had to scroll down a tiny bit.

And then a little more.

Her heart gave a happy leap.

Ooh, fun! There's my number again!

It was from when he'd texted her the location for today's hike.

He'd texted the other hikers, too.

Pretty much all of his texts were work-related.

A few were order confirmations from food delivery services. Others had to do with shipping acknowledgments regarding supplies he'd bought for his camp store.

It was really kind of a boring list. She wasn't sure what she'd expected to find. He'd told her he wasn't dating anybody, so it wasn't like she was going to discover some secret girlfriend. Not unless she went way back, and that would be really intrusive. Not to mention creepy. She couldn't do that.

She was tempted.

But, no.

Nell closed the app, and then there was another one staring her in the face.

Grant's photo album.

It kind of taunted her. That tiny colorful button.

It was probably all work stuff like he had on his Instagram.

Mostly landscapes with almost no people.

Boring. Boring. Boring.

He obviously had nothing on his phone he was ashamed of. He hadn't thought twice about letting her use it. So.

She stole a peek at the bathroom door and could hear the shower running.

What if she looked really quickly?

Just to see if…he'd taken any pics this morning when she hadn't been paying attention?

Yeah, that's it. On their group hike!

There might even be one of her, all decked out in her new hiking outfit. On the summit before that sudden cloudburst had changed the course of the hike—and left her looking like a drowned rat, she was sure.

That would be fun to see.

It would also make her looking through his recent photos perfectly legit, because she'd only be searching for herself. Yeah. That wasn't stalkerish in the least. It was more like a sign of healthy curiosity. Everyone liked seeing photos of themselves. When they were flattering ones, anyway. The unflattering ones were what all your supposed friends tended to post on social media. Sigh.

Nell tapped the album icon and frowned.

Well, that's about as disappointing as his text list.

She scanned through the photos, scrolling with her index finger.

It was pretty much what she should have guessed.

Lots of nature stuff. Summits. Rivers. Rapids. Mountains. Camping. Cliffsides.

There were tons of vistas and scenic views.

Others, though, included athletic-looking people doing adventuresome-seeming things—

Wait. Was that Grant hanging off a cliff?

She enlarged the photo and saw that it was him rappelling in what looked like a desert environment. Maybe somewhere in the southwest. Hang on.

Another photo in the same group showed Grant standing on top of a giant rock pedestal formation shaped like an arch. He posed proudly with a bunch of others all in rappelling gear. The woman right beside him stood awfully close.

Nell enlarged the pic, and her eyes nearly fell out of her head.

She was *gorgeous*. Tall. Slim but muscular, and with a long dark braid brought forward over one shoulder and beneath her climbing helmet. She wore fingerless rope gloves, a tank top, and biker shorts, exposing tanned and toned arms and legs.

Grant's arm wrapped around her waist, and he was beaming.

Like, totally lit up on love.

Oh nooo. That's what I have to live up to?

She flipped through more photos, and there were others of Grant and the brunette together looking extra couple-y. Yuck.

She checked the time stamp.

The photos were from a year ago.

She scrolled forward.

Nell's stomach roiled, and bile rose in her throat.

There were two more pictures from just last summer, and they were taken at this cabin. One showed his ex looking super pretty at the kitchen table, dressed in a really large T-shirt that covered the tops of her thighs and that probably belonged to Grant. Her dark hair was long and loose, and she wore a dazzling smile and not much else. Her bare legs crossed in front of her as she hovered over her breakfast plate, holding a half-eaten bagel slathered with cream cheese.

Nell frowned. But the second photo made her want to weep.

It was a shot of this woman at the waterfall. She stood in the stream knee-deep and near the cascades in a really tiny bikini. She looked like a celebrity, honestly. She was laughing and flinging water toward the camera with her perfect hands. A few droplets had landed on the lens and were right there in the picture, making the virtual moment seem so present and real.

Nell's chin jerked up. It had gotten quiet.

Too quiet.

The shower was no longer running in the bathroom.

She dropped Grant's phone like a hot potato, then had to scoop it up off the hooked rug. Her movement caused her foot to slide off the pillow, which jettisoned to the floor, and her ankle slammed down on the chest, just as the bag of frozen peas crashed to the wood floor and split open.

Oh no!

Soggy tiny green balls rolled everywhere, including under the sofa.

She shut Grant's album app and placed his phone on the chest, sliding it far, far away from her as fast as she could.

Too far.

Eeep!

Her elbow hit the stack of magazines, and it slid into a heap on the floor, landing on top of the frozen pea bag.

Nell set her feet down in front of her, her heart hammering.

She lowered the right one too fast and too hard.

Ow, ow, ow!

Something *clicked*.

The bathroom door popped open, and Grant emerged, steam fogging up the small space behind him. He looked really handsome in a fresh pair of jeans and a sweater. He stopped toweling off his hair to goggle at the mess. "What happened here?"

Nell righted herself on the sofa, crossing her arms like she'd been doing nothing wrong.

Like sneakily spying on Grant by going through his phone.

"Looks like a tornado hit."

"Er, not a tornado, exactly." She winced. "There was a breeze."

"A breeze?" He scratched his head.

"Yeah. I thought I heard someone at the door—"

"What? Out here?"

"It was a bird."

He dubiously eyed the door. "Are you sure it wasn't a bat?"

"A bat? Um. Maybe." She puffed out a breath.

"I've had problems with bats before." He cocked his head. "Was it a big one?"

She panicked. "I couldn't tell. I just saw—shadows. Wing-shaped shadows." A trickle of sweat ran down her temple. She wiped it back, pretending to be fiddling with her hair.

His brow creased. "But it didn't get inside?"

"No, no. I quickly shut the door, but not in time to block the wind."

"It can get kind of gusty up here," he conceded with a forgiving look.

Nell's pulse beat double-time. She licked her lips. "I'm so sorry."

She started to scoot off the sofa, but he held up his hand. "Don't worry about it. Sit tight. I'll get the magazines." He stepped forward, and something squished beneath his bare feet, sliming up between his toes. He made a disgusted face and lifted his foot, staring at it. Then he lifted his other foot and stared at that one, too. "Wait, are these peas?"

Nell cringed. "Sorry. The pea bag just kind of split open."

He scanned the floor, and his eyebrows arched. "I'll go and grab the broom." He used his towel to wipe the green grime off the bottoms of his feet, then tossed it back into the bathroom, where it landed across the sink. He returned with the broom and dustpan an instant later. "Wow, what a mess, huh?" At least he didn't look mad. He was chuckling.

"Ha-ha, yeah. The whole room just kind of—exploded."

Nell was already on her knees, picking up the magazines. She had to help somehow. Why did he have so many of these, anyway? There were dozens and dozens.

He swept up the peas and dumped them in the kitchen trash can.

Then he came back to help her with the magazines, some of which were wet. The ones that had been directly over the pea bag, anyway. He grimaced at those and set them aside, probably aiming to dump them in the trash or the recycling. He collected the dry ones and stacked them back on the chest.

"So," he asked. "Did you at least find your tent?"

Oops. "Not yet. I was just about to look."

His dark eyes twinkled. "You found a game for us, then?"

She blinked. "Ah. Yep." She hadn't exactly gotten around to looking at the games, but she couldn't tell him that because he'd wonder what she'd been doing all this time. How long did it take to send one text message to her sisters—and chase away a phantom bat? Less than five minutes, and he'd know that.

He stood, straightening the magazine stack on the chest. Then he picked up the soggy frozen pea bag, which was mostly empty, and carried it to the trash. "Great. What is it?"

"I want to surprise you." And also surprise herself. She sat back on the sofa as he returned from the kitchen. His gaze landed on his phone, and she leaned forward, handing it back to him. Then she casually reached for the pillow, which was still on the floor, and returned it to the chest, giving it a little pat. Her palm came up damp. That was probably pea juice or something. *Gross.* She was not putting her foot back on that.

He watched all this without comment and returned to the topic at hand: game-playing.

"Okay," he said, sitting in the armchair. "But, since there are limited choices, I might be able to guess."

"Yes," she said cagily. "Why don't you do that? Guess!"

"Now, you're being sly." He shook his finger at her. "You probably picked your favorite…"

"Uh-huh." She nodded. "I did."

He slipped his phone in his jeans pocket. "Hmm. Is it older or new?"

"Old." She tried to finesse this. "From the looks of the…box."

"Aha! So it's *not* Pictionary. That one's in a tin."

"It's still in a box, though."

"Yeah, no. Not really." He shook his head. "I'd say it's in more of a container. But that's okay. Pictionary's pretty hard to play with two people anyway." He thought a moment longer. "Can't be cards." His eyes searched the ceiling. "Is it Jenga?"

"No." She kind of liked Jenga, but if she said yes now, she'd never learn what else was in that chest, and she was supposed to have been going through it practically the whole time that he was in the shower.

"Checkers?" Ooh, she hadn't played that in years. How many other games were left?

When she didn't answer, he volunteered. "If it's not checkers, there are only two others."

She grinned, congratulating herself on navigating this tricky situation so seamlessly. "Exactly!"

"Battleship?"

"Close." She pulled a face. "But no dice."

He chuckled. "So then, it has to be—Scrabble."

Yes. Her heart did cartwheels because this was seriously a major score. "I *love* Scrabble," she said in all earnestness. It was better than doing a crossword because you were in competition with someone else. Plus, she liked the fun challenge of having to make words out of randomly chosen letters. "I play online all the time," she said, because—honestly—she had no other real people to play with. No one she knew was into word games of any sort.

"Do you?" He grinned. "That's cool. I like Scrabble, too." He sank his hands in his pockets. "I mean, used to. Haven't played in a while."

"I could give you a refresher course, if you'd like?"

"Sure." His dark eyes sparkled. "There is one issue, though."

Her eyebrows rose.

"My game's missing some of its letters."

"Most or just a few?"

He chuckled. "I think that we can manage."

CHAPTER NINE

Grant placed another log on the fire and switched on a few living room lamps, and also the overhead light in the kitchen. Dusk fell outdoors, and darkness crept in through the cabin's windows, casting long shadows across the floor. He set Nell up at the table with her foot propped on a sofa pillow on another chair. She had the Scrabble game in front of her.

He reached into the freezer for a cold pack. "That bag of peas was kind of shot, so I thought maybe we should move on to corn."

She giggled. "I was about to say something corny, but I didn't."

"Come on, Nell. Don't be a cornball."

"Ooh, look at you. Fast with the quip."

"I can be punny when I want to be. Just lend me your ears."

Her eyes twinkled. "You're a cornucopia of humor, Grant."

"Well, shucks."

She laughed harder. "You're a-maize-ing."

He chortled at her quick comeback. "There's a kernel of truth in that."

Susan hadn't been into wordplay or Scrabble. None of his other former girlfriends had, either. Hanging out with a woman who liked cheesy puns as much as he did was refreshing.

"I do eat corn, though," she said lightly. "It's not like it is with the peas."

"Well, hold yourself back," he teased, waving the bag at her. "It needs to do its job here." He draped the bag across her wrapped ankle and positioned it so it would stay in place.

"Thanks, Grant," she said. "You're being really sweet in taking care of me."

"I'm happy to do it," he said, because that was the truth. He liked tending to Nell. Her cheerful presence had been a welcome surprise. Plus she'd kept him immensely entertained with her wild camping stories. He could not picture any of the Delaney sisters in a tent. Least of all Nell, judging by what she'd selected as a hiking outfit.

He'd been mindful of having her ice her ankle off and on every twenty minutes or so, and his visible observation indicated that it had helped with the swelling. With her kind of injury, "RICE"ing for the first twenty-four hours was key. Rest. Ice. Compression. Elevation. He'd keep working on that, hoping she'd be much improved by tomorrow.

He filled both their mugs with steaming water from the kettle on the stove. "We've got two choices for tea. Earl Grey or Pumpkin Spice."

"Ooh, Pumpkin Spice sounds autumnal. I'll take that, please."

He opened two paper packets and dropped a teabag into each of their mugs, carrying Nell's over to her at the table.

"I don't suppose you have cream, even the pow-dered stuff?"

"No, but I've got honey."

"Honey would be great."

He opened a cabinet and produced a jar of

honey, placing it on the table with a spoon. "I also have lemons." Lemon with honey and pumpkin sounded kind of good, a tempting fall-like blend.

"Yeah?"

"In the refrigerator. They have a long shelf life, and I use them sometimes when I'm making fish."

"Other than fish, what do you cook?"

"Grilled stuff, mostly."

"Do you have a grill here?"

"Actually, I do. It's in the storage closet off the back stoop." He hadn't used that grill in a long while—not since the last time Susan was here. If Nell was staying longer as a girlfriend and not just overnight as an emergency houseguest, he'd be tempted to lay in groceries and make her a nice sirloin steak. Maybe if they started dating, he could do that another time. He'd already invited her out to Mariner's, and he looked forward to making that happen.

He opened the refrigerator and pulled out a lemon. "Yes or no?"

"Sure, but only if you're going to cut it anyway."

"I was going to do that later for dinner," he said. "So, might as well."

He removed a small cutting board from a drawer, along with a serrated knife, and sliced into the lemon, releasing a burst of citrusy scent into the air. He offered Nell a lemon wedge, and she squeezed its juice into her mug with a spoonful of honey, preparing her tea. He did the same when he joined her at the table.

They both took careful sips of the steaming liquid.

"This place is very cute." She glanced around the cabin. "Homey with the fire going in the woodstove."

"Yeah. I make sure to keep lots of firewood on hand. Especially in the fall and winter."

"I bet it's freezing up here in December."

He chuckled, thinking of ways to keep her warm. Like wrapping his arms around her and snuggling down under the covers. But he didn't want to push her or take advantage of the situation. "I've got lots of heavy blankets."

Her eyes darted toward the bedroom, and she blushed.

"But don't worry about that for now. The temps are mild enough, and you're getting the bed," he said to reassure her. "I'll take the sofa."

"Oh no. I can't let you—"

"Nell," he said. "I offered. Besides that, we can keep your ankle better elevated in the bed." He studied her sympathetically. "How's it feeling?"

"Still hurts a little."

"We'll give you more meds with dinner. In the meantime, we'll keep icing it."

He slid the Scrabble game over and removed the lid. Then he lifted out the turntable-style board and put it on the table between them. It was made of heavy plastic, and each game square was partitioned off by shallow sides, made to hold each tile in place so it wouldn't slide.

"Cool board. Where did you get it?"

"It was my mom's. We had it when I was growing up."

She lightly touched its edge, making it pivot. "Nice. It rotates around?"

"Very handy." He nodded. "Especially in cut-throat games."

"So you play cutthroat games, huh?"

"Okay, I'll admit it." He grinned. "I'm competi-tive."

"Oh yeah?" She grinned, too, and his heart thumped. "Well, so am I." She looked like she want-ed to say something more. "Grant, about that—"

"Yeah?"

But then she lost her nerve. She noted the score-pad and pencil in the box. "Er. Want me to keep score?"

His mouth twitched. "Only if you don't cheat me."

She gasped in mock shock. "I never cheat." She arched one eyebrow. "Do you?"

He chuckled. "Not anymore."

"What's that mean?"

"Long story." He figured he'd share it with her eventually. It was really pretty silly, and he'd been a goofy kid. Kids did things. Nell had probably pulled a few shenanigans, too.

"Hmm." She removed the scorepad and pencil from the box and set them beside her, and he hand-ed her a rack to hold her tiles. Once she was ready, he picked up the red velvet sack containing the let-ters and shook it before prying open its drawstring so she could select her tiles.

She placed seven tiles on her tile rack, shielded from his view.

He did the same. When he was done, he took the box and its lid, depositing them on the counter be-hind him.

Nell sipped from her tea, but her eyes were on him. "How many letters are missing?"

"Six."

"What happened to them?"

He gritted his teeth, deciding he might as well tell her. It was forever ago anyway. "I…disposed of them as a kid."

She blinked. "Disposed?"

"My mom was a killer Scrabble player," he explained. "She's the one who taught me the game. And, uh. Let's just say she was very good at beating me."

"Oh no." She giggled in disbelief. "You didn't?"

Heat spread from his neck to his face. "I'm afraid that I did."

"Wait. What did you do with them?"

"I buried them in my backyard."

She cackled. "What?"

"But only after hiding them in my sock drawer for a while. I became paranoid Mom might find them."

"Why not just throw them in the trash?"

"Too risky. What if they spilled out and I was discovered?"

She laughed, evidently trying to imagine this. "So you dug a hole." She motioned like she was using a shovel. "And buried them?"

"It was a decent service," he said reflectively. "Very solemn."

"You did *not* hold a funeral."

"Oh but I did." He placed a hand on his chest. "May they rest in peace."

She roared and gripped her sides like they were

splitting. "You were such a weird kid!"

He chuckled along with her. "Like you never did anything weird. Sure."

"I didn't cheat my parents."

"How about your sisters?"

"Well, I wouldn't call it cheating, exactly." She shrugged sheepishly. "But I guess I did deceive them. Charlotte especially. There was that one year where I helped her with her Halloween candy."

"*Helped* her with her candy?" Grant hooted, glad to know she wasn't a saint, either. "See there? I *knew* it. I knew it!" He shot her a smug look. "You're not so perfect yourself."

"Never said that I was. And anyway, it's not like you think," she said, her cheeks pink. "Misty came down with a sudden fever that year and couldn't go trick-or-treating. So Charlotte and I offered to share our candy with her. Only, after Charlotte went to bed, I refilled her plastic pumpkin so she wouldn't suffer."

"With candy from yours?"

She nodded.

"Didn't Charlotte notice the next morning?"

"Oh yeah, she did. But I said the Great Pumpkin had come by and worked some Halloween magic."

Grant chuckled at her impish grin. "Did she buy it?"

"Yeah." Nell chuckled, too. "She actually did."

"Wow, Nell. That was pretty altruistic for a kid." There he'd been kind of hoping she'd share some dirt, but even her stories about being naughty were charming.

"I was always looking after them. I wanted to."

She smiled, and he could tell that she meant it. Nell had such a caring instinct.

"How old were you?"

"Eight. No. Nine." She locked on his gaze, pondering something. "So, how about you? Did you ever fess up? About those missing Scrabble letters?"

"Didn't have to." He shook his head. "Mom had me totally figured out."

"Yeah? What did she do?"

"Nothing."

"Nothing?"

"We kept playing, and she acted like she didn't even notice those missing tiles. Mom was cool that way. Or maybe she decided to let my own guilt punish me. It didn't seem to matter much, anyway. She kept right on winning."

"So. Which letters did you steal?"

"All of the Us at first. Mom was lethal with that vowel. She had a way of combining it with certain consonants and placing the words on high-value squares." He shrugged. "Once all the Us disappeared, she still won. That's when I knew that the Q and Z had to go."

"Two high-ranking letters."

He nodded. "Ten points each."

Nell shook a scolding finger. "You were such a sneaky cheat."

"Hey! I take offense at that," he said, but he was laughing. "But, yeah. Probably so."

"How old were you?"

"Ten? Maybe eleven? Come on." He held his hands out in front of him. "She was always coming up with tricky words. I had to do something. When I had a Q, all I could think of was words that took Us, like Queen or Quota or…I QUIT."

Nell roared at this. "But the Us were missing in action by then?"

"Exactly." He grinned at the funny memories. "Meanwhile, Mom still stunned me with words like QI, 'a vital force inherent to all things,' and QINTAR, 'a monetary unit of Albania.'"

"I like qintar," she said. "I'm going to use that."

He shook his head. "Then there was Z and obscure words she came up with like ZA."

"Meaning pizza! Not so obscure. That's a great two-letter word." Nell smiled. "It's really helpful when you play online—"

"If you're talking about those tabs you can click to get acceptable two-letter-word choices, there's no such luck here."

"Ooh, we're playing hardball, are we?"

He got his game face on. "Yes, ma'am. Not only that…" He lifted a thick paperback dictionary off the table. It was dog-eared, and the worn cover had seen better days. "If it's not in this book, it doesn't count."

"Wait a minute. How old is that dictionary?"

"It's an official Scrabble one."

"Yeah, but from when?"

"That's not important." He leaned toward her. "Are you backing down from the challenge?"

She leaned toward him as well. "Not on your life." Heat stirred in her eyes. "Are you?"

His pulse thrummed in his ears. "Nope."

She set her chin. "Good."

"Nice to see I'm not the only competitive one

around here."

"So, you love a challenge, huh?"

The twinkle in her eyes sent heat skittering through his body. "Sure do."

She squared her shoulders. "Same here."

Now he was curious. He leaned back and studied her. "What's the biggest challenge you've ever tackled?"

"You first."

He though on this. "Doing the Overland Track in Tasmania."

"Whoa." She stared at him, impressed. "You were in Tasmania?"

"Yeah. I studied in Australia my junior year of college. Jordan did, too. That's how we met."

"That's so cool." She viewed him admiringly, and he liked it. A lot. "I didn't know you'd traveled. I mean, I remember you going to college in Chicago."

"Yeah. And you studied where? In Vermont?"

"How did you know?"

He chuckled at her slack-jawed expression. "Bumper sticker on your car."

"Aha!" She laughed. "Yeah, I majored in accounting. You?"

"Environmental Science."

"That makes sense. Did you always want to open your own camping store?"

"It was my dream."

"And now that dream has come true."

Her sweet smile warmed him. He pushed back in his chair, wanting to know more about her. "So how about you? Your biggest challenge?"

She rolled her eyes, but her cheeks turned pink.

"Um…probably signing up for your hike today."

This intrigued him. He couldn't fathom why she'd sign up and pretend to have experience. "Seriously? Why?"

"I wanted to try hiking out. Do something different."

He chuckled, recalling the price stickers on her clothing. "I kind of gathered you were a novice."

"It wasn't only that." She shyly dropped her chin, then peered up at him through her eyelashes. "I also wanted to see you."

His heart thumped. "What?"

"Yeah. I remembered you from high school and was kind of wondering what you were up to." She winced. "You're not mad?"

"Mad?" Was she kidding him? He was flattered. She'd gone to great lengths trying to impress him with her supposed outdoorsy ways, though truth be told, he'd have been happy if she'd shown up without a clue and owned it. "No. Not at all, but why didn't you say something sooner? Reach out?"

"Um." She bit her lip. "I'm not the most reaching-out type of person." Her face was the color of a ripe tomato. "I never tried to contact you before because I was worried, I guess. That you'd think I was weird."

"I'm not exactly in a position to call someone weird, now am I?" He gestured at the board between them. "Not after telling you I buried *Scrabble letters*."

She giggled, seeming to relax. "Had I suspected *that* level of weirdness, I'd have been on your doorstep ages ago."

If only. He crossed his arms. "Regardless of the timing, I'm glad you did it. Otherwise, we wouldn't be here now."

"Yeah, I wouldn't have ruined your hike."

"You didn't ruin it." His voice grew husky. "At all."

She blushed under his stare. So interesting that she'd apparently crushed on him and that he'd never known. He studied her, intrigued by her complexity. "My only regret," he said after a lull, "is that you didn't sign up earlier."

"Oh yeah?" Her pretty blush deepened.

Grant set his elbows on the table and leaned toward her. "Yeah."

Sparks flew between them as she held his gaze. Nell Delaney, of all people. She was funny and smart and fast with a quip. The thought of playing Scrabble against her was exciting somehow, but not nearly as energizing as having her with him here at his cabin. So, she'd tracked him down after wanting to see him. Were things working out the way she hoped? Because he sure liked where things seemed to be going on his end.

Oh, how he ached to reach out and touch her, cup his hand to her sweet round face. Stroke his thumb across her cheek, tracing that smattering of freckles. The ones that made her look so cute and sexy all at once. She was so close now. Her incredible lips just inches from his mouth.

A log popped loudly in the fire, and they both pulled back.

Grant's temperature spiked. He'd fallen completely under her spell for the second time today. If it happened again, he wasn't so sure he'd recover.

Or be able to resist making a move. But only if she wanted that, too.

From the look in her eyes, it seemed like she did. Maybe she'd been curious about him before, but now that she was getting to know him, was she liking him even better?

She combed her fingers through her hair, and her curls tumbled past her shoulders. She stared down at the Scrabble board, evidently searching for something to say.

"So, it was your mom," she said, sounding a little breathy, "who taught you to play?"

Great. No better way to douse ice water on romantic interest than to mention someone's parents.

"Yeah." Grant cleared his throat. "That's right."

She paused a beat, then asked him, "What was her best move?"

"Best move?" His body still buzzed from their earlier exchange, but he did his best to address her question. There'd be more time for romance later. He hoped. It wasn't like they had to rush this. Grant was cautious, a big believer in taking things slow. He searched the annals of his brain, stumbling across a recollection. "Hmm. Probably ZEBRANO."

She wrinkled up her nose. "What's that?"

"A tree having striped wood."

She chuckled. "Oh no! That's a seven-letter word."

"Oh yeah." He grinned. They were back to light-hearted fun, and that was fine with him for the moment. "Fifty bonus points for using all seven tiles, *and* she played that on a Triple Word Score."

Nell smiled. "She sounds great, Grant. I wish I could have met her."

"Yeah, she was. And you know what? So do I." He studied Nell, thinking about how much his mom would have liked her. And vice versa. "She was AMAZING."

"Seven-letter word using a Z." She grinned a devilish grin, and he wanted to kiss her so hard. But he decided to work on that later. "I think we're ready to play."

He rubbed his hands together, eager to get started. "No mercy?"

She met his eyes, and there was daring in hers. "No mercy."

Grant's heart skipped a beat.

He liked the sound of that. He'd never met anyone like Nell Delaney. That was for sure. "Okay, honey," he said. "You're on."

• • •

"Nooooo!!!"

Grant's groan echoed through the cabin, bouncing off the knotty pine walls. He raked both hands through his hair and threw back his head. "You slaughtered me."

Nell laughed, pleased with the outcome. Still, she tried to be gracious about it. "A twelve-point win isn't an annihilation, Grant."

"Might as well be." He chuckled and shook his head. "There was no coming back once you played GHERKINS."

"Guess you got yourself in a pickle by opening

up that S," she teased.

"Touché, Nell. Touché." He sat back in his chair and crossed his arms. "I give you all the credit. You didn't even need those Us, the X, or the Z."

"Now, if the K disappears…" She rolled her eyes.

Grant belly laughed. "No worries there. My cheating days are done."

"Yeah." She sighed happily. "Mine, too."

She helped him pack up the game, unable to believe the difference that twenty-four hours made. Just yesterday evening, she'd decided to sign up for Grant's hike, and today he'd said he was awful glad that she had. And the way he'd looked at her had made her skin tingle all over. A flurry of nerves settled in her belly. She might actually do this. Get Grant to fall in love with her—organically.

They shared the same sense of humor and loved word games.

And the way he'd tended to her had practically made her melt.

Her heart sighed every time he asked how she was doing or made some small effort to ensure her comfort. He really was a wonderful guy. Nell was pleased that she'd chosen so perfectly. She could have wasted years and years crushing on someone who turned out to be a really horrible person in the end. But no. He was everything she'd hoped for.

Grant Williams was a stellar guy.

He was more than a star.

He was an entire constellation.

And he lit up her night sky.

Maybe someday soon, she'd also be lighting up his.

She smiled, imagining them on a fabulous camping trip somewhere. Just the two of them alone together. She had no idea that Grant had hiked and camped outside the United States. That knowledge only made him more interesting. It was thrilling that he seemed to find her interesting, too, even though her hobbies were fairly boring compared to his: basically just knitting, Scrabble, and reading.

At least they shared their Scrabble fixation. Playing with him had been super fun, especially playing in person where she could watch his changeable expressions. His furrowed brow and the look of concentration on his face when he was anticipating his next move, or the sneaky gleam in his eyes when he was about to play a high-scoring word. She'd loved being party to all of it. But most of all, she adored hearing him laugh. They'd had a great time together, and more than once, Grant seemed momentarily struck by the fact, judging by his expression.

"Hungry?" he asked her from where he stood in the kitchen. He'd been washing out their tea mugs and putting them away.

Her stomach rumbled. "A little."

"How about I make us dinner?"

"Can I do anything to help?"

"No, it's pretty basic. Just some French fries and fried fish."

"Fish and chips?" She grinned. "Sounds yum."

"You like trout?"

"I don't think I've ever eaten it."

"You're in for a real experience, then."

"Oh." She had no idea what he meant by that,

but she was willing to go along with the menu. He was cooking for her, after all. "Good."

"Why don't you relax on the sofa and check out some of those magazines? Or, better yet, work on that knitting project of yours? That hat looks almost done." His dark eyes shimmered, and her heart gave a lovesick leap.

"Yeah, it is," she said, lost in his dreamy gaze.

She couldn't wait to give it to him.

CHAPTER TEN

Nell casually flipped through some of the magazines, but she was more interested in the catalogues she found for equipment and clothing than in the long, boring, exceedingly jargony articles about taking a pilgrimage called "Camino de Santiago" across the Pyrenees mountains from France into Spain, or scuba diving along the Great Barrier Reef in Australia. Those excursions were fine if you didn't mind developing calluses on your feet from walking nonstop for two weeks or risking your life by swimming in shark-infested waters.

Other pieces profiled domestic adventures, many at National Parks, and yeah. There was a fair share of camping. Along with climbing, kayaking, and other things, too. Her mind wandered back to that photo of Grant's ex in that tiny bikini, and she frowned. Not that she was jealous or anything. The woman wasn't even in the picture anymore. Except, she was probably implanted in Grant's memory. Like a sneaky little seed from his past that might decide to bloom at some inappropriate moment. That could be a problem if he started making comparisons between her and Ms. Mountain-climbing Woman.

Nell told herself to buck up and stop thinking negatively. She was the one here with Grant. Not old what's-her-name. She thumbed through a merchandise circular, picking out several outfits that she liked and that fit her figure. Many also went with her knits. Nice! She spotted a flannel shirt called a Boyfriend Borrow, marketed to women. It looked like a man's button-down shirt with cuffs and a collar, and it had a fun plaid pattern on it in blues, purples, and greens. Although she generally wore more frilly tops, something like this was a better call for a rugged outdoor adventure. It would also go with her coloring.

Ooh! She could get some of those cool duck boots, too, along with a green down jacket.

She was tempted to order it all for her proposed camping trip with Grant.

With my sisters?

Uh, no.

What was he thinking?

That would be like having two nosy chaperones along. That would also be in summertime, since that's what she'd told him. So flannel was out. Or maybe it could work for chilly evenings and mornings? But seriously. What was the point? The entire camping trip was fiction, and they wouldn't be going anyway. Not in a group, if she could help it.

If Nell went camping with Grant, she'd want him all to herself.

Ooh, that double sleeping bag looks cozy.

"Find your tent?" he asked from the kitchen. He stood at the counter, coating fish in a flour mixture. He had his sweater sleeves pushed up and appeared in his element. A frying pan sat on the stove, and the French fries baked in the oven, their fast-food scent filling the air.

"Not yet." She gave him an apologetic shrug.

"Without Misty's keen eye, a lot of them kind of look the same."

He chuckled. "Maybe you should do something else?"

She nodded and turned back around, reaching for her purse, which sat on the floor beside her. This year, she finally was going to give Grant the birthday present she'd made him. In person, and he was going to love it. She could tell. He'd admired the hat after he'd joked around with it, trying it on. He didn't know it was for him then, but he'd learn that soon enough.

Just five more days.

She'd never celebrated a birthday with a boy-friend before; if they became an item by then, this would be a first. She'd even bake him a cake! Then her hint to her sisters about them being exclusive would become an actual fact. That would give her three more weeks to work on the getting-engaged part. Assuming he even fell for her in the first place, and then didn't bolt the moment he learned about Aidan.

She owned a cute country cottage by a cranberry bog. Grant would probably like it a lot, since it was out in nature and not smack-dab in the center of town. She knew he rented a small house near his store. That was on the outskirts of Majestic, too, conveniently not too far from Nell's. She could ask him over for a birthday dinner on the seventh. After this time spent together at his cabin, then their date at Mariner's—which she now knew for sure was happening—the invitation to her place would be like icing on the cake.

Once she told him about her parents losing Bearberry Brews and their house, he'd surely understand why she and her sisters had made that extreme bet. The wager hadn't been undertaken lightly but out of desperate necessity. By the time she told him about it, she hoped he'd be too invested in her to be angry that she'd not been totally honest when he asked why she signed up for the hike now and not before. And hopefully he'd not break her heart by leaving her to Aidan. Only time would tell on that one, and she knew she had to be prepared to face the consequences if things didn't work out.

She sighed and examined her project, deciding in her heart that she was going to give Grant this hat one way or another and tell him how she felt—how she'd always felt—about him. The bet had just been the kick in the pants she'd needed to reach out. She hoped that he'd be pleased and return her feelings, but if he didn't, she would just have to deal with that harsh reality and move on. She lifted her knitting needles and got to work, dreaming up all the other things she could make Grant, in the event of the happiest outcome.

Maybe she could try a cardigan again? She could knit one to match the hat. A knitted scarf, too. Nell grinned at another idea. She could make a matching set for herself. His and hers knitted outfits that they could wear at the cabin when they took their couple's getaways. Her heart warmed at the precious image she painted in her mind:

Grant in his knits, appearing extra handsome with wisps of his wavy blond hair peeking out from under his birthday hat. He had a thick, warm scarf wrapped around his neck and wore a buttoned cardigan sweater over a turtleneck and jeans. He hugged her from behind, leaning forward, and Nell giggled, glancing over her shoulder into his adoring dark eyes. With her knitted hat, scarf, and cardigan being carbon copies of his, they'd look just like models on an adorable Christmas card, or a book cover, even. A romance novel cover, no question.

They'd have to take a selfie of that for sure.

"How are the lima beans holding up?" Grant asked, bursting her fantasy bubble.

Nell stared at her ankle, which was propped on a pillow on the chest and had a bag of frozen lima beans on it this time. The corn had long since given up the fight.

"Pretty well," she said. "My ankle's actually feeling a little better."

"Good. That's great to hear." He laid the fish in the frying pan, and oil sizzled. A mild fishy aroma wafted toward her. It wasn't unpleasant, but it was sort of gamey. It smelled different from other fish Nell had tried before. "I hope you don't mind skipping the veggies tonight. We don't have a ton on hand, so we should probably save them for medicinal purposes."

She laughed. Kids everywhere would love that excuse for getting out of their dinner veggies. Maybe if this worked out the way she hoped, there'd be a little Grant or a little Nell claiming a higher purpose for their veggies someday.

• • •

The evening got dreamier when Grant announced it was time to eat.

She hobbled over to the table.

"Everything looks so nice."

"My lady." He gallantly pulled back her chair, then helped scoot her in once she sat down. Afterward, he propped her leg on another chair using a pillow. He handed her two ibuprofen, and she took them with the water he'd already put on the table.

"You're being very attentive," she said with a flirty edge, and he noticed.

"That's because you need tending to." He smiled, and her stomach fluttered. "We'll add more ice in twenty minutes."

She'd never had anyone treat her this way. Just like the royal princess she'd imagined back when she'd assumed her mother's announcement about Aidan was a joke. After a lifetime of taking care of her sisters and putting everyone else first, being pampered was a feeling she could get used to.

He set a dinner dish down in front of her. It held a mound of French fries and a huge portion of fish that stretched across the width of her plate. Thank goodness the fish's head had been removed, but it still had its tail attached. Nell's stomach roiled. The closest she'd come to eating a whole fish before was fish and chips, and that was cut up in pieces and heavily floured and fried. You could even have mistaken it for chicken nuggets, if it hadn't tasted so nasty.

This specimen in front of her definitely looked like a fish, not poultry. A completely decapitated fish at that. A wave of queasiness crashed over her. Still, Grant had worked hard to prepare dinner, so she couldn't very well turn up her nose at it without seeming ungrateful. Since she couldn't very well hold her nose, maybe she could stealthily hold her breath when she swallowed. He probably wouldn't notice.

He'd set ketchup, tartar sauce, and some of that cut lemon on the table. Good. She'd use lots of those, and maybe they'd cover the fish taste. Grant served his plate and dimmed the kitchen lights a little. Flickering light trailed into the kitchen from the woodstove, and the candle's flame danced between them.

He'd gone to extra trouble to make this meal special, and she appreciated his efforts, so she'd do her best to get behind the meal choice.

"The fish looks great," she said politely as he sat down. "Thank you."

He issued a word of caution. "You need to be a bit careful when you chew. It's tasty but it can be bony. Let me show you a little trick."

He picked up his fork and grabbed hold of his fish's tail with his other hand, while the fried fish laid sideways on his plate. "Just lift the tail," he instructed, "and stick your fork into the underside like so." He did this, pinning the bottom part of his fish in place.

"Then you divide the fish into two halves by using the tail as a tab to pull back the top layer." She watched, horrified. This was worse than high school biology. Her gaze stayed glued to the plate as he set that upper portion aside, skin side down.

"Don't forget to check for bones." He did and picked out a scattered few from the flesh with his fork prongs. "That was part one." He met her eyes and grinned.

Nell pursed her lips, admiring his skill but wishing he was teaching a different lesson. Like one on how to best carve a standing rib roast or something. "I'm taking notes." She forced a smile, and he grinned again, apparently appreciating her rapt attention. If she didn't focus so hard, she would probably throw up. She'd had a goldfish once. Lots of years ago. It was much smaller, but still. Just the idea.

"Now that the fish is cooked," he said, "the spine should lift out easily."

He examined the bottom portion of his fish, prying his fork tines beneath the tip of the nearly intact spine at the tail end. With a lever-like move, he raised the tip of the spine, separating it from the meat and pinching it between this thumb and index finger.

"You grab the end of the spine like this and slowly…peel it back." When he did, the spine rolled right out of the fish, attached bones and all. "Ta-da!"

OMG, she felt lightheaded. All around her, she saw sparkly stars. But no! She needed to applaud this. Just look at his face. So proud.

She clapped her hands in enthusiastic approval, only stopping once or twice to cover her mouth. "Yay!" She squeezed lemon into her water to help settle her stomach. "Is there a reason you don't take the bones out first when you clean it?" she asked after taking a sip. That little fish skeleton sat on the

side of the plate, just lying there. All bony and whatnot. She added another squeeze of lemon to her
water. Then one more.

"Trust me." He winked, and her skin tingled
weirdly. Her stomach was in one great big knot,
though. Her throat felt kind of tight, too. "It's easier
this way." He motioned to her plate. "You'll need to
check both fillets with your fork and pry out any
bones that got left behind. Shouldn't be too many."

"Ahh, great!" She nodded and stared uncertainly
at her plate. At least she had a giant helping of
French fries. Maybe she could ask for more, then
bury some of the fish under those and extra ketchup.
After she'd cut her fish into portions and then slid
those around on her plate.

Oooh, but the smell. Grant said it was mild, but
so was salmon, according to everyone, and even that
made her queasy. When it came to shellfish, forget it.
She couldn't harm a creature that came from the sea.
Maybe she could say she was the opposite of a pes-
catarian? A "landatarian" or something like that?
Nell kicked herself for not thinking of this before.
Now she was stuck.

He chuckled and switched his plate with hers.
"Here, why don't you take mine?"

Her pulse pounded. His portion was even larger
than hers. "Oh no, I couldn't."

He grinned. "I insist."

The big fish taunted her, telling her she had to do
this. Whether she wanted to or not. "That's so nice of
you," she said feebly. "Thanks."

"No problem."

She added some tartar sauce and lemon to her

plate. A couple of squirts of ketchup, too. Then she added more ketchup and tartar sauce. Gobs more. She poked at her fish with her fork, gauging how to tackle it. "Do you eat the skin?" *Please say no. That would be seriously gross, like her parents eating whole soft-shell crabs. The barbarians.*

"Only if you want to. I do, but it's a personal thing. Don't feel I'll be offended."

Whew. "Oh! Okay." She suspected these were fresh fish, which made sense, since this was his fishing cabin. Still, she hadn't seen any of his fishing gear around the place, but maybe he kept that outdoors in that storage closet he mentioned. "Did you catch these here?"

"Yes, ma'am. Near where we saw that rainbow today."

"So, they're rainbow trout," she teased.

His mouth twitched. "In a manner of speaking." He helped himself to tartar sauce and lemon, too. "Seriously though, this fish is a type of char, so in the same family as salmon. Tastes like salmon, too, and it's really good for you. High in omega-3s."

That sounded healthy enough. Maybe she could stomach this.

She loaded some fish on her fork and added tartar sauce, then squeezed lemon juice on top. Some less-sensitive individuals probably wouldn't be bothered, but the fish still reeked to her. She held her breath as the forkful grew nearer, and then she quickly shoved it into her mouth. The faster the better so—*ooh, no, noooo. Ugh. Ew*. When they were kids, Charlotte had had a cat, Ginger. The canned food they gave her reminded Nell a little of… She set down her fork.

Grant watched her expectantly. "Well?"

She chewed deliberately, just in case he'd missed a bone. "Ooh," she said, running out of air. How long could one woman hold her breath? Maybe longer if she was in shape, but Nell wasn't. "Mmm, good." She'd never tell him what she really thought and risk hurting his feelings.

His grin lit up the kitchen. "I'm so glad that you like it. The freezer's full up."

Nell swallowed everything in her mouth in one huge gulp, then chased that with a lot of lemon water. "Nice!"

"Yeah. If we were staying here longer, we could have it again."

She added more tartar sauce to her plate. Lemon, too. "It's a shame we're going tomorrow, then." Ketchup? Where's the ketchup? Oh, there. She shook-shook-shook some onto her plate, covering her fries and some of the fish. Then she started cutting and moving things around, just like she'd planned. But first, she loaded a few forkfuls of fries into her mouth, because she was basically starving.

"Yeah." He frowned, looking handsome in the shadows. "Sure is."

"Do you cook this when you're camping?" she asked, starting to worry. While the initial couple of bites had been difficult, she'd muster through them. The more the flavors built up on her tongue, though, the more unpalatable they became.

"Oh yeah," he said. "Trout is delicious cooked over a campfire or on a portable camp stove. You just wrap it in foil and add some lemon."

"I bet that's tasty." *Or not.*

She scanned her plate and the enormous fillet, which she'd barely touched, and picked up a French fry. Then she ate another one, dousing it with ketchup. That sort of took the fishy taste away, but not entirely.

"Maybe I can make some for you and your sisters on our trip?"

Wait. He was back to that again? Grant really did seem to have a fixation on that camping trip. And about tents. "I'm sure they'd love that," she said, fully aware the trip would never happen. Not if she had anything to say about it, anyway.

She picked at her fish, and his forehead creased.

"Is something wrong?"

"No, no. Everything is so, so good. I'm just…" She lifted a shoulder. "Not as hungry as I thought I was."

"No worries," he answered cheerfully. "We can save any leftovers for breakfast."

Nell's stomach roiled. "Breakfast?"

"Goes great with grits."

She grinned tightly. Maybe she could find a way to just eat the grits part.

"Did you eat much fish growing up?" he asked her while continuing to polish off his meal. He seemed oblivious to how little she was eating, which was good. Except that she was actually hungry. She ate more fries, and then another bunch of them, stuffing them in her mouth.

"Um." She chewed behind the back of her hand. "Not a ton. My dad did most of the cooking, so we ate lots of Irish food. Like colcannon, bangers and mash…"

"What's colcannon?"

"It's made from potatoes and cabbage. It's one of those comfort foods. Really satisfying." She'd give anything to have some of that now. She took another forkful of French fries, noticing she'd nearly cleaned her plate. Of those, anyway.

"Want more fries?" he asked her.

"No, thanks. I'm good." She patted her belly. "Really stuffed all of a sudden." Maybe she could sneak out here and make a PB&J after they'd gone to bed? If Grant was a really sound sleeper. And she didn't stumble into a bunch of furniture while bumbling around in the darkness and hopping on her one good foot.

Okay. Bad idea.

"I'll wrap up your fish in case you get hungry later. Don't feel like you have to wait until breakfast."

"Great. Thanks."

"So you ate Irish food, hmm?" He continued working on his dinner. "Maybe you can make something for me sometime?"

Nell couldn't wait to have him over to her place. "I'd love to."

He cocked his head and studied her before changing the subject. "What do you do in your free time, when you're not knitting and playing online Scrabble?"

"I read."

"Oh yeah? What? Maybe we have some favorite authors in common?"

"Mostly romance novels." Heat warmed her face, and he chuckled.

"Okay then, no. Maybe not."

"Do you watch shows?" she asked. "So many great ones right now."

"Let me guess…" He shot her a teasing stare, and she playfully lowered her eyebrows.

"Don't judge me. I watch lots of shows. Comedies. Thrillers."

"Yeah, there are some good ones. Especially those Nordic mysteries."

"No way." She grinned. "I watch those, too!"

They discussed a number of series, discovering they watched a lot of the same shows, including British police procedurals.

"Wait." He held up his hand. "I still haven't seen the last episode, so don't spoil the ending."

"You're up to the trial?"

"Yeah," he said. "A real cliff-hanger."

"All right," she said. "I'll wait for you to see it, and you can tell me what you think. I kind of guessed the ending, because the chief inspector—"

"Nell, stop," he said, chuckling.

"Oops. Sorry." She'd been carried away with the storyline. Her sisters didn't watch any of the same things she did, so it was fun having someone to gush over her favorite police procedurals with. While Nell didn't enjoy the grisly crime aspect, the shows she watched tended to leave any actual violence off-screen. It was the solving of the crimes that intrigued her, almost like working a puzzle—or carefully strategizing her next Scrabble move.

Is this how it'd always be with Grant? If so, a marriage with him would be wonderful. They'd laugh together and joke about puns and go on nature hikes—because she *would* get better at them. He could teach her how to camp. She could teach him how to win at Scrabble. Against other people, at least, because no way was she giving up her title. There'd be many more rainbows in their future. It was okay if she didn't like trout. He didn't like crunchy peanut butter. Or coffee. That wasn't any sort of deal breaker.

He started to clear the table, and Nell felt awkward doing nothing. "I don't suppose you'll let me help put things away?"

"You, little lady, are not to lift a finger." He motioned toward the sofa. "Go on over there and get comfortable. I'll join you in a bit."

. . .

Grant scoured his frying pan, chuckling at Nell's reaction to eating trout. He got that it wasn't her favorite, but she'd been too polite to let on. Still, after her hiking and camping embellishments, he couldn't help but give her a hard time. As for the fish itself, he understood that game fish wasn't for everyone. Nothing tasted better to him than when it was cooked right on the spot near where he'd caught it.

His dad had taught him fly-fishing when he was about eight. In those days, his dad still liked the outdoors. When his dad lost his factory job, though, he started to sour on a lot of things, including recreational activities. His dad's primary recreational activity became booze.

Grant dried and put away the frying pan and cookie sheet, and he turned to handwashing the dinner dishes next. His cabin was basic, so he didn't have a dishwasher. Most times, he didn't really need one, since he was up here by himself.

He glanced over at Nell, and she seemed happy, knitting on the sofa by the fire, and her presence made his rustic retreat seem more like a home. He did wish his mom could have met Nell. She would have loved his cabin, too, appreciating its seclusion and gorgeous nature views. Unlike his dad, Grant's mom had never lost her love for the outdoors or adventure.

He finished with the dishes, putting them away after they were washed and dried, then called out to Nell. "Want more tea?"

"Sure!" She started to stand, but he stopped her.

"I'll fix it. Then I'll come and sit with you by the fire."

Her whole face colored. "That would be nice."

Yeah, it would.

CHAPTER ELEVEN

Nell sat on the sofa sipping her tea while Grant relaxed nearby in his armchair.

She wished she could think of a way to get him to come and sit with her. "I can make room?" she said, scooting over. "If you want to move a little closer to the fire."

Awkward. But there. She'd said it.

Grant studied her a beat, but then he smiled. "All right."

He stood and carried his tea over, settling in beside her. She set down her knitting and then opened her purse and tucked it away.

"Looks like you're almost finished with that hat."

"Yeah."

"It will look good on you."

"Oh no, it's not for…me."

His eyebrows arched. "Boyfriend?"

She playfully shoved his arm. "I haven't got one of those. I told you."

"That just goes to show how lame the guys in Majestic are."

She laughed. "Well, in that case, the women are pretty lame, too."

His dark eyes sparkled. "Where've you been hiding all of my life?"

She could have said *in plain view*, but she didn't. "I haven't been hiding. I've been right here."

"Yeah, but I didn't really know you before." He

sighed and studied the ceiling. "Think of all that time wasted."

She giggled. "How do you know the timing wasn't right until now? Maybe we were just polishing up our game-playing skills and our sparkling personalities first."

He chuckled. "You, Nell Delaney, might have a point."

"Besides which." She grinned up at him. "Now that I've thoroughly trounced you in Scrabble, there's nothing to say wc can't have a rematch."

"I'd be up for that," he said with a grin.

"Hmm, good thing I sensed an opening in your super busy schedule."

"My schedule's not that busy."

"Not dating much, huh?"

"Not at the moment."

She frowned, insecurities niggling at her. Of coursc he was dating—some. He'd only said he didn't have a girlfriend, not that he was a monk. Grant was the least monk-like looking person she knew. "You've probably had loads of other girl-friends before now."

"I wouldn't say 'loads.'" He shrugged. "I've had a few." He turned to her. "You?"

"I've had a few girlfriends, too, but I mostly hang out with my sisters."

He chuckled at her reply, and his eyes glinted. "You're avoiding my question."

Yeah, she was. How embarrassing to reveal her romantic history.

Which basically didn't exist.

"All right," she finally said. "I was involved with

someone briefly, but in the end it didn't go any-where."

"I can't say that I'm sorry." He sipped from his tea. "Who was he?"

She blinked at the bluntness of the question.

"I'm sorry," he said, backpedaling. "You don't have to—"

"Karl Kramer."

Grant blinked. "The butcher?"

"Yeah. He's more of a charcutier. Works with restaurants and such."

"Huh." He cocked his chin. "Did he cut you any discounts?"

No. He'd kind of cut out her heart, but she de-cided not to mention that part. "Ha-ha, but no. Not really."

"How long were you guys an item?"

"We made it through our third anniversary."

He digested this. "Three years, whoa. That's a long time."

"Actually." She winced. "It was more like three months."

"Oh, sorry." He set down his tea. "What did the slimebucket do?"

She giggled at his assumption that the breakup was Karl's fault, because in truth it had been. "I don't know," she said. "I think he wasn't interested in getting serious."

"Were you?"

"In a way?" Her shoulders sagged. "But in a way not." Because in the back of her mind, Karl was al-ways in second place, right behind her number one fantasy choice, Grant. She'd always assumed Grant was out of her league, believing she'd never appeal to someone as talented and athletic as him. From the outside, they seemed very different in so many ways. Now that she was getting to know him better in person, Nell understood that she and Grant weren't as different from each other as she'd believed.

"Well, I'm sorry Karl let you down. But not sorry, too, if you know what I mean." He laid a hand on her sweatshirt sleeve. "You could be Mrs. Kramer right now. Loading up on prosciutto and salami! I mean, seriously." He rolled his eyes. "Who needs all that meat, anyway?"

She laughed. "Thanks. You know, you're very good at making everything better."

He locked on her gaze, and his eyes danced.

"So are you, Nell. So are you."

The way he looked at her was so adoring, so blatantly interested, it was almost overwhelming to absorb it. It was like staring directly into the blazing sun. So much blinding white light. The sensation was oh so new to her and super wonderful.

She blushed and dropped her chin.

He reached out and tipped up her chin with his fingers. "I meant that, Nell." His voice grew husky. "Karl's loss is my gain."

"What about you?" she asked softly.

He withdrew his hand and picked up his tea. "You're asking about past relationships?"

She nodded. "You said there were a few?"

"There was really no one important."

"You're thirty-two," she said. "There must have been someone?"

"Okay. There was Carol in college." He blew out

a breath. "And then there was Susan."

Nell guessed at once who Susan was. She tee-tered on the edge of how much she wanted to hear about her, though. What if merely talking about her brought back all sorts of happy memories for him? What if he started regretting letting her go? She decided to steer clear of Susan for now and ask about the college one. "What happened with Carol?"

He shrugged. "We graduated and each went our separate ways. I always wanted to come back to Majestic, and she took a job on the West Coast. We tried the long-distance thing for a while, but it was hard to maintain."

"That does take commitment."

"Yeah, and anyway, Carol wasn't into any of the same things that I am. She was never interested in camping or anything like that." He shared a tender smile. "She wasn't like you."

Heat flooded Nell's face. "Uh, Grant?"

"Yeah?"

"About the camping…"

"It's okay if you're not really expert level." His eyes twinkled. "The important thing is that you enjoy it."

She felt trapped. "I, uh, do," she said, because she knew she was going to totally love it once she started going with him. "It will be fun for us to go sometime." She bit her bottom lip. "But, um, maybe without my sisters?"

His grin was so sexy, she felt it in her bones. "I like that idea even better."

But before she could completely melt, Grant glanced at his mug, which was empty. "Would you like some more tea?"

"Sure. Why not?"

"Why not indeed?" He got up and collected both their mugs, walking to the kitchen. "Susan was another story," he said when he turned on the kettle. He took the tea and honey from the cabinet, then came back to sit with Nell while the water heated up. She noticed he didn't have a microwave. It was a very basic kitchen, but it suited the cabin's vibe.

He sat down on the sofa and sighed. "Susan and I dated off and on for about two years."

Nell swallowed hard. It was the off and on part that she didn't like so much. What if Grant was only temporarily *off* with plans to go *on* again? "And?"

"And." He exhaled sharply. "I decided I liked things better when we were 'off.'"

Whew.

"She was…" He stroked his chin and continued. "Difficult to be around sometimes. Mega bossy. It was her way or the highway, so I took the highway. Finally, I took it for good."

"I'm sorry." She was, too. Even though she was glad he was firmly over Susan, she detected a hint of hurt in his voice. It had to have been hard to finally make the split. She waded into her next question carefully. "How long ago did it end?"

"July?" He set his chin. "No, wait. Early August."

Nell's heart hammered. "Like a month ago?"

Oh, nooo. I'm his rebound girl?

"Yeah." He nodded. "That's right."

Nausea bubbled in her belly. That didn't sound like being "off again" for very long.

What if his glamorous ex resurfaced?

"Funny thing is," Grant said, "she's already engaged."

Whew! "That fast?"

He nodded. "Turns out, when she wasn't with me, she was back with her old boyfriend, Paul."

"She was kind of a boomerang, huh?"

Grant laughed. "You know what? She was." He raked a hand through his hair. "And, after a while, I got pretty tired of playing games. I guess Paul's all-in, though." There was no rancor in his tone, only reflection. "Good for him."

Nell felt like a huge weight had been lifted. She shrugged. "Good for them both."

Grant reached out and took her hand, and her whole body heated at his touch.

"Good for them both," he repeated, his gaze on the fire. He held her hand firmly, and she squeezed his back, feeling so united. Like they were a team against the boomerang women and butchers of this world.

The kettle whistled shrilly, and Nell regretted letting go of his hand.

He seemed just as reluctant to break contact. Their connection had felt so right. So warm. Tender and reassuring. "Guess I'd better get that." He winked, and butterflies fluttered in her stomach. "Don't go anywhere."

• • •

Grant prepared their tea, brooding over Karl Kramer. He was glad the guy was out of the way. The idea of Nell being with him—or anyone else—sent a searing surge through his gut. At least she wasn't seeing anyone now, and he was glad. Nell Delaney was a very special woman. And the more he got to know her, the more amazing she seemed.

He grabbed a pack of frozen mixed vegetables from the freezer and brought that to her along with her tea.

She accepted the mug he handed her and perused the veggies. "Ooh, it's a medley this time."

He chuckled. "It's good to mix things up." He positioned the bag around her propped-up ankle. "Looks like the swelling's gone down."

"Yeah, it's feeling much better."

"That's a really good sign."

He retrieved his tea from the kitchen and joined her on the sofa again. He'd liked holding her hand before and intended to do it again. "So," he said casually. "Where were we?"

He held out his hand, and she smiled, lacing her fingers through his. "Right about here."

He chuckled and brought their linked hands to his lips, giving the back of her hand a kiss. A pink hue arched across her freckles like a pretty little rainbow.

"You've been so great," she said. "So nice to me."

He stared into her incredible brown eyes with those amber highlights. "Well, you deserve it."

She pursed her lips. "You'd better be careful, Grant. I might think you're flirting with me."

"You don't have to guess," he growled. "I am."

She blushed even harder and hung her head, but he could tell she'd liked the compliment.

After a moment, she looked up.

"So," she asked. "When are we going to Mariner's?"

"When would you like to go?"

"Anytime that's good for you." Then she amended, "As long as it's soon."

He squeezed her hand. "We can go as soon as you'd like."

"Tomorrow's Sunday," she said. "By the time we both get home, we'll probably both have catching up to do."

"Yeah, and you probably should rest that ankle another day or so, anyhow."

She frowned. "Mariner's is closed on Mondays."

His eyebrows rose. "Tuesday, then?"

Her smile sparkled. "Tuesday would be awesome."

"Great. Consider it a date." He lightly thumbed her nose with his free hand, and she wrinkled it up, looking the cutest.

She tilted her head, and her long reddish curls spilled sideways, shimmering in the firelight. "I'm excited about going on a date with you."

"I'm excited about going on a date with you." He paused to consider how beautiful she was, even sitting there wearing his baggy sweat clothes. "What time do you get off work?"

"A little past six."

"Okay, good. Want to say seven?"

"Sure."

"Want to meet there, or—"

"I'll probably want to go home and change first."

"Yeah. Where do you live?"

"On Galloway Ridge near the cranberry bog?"

"Oh yeah. I know it. You rent that little cottage at

the end of the lane?"

"Not rent it. I own it."

He admired her. "Well, look at you."

She giggled. "It's actually not far from your store."

"Just what I was thinking," he told her. "Why don't I pick you up?"

"Sounds great."

"I'll make a reservation for seven thirty to give you extra time."

She sighed. "Can't wait."

Grant was glad to have that settled. He leaned back against the sofa and picked up his tea while still holding Nell's hand. She drank from hers, too, and they both studied the leaping flames in the woodstove for a bit. After a while, he became curious about her job and her family.

"How do you like working at Bearberry Brews?"

"Truthfully?" She grinned. "I love it. It's great working with my sisters and my parents. Lucas, too. He's been with us since he was fifteen. His dad died in a fishing accident, and he needed the cash to help his mom look after their family."

"That's sad." Grant frowned. "For Lucas."

"Yeah, but he did okay. You know? Really pulled through. If it hadn't been for him, his little brother, Ramon, wouldn't be doing so well." She smiled proudly, her affection for the Reyes family clear. "Word is, he's college bound, thanks to Lucas's tutoring."

"Who's your barista? She seems nice."

Nell smiled. "You must be talking about Mei-Lin. She and Misty have been best friends forever, and she works at the café part-time. She's in grad school online to become an ESOL teacher."

"ESOL?"

"English for Speakers of Other Languages."

"Oh yeah. I think they used to call that ESL back in our day." He chuckled like that was so long ago, and maybe in some ways it was. "Sounds like a nice work environment," he said. "We've got a great crew at my store, too, including Jordan. He's the best."

"He's not native to Majestic, is he? I mean, I don't remember seeing him around before last year."

"Right," Grant said. "He moved here from Chicago. Wanted to live somewhere more outdoorsy so he could pursue his interests."

"Of?"

"Being outdoors." Grant laughed good-naturedly, and then he studied her a moment. "Doesn't that ever get tight, working with your family? Jordan and I are friends, but it's hard to imagine me working with a brother. I mean, do you and your sisters ever get on each other's nerves?"

She smiled. "Sometimes, but not as much as we used to. When Misty, Charlotte, and I were teenagers and all living at home together *and* working part-time at the shop, things could get a little iffy then."

"Iffy?"

"Charlotte's our marketing genius, and she's always been the creative one, which means she creatively often thinks she's right."

He chuckled. "Is she?"

"Not as often as she believes." Nell shook her head. "Charlotte's headstrong but very sweet underneath."

"And that's not you?" he joked.

"No, that's not me. I'm the oldest, so the most mature. Always the peacekeeper."

He nodded. "Noted. How about Misty?"

Nell blew out a breath. "Oh boy, hmm. Misty is the baby, and sometimes she acts like it. She was more spoiled because she came last. Everything's come easy for Misty, including boys."

He laughed and shook his head.

"Charlotte's pickier. She tends to dump men, while Misty draws them like moths to a flame. Both are very smart and accomplished. Misty maybe could have done more. She used to talk about going to design school. For fashion or something like that."

"So Charlotte's not the only creative one?"

"No." She pursed her lips. "You're right, but Misty's never done anything with her talent. She won lots of art awards in high school, though."

He leaned toward her and nudged her shoulder with his. "You're leaving yourself out in the creative arena."

Her eyebrows rose. "What do you mean?"

"Your knitting, Nell. You make things with your hands. You're creative, too."

She chuckled like she'd never considered this. "I guess you're right."

"Have you ever thought of selling anything?"

"Oh, I already have. On Etsy."

"See? That's very cool."

She blushed. "There you go, complimenting me again. Thanks."

Clearly she'd not been complimented enough in her life—something he intended to remedy. "Where did this creative streak come from?" he asked her.

"Your parents?"

"My mom is a photographer, but only as a hobby. You know those photos at the café?"

"The black-and-white shots?" He'd seen them and they were spectacular. "She took those?"

"Yep. Every one."

"Wow. She's got an eye."

"That's what I think, too."

"Has she ever considered going professional?"

"Not really. She doesn't have time. She helps my dad run Bearberry Brews. She and he do the coffee roasting and come up with the blends. They also manage the business and oversee its operations. They've been working that way together since they opened up shop."

"How long ago was that?"

"I was in kindergarten, and Misty was a baby, so, hmm. Maybe twenty-five years?"

"I think it's great that they've stuck with it. So many small businesses don't make it these days."

She frowned. "I know."

"Hey." He tightened his grip on her hand. "I didn't mean to be a downer. I know you said times have been tough at Bearberry Brews, but they'll improve."

"That's what we're counting on." She seemed eager to change the subject. "You mentioned your mom was outdoorsy like you are. What kind of things did she like to do?"

He was fine with this topic because he liked talking about his mom, and there hadn't really been anyone in his life interested in hearing about her. "Ride bikes, for one thing. She's the one who taught me to ride without my training wheels on, and boy that was a challenge."

"Oh, no. Poor baby Grant." Her face scrunched up. "Did you fall a lot?"

"I still have one of the scars." He let go of her hand and rolled up the left pants leg of his jeans. He pointed at a disfigured area above his left ankle. "See that line and those little dots? That was from a bicycle pedal. Twenty stitches."

She winced. "Ouch."

He chuckled warmly at her response and held her hand again. "It didn't put me off from riding. My mom made me get right back on my bike the very next day."

"What? The next day?"

"Yep. She was a toughie. But that was good." He rubbed his jaw at the fond memories. "That helped *me* toughen up."

"What else did she like to do?" she asked. "Your mom?"

"Camping, for sure. She and Dad took me a lot when I was little. When the two of them met, they were big backpackers. Spent their honeymoon in Yosemite."

"Really?" She seemed intrigued. "Was she a fisher…woman, uh…person, too?"

He grinned at her efforts toward gender neutrality. "No, that part I got from my dad. He taught me to fish when I was a kid. Those were good times." He frowned. "That was before things changed."

Her face was lined with compassion. "I'm sorry, Grant."

"Things happened." He sighed. "First, Dad got let

go from his job at the factory. Then Mom got her diagnosis and had to stop teaching."

"What did she teach?"

"High school music."

"Was it cancer?"

His heart ached at the painful memory. "They found it pretty late. There wasn't a lot they could do. She tried, though, but treatments were expensive, even with insurance. That's when my dad started falling apart."

She scooted toward him on the sofa and rubbed his arm. "That must have been a terrible time."

He was comforted by her touch and leaned into it. "It was, but we got through it. I mean, I did. My dad was never the same."

She got a distant look in her eyes. "Yeah, I know what you mean."

"Nell? What is it?"

She shook her head, seeming to bring herself back to the conversation. "It's nothing. We were talking about you and your family."

"No, seriously. I want to know." He wrapped an arm around her shoulders, sensing a hard story was coming. She sagged against him, and he held her closer.

"Something similar happened to my dad. Nothing as horrible as cancer. I don't want to diminish what you all went through."

"It's all right." He hugged her tighter. "Tell me."

"He had a business partner, John Strong. They started Bearberry Brews together and were really close. Both our families were really great friends. Well, our parents were, anyway."

"Did the Strongs have kids?"

"One son, Aidan." She searched his eyes, looking like she wanted to say something more, but then she didn't.

"What happened to your dad?" he asked her.

"Mr. Strong cheated him in business. My dad is such a kind person, nice as the day is long, but that also makes him a little naive, and I'm afraid Mr. Strong took advantage."

"How?"

"By giving him the coffee shop in Majestic in exchange for global distribution rights."

"Hang on." He raked a hand through his hair. "Bearberry Coffee. That sounds familiar somehow, and not just because of your shop."

"Yeah. They distribute to specialty grocery stores. Co-ops and the like."

"Oh yeah, I remember the packaging. It's like your store logo but more streamlined, with berries and missing the bear silhouette rising up to eat them."

"Right. They operated off of the company's initial recipes. The first blends my parents and the Strongs concocted together. Afterward, my folks went on to develop new coffees, but the international business stuck with the basics because that's all they'd gotten rights to."

"So," he asked. "That's you guys, then? Everywhere in the stores?"

"Would have been us, but no. There was a split between the families and the businesses, with the Strongs becoming billionaires after moving to London, and the Delaneys receiving no share of those profits while they stayed here. After that, the two families became enemies."

"Oh no. For how long?"

She was quiet a moment. "The wounds still linger. The point is about my dad and what Mr. Strong's deception did to him. He didn't start drinking—nothing as drastic as your dad—but he did change, and not for the better. He just became unhappy in a way. Less cheerful and optimistic than he used to be."

"And now? How's he doing?"

"Okay, just not the same as before, and the café is struggling, like I told you. That doesn't help his outlook."

"It will come back, Nell." He gave her an affirming hug. "Things will get better."

"I'd like to believe that," she said.

He hoped that for her, too. They sat together in silence, the warmth of their bodies mingling in a way that comforted him. Grant never talked to anyone about his family, but sharing things with Nell had seemed natural. He was glad she'd felt comfortable talking to him about private things, as well. The fit between them was so easy and right. It felt good being with her and having her beside him.

"I think it's cool about you and your family," he said. "All being so close."

"Yeah, it's nice."

"You think you'll want a big one, too?" She gazed up at him, wide-eyed. "I mean, someday."

She smiled softly. "Someday, sure. But not hugehuge. Not sure how many diapers I want to change."

He chuckled. "You make a good point."

"Of course, I won't be the only one diaper-changing."

"No?"

Her eyebrows arched. "I'd be expecting some help from my partner."

"Sounds fair."

They were both quiet a moment, and then she asked him, "How about you? Want kids?"

"Yeah, probably. I think that would be nice. Assuming I found the right woman. The right person for my wife." If he hadn't already.

"You'd make a pretty great dad," she murmured. "Based on your skill level."

His eyebrows rose.

"Applying frozen vegetables to injuries."

He laughed. "Yeah, there's that."

She squeezed his hand and said wistfully, "Kids get into lots of things."

"Don't I know it."

"Like burying game pieces in their backyard."

"Hey!" He poked her in the ribs, and she giggled. "Still hurts my feelings that you had the audacity to beat me with my own board at my own cabin."

She playfully rolled her eyes. "Does not. You enjoyed the fierceness of our game."

He chuckled. "You're right. I'm over it."

"Good to know you don't hold grudges, then."

"Not generally, no. Guess I'm like my mom."

"Noted." She sighed and laid her head against his shoulder, and his heart pounded in a steady rhythm. Everything about this felt right. Him and Nell together.

A hush fell over the room, and flames flickered in the woodstove.

He brought his hand to her cheek and turned toward her, gazing into her pretty gold-and-brown eyes. "I feel like something's happening here."

She reached up and touched his hand, pressing it against her soft skin. "I feel it, too."

He'd been drawn to her before, but this time there was no fighting this tide. Her pull was stronger than the tug of the ocean, and he was a man lost at sea.

He grew nearer, dipping his chin toward hers. "Nell, can I kiss you?"

Her voice was breathy when she answered. "I think I'll die if you don't."

His lips brushed over hers, and they were satiny smooth and inviting. She sighed, and he kissed her again, firmly planting his mouth against hers.

She turned toward him on the sofa, and he took her in his arms. Something thudded onto the floor— probably the bag of frozen vegetables—but he didn't care.

He tightened his embrace, and she molded into him, kissing him sweetly at first and then with more passion as they became swept up in each other. And then they were off to an oasis of their own, just the two of them with emotions crashing down on them in wave after tumbling wave.

"Oh wow," she murmured breathlessly. "You kiss like a waterfall."

"Oh yeah?" That was absolutely the best compliment any woman had ever given him. "Then, honey," he rasped. "Let's dive back in."

Her pale cheeks grew rosy beneath her faint freckles, and her pretty eyes sparkled in the firelight. He gazed into her eyes, amazingly lost—and found—there. His heart warmed when his mouth met hers. Then it heated up some more, and then another notch, threatening to burst into flames. If he was going down, then he was taking her with him.

He pulled her closer, threading his fingers through her long and silky hair, kissing her like there was no tomorrow. Because in his mind there wasn't.

There was only this moment and tonight.

CHAPTER TWELVE

Grant woke up the next morning on the sofa, his whole body humming from the fiery kisses he and Nell had shared last night. This was fantastic. This was wild. He was happier than he'd ever been. And it was all because of her.

He cradled his head in his hands, recalling every sweet moment. From the second he'd first seen her dressed in *so much pink*…to the panicked look in her eyes on that summit…to when she'd landed on him in the rain and he'd had to carry her down that mountain. And then she'd been here, lighting up his cabin like an ocean sunrise.

He sat up with a jolt.

Wait.

He slammed back against his pillow.

I think I'm falling in love.

Grant scanned the low ceiling with what he was sure was a very goofy grin, but he didn't care. This was life-altering stuff. Nell made him feel good. She made him feel alive. She made him want to race right outside into the meadow and shout it up against the mountains.

But, no. He wouldn't do that.

He peered toward the bedroom and saw the door was shut.

She was still sleeping.

Oh man, it was a shame they were going home today.

He held on to the hope that the roads might not have cleared, but he knew that was a long shot. Maybe not for the bridge but the back way. Since the rain had stopped midday, the flooding was bound to have subsided by now. He didn't know about the tree, though; some good Samaritan might have moved it out of the way. And, even if it was still there, Grant kept a chainsaw here in his storage closet.

He sat up again, feeling inspired. Of course, that's what he should do.

Go check that backroad and clear it, if it hadn't been cleared already.

Then he could go into town and get Nell a little surprise: a cup of morning coffee like she was used to having. He knew her favorite kind. He could get danishes, too. Yeah. A nice little breakfast for both of them. He'd pick it up at Bearberry Brews. Maybe he'd stop at the market and nab a few groceries, so he could make her something special for lunch because, no doubt, she'd rather suffer through another meal of trout than risk hurting his feelings.

He chuckled. Someday soon, he hoped to convince her she suited him just fine as is—her complete dislike of trout, a total lack of camping knowledge, and all.

There was no reason they had to rush out of here today. Neither of them was working until tomorrow, although he probably should swing by Blue Sky Adventures to make sure it hadn't incurred any damage during the storm. It was a thirty-minute drive into town, so he could get all that done in an hour and forty-five minutes if he worked quickly. Max, two.

Grant checked his watch. It was a little after six, and the sun wasn't even up yet. Bearberry Brews opened at seven. He needed to get going.

· · ·

Nell opened her eyes as sun streamed through the windows, creeping through the slatted blinds. What time was it, anyway? Her instinct was to check her phone, but then she remembered that the battery had died.

She scanned the room in a groggy state, then peeked under the covers at Grant's sweat clothes. It had gotten cold in this room overnight, being away from the woodstove, so she'd been glad for the extra blankets he'd given her.

It had taken her almost an hour to cool down from his heated kisses, though.

Only in her *dreams* could a guy kiss that way.

If that was just kissing, she could only imagine other things, but she tried hard not to, because even the fantasy of her and Grant together made her flush with nerves. She was sure she'd be okay when the time came. More than okay. Ecstatic. Grant definitely seemed to know what he was doing, and she was happy to let him take the lead. Then, she could take command next and give him sexy orders in the bedroom, like some of the heroines in the novels she read. Nell giggled at her naughty thoughts.

If her sisters only knew how well this was going! She couldn't wait to tell them. Even though they were in competition with each other, she knew in her heart they'd be happy for her. She'd never had a true love. Had never been in love until…

Wait.

Her heart pitter-pattered.

She kicked her feet excitedly under the covers, then winced.

Ouch. Ow. Ow!

She'd kind of forgotten about her twisted ankle. Until now.

Ugh.

It throbbed a bit, but not as much as it had at first. Nell pushed back the covers to examine it. She lightly touched the athletic tape, pressing down on it from different angles. Hmm. It was definitely doing better today. It almost didn't hurt at all when she didn't move much.

Maybe she should try standing.

Argh. That smarts!

She sat right back down again, contemplating her leg.

Her ankle was tender and a little achy, but at least it wasn't hot and throbbing anymore. So that was an improvement. By this time tomorrow, she'd probably be improved even more. She'd probably also be back at her house by then. Nell frowned, wishing in a way she could stay here, at least for one more day. She couldn't wait to see what Grant's plans for this morning were. Was Grant going to pamper her again? Maybe make her an amazing breakfast? She'd love that. Anything but fish.

She drew in a deep breath and stared around the room, still in a haze. This wasn't a dream. She was really here at Grant's cabin with him, and things couldn't be better. He was so much more than she'd expected, in all the best ways. Very genuine and funny. He could definitely keep up with her quip for quip. She'd loved engaging in wordplay with him, both in telling jokes and then when beating his socks off in Scrabble. He'd been a good sport about it, but she could tell he'd hated losing. Nell understood those instincts. She liked winning, too.

From the breadth of his outdoor knowledge, he was obviously smart and skillful. But, apart from being rugged, he'd been tender in looking after her, too. He'd bandaged her twisted ankle and carried her down that mountain, then had taken extra care in icing and elevating her injury. Also, in giving her medicine. And here she was, already feeling better, thanks to him. Seeing that waterfall had made her heart so light, and he'd obviously had fun being with her. Otherwise, he never would have suggested taking the selfie.

She'd loved telling him about her family and Bearberry Brews, and she had enjoyed learning about his mom and some things about his childhood. About those former girlfriends, though? Not so much. But that was okay. What mattered was the "former" part. Neither of them was in the picture any longer. But she was. Yay!

She was especially glad to be here last night when his dreamy kisses had swept her away.

Grant was treating her royally, even cooking for her. He couldn't help that fish wasn't her favorite or that she preferred chunky peanut butter. They could work around those things. Nothing too major.

He seemed so easygoing. Even in letting her borrow his phone. If he only knew. Nell's face heated.

She would never ever peek at his photos again. Or his text messages. Not unless it was his idea and he had something important to show her.

Who knows where things would go between the two of them after their intimate talk and hot kissing session last night? Grant had already offered to take her to Mariner's and had also asked about her cooking him dinner. Those things had to mean he was liking her at least somewhat. Hopefully, more than "somewhat." When he'd said *I feel like something's happening here*, she'd felt it, too. Boy oh boy. 100 percent. This time, it wasn't a crush, or all in her head, or only one-sided. The way that he'd looked into her eyes said it was happening for him, too.

Tiny tingles raced down her spine. *Ahhhh. We're falling in love!*

She balled her fists up against her mouth so she wouldn't squeal out loud.

The sensation dazzled her like an array of bright colors. All sparkly and glittery. *And dizzying.* She felt lightheaded, like she was walking on air.

Her stomach growled.

She was also probably hungry.

With her hoping for Grant to become her life's partner and everything, she didn't want to hurt his feelings. But no way on earth was she having that nasty fish for breakfast this morning. Maybe he was still sleeping and she could sneak out there and fix herself a PB&J before he woke up?

She was sorry to most likely be going home today, but her time here with Grant had given them a great start. All she had to do was make sure that everything kept going smoothly during the next few days, until she could work up her nerve to tell him about Aidan. She'd considered broaching the subject when they talked about the Strongs last night, but the moment hadn't seemed right. She hadn't wanted to drop the bombshell that could ruin everything by making Grant feel pressured.

What she wanted was for Grant to love her with his whole heart, and not because of the wager between her and her sisters. Because if he didn't get to know and care for her true self, then what was the point? As much as she'd always wanted him, Nell now saw a much harder truth. She didn't just want Grant to love her back—she needed him to love her for who she was inside. Which was why she was going to tell him about the camping today. And she was going to have to tell him about Aidan soon.

Nell got up out of bed and hobbled over to the door, able to put her right foot down occasionally. That was progress. But, when she peeked into the living area, she didn't see Grant. The blanket he'd been using was folded neatly and stacked in the armchair with his pillow. She glanced toward the kitchen, but he wasn't there, either, and the bathroom door was ajar.

Nell skip-hopped to the front door and pulled it open.

Morning birds chirped, and a cool breeze rippled through the trees.

What? His SUV's missing.

Her pulse pounded, and she told herself not to panic.

He's probably gone to check the roads.
Yeah, that's it.

Good time for her to hightail it to the kitchen and make a sandwich. That way, when he made fish for breakfast, she could legit claim she wasn't hungry.

She'd make herself a cup of tea, too.

Fifteen minutes later, Nell sat at the kitchen table, drinking her tea. She'd gobbled down that PB&J in record time, so afraid that—at any minute—he might walk in. But he hadn't, and now she was beginning to worry.

That's when she saw the note on the front of the refrigerator.

He'd pinned it there with a magnet, and she'd missed it before.

Gone out for an errand.

Be back soon.

XO

Her heart fluttered at the X and the O.

And then it fluttered again.

Okay, this was good. This was fine.

She'd have time to shower now and get back into her hiking clothes.

She'd washed the running pants out in the sink with her undies yesterday, and they were hopefully dry. At least she'd look more presentable when Grant got back. Plus, she'd be ready to go. She frowned, sorry to be leaving this cozy little cabin.

With any luck, she'd be back here again.

She sighed contentedly.

Loads and loads of times with Grant.

• • •

Grant sauntered into Bearberry Brews, feeling pleased with himself. He'd used his chainsaw to clear the road in less than ten minutes, doing his first good deed of the day.

Now he was about to perform another.

This was going to be a huge surprise for Nell. She'd probably cover him in kisses with her thanks.

If he was lucky.

He glanced around the quaint space, seeing it was mostly empty. Not surprising at this hour on a Sunday. A blond woman with a ponytail worked at a table with her ear buds in, and a guy with a beard sat reading his tablet in a comfy armchair in the corner. The panorama through the window beside him showed a sandy slope dotted with wavering grasses and gulls soaring through a clear blue sky.

The front-facing windows looked out toward the street and, beyond that, the ocean. A stone stairway with an iron railing led down to the beach. He noticed that Mrs. Delaney had captured a dramatic shot of the steps looking upward toward the towering cliffs.

She really did have talent.

"Can I help you?"

Grant faced the counter and the dark-haired guy who'd asked. Lucas Reyes. "Ah, yeah. Hey, Lucas."

"How's it going, man?"

"Can't complain." Which was the understatement of the year. Grant was floating on air. "You?"

"Same." Lucas gave him a pleasant smile, and Grant studied the treats in the pastry case, then reviewed the menu on the chalkboard.

"I'll take one of those bear claws, please. And,

a...hmm. Cranberry orange scone. Also a chocolate croissant," he said, thinking that looked delicious and that he'd have that for himself, since Nell wasn't big on chocolate.

"To go?"

"Yeah, thanks."

The woman behind the register was distracted by her phone. She wore a stud in her nose.

There's Misty.

As Lucas bagged his choices, he asked, "Anything else?"

"Yes. I'd like the largest size you've got of Blueberry Cheesecake Pralines and Cream."

A brunette backed out of the kitchen carrying a stack of clean dishes and mugs that she set on the counter near Lucas. "I'll get it!" She stared at Grant with big blue eyes. *And there's Charlotte.* "Grant, hey!"

"Hi, Charlotte." He smiled politely, figuring it couldn't hurt to be nice to Nell's sisters. He and Nell could start dating soon. Exclusively, if she agreed.

Misty set down her phone, looking surprised. "Grant. What are you doing here?"

Wasn't that obvious? "Picking up breakfast."

"For Nell? Aww." Misty pressed her hands to her heart. "Aren't you the *sweetest*."

Lucas watched their exchange in an odd way, and Grant got the feeling he was paying extra special attention to Misty.

Hang on. Was Lucas crushing on her?

If he was, Nell's youngest sister was oblivious.

A woman with graying hair made her way out of the kitchen juggling several one-pound bags of freshly roasted coffee beans in her arms. "Oh Misty! Can you please—" The shape and color of her eyes reminded him of Nell's. "Grant?"

He nodded deferentially. "Good morning, Mrs. Delaney."

"Good morning."

Seconds later, an older guy with a round face emerged through the kitchen door, carrying more bags of coffee. "Hello. You're Nell's friend, aren't you?"

"Yeah, Mr. Delaney. Good to see you."

Lucas relieved Mr. Delaney of his coffee bags and began helping Misty stock the shelves near the register with the bags she'd taken from her mom.

An awkward silence ensued as they all watched Grant. He felt like a fish in a fishbowl. What? Was it written all over his face? Maybe he had that lovesick puppy dog look? Charlotte grinned with a knowing gleam in her eyes.

Yep. Guess so.

How embarrassing.

"One Blueberry Cheesecake Pralines and Cream coming right up. Extra-large." Charlotte winked at Misty, then turned to Grant. "Whipped cream with that?"

He shifted on his feet. "Sure."

Lucas shook his head. He was apparently used to these family dynamics and secret code messaging between the Delaney sisters. Grant suspected Nell could send and receive those, too. Telepathically.

Charlotte got busy making the coffee. "How's Nell doing?"

"Actually, a lot better."

Misty blinked. "Better?"

He studied their perplexed expressions. "Didn't she tell you?"

"Tell us what?" asked Charlotte.

"She fell, or stood, really. Got up too fast and twisted her ankle."

"Got up?" Charlotte asked, latching on to that detail. "From where?"

"Yeah," Misty said. "What were you guys *doing*?" She grinned at Charlotte, clearly getting the wrong impression.

Not good. Especially in front of Nell's parents.

His ears burned hot.

"She had a minor accident on our hike," he explained. "Slightly rolled her ankle."

"Oh no." Mrs. Delaney frowned. "Poor Nell."

"But she's going to be okay?" Mr. Delaney asked with a furrowed brow.

Charlotte placed the paper coffee cup on the counter and snapped on the lid, waiting on his reply. Lucas watched him like a hawk, too. So did Misty.

"Yeah, yeah. She'll be back on her feet in no time."

"Well, I think it's very sweet," Charlotte said. "That you're taking care of her."

"It *is* sweet." Misty chuckled. "Don't forget to keep that up in the future!"

Charlotte shot dagger eyes at her, and Misty winced.

What was that all about?

Grant paid Misty for his pastries and the coffee, and she gave him his change. All the while, she sent him subtle looks like she was in on his big secret.

Only he didn't know what that secret was. Unless it was about his interest in Nell, which was blatantly clear to her family by now. And Lucas, he guessed. Which he was glad of. He didn't need Lucas thinking he was interested in Misty—only one Delaney woman had his eye. The one who'd claimed she did a lot of camping with her sisters, he remembered suddenly, which he suspected was a big farce. Maybe he could prove it.

"Misty," he said. "What kind of tent do you all use?"

She stared at him blankly. "Huh?"

"He's talking about *camping*," Charlotte told her in a sing-songy way. "You know, our annual trips with Nell?"

"Er." Misty panicked. "It's a—triangle one?"

Grant didn't know whether to laugh or frown. Misty's camping vocabulary was about as good as Nell's. So that story clearly wasn't adding up. Apart from that, Charlotte and Misty were both acting a little strange. Like they knew something that he didn't. Maybe before Nell's phone died, she'd texted them about how great things were going with him. She might have even sent them that rainbow selfie.

Mr. Delaney appeared lost. "We're going camping?"

"Not you, Dad." Charlotte patted his shoulder. "It's a sisters' trip."

"Good," Mrs. Delaney said. "I can't imagine sleeping on the ground. Not at my age." She stretched out her back. "I need to get back to the roaster, but great seeing you, Grant." She gave him a sly smile. "Thanks for helping our Nell."

He sighed. Well, that cat was pretty much out of the bag. That had to be what Charlotte and Misty were giving him funny looks about, too. He should have guessed he'd tip off her family by coming here. Not that he was ashamed of his involvement with Nell. It was just a little awkward being the center of so much scrutiny from her family.

"My pleasure, Mrs. Delaney."

"Oh Lucas," Mrs. Delaney said. "If you don't mind lending a hand?"

"No problem," he said, walking after her. He took one last look at Grant, then at Misty, and Grant guessed he was slightly protective. Nell had mentioned he was like family. Grant was pretty convinced Lucas thought of Misty as more than family, though, whether or not he was going to let her know it.

Mr. Delaney stopped to peruse Grant on his way to the kitchen. Grant sensed he was summing him up and gauging his "intentions." "You take good care of my Nelly, now. She's pretty special to me." He glanced at Charlotte and Misty. "All of my girls are."

He swallowed hard. "Yes, sir. I will," he said, fully intending to. As soon as he got out of here, which would hopefully be soon. The walls seemed to be closing in on him.

The others left, and an attractive woman he now knew was Mei-Lin exited the kitchen. She carried plates loaded with breakfast burritos over to two customers seated by a table in the corner. She returned to the pastry case and grabbed some empty bags.

"Hello there," she said, grinning at Grant.

"Uh, hey."

"You're Nell's friend, right?"

Awesome. Not. His relationship with Nell had obviously spread through the shop. He could only hope it wasn't already all over town. That would be embarrassing, since he and Nell hadn't totally figured it out yet. "Yeah. We… She and I are spending time up at my cabin."

"Ooh, nice." Mei-Lin waggled her eyebrows, then got to work selecting items to drop into pastry bags, presumably for the clients at the table who were taking them to-go.

Grant was pretty ready to skedaddle himself. Everyone who worked here seemed to know his business, which was uncomfortable to say the least. He picked up his own pastry bag and the coffee, eager to get back to Nell. "Well," he said to all the women, "good seeing you."

"See ya, Grant," Charlotte said with a cryptic smile.

Misty batted her eyelashes. "Give our love to Nell."

Grant was almost to the door when he heard Misty whisper to Charlotte.

"Lucky Nell. Now she won't have to marry Aidan."

"*Mist-y, shush!*"

A lead weight settled in his stomach.

Why was Nell lucky, and what did that have to do with her not marrying somebody called Aidan? Grant whirled back around, and both sisters stared at him, shell-shocked. The look on their faces said he'd caught them red-handed. But at what?

His heart hammered. "What's going on?"

Charlotte pursed her lips, then exchanged an excited glance with Misty. Whatever Misty was giddy about, Charlotte appeared stoked about it, too.

"Um." Charlotte bit her lip. "We were just talking about—"

"Your engagement," Misty blurted out, her face bright red.

Charlotte gasped, but it was too late.

Misty had blown the big secret she'd been holding in.

"My *what*?"

Charlotte widened her eyes at Misty, and Misty winced. "Your engagement," she said. "When Charlotte mentioned the ring, Nell didn't deny it."

Ring? As in, they thought he and Nell were getting *married*?

Before Grant could blink, they'd scurried around the counter and were racing straight for him with their arms outstretched. They latched onto him with hugs, shielding their hushed conversation from their customers.

"We're so happy for you," Charlotte whispered.

Misty squealed softly. "You and Nell—who knew? I mean, we did, of course. But now that it's official, yay!" She and Charlotte bounced on their heels, shaking Grant in their embrace like a diner milkshake.

Me and Nell? Future husband and wife? No.
Where on earth did they get that idea?

"You're such a prince," Charlotte wailed, an emotional mess.

Wait. Was she *crying*?

"Yeah." Misty squeezed him the hardest. "The best." Her voice cracked, too, and his heart lurched. The room kept spinning around and around as Nell's coffee sloshed in its cup. He tightened his grip to hang on to it and the pastry bag.

Charlotte and Misty stopped jostling for a moment, and he got his bearings, the café coming back into focus.

"You're talking about…" He broke out of their hold. "My engagement to…Nell?"

He sent a panicked glance around the café to find Mei-Lin grinning at him. "Congrats," she said, like she knew all about something he didn't. Then she pushed her glasses back up on her nose and turned away, handing a newly made coffee to a waiting customer.

"I know we're not supposed to talk about it yet," Misty said, "so *shh* that we told you we know."

Charlotte dabbed at her eyes. "Mom and Dad don't know, either, so double *shh*."

Count him in among the clueless.

He was still stuck back at the beginning of this mess. Him and Nell engaged? What would possess Nell to tell her sisters that? He felt like his brain had been buffeted around by the wind, knocked back and forth and then every which way. He didn't know up from down or left from right anymore. But he did have the presence of mind to understand he wanted more information, so he decided to play along.

"When did Nell share all this?"

Charlotte leaned toward him, keeping her voice down. "Yesterday."

"I mean, she didn't say you were *engaged* in so many words." Misty rolled her eyes.

"But we got the gist of it," Charlotte said.

Misty spoke quietly to Charlotte. "Guess Nell really knew what she was doing in signing up for that hike."

Wait. *That little sneak.* So, Nell had set things up on purpose? Meeting him on the hike, their lovey-dovey times at the cabin? All of it, even her ankle? No. She probably wouldn't have gone that far. That part must have been a real accident. But why?

Charlotte pulled a face. "She must have told you everything, huh?"

Uh. No. It was painfully clear she hadn't.

Misty poked him in the chest. "And you stepped up like a gallant knight to rescue her."

"If you hadn't proposed," Charlotte said, "Nell might have been stuck with...you know." She grimaced like she couldn't bear to say his name.

"Aidan Strong," Grant said deadpan, putting this weird jigsaw puzzle together.

"Yeah, him," Misty said grimly. "By losing our bet."

"Which bet is that?"

"The one about us having to find husbands first so we don't have to marry—"

Charlotte cupped a hand over Misty's mouth. "Wait. Nell didn't tell you?"

Grant paused and then said coolly, "Oh yeah, she did. Of course." His mind worked quickly, putting the whole twisted scheme together. Nell had said that Bearberry Brews was in financial trouble, so maybe this marriage to Aidan had to do with that.

The arrangement between the two families could be more professional than personal, a company merger of sorts. A business marriage versus a love match. He decided to test his hypothesis. "This is all to help your café, right?"

"Right," Charlotte whispered.

"And our parents," Misty said.

"Which is why," Charlotte added, "they can't know."

"Dad would never go for this."

Grant couldn't say that he blamed him. "Or your mom?"

They stared at each other and hedged.

Misty said, "Er."

Then Charlotte answered. "Not her, either. The bet was just between us sisters."

"And Aidan doesn't know which of the three of you it will be?"

Misty shook her head. "Not yet."

"I'm just amazed he agreed to it." Grant paused. "I mean, not that all of you aren't great."

"Yeah," Charlotte said. "At first, we were surprised, too."

"But, you know." Misty lifted a shoulder. "Guilt."

Over the Strongs cheating the Delaneys out of billions, he supposed. "Right." So how much guilt did Nell feel for not telling him about this wager? She and her sisters were in a race to get married so they wouldn't be saddled with Aidan? His head reeled. Wow. He didn't know if he should be offended or flattered for having landed at the top of Nell's must-marry-soon list. He also questioned what was so horrible about Aidan, since they were all scrambling to avoid him.

"We're so excited," Misty said, "and honestly not upset at all."

Charlotte nodded. "Nell's happiness is our happiness. We only want what's best for her—and you."

Grant eyed them both askance, and Misty winced. "It's true we were fending for ourselves, too, but neither of us has made it that far. I mean, dates, sure. Yeah. But engagement! Woo!" She nudged him playfully. "You're a fast worker."

Charlotte crossed her arms and studied him. "Looks like he didn't want Nell getting away."

"Sure didn't." Grant grinned pleasantly. Privately, though, his gut twisted. Just this morning, he'd believed they were falling in love, when all along she'd just been playing him in her attempt to snag a husband ahead of her sisters. There had to be a timeline on this.

"I hope it doesn't seem like we're rushing things," he said cagily.

"No, not rushing at all," Charlotte said.

"Yeah." Misty grinned. "Thirty days is longer than they get on some reality shows."

Wait. Thirty. *Days?*

Grant coughed into his hand. "It is," he agreed.

"Still," Charlotte said. "It's a good thing you and Nell jumped in right away."

He grinned tightly. "With both feet."

So, Nell was under extreme time pressure. No wonder she'd come on so strong. She could have picked anyone in Majestic, but she'd chosen him, tracking him down like a big buck in hunting season, and he'd foolishly walked into her trap. He might as well have worn a bull's-eye on his chest when she'd caught him in her crosshairs with those golden-brown eyes of hers.

He barely held in a scowl. Finding out the girl he'd let down his guard for, who he thought he might *love*, had been manipulating him the whole time felt pretty lousy. More than lousy. Irritating. His jaw clenched. No, worse. He was angry.

There was just one thing he needed to know: why *him*? Because he was young and single and there weren't that many eligible guys in Majestic? She possibly remembered him from high school as being a decent guy. Even though they hadn't really known each other much at all, they had vaguely known about each other. So when she went scouting for a husband, maybe she figured he'd be okay.

Wait. What if he *wasn't* "okay"?

A light bulb went off in Grant's head. One in the shape of a curveball Nell wouldn't expect. Maybe she wasn't the only one full of surprises. He could pull a trick or two out of his hat. His heart thumped harder as the idea fermented in his brain. If he came off as a horrible prospective mate, Nell would want nothing more to do with him. He wouldn't have to be the jerk who dumped her and potentially sent her packing to London. She'd realize trying to trap Grant was a huge mistake first, then summarily dump *him*. Toot sweet. Stellar plan.

Unlike his dad, who'd failed at commitments, Grant took pride in honoring his word, and he'd promised the Delaneys he'd look after Nell. And he would—right up until she decided he was not the man for her. All he needed was a little more "quality" time with Nell to convince her she'd bitten off more than she could chew. And, boy oh boy, he intended to be a mouthful.

He wouldn't shout or stomp around like a Neanderthal, but he wouldn't exactly be modern-day marriage material, either. He repressed a chuckle, imagining the various shenanigans he could pull to drive her away. The prey would be outfoxing the fox then.

Yes. This plan was sounding better by the second. He just needed to set it in motion.

"You know," he said to Charlotte and Misty. "Nell could probably stand to rest up a bit longer at the cabin with that hurt ankle of hers. And honestly? I don't mind taking care of her. So, if she decides she wants to stay, I can take off work for a few more days. Besides," he said, layering on more sugar, "that would give us a great chance to plan our wedding. You know, all those millions of important little details."

"Aww," Misty and Charlotte gushed together. "*Grant*."

"I think that's a great idea," Charlotte said.

"The best idea," Misty agreed. "We can cover for her here."

"She left her car on the mountain, though, so someone will need to go and get it."

"She keeps an extra set of keys here," Charlotte said. "Misty and I can pick it up after work."

"Great," Grant answered. "I can drive Nell home when she's ready." He repressed a grin, thinking that was going to be sooner rather than later. He'd need to stop and pick up a few things on his way back to the cabin, but that was easy enough.

"Where's her car?" Charlotte asked him.

"At the lot near White Pines Overlook," he said. "I don't suppose you also have a key to her house?"

"It's on the key ring," Charlotte said. "Why?"

"Would it be too much trouble for you to bring Nell some extra clothes and maybe her phone charger when you go get her car? My cabin's right on the way."

"You're so thoughtful." Misty had stars in her eyes. "We'll be happy to do that."

"Just text us directions," Charlotte said. "The last digit of my phone number is one up from Nell's."

"Sounds good," Grant said. "Thanks!"

• • •

Grant was in the middle of checking out at the market when the stocky cashier, Mrs. McIntyre, lowered her glasses. "Is it true what I hear about you and Nell Delaney?"

Her husband finished filling the morning newspaper bins and strolled over. "Getting married, I hear," he said with a big grin.

Grant stared at the stacks of newspapers. "Did it make the *Seaside Daily*?" he asked, only half kidding.

Mrs. McIntyre smiled. "No, sweetie. We heard from our son Sean, who's been seeing Misty."

Huh. Wonder if that guy knows about the bet.

Mr. McIntyre's eyes twinkled. "I always did like the Delaneys and Nell." He began bagging Grant's groceries and helping his wife. "Nice family."

"Yeah." Okay. So. It was worse than he feared. This was no longer just between him and the Delaneys. Word had gotten out in Majestic that he was getting married to Nell, and with the McIntyres in possession of the information, it would soon spread like wildfire all over town. Before long, everyone from the pastor to his postal carrier would be offering their heartiest congratulations.

Grant could deny that he was engaged, but at this point folks might not believe him. In any case, he'd hate to hurt the Delaneys that way, especially in light of what they'd been through. It wasn't their fault that Nell had messed up. Problem was, Grant's pedigree wasn't exactly pristine, so everyone would assume he'd been the one to break things off when the word got out. It'd be *his* fault the Delaneys got hurt, even if it wasn't.

Which was why his plan was necessary.

Nell wouldn't know he knew about her claims of an engagement or that ridiculous bet she'd made with her sisters. Oh no. He was going to very patiently wait for her to explain the whole situation to him, before gladly driving her home—or to the airport, if that's what she preferred.

Mr. McIntyre set the last of Grant's bags in his shopping cart. "Give our regards to Nell, now."

Mrs. McIntyre tittered. "I hope we get an invite to the wedding!"

He waved over his shoulder and headed out the door.

The invitations for the wedding-that-wasn't were never going to make it in the mail.

• • •

Grant stopped by Blue Sky Adventures next. He wanted to make sure the store had survived the storm, but more importantly than that, he was on a mission. He was glad to see Jordan's SUV in the parking lot, because he wanted his friend's advice. He found Jordan in the back room, unpacking some new climbing equipment—helmets and other kinds of gear.

Jordan looked up from his work. "Hey, man. What's up? I thought you and Nell were up at the cabin?"

"We are up at the cabin, and things were going great." Grant frowned. "Until they weren't."

"Oh no." Jordan searched Grant's eyes. "Is Nell okay?"

"Physically? Yeah. She's on the mend, I'd say." He shook his head. "Mentally, though, she's very tricky."

"Nell Delaney, tricky?" He shot Grant a doubtful look. "That seems kind of a stretch."

"What's a stretch is what she told her sisters—and, by extrapolation, the whole town," he groused. "Apparently."

Jordan crossed his arms. "What's that?"

"That she and I are engaged."

Jordan hooted with laughter.

When Grant scowled, his friend's humor faded, and he pursed his lips. "Oh, sorry. But seriously, Grant. Why would she do that?"

Grant ran a hand through his hair. "It has to do

with some crazy bet between her and her sisters. Their family business. And—you won't believe this—a marriage of convenience to some dude in London named Aidan."

"Marriage of…?" Jordan squinted. "You mean, people still do that?"

"Yeah. At least it seems the Delaneys do."

"They're all good-looking women," Jordan noted. "And seem nice and smart."

"Exactly. You'd think that they'd have choices. I just never expected Nell's choice to be *me*."

"And that's a bad thing because?"

"Because it makes me the subject of a bet, Jordan." Grant raked a hand through his hair. "It's not like Nell's interested in me for me."

"How do you know that?"

Grant blew out a breath. "Even if she is, there's some kind of timeline involved, and I don't do timelines. Or pressure."

"I certainly get that part. How long's the timeline?"

"Thirty days."

Jordan's eyebrows rose. "Okay, you're right. That's short. What's supposed to happen by then?"

"Nell's supposed to be engaged to someone if she doesn't want to marry British dude."

Jordan grinned broadly. "Twisted."

"You bet it is, which is why I have to put a stop to it."

"Are you sure you want to?"

"Are you kidding me?" Grant said. "Of course I'm sure."

"I thought things were going well up at the cabin?"

He huffed. "That was *before* I knew I had a groom's bounty on my head."

"Gotcha." Jordan's shoulders sank. "So, what are you going to do? Talk to her? Call the whole deal off?"

"No." Grant set his chin. "I'm going to let *her* do that, thank you very much. You know how it was for me, growing up under my dad's dark shadow in this town. I've finally built my reputation here. Have a good business. Friends." Grant sighed. "I'm not going to toss all that away by having word circulate around Majestic that I'm the scumbag who dumped sweet little Nell Delaney. As it is, when she has to tell people she dumped me, they'll already assume it's my fault, no matter what I say."

"That would just be a rumor."

"You're still fairly new here," he told Jordan. "In Majestic, rumors are generally suspected to be based somewhat in truth. And anyway, I don't need the hassle of deflecting the untruths. I'd rather leave that unsavory task to the woman who apparently started it all: Nell. I don't know why she'd let her sisters think we're engaged. Probably so they'd let her out of that bet. But now she's going to be the one to tell them that we really aren't. Not only that, she's going to be sure to tell the whole town. Because, trust me on this, once I get back to that cabin, Nell Delaney is not going to want to marry me. She'll be running for the hills."

"Uh-oh. I don't like the look in your eyes. What do you have in mind?"

"A lot of things, actually." Grant chuckled and rubbed his hands together. "Like making myself impossible to live with." The plan had really started coming together on the drive to Blue Sky Adventures. Far from being mean, he intended to be Mr. Sunshine, all sweet and lovey-dovey on the outside. Cloyingly so.

"Slow down there, friend."

"I'm not talking *bad* stuff," he told Jordan. "More like absentmindedly inconsiderate, while blinding her with overbearing cheerfulness. I also might throw down a challenge or two. Ones that I know would drive any reasonable woman away. And I do believe Nell to be that, despite her current lack of judgment."

Jordan frowned at him. "Two wrongs don't make a right. If you feel she's tricked you, maybe the best way to respond is not by tricking her in return."

Grant stood up a little straighter. "I won't be tricking, exactly. More like encouraging her to see that I'm not the right guy for her."

His friend blew out a breath. "Don't say I didn't warn you when this backfires."

Grant set his hands on his hips. "And just how is it going to backfire?"

Jordan's eyebrows shot up. "Do you want the whole list?"

"No," Grant grumbled. "What I want is your help in picking out a tent."

"What kind of a tent?"

"The most ridiculously complicated one we've got."

CHAPTER THIRTEEN

"Sweetie pie! I'm home!"

Well, that was different, but Nell secretly liked that he'd picked a pet name for her. He was obviously happy to see her, and she was desperately glad to see him. He'd been gone for hours.

Nell hobbled toward the front door and hugged him around the neck.

He hugged her back, lifting a large paper cup in one hand. "Easy there. You'll spill your coffee."

"Coffee?"

His dark eyes twinkled as he shut the door behind him. "I brought you your favorite."

Nell accepted the paper cup, and a familiar smell flooded her senses. Blueberries, toasty nuts, and caramel with heavy cream. Her mouth watered. She took a sip, and it had gone lukewarm with the whipped cream dissolving in the liquid. Still, it was delicious. "You went to Bearberry Brews?"

"I did," he said proudly.

"Thank you." She took another sip, grateful to be drinking coffee again and not tea. If he'd had a microwave, she would have heated it up, but since he didn't, she was happy enough to drink it room temp. "The roads, then? They're cleared?" She tried to hide her disappointment, but judging by how his expression turned sympathetic, he detected it.

"Chin up." He shot her a smile. "That doesn't mean we have to go anywhere—yet."

"What?" She noticed he had a paper bag in his hand. Ooh, had he brought her some treats, too—

Hang on. If he'd been to the café, then he'd probably seen her sisters.

Her heart pounded. What if they'd said something to him about the bet?

"Why don't we go sit down at the table?" he said.

"Grant," she said as they headed to the kitchen. "Who did you see at Bearberry Brews?"

He shrugged. "Pretty much everybody."

Her pulse skittered. "Oh."

He set his jaw, thinking. "Charlotte, Misty, your parents. Yeah." He met her eyes. "The whole happy family. Plus Lucas and Mei-Lin."

She exhaled internally. Okay. That was good. If everybody was around, then her sisters wouldn't have blabbed about anything.

"They were all sorry to hear about your accident and hope you feel better soon."

"You told them about my ankle?"

"Yeah." He frowned. "I kind of did. Why didn't you?" He gazed at her in a penetrating way that set her nerves on edge.

She flipped back her hair. "I didn't want to worry them."

"That is so you. Considerate to a fault." He glanced at the stove top, where a fresh loaf of apple bread was cooling. "Well, what have we here?" he asked, sounding pleased. He walked over to the loaf and inhaled deeply, then glanced at her. "It smells amazing. What is it?"

"Apple bread. My recipe's technically for applesauce cake, but since you didn't seem to have a

Bundt pan around, I cut the recipe in half and used the loaf pan under the stove." She made her way over to the table, taking care with her right foot. "I hope you don't mind that I used some of your ingredients. I found a couple of apples in the fridge that looked like they needed to be eaten."

He laughed. "Yeah, those have been there for a while."

"And anyway." She shrugged. "You had oil, sugar, and self-rising flour."

"But no eggs?"

"I substituted applesauce for those. It's a vegan trick." She knew about that from when Misty had dated a vegan named Devon. Her sister had told her all about the extra efforts she'd made in baking for him. Nell had tried some of the plant-based replacements for hot dogs and such and—honestly—was not a fan. If eating meat, dairy, or whatever was an issue for someone she cared about, of course she'd make accommodations, too. But she wouldn't have to worry about that with Grant. He'd pretty much assured her he ate everything. "I noticed you had some mini packs of applesauce in the cupboard. I kind of had to use them all. I hope that was okay?"

"More than okay. Thank you, Nell." He appreciated the cinnamon scent in the air. "I see you found my cinnamon, too."

She chuckled. "It was next to the oatmeal. I found cloves and nutmeg, too."

He sniffed the air. "That's what smells so delicious. Yeah, I keep those around for eggnog and such at Christmas." He set his hands on his hips. "I didn't know you were making me breakfast."

"I would have made bacon and eggs if you'd had them."

"Fantastic." He winked. "I'll take a raincheck."

"What?"

"Just let me bring in the groceries."

"You went to the store?"

"Yes indeed-y. I did."

Her smile faltered a bit. He was super perky this morning, but that was a good thing, right? He seemed in great spirits about having been into town, and now he was stocking up. For what, though?

He pointed to a chair at the table. "You sit right down and rest that ankle of yours until I bring everything in."

"Everything? How much is there?"

"A lot."

"But why? If we're—"

"Ah, ah, ah," he said. "No talking negative. I definitely don't want to leave here. Do you?"

She gulped. Was he suggesting what she hoped he was—that the two of them could continue playing house a little longer? "No...?"

He sat down at the table with her and took her hand, setting his pastry bag aside.

"Nell," he said with an earnest look. "I've been thinking a lot, ever since our *wonderful* night together last night. And our *beautiful* day together yesterday. The waterfall. Your smile. Everything."

Oh wow. Her pulse fluttered. "Really?"

He held her hand tighter. "I told your sisters that I want you to stay here for a few more days so that I can take care of you."

Her jaw dropped. "Wait. You did?"

"Yeah. But it's not only that." He grinned. "There's more going on between us. I feel a connection. A very special connection. It's almost cosmic. And Nell." He dove into her eyes, and her heart thumped. "I think we should explore it."

She squeezed his hand, almost dizzy with joy. Was this actually happening? "I feel it, too."

"Do you? That's wonderful."

Hesitation needled its way into her happiness. "But wait. What about your job and my work?"

"Charlotte and Misty said not to worry about coming in. They want you to rest and recover here, and they'll cover for you at the café. For my part? I'm my own boss." He chuckled. "I can do what I want."

"But don't you have adventures scheduled or something?"

He patted her hand. "I've already rescheduled them."

"Wow. I don't know what to say." Happiness fizzed through her, like sparkling champagne bubbles. "That's really sweet of you. All of this is."

"Not as sweet as you are." He bent forward and gave her a peck on the lips. Her face warmed all over—and other parts of her body, too.

"Here's what I'm thinking," he said, his voice husky. "I know it seems very early on and like maybe I'm rushing things, but I think that you and I"—he motioned between them—"should be exclusive." He took both her hands in his. "What do you say?"

Nell gulped. Okay, not only was this happening, it was happening *fast*. But that's what she wanted—no, *needed*—right? "I'd say that's…that's what I want, too."

"Excellent." He brought both of her hands to his mouth and kissed them. He peered up at her and paused. "This isn't going too fast for you?"

In any other situation, yes. But when it came to how she felt about Grant now that she'd gotten to know him… "Not at all."

"Some people can be reckless," he said. "Jump into things. Rush in headlong without thinking." His dark eyes twinkled. "But that's not us."

Nell licked her lips. Maybe it did feel kind of rushed, but that was okay. When true love was there, who were they to question fate? Their time together must have made a huge impression on him, just like it had left its mark on her. One day and exclusive— on this fast track, becoming engaged by month's end didn't seem like such a huge stretch.

She'd just need to adjust to this breakneck-speed pace.

"I think timelines can be artificial," she said, more to herself than him, her face warming. "People can say you have to date for so long before becoming serious, and then wait X amount of time before taking the next step."

"But you're not one of those?"

"I'd say it's very individual," she said. "Depending on the couple." She watched *The Bachelor* and *The Bachelorette*, and those dating timelines were compressed. Granted, those couples rarely made it, but that was TV.

He sat back in his chair and threw open his arms. "Who's to argue with love, Nell? Certainly not me."

Love? She swallowed hard. "Grant, what are you saying?"

His grin widened. "I'm saying let's give this a chance. See how we do. Who knows how things might go from here if we're compatible?"

Wait—*if*? Now he had her confused. "But I thought we were?" She paused. "Compatible."

He rubbed his cheek. "Scrabble? Yeah, that's good, but Nell…" He leaned toward her. "I'm talking about our ability to live together. Cohabitate. For the long haul."

She felt lightheaded. "You mean, while being married, right?"

He thumbed her nose. "Now let's not go jumping any guns here." He pushed back his chair and stood. "But, if we find we really get along…" His eyebrows rose. "You never know."

Okay, that sounded doable. She could work with that. Yes, they'd need to keep things speeding along if they were to be engaged by month's end, but if he felt as strongly as he seemed to be saying he did, he'd be *putting a ring on it* soon enough.

Take that, Charlotte.

Nell gathered her frazzled thoughts and tried to fully soak in the morning's developments. Somehow, even with her abysmal attempt at hiking and even worse attempt to sound like a camping whiz, she'd hit a homerun.

Operation First Bride was rocking it.

I'm going to marry Grant!

Hopefully.

"Now," he said, "let me go grab those groceries before everything melts."

"Want help?"

"No, you stay put. Maybe you can help put things away, though." He studied her outfit. "I see that you're back in your hiking clothes."

"Yeah, I washed them out, and they dried over-night." If she was staying there, she wished she had something else to wear besides Grant's sweats. But those would do if she could spend more time with him. She shrugged. "I thought you were taking me home today, so."

"Not to worry. Misty and Charlotte are dropping by this evening with some more of your stuff, and your phone charger."

"Oh? Are they? That's great." Unless they brought up the bet by accident. That would be a disaster.

Which meant she'd be worrying about any slips until the moment they walked back out the door. Super fun.

"Yeah. I figured you'd want to have some of your own things while we're settling in." He winked. "Nesting."

Her eyebrows arched. "Nesting?"

"Just like two little lovebirds, Nell. Lovey-dovey."

Her heart fluttered, except this time the giddiness was tinged with a hint of panic. There was that "love" word again. Twice, even.

She totally wouldn't mind getting a little more lovey-dovey with Grant. Soon. She just needed to find her footing in his accelerated timeline, and fast.

"Thank you for thinking of that, Grant." She gave him a tentative smile. "Um. Do you think I could borrow your phone to text them a list of things to get?"

"Good idea. Text away!" He handed her his phone. "I want you to be comfortable for the duration of your stay." His eyes swept over her slowly. "But please don't set your departure date yet. I've got another surprise for you."

She blinked. How many more surprises could she take in one morning? "You do?"

"Sit tight. I'll share in a bit."

Dazed, Nell stayed at the kitchen table and sent a quick note to her sisters. She kept it specific to a short list of clothing and some toiletries and didn't mention anything else, in case Grant went back and read it later.

Charlotte answered first.

We're happy to help out!

Misty followed.

See you soon!

Nell weighed her options but decided not to reply to cither one.

Better to wait until she had her own phone or saw them in person.

• • •

Grant hauled in bag after bag of groceries, trying not to chuckle at Nell's stunned expression. Nesting. That genius idea had been totally inspired, and it had come to him on the fly.

"Whoa," she said. "How long are we staying?"

"How long would you like to stay?"

"Um." She pursed her lips, seeming reluctant to offer an opinion. Which was okay by him. He was happy to play this by ear. Especially since he wouldn't have to play it for too long. He was pretty sure she'd be gone by this evening.

The houseful of groceries he'd have left over would totally be worth it.

He grinned. "Most of these are cleaning supplies, anyway."

"Cleaning?"

"Yeah." He glanced around the cabin. "This place probably needs a little sprucing up."

"Oh."

"Now that we're officially together." He winked. "You can officially get to work."

Her mouth dropped open. "What?"

He laughed warmly. "No worries, sweetness. You don't have to get to work right away. I know you've got your ankle problem." He frowned. "How's it doing, anyway?"

"Oh. Um, actually. A little better today." She watched him stow a ten-pound bag of ice in the freezer. "Is that for my ankle?"

"Nope. The ice is for fishing." He handed her a shopping bag. "This is for the ankle. Your frozen veggie days are done."

She took the bag, curious now. "What's this?"

"A real ice pack. The sooner you heal, the sooner you can participate as a full partner in our relationship."

She paused. "Partner?"

"Yeah, by pulling your weight around here. I mean, there's nothing actually wrong with your left ankle, or your arms or hands for that matter. We'll need to *pull together*, Nell, to make this whole thing work. Be a team!" He raised his fist in a fake cheer.

"Oh." She blinked. "Oh, sure."

He reached into one of the bags he'd set on the counter. "Look what was on special."

She goggled at him as he pulled out six mesh bags of Brussels sprouts. "Wow. Um. That's a lot of Brussels sprouts."

Yes, it was. He let his face fall. "Oh no. I totally forgot. I'm sorry, Nell. You don't like these, do you?" He gave his best dejected frown and walked to the trash bin. "I'll just ditch them in the—"

"No, don't! That's wasteful."

He turned to her. "Yeah, but…" He wrinkled his nose. "They're going to stink up the house, and you hate them."

She grimaced. "I didn't mean that so…absolutely." A lie. He knew it. But he also knew she wouldn't have the heart to disappoint him.

"At least I didn't get peas! Not even the frozen kind."

"Thank you." She laughed, and he was still kind of charmed by it, but he told himself to toughen up and remember his mission. He reached for the tofu hot dogs next and set those on the counter, along with the hot dog buns.

"I got your favorite campfire meal."

"Oh nice! Hot dogs?"

"Yes, ma'am. I'd planned for us to cook them tomorrow during our camping day."

Her eyes went wide. "We're going c-camping?"

He chuckled at her horrified look. He couldn't wait to find out just how little she actually knew about tents and such. "Not going anywhere but here." He glanced at the grocery bags. "Hey, would you mind putting the cold stuff away so I can bring in your surprise?"

"Uh, sure." She scrambled to her feet and hopped over to the counter. He noticed she was putting more weight on her right foot, which was what he'd hoped. He felt mildly guilty about giving her a hard time when she was injured. Not that guilty, though. All things considered.

As he headed for the door, he said, "I got marshmallows, too. And graham crackers."

"Sweet. For s'mores?"

"You don't have to eat the chocolate." He stopped walking and hung his head. "Oh man."

"Grant? What is it?"

He gestured toward the pastry bag on the table. "I bought us a few treats this morning at Bearberry Brews, but I got so hungry running errands I wound up eating some of them myself."

"That's no big deal. It's fine."

"Yeah, except." He shrugged. "The only one left is chocolate."

She hopped back to the table and peeked into the bag. "Ooh, it's a croissant! I love those." She pulled it out and took a big bite to demonstrate. Her lips scrunched up a little funny when she chewed, but he gave her full credit for making the effort. It actually made her look really cute. Grant stopped himself, reeling back those positive thoughts.

Focus. Focus.

"Didn't you say you hated chocolate?"

"Not all of it." She wiped her mouth with the back of her hand. "I like it fine when it's combined with other things like yellow cake and, uh…croissants."

"Whew." He ran a hand through his hair. "And here I was sure I'd messed up again."

"Grant," she said, her expression softening. "You could never 'mess up.'" Her golden-brown eyes shone, and he wished she wouldn't do that: look completely adorable. That didn't help his resolve at all.

"Thanks, Nell."

Now let's just see how long your sweetness can last.

She opened the refrigerator door and picked up the hot dogs. "Oh. These are tofu."

"Yeah. Is that a problem?" *Please let it be a problem.*

"No. No problem." She examined the bacon next, and it may have been a trick of the refrigerator lighting, but he swore she went a little pale. "Wait. Is this vegetarian bacon?"

"Didn't I tell you?" His eyebrows rose. "I'm a pescatarian."

She leaned into the refrigerator door. "A pesca — what?"

He chortled to himself. "A pescatarian. It's like a vegetarian, only I eat fish."

Her forehead wrinkled. "But didn't you say you'd had the lamb stew at Mariner's?"

Argh. He forgot about that, but he found his way around it. "I've just heard the stew is delicious. From loads of people. Figured they couldn't all be wrong." He tacked on a laugh for good measure.

She looked like she was trying to recall their conversation. "Same with the corned beef and cabbage?"

"Yep." Sweat threatened to pop on his brow. How many things had he mentioned in that one conversation?

"So then." She processed this. "You don't eat meat?"

"No meat. Only fish."

"But…what about the grilling?"

"What grilling?"

"You said you liked to grill out?"

The woman had a mind like a steel trap. "I do like to grill out: tofu hot dogs. And other things, like…tofu kabobs. And veggies." He nodded to himself. That sounded like something a pescatarian would cook. Hopefully.

"Well, okay." She seemed to be processing all this. "I think that's great. Save all those cows and pigs."

"And sheep," he said. "Mary and her little lambs. You don't want to forget about those."

She swallowed hard. "Sure wouldn't."

After a pause, he added, "Or the chickens."

"Absolutely." She smiled tentatively. "Save them, too."

He frowned. "There will be no turkey at Thanksgiving, I'm afraid."

"Maybe we can find you a tofu version?" Her expression shifted from disappointed to hopeful. "Or. Isn't there another poultry substitute? What's it called? Seitan?"

"I mean, I can't—" He balled his fist up to his mouth like he was about to retch. This one was going to have to be good. "Can't bear the sight of it. Or the smell. Of any poultry, really, real or fake. Reminds me of Robby."

"Who's Robby?"

No one he knew. But she didn't need to know that. "My little red rooster." He broke down a bit, his voice cracking, and he shielded his face with his hand. He sneakily peeked through his fingers to see if she was buying it.

Nell's expression was a combo of dumbfounded and horrified. "So, he was…?"

Grant sniffed. "My pet as a kid."

"Oh no."

"He used to ride on my shoulder." Grant gave a wistful look and patted his shoulder. "Right up here." Judging by the sympathy rolling off of her in waves, he was actually pretty good at this. The more he spun this tale, the more she believed him.

"What happened to Robby? I mean, I understand if it's too painful to talk about," she rushed to add, "but I'd like to hear about a pet who obviously meant a lot to you."

His heart stumbled a bit. Why did she have to be so darn caring? He schooled his emotions and dug back in. "My parents wouldn't tell me. They said he went to live 'on a farm.'" He lowered his eyebrows. "I think we both know what that means."

Her shoulders sagged. "Oh, Grant. I'm so sorry. Not to worry. There won't be any turkey for our Thanksgivings, tofu or otherwise."

You've got that part right, sweetheart, because you and I are going to be way done by Thanksgiving. Finished before Halloween.

She peered into a grocery bag and pulled out the eggs and cheese. "Guess you're not a vegan, then."

She somehow looked relieved. Although she did say that thing about the vegan egg substitution, so maybe his feigned dietary restrictions wouldn't throw her as much as he'd hoped.

Though, from the wide-eyed way she was staring at the tofu hot dogs, they would. He resisted a chuckle and headed for the front door. "Don't go anywhere. I'll be right back."

• • •

Grant went outside, and Nell returned to unloading the groceries. Wow. Who knew about the rooster thing? Robby, huh. This could pose a problem in the Delaney house. Her dad prided himself on his Thanksgiving turkey and homemade oyster stuffing. Nell generally skipped the stuffing due to the oysters, but the turkey was always divine. Never mind about that. She could worry about Thanksgiving later.

If she and Grant got married, they'd work out a compromise. Her heart sank. She couldn't imagine skipping the traditional holiday meal with her family, though. Then she told herself not to get carried away. Robby was clearly a traumatic childhood memory for Grant. They'd find a way to make accommodations.

That's what you did for the person you loved: accommodate!

So, he was a pescatarian who ate a lot of fish. So what?

She liked to knit, and he didn't.

They had their differences.

She just hadn't counted on there being so many of them.

Nell dug into another grocery bag, hunting for that "cold stuff" he'd mentioned. While she was trying not to worry, sneaky little doubts began creeping into her mind. Like her not knowing Grant as well as she'd believed yesterday. Then she remembered the cold pack he'd brought her and the coffee. He'd remembered her favorite kind!

Maybe she wasn't picky enough due to her lack of experience, but as far as she was concerned, Grant Williams was a prince. *Her* prince, and if things kept progressing the way they had in barely twenty-four hours, she and Grant were going to have their fairytale ending, just like the heroes and the heroines in the books she read.

True to his word, Grant hadn't bought peas. Only a few replacement bags of the other frozen vegetables. And milk. It was almond milk, but that was okay.

Wait.

She opened the deli drawer. Yep. The cheese was lactose free. No worries. She could adjust. Misty'd done okay with Devon, and she'd do just great with Grant. And anyway, it wasn't like they'd always have to eat the same things. They were individuals with their own tastes and preferences.

Grant ambled through the front door, his arms loaded down, and she stepped back.

What was he carrying? He looked like an army ranger about to deploy.

He had an enormous backpack on his back and all sorts of odds and ends dangled from it, including what looked like a bedroll and a portable camp stove. He held a sleeping bag in his arms and a duffel bag and had a large pocketknife of some kind clenched between his teeth.

She jumped back at the sight. "What's all this?"

He mumbled and motioned with his head, and she very carefully removed the pocketknife from his mouth. She studied it, seeing it had lots of pull-out thingies. She popped one up that looked like a bottle opener.

Grant grinned broadly. "Surprise!"

She closed the knife and flinched when the bottle opener sprang back into place.

"Careful," he said. "Some of those are sharp."

"Er..." She surveyed him up and down and peeked behind him. "What's all this?"

When he'd said he had a surprise for her, she didn't know what she'd expected. Maybe flowers or something. Definitely not camping equipment.

"Our supplies for camping day. Tomorrow, you're going to show me what you know about camping, and then I—"

She touched his sleeve. "Grant."

"Huh?"

"I'm really, really sorry, but I need to tell you something."

His eyebrows arched. "It's not about us? You haven't changed your mind?"

"No! Far from it. It's just about the camping?" She lifted a shoulder. "I might have exaggerated a little."

"How so?" For his arms being so loaded down, he didn't seem to be suffering. He really was a strong guy. She guessed he'd more than proved that the two times he'd carried her.

"When I told you I went camping with my sisters." She licked her lips. "That wasn't exactly true."

"What? You're kidding." He scrubbed a hand down his face. "Is that why Misty looked so confused when I asked her about the tent?"

"Oh. Um. Did she?" Nell bit her lip. "And did you?"

"Hang on," he said. "Let me set this stuff down in the bedroom. We won't be needing it until tomorrow anyway."

"Oh. Okay."

He trudged through the living room, grumbling about something to himself, and Nell feared it was about her and camping. "I'm really excited to try it, though," she called after him. "Can't wait!"

He deposited his gear and returned, pausing on the threshold. "So. You lied about the camping?" He appeared a bit dazed but also crestfallen, and Nell felt awful for disappointing him.

"I didn't mean anything bad by it. I promise. I was only…" Her chin trembled. "Trying to impress you."

"Nell. You don't need to try so hard." His eyes glimmered dimly. "I already told you that."

"I know, and I'm sorry."

He pursed his lips and folded his arms across his broad chest. His gaze swept over her, settling on her face. "So. What other stories have you told?"

Uneasiness washed over her. Uh-oh. "Stories?"

"I mean, okay about the camping. That's not such a huge deal. I can teach you."

"Exactly." She heaved a breath. "That's what I was thinking. It will be a fun project for the two of us. You teach; I'll learn. Just like how you showed me about deboning that fish!"

"So, when you said you were an expert hiker—"

Her pulse beat faster. "I'm not really an expert at that, either." Her heart hammered, and she feared this whole thing was going to blow apart.

Then Grant surprised her by chuckling out loud. His laughter was good-natured, too. Sweet and forgiving. "Honey, I had that one figured out the moment you stepped from your car." His eyes twinkled, and relief coursed through her.

"What? You did?"

"You need to be careful, Nell. Lies have a way of building on each other."

"That's...that's what I hear."

"You have built a campfire, though?"

"Um." She shrank back a little. "Not exactly."

He held out his arms. "Come here."

She hesitated.

"I'm not mad at you. Honest."

She took a baby step toward him.

"Closer."

And then another.

He walked forward and drew her into his arms, hugging her tightly. "There's nothing we can't get through together." He pulled back to gaze in her eyes. "Isn't that what you believe?"

"Yeah. For sure."

"Then great." He gave her a firm peck on the lips and released her, so abruptly she nearly stumbled. Nell caught herself and stood upright, shifting most of her weight to her left foot.

"Then here's what we'll do. We don't have to talk or worry about the camping until tomorrow. There will be plenty of time for you to practice then. Besides that, we've already got our work cut out for us today."

"We do?"

"Yes, but first." He rubbed his belly. "I'm famished. Do you think you can make us some lunch? Maybe some BLTs?"

"With the fake bacon?"

He chuckled. "It's not fake; it's tofu."

Of course it was. What wasn't?

She stared back at the kitchen, which was in a disarray with a lot of the groceries still in their bags. He might have offered to help. But he didn't.

He glanced at the kitchen. "I see you still have a lot to do, so I'll wait." He walked over to the stove and picked up the apple bread. "Maybe I can have a slice of this to tide me over?" He scanned the loaf. "Uh-oh. Oh no." He glanced at Nell. "Are those nuts in here?"

"Um, yeah. Walnuts, why?"

"Can't eat them." He shook his head. "Make my throat close up."

Nell's mouth dropped open, but then she shut it. "But the walnuts were in your cupboard next to the oatmeal."

"Those belonged to Susan."

"Oh." She frowned. "But didn't you say you like trail mix?"

"Right. Yeah, I do." Grant snapped his fingers. "Only I make mine with peanuts. Walnuts are tree nuts." He shrugged. "You can eat the apple bread, though. Or freeze it to take back with you later."

She crossed her arms. "I thought you said you eat just about everything?"

He rubbed his chin. "Within limits." He stared at the refrigerator and sighed. "No worries. I'll just grab an apple in the meantime." He opened the refrigerator, but they were all gone. She'd used every last one in that apple bread.

He turned to Nell, and she covered her mouth with both hands.

"Oh no. I used them all up with the applesauce."

He frowned when her cheeks sagged. "No worries, sweetie pie. I'll be fine until lunch. Why don't you finish up in here, and then call me when it's ready?"

"Where will you be?"

"Getting my fishing gear together." He grinned broadly and patted his chest. "After yesterday's heavy rainfall, the fish will be jumping."

CHAPTER FOURTEEN

Nell put away the last of the groceries and sighed. She ought to be happy about how things were going. She and Grant were exclusive, yay! Besides that, he'd asked her to stay on at his cabin so they could work on their relationship together, which sounded dreamy.

Still, today was a far cry from yesterday when Grant had been the pamperer and she the "pamperee." Not that she expected anyone to dote on her all the time, but the change had been so…abrupt.

She sat down at the kitchen table to rest her sore ankle after propping her foot on a chair and topping her wrapped ankle with a bag of frozen corn. The ice pack that Grant brought her was still in the freezer chilling up.

Grant cracked open the back door. "Is lunch ready?"

Ugh. She'd barely sat down. "Not yet! But soon!"

"Well, don't take too long. Daylight's burning!"

Sure. Nell picked up the frozen corn and dropped her right foot to the floor. *Ow!*

She should probably take it easy this afternoon. Maybe Grant would carry her down to the waterfall again so she could watch him fish? That would be relaxing and fun. She could even take her knitting and work on that. She only had a few more days before his birthday to finish his hat, and she was excited about giving it to him. He was going to be so surprised.

And in a much better way than he'd been surprised about the camping.

And the hiking.

But there, she'd done it.

She'd admitted the truth to him about both those things, and he'd handled the situation reasonably well.

Better than well. He'd been loving and supportive. Understanding, even.

Maybe it would be the same when she told him about Aidan?

She bit her lip. She hoped.

Nell got to work making the sandwiches, but the bacon cooked up really weird-looking and not crispy. Well, okay. If Grant liked things that way. She'd found potato chips when she'd put things away, so he wasn't a total health nut. At least they had that in common. She added some chips to their plates, and pickle spears, too.

Once lunch was ready on the table, she hobbled out the back door to find Grant. He stood on the stoop, going through his tackle box. A couple of fishing rods leaned against the house, and the storage closet door was open.

"Lunch is served!"

He looked up at her and grinned. "Great."

He joined her at the table, perusing his plate. "All looks good, thanks." He took a bite of sandwich and grimaced. He made a chewing motion, then paused and chewed again. "This bacon isn't cooked." He spit something out in his hand, and Nell gawked at him, horrified.

"What? Oh no."

"That's okay. I'll just pick it out." He took the tops off his sandwich halves and began to pick out the limp bacon. He dangled one piece by its end and made a face.

"I'm sorry." Nell winced. She took a bite of her sandwich and nearly gagged. He was right. It was nasty. She must have done something wrong.

"That's okay," he announced. "We still have fish."

"What?"

He walked to the refrigerator and pulled out a foil packet of leftovers from last night's dinner. "Want some of this?"

"Um, no thanks." She straightened her spine. "You know what? I actually kind of ruined my appetite with that croissant you brought me."

"Well, that's a shame." He slapped a cold slab of fish onto his sandwich and put it back together. He sank his teeth into it. "Now that's a sandwich."

Her eyes burned hot. It was the first meal she'd made him, and she'd failed at lunch. She'd also failed at that apple bread. Who knew he was allergic to tree nuts?

"Hey," he said. Then he spoke more gently. "Hey, Nell. It's okay. Not your fault, really."

"I'm sorry about the bacon."

He shook his head. "It's crap bacon anyway. You want a peanut butter sandwich? I bought crunchy."

Her heart warmed. "I saw that. That was thoughtful of you."

"See?" His mouth twitched. "I'm not such a bad guy."

"Are you kidding? You're a great guy."

"Thanks. I think you're pretty great, too."

She took a sip from her water, feeling better. Okay, so they'd hit a few minor speed bumps when he'd surprised her with the groceries and his boat-load of dietary restrictions. She'd had a few revelations for him, too, about the hiking and camping. So now they were even and could start fresh. Working on their compatibility. "So! We're going fishing?"

"We?" His brow furrowed. "You want to fish?"

She chuckled at his response. "Well, no. Not me personally."

He shook his head and kept eating. "Didn't think so."

"But I was thinking I'd tag along."

"What for?"

"To, uh. Keep you company?"

"Aren't you sweet?" He sighed. "But no. I'm afraid you won't have time for that."

Nell was thrown. "What do you mean?"

He pointed to the cleaning bucket in the corner of the kitchen. It was loaded with cleaning supplies. A mop stood beside it, along with a broom that had a dustpan clipped to its handle.

All the air left her lungs. "You want me to stay here and *clean*?" She breathed deeply and counted to ten. "While you go fishing?"

"Uh-huh," he said, like that was the most natural thing in the world.

"But I have a hurt ankle."

He frowned. "I know you do, which is why I brought the step stool in."

She turned to stare at the step stool he'd carried indoors when she'd called him in for lunch. It was short, maybe a foot off the ground, and had a cushioned top. He'd dragged it from the storage closet. "Ah." She tried to say something more, but she couldn't. She was speechless.

"It's very comfortable," he said. "You can sit on that while you work on the bathroom."

"What?"

He whispered, "It hasn't been cleaned in months."

Um. Yeah, she'd kind of noticed that but had been too polite to say anything.

"Same with these hardwood floors. They could use a good polishing."

Okay, this had to be a joke. "You're kidding, right?"

He scratched the back of his head. "Um. No."

"But honey," she said as sweetly as humanly possible, even though she gritted her teeth. "What about an equal division of labor? This *is* the twenty-first century."

"Exactly right." He stood and took his plate to the kitchen sink, dumping it inside of it. "Which is why we're dividing evenly." He strolled over to the cleaning bucket and brought it back to her, setting it down at her feet. It had a toilet brush protruding out of it, and he grabbed its handle.

She watched him wide-eyed.

Nooo. He wouldn't.

"I'm the hunter-gatherer guy. I catch the fish. I bring the groceries." He handed her the toilet brush. "You keep the home fires burning."

But oh yeah, he did.

Nell's jaw dropped.

Hunter-gatherer guy. What did he expect from

her? Maid service?

She tightly shut her eyes and tried not to scream. This was absurd. Even her dad was more fair-minded than this. He cooked and did the dishes. Laundry, too, lots of times.

Grant had to be pulling her leg.

But when she opened her eyes, he still stared at her, looking dead serious. He set his chin. "You have a problem with home fircs?" He sounded legitimately perplexed.

Nell's pulse pounded in her ears. "You. Want. Me. To. Burn down this cabin?"

"You're so cute." He chuckled and patted her cheek. "But no on burning down the cabin. Let's, uh…not do that part. What I meant was—" His gaze darted to the woodstove. "Literally, keep the home fires burning. When the woodstove goes out, it's a bear to get it going again, and it will get below freezing tonight."

Nell tried to work her mouth, but no words came out. Finally, she managed. "Woodstove?"

He nodded and thumbed over his shoulder. "The woodpile's out back, and there's a log splitter there if you need it. But be careful and don't overdo things." He glanced at her ankle. "We want you to mend."

"But, Grant. How can I—"

"You're resourceful." He bent forward and kissed her on her forehead. "That's one of your gifts."

• • •

Grant shut the back door behind him just in time to conceal his chortles.

He wished he had a picture of Nell's face when he'd handed her that toilet brush.

She'd looked like she wanted to scream, or clobber him with the toilet brush.

To her credit, she didn't do either.

He grabbed his fishing boots and the waders he kept on a hook in the storage closet, hoping he hadn't been too hard on her. He didn't really believe she'd clean the bathroom and polish the floors, much less chop wood. What he guessed she'd do was spend the next few hours steaming about what a jerk he was. Unfair in his expectations and chauvinistic, too.

By the time he returned from fishing, she'd be begging to leave.

Good.

She could catch a ride home with Charlotte and Misty when they stopped by.

Grant dressed in his fishing clothes, sliding his chest-high waders over his fleece jacket and jeans, and stepped into his boots, leaving his hiking boots in the storage closet. Then he strolled down the path leading to his favorite spot, his rod in one hand and his tackle box in another. A cooler handle hung from the crook of his arm. He'd filled the cooler with ice and would use it to stow the fish until he was ready to clean them.

It was a gorgeous afternoon, and puffy white clouds dotted the blue sky above the cascades. It was hard not to remember yesterday's rainbow, or the very different feeling he'd had in his heart when he'd been here with Nell. He recalled the selfie that she'd sent him, and his insides ached. He'd been one happy, carefree guy.

Misguided, though, and gullible.

Grant frowned, his heart hardening again.

Nell's pretty smile had all been for show. If it hadn't been for her race against time to find a husband, they might have actually stood a chance.

When was she going to tell him the truth about the bet with her sisters? She'd only fessed up about her camping and hiking inexperience under duress. He figured she was going to come clean about Aidan eventually, but he had no idea when.

Grant's heart gave a hopeful lift.

Maybe once she'd had enough of his cooking and cleaning expectations and couldn't take any more? He chuckled, betting that that time was coming soon. And, if by some great miracle she decided to stay after today, he'd move on to the next "C" in his plan, the one that came after Cooking and Cleaning: Camping.

Yeah, it was fine. Nell could keep her little secrets about Aidan and that bet a while longer if she wanted, and he could keep having fun making himself an unbearable guy. He didn't intend to apply any more honesty pressure, though. He'd leave that to Nell and her conscience.

• • •

Nell stared down at the toilet brush, her irritation building. She'd been sitting at the kitchen table for a while holding it. She didn't know for how long. The minutes just seemed to keep ticking by as she sat there in shock. Then she went from irritated to flaming mad.

All yesterday, Grant had been so tender and attentive. Today, she was his personal Cinderella. Emphasis on the cinders part.

Keep the home fires burning?

She couldn't believe he'd really said that, or the bit about him being a "hunter-gatherer guy." *Grrr.* The man had some nerve.

She wasn't fully recovered from twisting her ankle. Still, what? He wanted her to clean the bathroom and polish the wood floors? Seriously?

If she told her sisters any of that, they'd die. They'd also be furious on her behalf, lowering their opinion of Grant. She doubted they could lower their opinions any further than hers, though. Because her opinion of Grant was currently in the toilet. For real.

And to think, not even an hour ago, she'd been excited about their future together.

There would be no future if this was what he called wedded bliss. She'd rather marry Aidan and live a lonely life in London than align herself with a misogynist who didn't understand the meaning of equal partners in a relationship.

Grant was so not the person she remembered from yesterday. It was like he'd done a complete one-eighty after he'd gone into town.

Wait a minute.

Nell gaped at the toilet brush.

No way. Her sisters wouldn't have.

Or maybe they had?

What if neither Charlotte nor Misty had *meant* to mention the Aidan bet, but it came out inadvertently somehow? Misty did have a tendency to blab, even though she didn't do it on purpose. Maybe she'd sent Grant some weird signals or slipped in a subtle congrats about how well things were going between them? Gah. Maybe she'd even mentioned her selfie in his boxers! Nell face-palmed, really hoping that Misty hadn't. Charlotte, either, for that matter. With her folks around, it was doubtful her sisters would have said that much. Or shown him pics.

She hoped.

But whatever they'd said—because at this point, them blabbing was the only reason any of this made sense—they'd somehow tipped off Grant that she'd intended to win him over quickly. Thereby irking him *hugely*.

So hugely that all of a sudden he was determined to get rid of her.

She waved the toilet brush like a wand, getting it.

He's trying to shove me away by making himself impossible.

She gestured toward the cleaning bucket with the toilet brush, then toward the bathroom, sweeping her arm across the hardwood floors.

Really impossible.

Her cheeks steamed.

She couldn't remember ever being this worked up.

Okay, fine! So. Grant didn't want her and was going to make that perfectly clear—in his twisted, underhanded way. Only, now that she was on to him, she wasn't going to make things so easy. She got what this was. A vain attempt to punish her for what he probably saw as *her* tricking *him* into falling in love. He was going to show her just how unpleasant being married to him could be. Not at all a bed of roses. More like a thicket of thorns.

Her jaw clenched.

Of course. That sneaky man.

This was all a wicked scheme.

That's what all that compatibility talk had been about. It was no small coincidence that he'd started gently insinuating how ill-suited they might be for each other immediately afterward. Were all those dietary restrictions he'd claimed real, or was he just trying to invent more trouble for her?

He'd been inconsiderate about not helping to put the groceries away and about his expectations for her making lunch, too. Then he'd gone off to relax and go fishing while leaving her to do the grunt work here.

Partnership. Pull your weight. Compatibility.

Grrr. If he'd planned all this, that had taken some time. No wonder he'd been gone so long this morning. He'd been putting his whole dastardly plan together.

Who knew he had it in him?

She eyed the toilet brush. Seems she had quite a bit more to learn about Grant Williams.

Starting with how best to make him pay for this little game of his.

He was trying to push her away? Great. Let him! Why would she even want a relationship with a schemer like him anyway? He didn't even give her a chance to explain! But first, she planned to cause him quite a bit of grief by giving him a taste of his own medicine. She would *not* let Grant get away with making her feel foolish.

No. He was going to be the one feeling foolish by the time this was all over.

Nell didn't have a lot of experience in the love department, but she did have the love of her family, and she also had her pride. Grant wasn't going to strip her of either of those. She was ready for this. He wasn't going to get away with making *her* out to be the quitter. She had a lot more backbone than he knew, and she was feeling more empowered every day.

Two could play at his little game. Let him be the one to call this whole thing off. Not her. She wasn't going to break him with spite; she was going to kill him with kindness. And if he possessed any decency at all, his guilt would eat him alive. He'd feel guilty over putting demands on her and twice as bad about being the one to break things off. Because she would be unfailingly perfect. For the first time ever, maybe.

Nell's confidence surged. Hey, it was only one toilet, and the rooms were small, so there weren't a ton of hardwood floors. Grant probably guessed that she'd be mad and refuse to clean his cabin, which she was within her full rights to do.

It was also her prerogative to be the sweetest domestic goddess he could have ever envisioned. She was not going to cave. She was going to make this grungy little cabin gleam like a palace. She giggled at what Grant's expression might look like when he got back and found the place spotless. What would he say or do then?

Operation First Bride was now Operation Ditch Me.

The only question was, how long would it take for Grant to crack?

• • •

Nell limped back into the kitchen carrying the cleaning bucket and the mop. Scouring that tiny bathroom had been hard work, but it looked so much better now. It glistened.

She tightened the band on her ponytail holder, examining the cabin's wood floors.

Those gleamed, too.

Embers glowed faintly in the woodstove.

Oh no. She'd totally forgotten to stoke it. Soon, it would be getting dark outside, which would mean Grant coming back. She hunted around near the hearth, but there was only one small log in the log holder. That wouldn't be enough. At least there was more wood outside.

Nell put on her jacket and boots, discovering the right one fit on more easily. Even after all her moving around, her ankle appeared to be doing better. It was probably helpful that she'd sat on that step stool while doing a lot of her cleaning and that she'd been on her hands and knees while polishing the floors. She grumbled, knowing she could never tell her sisters about that.

She was glad Charlotte and Misty hadn't shown up early and caught her cleaning house. They would have hustled her out of there so fast, but that was just because they didn't understand what was going on. Nell did, though, which was why she was going out to grab that wood. She would not be dumping Grant Williams. Not today; not ever.

She ambled awkwardly out the back door and

over to the woodpile on the far side of the fish-cleaning station, but none of the wood pieces were small enough to fit in the woodstove. They looked more like sections of a tree trunk that had been halved, some of them quartered. She spied a long-handled axe leaned up against the woodpile.

So that's what he meant by a log splitter. O-kay.

It looked a little intimidating, but she'd always been the kind to learn by doing, and she wasn't afraid to give this new task a try.

She scooted over to the log splitter and hoisted it into her hands. It was heavy, but she could wield it. Yeah. She could do this. It might actually be kind of fun.

She took a big chunk of wood and stood it on end.

Then she stepped back a bit and raised the log splitter.

Whoof!

She brought it down with a *whack*, and the log split in two.

Nell stared at it, amazed by her success.

Not only that, the action had felt good, empowering.

Hey. She was going to do it again.

And again.

And again.

Each time she split a log, she got better at it. The work also helped her take out some of her frustrations. And she had a few minor ones, if she was being honest.

Cleaning the bathroom hadn't exactly been a joy, for example.

Whack.

The floor polishing had made her knees and back ache, too.

Whack.

There'd be no Thanksgiving turkey in her future—ever?

She couldn't exactly blame Grant about Robby.

Wait.

She recalled his pasted-on pout.

He'd totally made that up!

Whack. Whack. Whack!

The piece of wood splintered into more than a dozen pieces.

Okay, maybe that was too much chopping.

She exhaled, feeling better.

At least she'd made good kindling.

CHAPTER FIFTEEN

Grant was pleased with his haul. He'd caught over a dozen fish and had thrown about half of them back, keeping only the big boys. He'd gutted and cleaned them streamside to avoid making a mess at the cabin. He wasn't callous enough to ask Nell to clean up his outdoor fish-cleaning station, too. He did have some heart.

A heart that he'd have to guard a lot more carefully in the future. Apart from the occasional girlfriend, including boomerang Susan, he'd mostly been a solitary man. Solitude was what he craved and what he enjoyed. He'd never had trouble being his own best company. Just yesterday, he'd started wondering if he should change that.

He'd been so comfortable with Nell the previous evening that he'd started to believe he'd found that kind of compatibility with her. And then, once he'd kissed her, he'd become convinced he had. Her affection had been more than physical. He'd believed there were deep emotions attached. He'd sensed that he and Nell were on the brink of a once-in-a-lifetime thing, the kind of relationship most people only dream of.

But sadly, he'd been mistaken.

The sun had not completely set, but it sank low on the horizon, grazing a mountain ridge. When he approached the cabin, he saw smoke curling through its chimney pipe. At least she hadn't let the fire go out. So that was something.

She was probably sitting by the woodstove knitting on that hat of hers and stewing about what an ape man he was. By the time he showered and changed, her sisters would likely be on the doorstep, which was great with him. He knew what he was cooking tonight, and it was pretty clearly something Nell didn't like. Fresh-caught trout.

"Guess what's for dinner?" he announced, opening the front door. He left his gear on the front porch and planned to stow that away after depositing his cooler of fish in the kitchen.

But when he walked inside, he stopped on a dime.

Where was he, and what had Nell done with his cabin?

She glanced at him from where she sat on the sofa with a beautiful grin. Her hair was long and damp, and it looked like she'd recently showered. "Well, hi there! Good fishing?" She held her knitting in her lap with her two knitting needles poised in the air. Her foot rested on the chest with the ice pack positioned on top of her wrapped ankle.

Low flames leaped in the woodstove, and their glow filled the room, which had been completely tidied up and apparently dusted. The kitchen was clean, too. And the floors beneath him shone. They smelled good—like oil soap. The entire place had a fresh scent, a mixture of lemon and pine.

"Wow, Nell." He was flabbergasted. "You did all this?"

She proudly squared her shoulders. "I did."

"But why?"

"Because we're dividing the labor," she said sweetly, and his heart pinged.

Uh-oh.

No, no. Stop that.

"You're the hunter-gatherer guy." She batted her eyelashes at him. "And I'm your domestic goddess."

Okay, of the many things he'd expected, it wasn't this.

"You, uh." He looked around the room again, noticing the door to the bathroom was open. Shiny porcelain and gleaming fixtures glinted back in his direction. "Cleaned the bathroom, too?"

"I don't mind being your goddess, Grant," she said in sultry tones.

His heart pounded. Wow. That sounded sexy.

"As long as you'll be my Greek god."

Grant shifted on his feet, weirdly excited by that proposition. Then he told himself to snap out of it. She was just playing him. She couldn't mean it.

He stared at her, and she smiled ever so slightly in a come-here-baby kind of way.

Grant backed up a step. Then two steps. Three.

She's very cunning; I'll give her that.

A bitter scent wafted toward him. Strong and cabbage-like. He detected garlic, too. "Is something cooking?"

She motioned toward the stove with her knitting needles. He saw that the window over the kitchen sink was cracked open a few inches. "I'm roasting you some of those Brussels sprouts you bought." She grinned. "Two whole bags."

"Two?"

"I won't eat any, so." She shrugged. "I figured two

were enough."

"Yeah. Um. More than plenty." This was not going at all like he'd intended. Instead of being steaming mad, she seemed relaxed and happy. Carefree and lighthearted and even more into him than before. Not less. This was so weird.

"What have you got in the cooler?"

"Trout."

"Might have guessed." She cutely rolled her eyes. "That will go really great with those Brussels, huh?" She pointed to the floor behind him and giggled. "Uh-oh."

He turned around, seeing he'd tracked mud all across the newly polished floors. Forward—and backward. That made him feel like a jerk after all her hard work. "Oops. I'm sorry about the muddy footprints," he said. "I'll mop them up." He bent toward the floor, swiping at the muddy tracks with the bandana he'd tugged from his pocket.

Her eyebrows rose like she couldn't believe it.

"I'm not that big of a jerk, Nell." Then he remembered his request with the toilet brush and got that, yeah, in her mind he probably was. "I mean." He stood, swallowing hard. "Usually."

"I get that part," she said slyly. "You were just playing your *role*." She emphasized that last word like she was trying to tell him something. Wait. Was she onto him? Already? But no. If she was, then why did she seem so darn cheerful about things? Sitting there on the sofa all happy-looking, like every red-blooded man's dream. Or fantasy. Okay, that god and goddess image was really starting to fuel his brain. She 100 percent had the body for it, and the face, with those sweet, sweet freckles, her plump pink lips and those golden-brown—

No. Grant put up a mental stop sign and slammed on the brakes.

Somehow, though, he didn't come to a full stop.

It was more like a rolling stop—the kind you take casually.

When you think no one is looking.

And there is no CCTV in the area.

If he'd been actually driving his SUV, he probably would have gotten a ticket.

"No problem," she said about his muddy footprints. She motioned with her hand like she was urging him along. "Go on then. Come around the other way, but leave those muddy boots outside."

His whole body flushed. She could have told him to do *anything* with that commanding look in her eye and he probably would have done it. Forget the goddess part; maybe she was an enchantress.

Grant swallowed the words before he could say *yes ma'am.*

He shut the front door, dazed.

What's going on?

How had his plan backfired? And why did he suddenly feel guilty for messing up the hardwood floors? This was his cabin. He could trash it if he wanted to.

Although he really wasn't inclined to do that. He'd never seen it looking so good.

Grant circled to the back stoop and got out of his boots and waders, hanging his waders on a hook in the storage closet.

Okay, so she'd cleaned the cabin.

That was all well and good.

That didn't mean she was an admirable person who deserved his forgiveness. She just really didn't want to marry that Aidan guy. That's all.

His gaze tracked to the woodpile, and his jaw dropped.

Hang on.

She chopped *wood*?

He stepped into his hiking boots and walked over to examine the damage.

She'd smashed the daylights out of one piece. What had she been thinking at the time? He swallowed hard. Maybe he didn't want to know. Especially if she'd been thinking about him.

Nell appeared at the back door. "Want me to clean those boots?"

"What?"

Her gaze landed on the boots on the stoop. "They're caked with mud. I can wash them off with the hose if you want."

Wait. "I thought you were roasting Brussels sprouts?"

"I'm good at multitasking." She grinned, and his heart stuttered. He could just bet that she was. She could probably cook and clean and do that domestic-goddess thing to him all at once. And cast a spell on him, too. Oh man, this was tricky territory.

Red flashing danger lights glared in his head.

He gulped. "O-kay," he said slowly. "Sure."

She took his boots and carried them, sort of limping/skipping over to the hose caddy, where she cranked on the spigot. Then she stood back and began washing down his boots using the nozzle attachment. She swished the hose from side to side, her backside swaying with the motion. Grant tried not to think about that. He tried to figure out what she was up to instead.

He set his hands on his hips. "Has something come over you?"

She looked up. "Like what?"

This was not the Nell from yesterday. This was like Super Nell on cleaning steroids. "I mean, why are you being so…"

"So what?"

Flirtatious? Alluring? Awesome?

No. None of those would work.

He hunted desperately for the mental stop sign, then—whew!—found it.

He cleared his throat. "Easygoing?"

Her eyes sparkled. "Because I'm an easygoing person."

"Don't think so."

"What?"

"I think you're up to something."

"Oh yeah?" she asked impishly. "Like what?"

"Like I don't know. Something."

She held a devilish gleam in her eye, and his pulse raced. It was like the sense that animals get before an earthquake hits, or the calm before a storm.

"You mean, this?" She wheeled the hose on him, dousing his chest with an icy blast. The water was freezing cold.

"Hey, stop!" he yelled, but he was laughing. What had gotten into her?

She giggled and sprayed him harder, showering

him from top to bottom. "Looks like you need some cleaning off, too."

Gooseflesh rose on his arms. "Nell," he growled. "You'd better watch it."

She giggled more. "You wanted me to clean today, so now I'm cleaning."

He leaped after her, and she dropped the hose and raced away. But she wasn't fast enough with her compromised ankle. He caught her by the waist. "So you think this is funny?"

He tugged her up against him, her back against his chest.

She doubled forward, cackling harder. "Yeah. Yeah, I do."

He nabbed the hose off the ground and shot a burst of frigid water down her back.

"Argh! Ooh, you!" She spun on him and yanked the hose away, dousing him in the groin.

He yelped. *Crap that's cold.* "Oh, now that's playing dirty."

She laughed. "Not as dirty as you play."

He latched onto her and pulled her close, her chest pressed to his. His heart boomed like a thundercloud, and tiny electric tingles coursed through his veins. Her clothing was soaked, and so was his, but he was anything but cold. He was sizzling. Hot. His muscles tensed.

"Want to play dirty, Nell?"

She dropped the hose to the ground. It shot a steady stream of water across the backyard.

A blush swept her cheeks, highlighting her freckles.

Damp tendrils framed her face.

Man, she was a beautiful woman.

Tempting. Infuriating. Desirable.

His breath pulsed into the air.

Hers did, too.

"Yes," she said.

And all he could think about was kissing her senseless.

CHAPTER SIXTEEN

An earsplitting wail emanated from the cabin.

Nell blinked up at Grant. "What's that?"

He blanched. "Smoke alarm."

Misty and Charlotte appeared around the side of the cabin, racing toward them. Misty had a small athletic bag slung over her shoulder. Nell whirled toward them. She hadn't even heard their car pull up. Then again, she'd been a little distracted.

"Guys! Guys!" Charlotte shouted.

Misty stared at Nell and Grant, observing their saturated clothing. Then she looked down at the running hose. "What the heck?"

Charlotte waved her arms, capturing their attention. "Something's burning."

Grant shut off the spigot and darted into the house ahead of the group.

Black smoke spewed from the oven, emitting a noxious smell.

"Oh no!" Nell groaned. "The Brussels sprouts." She switched the oven setting to "off" and popped open the oven door, pulling out the cookie sheet using an oven mitt. Charred black balls sizzled and rolled sideways, sending their stench exploding into the air like a stink bomb.

Nell covered her nose and mouth.

Grant chuckled. "So much for multitasking!" he called above the noise. The glimmer in his eyes showed he was teasing. Still, Nell felt bad about smelling up the kitchen—and the cabin. More than ever. Ugh.

Grant shoved the kitchen window open farther, then pulled the front and back doors open wide, before reaching up to silence the blaring smoke alarm positioned over the back door. Charlotte and Misty helped clear the air by waving dish towels around while coughing and choking and covering their mouths.

"Ew," Misty said. "Smells awful in here."

Charlotte wrinkled up her nose. "Um, yeah. Nasty." She shoved her dish towel under the kitchen sink, dampening it, and then waved it around some more. She turned her gaze on Nell and Grant, examining their sopping clothing. "What were the two of you doing?" Her eyebrows arched, and she got a mischievous look in her eye like she could guess.

Cold trickles ran down Nell's back. She was drenched, and Grant was, too, but he was more soaked on his front side. She giggled at the wet splotch on his jeans and the saturated stripes on his shirt. Droplets dripped from his hairline, ears, and chin. They were both leaving puddles on the floor.

He wiped his jaw with his hand, staring at Nell, and Nell flushed, turning to Charlotte.

"I was cleaning off Grant's fishing boots, and things got...out of hand."

Grant cleared his throat. "Nell attacked me with the hose."

"Me?" Her face burned hotter.

Misty glanced down at Nell's ankle. "Wait a minute. I thought you were hurt?"

"I was. Am. *Argh.*" Pain shot through her ankle,

reminding her of her injury. She'd been so high on adrenaline earlier—first in her waterplay with Grant, and then during her fear over the fire—she'd nearly forgotten. "Maybe I moved around too much."

Grant nodded. "Or ran into the cabin too quickly."

Nell eased herself back toward the kitchen table and sat. "Maybe." She shivered, and Grant strode into the living area, retrieving the sofa blanket. He returned to Nell and draped it around her shoulders.

"Thank you." She stared up at him, and warmth flickered in his eyes. This was the Grant she knew and remembered. The one outside was one she'd like to get to know better, too. He hadn't even kissed her, and her whole body had been about to combust in flames. Given that she'd been doused in icy cold water beforehand, that was an outstanding feat.

"Aww," Charlotte said. "You two are really cute together."

"The cutest lovebirds," Misty crooned. "But wet ones. Water birds."

"Funny, Misty," Nell said, a bit embarrassed in front of Grant. She blushed, feeling conflicted. If she was trying to get him to ditch her, sexy water play probably wasn't the best way. Not that she hadn't enjoyed it.

Grant's neck turned red, and he cleared his throat. "You're freezing," he said to her. "You should probably get out of those wet clothes soon."

Nell tugged the blanket around her tighter. It had been folded over the arm of the sofa near the woodstove, and its heat warmed her through and through.

Grant went back to the woodstove, stoking it with a few more logs and giving her a second with her sisters.

"Sean and I are getting close," Misty said, keeping her voice down. "Maybe not as close as you guys, but, you know…" She shrugged. "Maybe soon."

Charlotte smirked, then whispered, too. "Misty's not the only one with a dating life. I just don't go broadcasting mine."

Nell's pulse fluttered nervously. Were Misty and Charlotte hinting that they were close to winning the bet? She scanned their eyes, and each sent her a self-congratulatory little nod.

Nooo. Not now. Not when I'm on Operation Ditch Me.

Then again, what else could Nell expect? Nobody wanted to marry Aidan, and her sisters didn't know she was mentally bailing on trying to win over Grant. They certainly wouldn't think that now, after catching her and Grant in that water fight. Nell decided to let them think what they wanted. It was better than them believing what they'd suspected at the beginning: that Nell would automatically lose their bet.

"Great place," Charlotte said, glancing around.

"Yeah," Misty concurred. "Looks like a sweet little getaway for two."

Charlotte nudged her. "Uh-huh, and three's a crowd. Four is even worse."

The group chuckled at her comment, and then Misty remembered the bag on her shoulder. "Oh yeah, here." She handed it to Nell at the table. "This is for you."

"Oh great. Thanks for bringing it by."

Charlotte's eyes lit up. "Nearly forgot. I've got something for you in the car." She exited through the open front door and returned minutes later holding a covered casserole dish. "Chicken parmigiana," she proclaimed. "Your favorite."

"Oh Charlotte," Nell said kindly. "You shouldn't have." Delicious scents seeped into the air, replacing the stench of burned Brussels sprouts with the tempting aromas of oregano, basil, fresh-grated parmesan cheese, and Charlotte's yummy homemade marinara sauce. She really was an excellent cook.

"It was no trouble," she said. "Things were slow at work this afternoon, so I knocked off a little early and went home to put it together."

Nell lowered her voice and sent eye signals to Charlotte. "No. I mean you shouldn't have." She rolled her eyes toward Grant and whispered. "Poor Grant can't eat chicken."

He returned from messing with the fire, smiling at the women. "Poor Grant what?"

Nell nodded toward Misty and Charlotte. "I was just telling them you're a pescatarian."

Charlotte frowned. "That's too bad." She stared at Grant. "I brought you and Nell some chicken parmigiana. My signature recipe."

"It's, uh, true about the chicken." He shifted on his feet and cut a glance at Nell. "But I do eat pasta! I'm sure I can have a bit."

"No." Nell shook her head and pried back the lid of the casserole dish. Thinly sliced pieces of chicken breast had been pounded flat, breaded, and fried, and laid on the saucy noodles and under the melted cheese. Fresh basil leaves sat on top. Nell's mouth watered. She was starving, and this looked and smelled so good. She covered the casserole and peeked at Grant. "We have to think of Robby."

"Who's Robby?" Charlotte asked.

He frowned.

"Grant's pet rooster when he was a kid," Nell said. She whispered the next part. "He went to live 'on a farm.'"

Misty's mouth dropped open. "Oh no."

"Yeah." Nell made a pouty face. "Which is why Grant can't eat chicken now. Or poultry of any kind."

"Yikes, no turkey?" Charlotte said. "Bummer at Thanksgiving, I guess." She sent Grant a sympathetic look. "I'm so sorry for your loss."

He squirmed uncomfortably. "Uh. Thanks."

Nell sighed. "No beef or lamb, either."

"There goes Dad's shepherd's pie." Misty sighed. "You're going to be missing out, but there are lots of vegan options, I suppose."

Grant grinned tightly. "Great."

"Thanks so much for doing this anyway," Nell said, handing the casserole dish back to Charlotte.

Charlotte frowned.

"No, don't." Grant reached out his hand. The group turned to him. "I mean, not after Charlotte went to all that trouble. And anyway, you can eat it, Nell."

Yes. That's just what she'd planned. *No more fish. Yay!*

"Oh, um. You're sure it won't bother you, having this in the house?"

"Life is all about compromise," he said with a magnanimous gleam in his eyes.

Misty and Charlotte gazed at him adoringly, and Nell had to keep herself from rolling her eyes. "Yeah. Sure is."

Misty surveyed the charred Brussels sprouts on the stove top. "Do you have something you can eat for dinner, Grant?"

"Oh yeah, tons. I laid in some groceries."

"Boy, did he ever." Nell winked at her sisters. "Including cleaning supplies."

Grant's neck reddened, and then his whole face went crimson, but Nell wasn't going to mention his macho-man assignment of duties. Not just yet. She could let him think she was on the cusp of that, though. "Grant has the most interesting ideas about partnerships—and divisions of labor."

He laughed uncomfortably and held up his hands. "No need to go boring your sisters."

"We're not bored," Misty said, her gaze pinned on him.

He squirmed on his feet.

"Cleaning, hmm." Charlotte took another appreciative glance around. "Well, things here look super clean to me."

"Yeah," Misty said. "All spic and span." She studied Nell, like she suspected something was up.

"We should probably get going," Charlotte said. "So you guys can get changed." She addressed Nell. "How long do you expect you'll stay?"

"Er…it's hard to say."

Grant arched his eyebrows at Nell. "Up to you."

Good. Because she was *not* about to walk out

now. Not when she was this close to winning by having Grant dump her. She turned to her sisters. "Not sure. I'll text you."

There was no good way to ask about what they had—or hadn't—revealed to Grant at Bearberry Brews in front of him, so Nell dropped it. She could always text them later, and at this point it hardly mattered.

She'd figured out Grant's game, and she was gaming him back. Very successfully, in her estimation. He'd appeared really tempted by Charlotte's chicken parmigiana. He'd practically drooled. Poor guy. She guessed he was famished, too. But he wasn't getting one bite.

Oh well. He evidently had more trout, and he loved that. Nell smiled, happy to leave him to it. She knew what she was having tonight.

Thank you, Charlotte.

Grant walked Charlotte and Misty to the door. "Thanks for bringing Nell's things by, and thanks for the dinner. I would definitely try some…" He glanced at Nell. "If I could."

"You're welcome," Charlotte said.

Misty dangled a key chain in her hand. "We're off to grab your car," she told Nell.

"Thanks!"

Grant rubbed his upper arms. "It might be good to grab a shower," he told Nell.

"Ooh, sounds romantic," Misty teased. "We'll hurry up and get out of your way."

"Come on, Misty," Charlotte said, dragging her along.

Grant gave an embarrassed chuckle. "Bye, guys."

Nell blew them a kiss. "I appreciate you!"

"We love you, too," Charlotte said. "Feel better."

Misty waved. "Bye!"

Grant walked over and shut the front door, leaving the back door and kitchen window open because the air was still clearing. "Want to shower first?"

"No. This time, you." Nell peeked into the bag Misty had given her. "I can put on my dry PJs and wait for my turn. Meanwhile." She stared at the stove top. "I'll dispose of the Brussels sprouts."

"Be sure to give them a decent burial," he joked.

She got his meaning. Put them in the compost pile outdoors and not in the trash, where they'd continue to stink up the house. And they did reek. Big time.

"Will do."

Grant grabbed some clothing from his dresser, then stepped into the bathroom, shutting the door. Nell used that opportunity to slip into the bedroom and change into her comfy flannel PJs. They were blue with polar bears on them, and they were warm and cozy after being so chilled. She put on clean socks and her fuzzy slippers, too.

She yawned. Wow. She'd exerted a lot of energy today with all that cleaning, but Grant's flummoxed expression had been worth every muscle ache. She rubbed her sore shoulders and back—she'd used muscles today she hadn't used in a long time. Maybe ever, when it came to the wood chopping. She chuckled to herself, pleased that she'd been pretty good at that. It was nice to enhance her skill set.

She reached the kitchen and lifted the now-cool cookie sheet holding the burned Brussels sprouts off of the stove top. Then, she pinched her nose and carried it toward the open back door. When she came back inside, the smell from the burned food had mostly dissipated, so she closed the kitchen window and back door, since it was growing chilly outside.

The water play with Grant in the backyard sure had been sexy. If that smoke alarm hadn't gone off, he definitely would have kissed her, apparently despite trying to push her away. She'd have welcomed his kisses, too. Even as angry as she was, every inch of her body had been aching for them.

Of course, her sisters would have arrived right then. Maybe it was better that Misty and Charlotte hadn't caught them in the middle of a hot make-out session. They didn't need to witness Nell and Grant's intimate interactions to guess there was chemistry between them. From the twinkle in their eyes, Charlotte and Misty had sensed it crackling through the air.

Nell's gaze snagged on the casserole dish on the counter, and her stomach rumbled. Between all the work she'd put in today and that very small lunch, she was starving. She lifted the casserole dish lid, and delectable steam flooded her senses. Charlotte must have pulled it right out of the oven before coming here because the casserole dish was still warm.

While her dad often baked Irish dishes, their mom enjoyed making Italian, since she was part Italian on her grandmother's side. Nell's late Italian great-grandmother had died years ago, but the family still enjoyed many of her signature dishes. Charlotte was probably the best cook of her sisters, and she was super talented at making homemade sauce.

Nell glanced toward the bathroom, but the shower water was still running. She probably ought to wait for Grant to eat dinner, but since he supposedly didn't eat chicken—she rolled her eyes—maybe she could go ahead and have a little.

Her belly clenched with hunger, and she looked down at her ankle, which was bothering her, too. She should probably take a few more meds for the ankle, but it would be best not to do that on an empty stomach. Nell hopped on over to the cabinet where Grant kept the dishes and removed some silverware and a spatula from a drawer.

Then she served herself a modest portion of chicken parmigiana.

Her stomach growled, and she added more pasta and another piece of breaded chicken to her plate. *There. That's better.*

She doubted Grant would blame her for getting started, and she wasn't going to eat what he was anyway. She yawned again, feeling even more exhausted than before, and carried her food and a glass of water over to the sofa, along with two ibuprofen tablets. She swallowed her painkillers first and then cut into a piece of crispy chicken, heaping that onto her fork with a swirl of al dente spaghetti coated in tangy sauce.

Oh yum.

Heaven.

The woodstove cast out its warming glow, heating her fingers and toes and making her toasty all over as she devoured her delicious dinner. The comfort food settled in her belly, leaving her happily satisfied. Really, really sleepy, too. She set her empty dinner plate on the chest and sat back against the sofa, pulling the sofa blanket over her.

Her eyelids drooped, and her head felt heavy. She didn't want to abandon Grant, but the heat from the woodstove lulled her deeper into sleepiness and relaxation.

She slumped onto her side and curled up contentedly under the sofa blanket, settling her head down on a sofa pillow. She'd just rest here for a moment until Grant was done with his shower...

• • •

When Grant came out of the shower in fresh jeans and a sweater, Nell was sound asleep on the sofa, looking so pretty with her long auburn curls fanning across her face that he had to stop and catch his breath. An empty dinner plate sat on the chest beside a water glass, and he saw that she'd had some of Charlotte's chicken parmigiana. Not that he blamed her for going ahead and eating. She had to be exhausted from all the work she did today.

He crossed his arms in front of him, admiring her beauty as well as her strength. He was still amazed that she'd chopped wood. She'd done a good job of it, too. Well, except for that one mutilated piece.

He pursed his lips, thinking about how much she'd surprised him. He'd thought for sure she would have called it quits after he handed her that toilet brush. But she hadn't. She'd even polished the wood floors and cleaned the bathroom without complaining. Even when he'd asked the impossible of her, she'd risen to the challenge. Why? Could she really like him that much, or was this more about her dislike of Aidan?

It was obvious by the way Nell and her sisters interacted that they loved each other a ton. He guessed they loved their parents and their family business, too. Otherwise, why would they go to such extremes to prevent it from going under? He supposed Nell and her sisters were being altruistic in their own way by keeping their plans from their parents, but if he'd been their dad or mom, he'd have wanted to know.

It seemed a lot to ask of the Delaney sisters. Or, at the very least, it was a lot for them to ask of themselves, and yet they'd all entered into an agreement that one of them—the losing one—would marry Aidan to help save Bearberry Brews. Grant sighed, knowing it was a nutty plan, but his heart also ached for the way it had forced Nell's hand. Maybe if she hadn't had the pressure, he and she would have met and started dating in a normal way. Instead, she'd gone out there like a cowgirl on the range looking to rope a guy—and her lasso had landed around him.

Grant wanted more for himself than being somebody's last-minute husband. Nell deserved more for herself, too. She had a bubbly sparkling spirit that would make her stand out in any crowd. A quick wit and intelligence, too. Besides that, she had a caring and compassionate side. He could imagine becoming friends with her, then more than friends; lovers. Even maybe something more.

In another universe, though. Not this one.

In *this* universe, he needed to keep his head on straight and remember that she'd played him, if not purely for her own gain, at least for the benefit of her family business. She'd set her sights on him as a husband placeholder so that spot wouldn't get filled by Aidan Strong. It would bother him less if he didn't like her so much, because it would make things a lot simpler when it ended.

He glanced into the kitchen, recalling that he still needed to deal with the fish he had waiting in the cooler on the back stoop. Maybe he should try to rouse Nell first to see if she was ready to go to bed.

"Nell," he said softly. "Nell?"

He stooped low and touched her arm, but she didn't budge.

She was out like a light and would likely sleep straight through till morning. He tried gently shaking her again, and her eyelids fluttered. But then she hunkered down even more beneath the sofa blanket, snoozing like an angel. She was pretty adorable all right.

He shook his head.

Adorable, but not the right woman for me.

Tomorrow, I'll have another chance to prove that to both of us.

He went into the bedroom and pulled back the covers. Then he returned to Nell, scooping her up in his arms. She mumbled and wrapped her arms around his neck, still in her dream world. Maybe she was dreaming about him. He'd certainly spent a lot of last night dreaming about her.

But that was before going into Bearberry Brews and talking to her sisters.

He set her down on the bed, laying her head on a pillow and tenderly covering her up, then stood in the shadows thinking as light flickered into the room from the woodstove.

Nell. Nell. If only you loved me.

But she didn't. Sadly, she was just pretending.

Well, he could pretend, too, for one more day.

He raked a hand through his hair, his heart brimming with sorrow.

They'd had such an amazing day yesterday. And even today, after all the hurdles he'd put her through, she'd managed to leave her mark on him. When he'd walked back into his spruced-up cabin, she'd caught him off guard—and branded him with that dazzling smile of hers.

Then later, he was sure they'd shared a moment after their water fight. Their exchange had been sexy. Intimate. Fun. For an instant, she'd let her guard down, and it was like he'd seen the real her. He'd slipped, too, revealing his emotions. Too many of his emotions. He'd nearly tipped his hand.

But he wouldn't slip up again. That would only prolong his misery. He needed to get Nell to go ahead and dump him so they could both go on with their lives. Tomorrow, he would ratchet things up to the point where she'd have no choice but to go.

• • •

Grant woke up in the middle of the night starving. He'd opted against frying the fish, not wanting to wake Nell with any banging around of pots and pans, and made himself a quick peanut butter sandwich instead. He wasn't in the mood for more peanut butter now, though. He craved real food, and not something made with tofu, either. Or anything lactose free.

He quietly stole into the kitchen and flicked on the light over the stove. Deliciously cheesy chicken parmigiana sounded awesome about now. He didn't care if he had to eat it cold. Maybe he could spread the remaining noodles out in the bottom of the serving dish after he fixed himself some. That way, Nell wouldn't notice that he'd eaten any. She probably hadn't counted the actual chicken pieces. Nobody could be that observant.

Grant located the casserole in the refrigerator and set it on the stove top, serving himself a nice big helping. Amazing aromas wafted toward him, and he couldn't wait to dig in. He used the serving spatula to carefully rearrange what was left and covered the casserole dish with its lid, tucking it back in the fridge. Then he settled down at the table for his late-night feast, which was absolutely as tasty as he'd hoped. More so.

He finished in record time, being pretty obviously famished. Now he was in the mood for something sweet. A little dessert would be nice. Aha! His gaze snagged on Nell's apple bread on the counter. He unwrapped it and held it up for a sniff. His mouth watered at the hints of cinnamon and apples. *Yes. This is going to be delicious.* Just the right little morsel to top off his savory pasta, the flavors of which still rolled around on his tongue.

He slid open a kitchen drawer and took out a large knife. He started to cut himself a moderate piece, then decided to make it bigger. *Who am I kidding? This looks incredible.* His stomach rumbled, and he took a bite. Yum. Such appley goodness. The crunchy walnuts were a superb touch. His mouth was having a happy little party—the fall fest kind.

It would be easy for him to take a smidgen more without Nell finding out, since she'd clearly had some earlier. Probably to keep her energy up while doing all that cabin cleaning—and wood chopping. Grant's spirits flagged, and he felt like a heel all over again for laying all that work on her. Then he tried to remind himself that no one had forced her to comply with his unreasonable requests. In fact, the goal had been for her *not* to comply.

"What are you doing?"

Grant jolted upright, cramming the huge slice of apple bread into his mouth until his cheeks bulged out like a chipmunk.

"Hmm?" he asked, spinning toward her.

Nell stared at him wide-eyed. "Are you eating something?"

He covered his mouth and mumbled, "Nuh-uh."

Then her gaze fell on the decimated apple bread loaf on the counter. "Oh yes, you are!" She gasped. "Grant Williams. You great big phony!"

He chewed fast and swallowed hard—a couple of times—forcing it all down. "I'm not a phony," he said from behind the back of his hand.

She gawked at him. "I thought you couldn't eat apple bread?"

"I can't." He brushed a few crumbs off his T-shirt. "Normally."

"What about the walnuts?"

Yeah, what about those? He thought fast. "Turns out those were black walnuts. I can eat that kind."

"Uh-huh. Right." She folded her arms in front of her, and he willed her not to look at the sink. Unfortunately, his will wasn't strong enough to control hers, because her gaze roved in that direction anyway.

"I don't believe it," she said, goggling down at his dirty plate and utensils. "Were you eating chicken parmigiana, too?"

"No, I—" He wrung his hands together. "It was just the noodles!"

"What about the cheese?" She arched one eyebrow, and he broke a sweat.

"I, ah…scraped that part off!"

"But, Grant—" Her eyes widened in horror, and then she blinked. "What about *Robby*? You said you couldn't even look at or smell—"

"Yes, yes. So true. That's why I had to—avert my eyes."

"*Avert* your *eyes*?"

"Yeah, like—you know—during a car crash?" Although this was feeling more and more like a train wreck every second. He shifted on his feet, feeling so called out. Talk about being caught red-handed. "Ahh… What are you doing up at this hour?" he asked, his throat scratchy.

Anything to change the subject. Seriously.

"I was hungry," she announced without a hint of apology. Her eyebrows rose. "Looks like somebody else was, too."

Okay. That didn't quite do it.

Grant rubbed the side of his neck. "Want some

more of that fish?"

"No, thanks. I think I'll have a piece of apple bread." She peered around him. "If there's any left."

"Oh yeah. Sure." He stepped aside, his face burning hot. His ears, too.

She cut herself a piece, then carried it back to her room on a napkin.

Before she left, she sent him a sassy little smile. "I'm glad that you like my cooking. Charlotte's, too."

"Nell?"

She stopped walking. "Hmm?"

"About Robby?"

"Yes."

"That was…um…a long time ago. So." He shrugged as she locked on his gaze.

"I'm sure it was," she said in the smug sort of way that told him she knew 100 percent what he was up to. Lying about Robby. Fibbing about his dietary restrictions.

She turned and sauntered away with her apple bread but paused in the doorway to the bedroom. "Oh, and Grant? I had *so* much fun cleaning today. I can't wait to see what you have planned for me tomorrow. Good night."

She flashed him a smug smile, and his stomach dropped. Man! Had she figured out his ruse that quickly? Or maybe she hadn't and she was just fishing? Trying to test out the waters to see if he'd crack, spilling all his truths about his nonexistent childhood pet and imaginary food issues? But she'd said the last bit about the cleaning with purpose. More purpose than anyone fishing for information could muster.

Which meant she probably had him completely and totally figured out.

Argh. Okay. This was getting out of hand. He was *not* going to let Nell get the best of him or act like she saw through him. No matter how momentarily exciting a few of their interactions had been. *She* was the one who'd tried to use him as her insta-groom, and he could not let himself forget that. Tomorrow, he was going to double down on his double down and make her want to walk out of here once and for all.

CHAPTER SEVENTEEN

Nell woke up the next morning feeling rested and happy. She stretched under the covers, and a few muscles ached. But that was okay. They were good aches. Well earned.

Wait. Why did she think that?

She opened her eyes and sat up in bed, remembering where she was.

At Grant's cabin.

She glanced around the compact room with its knotty pine walls and sparse furnishings. Her phone was on the nightstand, and she'd plugged it in. Oh yeah, when she came in here to change into her pajamas. She'd fallen asleep on the sofa afterward, and then Grant had carried her here and tucked her in. Her heart fluttered at the drowsy memory of being snuggled in his arms, and then the warm sensation of having the covers sweetly draped over her. She'd believed herself to be dreaming, thinking it couldn't be real.

Then, she'd awakened in the middle of the night feeling hungry and had caught him cramming his mouth full of her apple bread. Ha! The bread he'd claimed he couldn't eat. She giggled remembering the look on his face when she'd surprised him in the kitchen. She was pretty sure all that bunk about being lactose free and loving tofu bacon was a pure fabrication, too.

Grant was so full of himself and full of baloney.

She was *so* on to him. He didn't stand a chance of kidding her any longer. That didn't mean she wouldn't keep playing along until he completely gave up. He seemed to be softening last night. Maybe things were getting close to being over? Her heart hurt, and she had really mixed feelings about that. She didn't like the new Grant very much, but she'd begun falling for the old one. And she'd seen tiny glimpses of his former self last night.

She picked up her phone, seeing numerous text messages had come in from her sisters.

Charlotte: *Grant's so great!*

Misty: *What kind of hot games were you playing with that hose?*

Nell shook her head.

Misty again: *Hope you got that shower. Woo!*

Big wink-y emoji.

Charlotte: Frowny emoji.

Sorry he can't eat chicken.

Nell fell back against her pillow, holding her phone up in front of her.

She grinned a goofy grin and texted a pic to the group.

No reason to let them know that Operation First Bride had blown apart.

They'd probably gloat.

Thanks, girls. Love you!

Charlotte: *If that's not a woman in love, I don't know what is.*

Then Charlotte sent a pic of *her* face, grinning from ear to ear. She was also pointing to her ring finger.

Guess who's going to put a ring on it first?

Nell's heart pounded.

Charlotte?

But Charlotte didn't answer.

Misty did: *Grant! We want Grant! In his boxers.*

Nell's cheeks burned hot.

Sorry girls. For my eyes only.

Then Misty did something super annoying. She sent back a pic of *her* wearing someone else's boxers! They had little lobsters on them.

Misty! Are those Sean's?

Misty sent a kiss-y emoji.

Charlotte did, too.

That was so like her sisters to be competitive. And definitely like Misty to be a copycat. Really! Nell knew they loved her, but they obviously couldn't stand the idea of her taking the lead in winning their bet. If they only knew.

Nell's heart sank.

For an instant last night during their hose play, she'd found herself wishing that Operation First Bride with Grant had been back on. Then, afterward, he'd been so kind and caring in the kitchen. When she'd surprised him later eating her apple bread, he'd looked so adorably called out it was all she could do to keep from bursting out laughing. Those were the sides of Grant she found herself falling for again—darn it. But no. She needed to stay focused on her goal. She wasn't trying to win him any longer. Not if he didn't seriously want her. Her heart ached, and she felt so mixed up inside.

If she could only believe he cared, things would be different. But he didn't. Otherwise, he wouldn't still be playing this trying-to-get-rid-of-her game.

Nell sighed and stared at her phone.

The large clock on Nell's screensaver stared her in the face.

What? Eeep!

It's almost twelve o'clock.

How had she'd slept so late? She never slept in. Never, never, never. Oh no. She had to get up and get going to stay on top of her plan. Kill him with kindness. Right.

I can't wait to get up and chop more wood, or whatever it takes.

Okay, except for cleaning the bathroom again.

She probably wasn't up for that.

Doing the wood floors, either.

But that was fine. The cabin was already spotless. So.

If it came down to chopping wood, she was okay with that. She'd actually liked learning something new, and she'd been really, really great at it.

She pushed back the covers and sat up again, staring down at her ankle. Nice. It wasn't throbbing or hurting at all. She bent up her knee and reached for the athletic tape, deciding to unwrap it and take a look. When she did, it appeared to be normal.

Well, that's a good sign.

She placed her feet on the floor next and tried standing. Her right ankle had some residual pain, but it was very minor, so she could probably get by without her ankle being wrapped today. That was good, because she wanted to shower and put on the makeup her sisters had brought her. She couldn't wait to feel like herself again and wear girly clothes instead of Grant's sweats or those super-snug running pants.

She gathered her new outfit and bathroom stuff and started toward the door. Beyond it, she could hear Grant milling about in the kitchen.

She laid her hand on the doorknob, then halted, glancing around the room.

All the camping stuff was gone.

• • •

Grant looked up when Nell opened the bedroom door. "Morning, sunshine! How'd you sleep last night?" He stood at the stove, blackening some fish. Since he was lowering the boom today, Nell would be leaving shortly. No reason she couldn't enjoy a nice brunch first. Besides that, she'd probably need the sustenance to deal with the tasks he had in store for her.

"Like a rock, apparently." She laughed, then wrinkled up her nose, probably at the trout smell. She sent him a knowing look. "Having a full belly helped." She held a stack of clean clothing, a make-up bag, and a brush. Her hair was in a bit of a disarray, but her face appeared fresh and perky. "How about you? Sleep well, too?"

He flipped the fish in the skillet, ignoring the full-belly remark and her little smirk. The one that made her so infuriating and yet a whole lot enticing.

Yeah, she was definitely onto him.

"Yep, I did."

She grimaced. "Sorry I slept so late."

"No worries. You probably needed it." And there he went feeling guilty yet again. When he'd left her with that list of chores, he'd expected her to yell and scream—or at least fuss and grumble—and furiously push back. Not flit around his cabin like a frenzied cleaning fairy waving that toilet brush as her wand.

She goggled around the room and at his mounds of camping stuff. "What's going on?"

"Camping day," he said. "But first, brunch."

"Well. I can't wait for that!"

He chuckled. Rather than rising grouchy and sore, Nell was perpetually upbeat. How did she do it? What's more, why did her positive attitude tend to rub off on him? He felt happier when he was around her, even though he warned himself not to get sucked back in.

He was going through with today's plan. Period.

He forced himself to run through the facts. While she said she'd been interested in him before all this and had wanted to get to know him, could he believe that? Did it matter? She'd given them a frenetically fast goal of becoming serious. *Way* serious.

Grant didn't like being pushed or operating on other people's schedules. He made up his own mind about things he wanted to do and the women he decided to pursue. He was *not* going to let his defenses down and recklessly fall for a woman just because she was racing against a ridiculous timeline so she wouldn't have to marry some British guy.

No matter how much he liked her.

"Fish and grits and coffee okay?" he asked as she walked toward the bathroom.

She paused in the doorway. "Coffee?" Her wide eyes sparkled with gratitude, and he was glad he'd made her happy, in spite of himself. It wasn't like he was trying to make her mad at him, per se. He simply wanted the woman to pack up and leave him—and what he suspected would be his broken heart—in peace.

"Yes, ma'am. I made it in my French press."

She viewed the French press on the counter. "I didn't know you had one of those."

He chuckled. "You probably wondered how we were going to make the coffee when you put away the groceries and saw those coffee grounds."

"Yeah."

"Can I pour you a cup?"

"That would be great." She pursed her lips. "After I shower, though."

She basically had the ability to look gorgeous all the time, whether she'd showered or not. Even in the pouring rain, like she'd been on their hike, or drenched by the hose like she'd been yesterday after their water fight.

Full stop.

Now was not the time to consider Nell's attributes.

This was the day to construct the hurdles he knew she'd never surmount, no matter what game they might now be playing. So yeah, maybe she was onto him or maybe she wasn't. Though he heavily suspected the former. This wasn't even about compatibility anymore. Maybe it never had been. He and Nell were engaged in a knock-down-drag-out battle of wills. She might have beat him at Scrabble, but she wasn't taking the spoils in this war. He was. And, when all was said and done, Nell was going to be the one to explain the whole pseudo-engagement mix-up with the town. Not him.

He wasn't expecting a big blowup or anything, but he did anticipate Nell packing her bags and going home. Then, that would be that. She'd leave him, and he'd be off the hook. A free man by his birthday.

"All right-y," he said lightly. "Take your time."

· · ·

Nell emerged from the bathroom feeling like her old self again, her heavy damp curls falling past her shoulders. She deposited her PJs back in the bedroom, then came into the kitchen. Grant gave her an appreciative glance. She wore dark stretch pants under her woodsy green peasant blouse and had slipped her chocolate brown cardigan on top of that. The sweater was one of her more successful projects, even though it had taken her forever.

"Wow, you look nice."

"Thanks."

He studied her cardigan. "You knit that?"

"Yeah."

"Great job."

She giggled. "It's only great because this was the fourth time I tried to make this pattern. My first three cardigans were major fails."

He chuckled. "Well, this one looks amazing. And hey, you're walking normally."

She smiled softly. "Thanks to you."

He blew out a breath. "Look, Nell. About yesterday."

"Yeah?"

"I mean, it was really thoughtful of you to clean

the cabin and chop that wood, only…" His eyebrows rose. "I hope it wasn't too much for you."

"Too much? No." She shook out her hair. "Just don't expect that kind of service every day."

Something glimmered in his eyes, but she couldn't quite read it. "I won't." He poured her a mug full of coffee from the French press. "Want almond milk in that? I'm sorry I don't have regular milk or cream."

Dietary restrictions, hoo. She couldn't believe he'd invent all of that on purpose. "No thanks. Black is fine." She took a sip and set down her mug. "I'm sorry you're so limited on what you can eat. That must make it difficult for you when you camp and such."

"Oh no, not really. I can pretty much get what I need in town."

She shrugged, deciding to needle him. "Hmm. Yeah. I guess McIntyres' Market carries just about everything. Seems they even carry black walnuts."

His ears turned red as he stirred the grits. "They do."

Uh-huh. "So, about Robby—"

His chin jerked up. "Yeah, what about him?"

"I'm really proud of you and your progress, Grant."

"Progress?"

"Last night, you know." She nodded toward the refrigerator. "You finally came around and ate some poultry."

His eyebrows knitted together. "Uh no, not the chicken. Like I said, it was just the noodles—and the sauce."

"You're sure? Because I wouldn't fault you for taking one tiny nibble. Nobody would after all this time. Except…" She grimaced. "Maybe him." She made a pitiful little crowing sound.

Grant's eyes grew huge.

"He might still be out there, you know." She sighed. "Robby."

"Doubt that. It was such a long time ago."

"My sisters were crushed when they heard the story. They said to tell you they're sorry."

He did a double take at her, then focused back on the stove, adjusting the gas flames on the various burners. "Oh. That's nice. Very kind of them both."

"Misty wants to know how old he was."

Grant dropped the lid back on the grits pot, and it clattered. "Who? Robby?"

"In bird years, yeah."

He blanched. "What?"

It was all she could do to keep a straight face. He could always confess the truth, but Nell knew that he wouldn't. He was in so deep with his rooster story, there was almost no way out without him swallowing his pride and admitting he'd lied.

"Are those different from people years?" She pursed her lips so she wouldn't giggle. "Like, how it is with dogs?"

"Oh. Oh. That! Not sure." He set his jaw, pretending to ponder a memory. "I've never thought too much about it, really. When we got him, he was mature."

"Not a chick?"

"Nope, not that. Full grown." Grant's gaze darted toward the back door like he wanted to race right out of it. But she wasn't letting him off the hook that easily.

"He had his comb, then?"

He blinked like she'd spoken to him in some alien language. "Comb?"

She held her hand above her head and wiggled her fingers.

"Oh yeah, that!" He swallowed hard. "Well yeah. Of course, yes. He did."

"So he crowed?"

"Ah…yep!" His whole face flushed. "Cock-a-doodle-do!"

She held in a smirk. "Bet your neighbors loved that."

He stirred the grits again, only faster. "They were — very tolerant."

He was extra cute when he stumbled over his words. Too bad his reasoning was far from endearing. "Charlotte says she might be able to help you track him down, you know."

Sweat beaded his hairline. "You're joking."

"No. She has friends in Fowl Animal Rescue."

"Fowl?" His eyebrows knitted together. "Wait. Is that a real thing?"

She nodded, having the best time with this. And boy, he deserved it after making up that poor little rooster story. "Their records go back a long time."

"Yeah, but — this wasn't in Majestic."

"I figured that. There's an interstate database."

His jaw dropped, but he shut his mouth quickly. "I'm sure he's long gone by now. Long, long gone. That was ages ago."

Her eyebrows arched. "Might give you some closure?"

Grant turned off the skillet like he was ready to

close down this whole conversation.

"Ah, no. No, that's fine. That was kind of Charlotte, though. Really sweet of her to offer."

Nell patted herself on the back for her incredible control. If she weren't so strong, she'd be rolling on the floor laughing.

"I can tell it's still tough," she said. "Memories of losing your childhood pet."

He shifted on his feet and gave an awkward smile. "It is. But you know what they say—time heals old wounds."

Nell bit her bottom lip, holding back a roar of laughter. "All wounds."

"What?"

"The expression is *all*, Grant."

"Oh? Is it? Well okay then! Good to know."

Nell sat at the kitchen table. "Can I help with anything?"

He exhaled sharply, then drew in a breath, appearing grateful the Robby conversation was over. She kind of regretted that herself. She'd had the time of her life with it.

"Not at the moment." He shook his head. "But you can make the hot dogs later, if you'd like?"

"Ooh, we're having the hot dogs for dinner? Great." She wasn't sure how good they'd be. Hopefully better than the bacon, but at least they wouldn't be trout. She was tempted to bring up Charlotte's chicken parmigiana, since there was still a lot of that left, but then she decided enough was enough with the poultry teasing. She wasn't sure how much more of that Grant could take without literally flying the coop, and she didn't want him leaving just yet.

She intended to learn what he had in mind for today in his dastardly plan to drive her away so she could thwart it with Operation Ditch Me. She liked staying one step ahead of him. It made her feel empowered, and empowered was good. It was…freeing. All the years she'd spent worrying about everyone else, it felt nice to be powerful in her own right. She'd probably never go back to being the family fixer again.

Just because she basically only had work and her knitting didn't mean she had to drive everyone to their doctors' appointments all the time or run people's errands for them ceaselessly. She also needed to stop making lunches for her sisters, except for on special occasions. They weren't little kids in school anymore. Besides all that, Nell's special services would stop the moment she stepped onto that plane to London. She'd only be looking out for herself after that.

Oh yeah. She would also be helping her family. And saving their family business.

But those were just bonus points.

"Brunch is served."

She stared down at the plate Grant set in front of her, and her blowtorch-powerful thoughts flickered down to a dim flame. He'd blackened the fish, and it smelled a little spicy, with hints of smoked paprika and cayenne. He'd also loaded her plate down with grits. Her stomach lurched. People seriously did this? Eat fish for breakfast? Never mind that it was after noon. It was still kind of morning to her. But wait. She was strong. Tough enough to chop wood and wield that nasty toilet brush. She picked up her fork, determined not to let him see her flinch.

She roused her enthusiasm instead. "Looks yummy." At least he'd already deboned it for her, presenting her with two meaty fillets.

"I blackened it Louisiana style," he said, joining her at the table. "Goes great with grits."

She was glad there were lots of those, because that's what she intended to fill up on. "When did you learn about Louisiana cooking?"

"When we lived there."

"Oh?"

He shrugged. "Lived lots of other places, too."

"I heard you'd moved around," she said, "but I didn't know where."

He removed the teabag from his mug and wrung it out around a spoon. "New Orleans, Asheville—"

"North Carolina?"

"Yeah." He dropped the teabag onto his plate, which was even more loaded down with fish than hers was. "Savannah, Georgia, too."

"That's a lot of moving around for a kid."

"That was a lot of moving around for high school."

Her mouth dropped open. "You mean, when you moved here your senior year…?"

"I'd already been in three other high schools, yeah."

She took a sip of coffee. "I'm impressed you settled in so well." He began eating and motioned for her to go ahead. She planned to. Soon. She was working her way up to the fish by getting caffeinated first.

He shrugged. "I became a chameleon. I adapted."

He'd adapted amazingly as she recalled, being super popular and snagging a pretty cheerleader as his girlfriend. "What made you decide to stay in Majestic?"

He set down his fork. "I guess I decided I'd found my fit. I liked the small-town vibe and being on the ocean. So close to the mountains, too."

"It's a nice town." He stared at her plate. Okay. She couldn't put this off forever.

She took a tentative bite of fish along with a heaping forkful of grits. The smoky flavor had a bite and went a long way in disguising that fishy taste, especially when paired with strong coffee. She took another bite. "Mmm. Tasty!"

He grinned to beat the band. "Glad you like it."

She stabbed into her fish again. *There! Two bites! Good.* Ew. Wait. *Not so good.* All right. She was done. The rest of it she'd push around her plate and conceal under the grits. Maybe she could ask for more of those in a sec.

He'd stopped paying attention to her meal to focus on his own. Thank goodness.

"Yeah. So. Anyway," he said, already scraping his plate. How had he packed in so much food so quickly? "I've made some great plans for us today." He motioned toward the living room. "I thought as a part of our compatibility efforts, we'd work on camping."

That didn't sound too daunting. "Oh!" she said brightly. "Sounds fun." It was certainly better than being handed a toilet brush. She was trying to keep her cool here, but if he handed her another one of those, she couldn't 100 percent guarantee she wouldn't scream.

"I brought up everything we'll need to practice: a tent, a bedroll, a sleeping bag. Hey. Even a camp stove. If things go well..." He leaned toward her, his eyes twinkling. "Maybe we can even arrange our first camping trip together?"

"Oh, *nice*," she said, all the while knowing he didn't mean it. He was likely laying a trap by setting her up for failure with another ridiculously big ask. At least "practice camping" didn't seem nearly as bad as real-time cleaning.

"Yeah. It will be." He frowned. "That is, if you honestly decide you like it, because I'd hate for you to be pretending."

She set down her fork. "What? Me? Pretend with you?" She pouted, underscoring her hurt tones. "Honey-bunchy," she said, needling him on purpose, "why would I do that?"

A muscle in his jaw tensed. Apparently being called honey-bunchy wasn't half as much fun as him saying it to her. "Because you—" He shook his head. "I mean, you *did* pretend, Nell. You admitted as much. About the tent thing and the hiking."

She lifted her chin. "That wasn't so much pretending as exaggerating, Grant."

He huffed. "Then you 'exaggerated' a lot."

"O-*kay*." She leaned toward him. "But that doesn't mean I'm not eager to learn. I am!"

"Excellent." He grinned. "I was hoping you'd say that."

She sat back in her chair, waiting for him to lay this on her. Whatever it was, she was ready. "When do we get started?"

He folded his arms in front of him. "Not we, Nell. You."

She tried not to fume internally, but she still did. Of course it was only going to be her. She should have guessed that. "I don't understand," she said, feigning innocence. "You want me to set everything up?"

He nodded toward the back door. "There's a big clearing in the backyard that's the perfect spot for pitching a tent."

She gripped the table white-knuckled, like she was terrified, when she really wanted to roll her eyes. He thought he was sooooo smart. "You're planning to help me, right?" she asked, knowing full well he wasn't.

He took her hand. "I'd really love it if you could try this on your own. I need to believe your heart is in it. Besides, aren't you the kind who learns best by doing?"

She grinned so big her cheeks pinched. "I am."

Surprise flickered in his eyes. If he'd expected to throw her that easily, he had another thing coming. "But if you're really not into it…"

She squeezed his hand extra hard, and he jumped in his seat. "Oh no. I'm *totally* into it." She scanned the mounds of camping equipment, and her stomach fluttered nervously. Then she told herself not to give up. If she could wield a log splitter, she could do just about anything she put her mind to. "I can't wait to surprise you. Just like I did yesterday."

His dark eyes danced. "You sure did." He leaned toward her and spoke huskily. "You domestic goddess, you." He squeezed her hand, and heat pooled in her belly. She blushed, wishing he still didn't have the ability to have this effect on her. But he did, darn it.

Nell retrieved her hand, using it to tuck a lock of her hair behind one ear. Still, her pulse stuttered unevenly. He was so maddening. So impossible!

"Now." He thumbed toward the back door. "Go on out there and break camp like a pro."

So demanding. "What? Now?"

"No. You're right." He stared down at her plate. "You'd better finish eating your fish first. You're going to need all your energy. It might take you a while, since you're new at it, but no worries," he said. "Most of it is intuitive. Plus, the tent comes with instructions."

At least that was something. All she had to do was follow what they said. It would be like reading a recipe. Just one she hadn't tried before. She was going to do this—enhance her skill set even more. Then when she went off to England to marry Aidan or whatever, she'd be that much more of a capable person. "Okay, good."

He leaned toward her and thumbed her nose. "I can't wait to eat those hot dogs."

Wait. She was supposed to do that solo, too? "You want me to make a campfire?"

"Ooh, yes. Great idea."

Nell felt like she'd shot herself in the foot. That wouldn't have occurred to him if she hadn't suggested it.

"But you can use the camp stove instead if you'd like. Either one could be fun. Though it would be nice to have a fire going for us to make those s'mores later. In any case, you'll have plenty of time to get things organized before it gets dark."

She blinked, and he continued.

"Instructions for the tent are in the bag. Easy-peasy. You shouldn't have any problem at all. And here's the great thing: I got an extra-large tent for us to test out. Sleeps up to six people."

"Six?" She gulped. Maybe this wouldn't be as simple as she'd hoped. She drew in a deep breath. Things would be all right. This would be great. She was *not* going to let Grant prove her a failure. *Far from it, bucko.*

"Yep." He grinned. "That way, we can take along your sisters sometime."

"Oh, *great.*" There he went with that again. He was so incredibly annoying.

"Lucas, too, if he wants to go."

"Ah. Super."

"I don't suppose your folks would be interested?"

"Er, nope. Probably not."

He scraped the remaining morsels of the food off his plate and into his mouth, then stood, leaving his plate on the table. "If you don't mind cleaning up, I'd better make tracks."

"Wait." Her heart pounded. "Where are you going?"

"Fishing," he said like she should have expected it—and maybe she should have.

If they'd actually been working on their compatibility skills, she might have been irritated that he was constantly running out on her. But she got what he was doing, acting like being absent was his standard MO. No woman would like that. Especially not when she was the one left holding the laundry bag. And he clearly knew it. What a prince! Not. She couldn't believe she'd actually thought he was one once. If hindsight were foresight...

Whatever.

He stopped by the back door and winked. "Don't worry. I'll be back in time for dinner."

I just bet that you will!

Fortunately—for him *and* the floors—he slipped out the door before she had a chance to throw her plate at him.

CHAPTER EIGHTEEN

Grant chuckled as he got into his waders and boots. There was no way on earth Nell could pull off today's tasks. The tent he'd picked out was complicated even for experienced campers. Poor Nell would be completely flummoxed. He almost felt sorry for her, but not quite. He hadn't exactly appreciated her extended interrogation about Robby this morning over breakfast. The breakfast that he'd so nicely made her. She'd probably suspected the whole story was made up and she'd been trying to get him to admit it, but if anyone was going to break down with true confessions at his cabin, it was going to be Nell and not him. She'd likely reach her breaking point today. There'd be no workaround for her failing to put up that tent.

Camping was his number one thing. He owned a camping store, even. If she couldn't prove herself with that—and he knew she wouldn't—they could never be a team. In another world, her lack of experience with outdoorsy adventures wouldn't have mattered to him in the least. He could have helped her learn, sure. And he would have loved to do that if she'd been a genuine person with a good heart who was honestly interested in him.

Instead, she'd invented the charade that they were going to get married and now had evidently perpetuated it with her sisters. So fine. She could run straight to them and crocodile-tear cry on their shoulders when she told them the engagement was off. And, if by some miracle the camping challenge didn't work, he had a few more tricks up his sleeve.

One way or another, today would be the end of it. Grant could drive her home after dinner, or even before, if that's what she wanted. It was another beautiful fall day, and he intended to spend it engaging in his favorite stress-reducing hobby. He grabbed his fishing gear and headed down the hill, eagerly anticipating a peaceful and productive couple of hours away on his own. He'd deal with the fallout from Nell's camping catastrophe, and their impending "breakup" or whatever, when he returned.

• • •

Nell grumbled and set the smelly frying pan aside to soak. Then she washed and dried the sticky pot for the grits. She'd hoped to avoid cleaning for Grant today, but oh well. These were just some dishes, and she wasn't going to let him best her over this. He'd made the meal anyway, so her cleaning up afterward was actually an equitable division of labor. It would have been *nicer* if they'd agreed to it beforehand, but they hadn't.

She wasn't so sure about her camping assignment today, or what he intended to gain from it. He clearly believed that setting up camp would overwhelm her, but no, it wouldn't. She was smart and determined and really good at learning new things. She'd chopped wood, hadn't she? And she'd liked it. She'd probably like camping, too. Maybe she'd never do that with Grant after she got him to dump her, but at least she would have learned another skill. And

improving her skill set felt good! Made her more
confident that she could tackle anything. Even going
off to England to marry Aidan if it came to that.

Grant was still determined to get rid of her. But
she wasn't leaving until she was good and ready. And
she'd be ready when *he* said the goodbyes. She was
tougher than she looked. If Grant was going to
double down, then she was going to triple that. No.
Quadruple. Quintuple. Grant might be missing the
Q in his Scrabble game, but Nell fully had her wits
about her.

She'd had him so on the spot with her Robby
questions this morning, she wished she'd captured a
photo of his face. He'd been totally cornered,
trapped by his own lies, and yet he'd been far too
stubborn to tell her the truth. Grant Williams wasn't
the only one around here who could hold his
ground. She could, too.

Her gaze roved over the heap of camping equipment piled up near the sofa, landing on the tent bag.
It seemed larger than it had first appeared now that
she knew it slept six people. He'd obviously tried to
make this as hard on her as he could by selecting an
enormous tent. But that was okay. The tent came
with instructions, so that was good. She had them
spread out on the kitchen table and had been looking them over after Grant had gone. The tent setup
did appear rather complex, but she was used to intri-
cate work with her knitting. She could do this.

She tidied up the kitchen, deciding to leave the
frying pan for later. Once she got the tent knocked
out, she wouldn't need to start the campfire or make
the hot dogs until closer to dusk when he was due to

return. That was hours away, and she'd have loads of free time before then. That would give her a chance to take care of the pan, relax, and wrap up her knitting. Grant's hat was almost done, although she doubted very seriously that she'd be giving it to him at this point. He surely didn't deserve all the love she'd put into it, but maybe some lucky buyer on Etsy would.

Operation Ditch Mc had come with a lot more baggage than she'd anticipated, but step by step she'd been unpacking it all and staying her course. She couldn't wait to see the look on Grant's face when he got back and noticed the set-up tent and a campfire glowing. How long could he possibly keep this up? He seemed more and more guilty over his absurd requests, like he was secretly regretting his scheme. Well, good! Let his regret build up a little higher, to the point where he'd admit what he was doing and apologize for it.

And if he wouldn't? That was fine, too. No way on earth did she want to have a future with him any longer. He'd totally blown that chance.

She dragged all the camping stuff into the backyard, but unlike Grant being able to haul everything at once, she had to make three trips. Four, if you count the fact that she carried the camp stove and its small butane tank separately. She had this irrational fear of dropping the butane tank so it exploded in flames. She'd already set off the cabin's smoke alarm once; she didn't need to catch the entire building on fire, despite the fact that she'd joked about that with Grant earlier. She understood now that had been a lame joke.

There! She finally made it. The day was crisp and clear and only a tad chilly, so she was warm enough in her cardigan, not needing her jacket as an extra layer. She undid the bedroll and unrolled the sleeping bag on top of it. Hmm, that's funny. There was only one bedroll and a sleeping bag, and not two of each. Maybe that didn't matter, since this was just for practice. In any case, the sleeping bag would give her someplace to sit while she figured out the tent setup.

First, though: campfire.

She hunted around by the edge of the woods, locating several mid-size stones. She hauled them over, forming a ring near the bedroll. Then she went back into the woods, picking up sticks.

If she had been camping with Charlotte and Misty, this would have been her number one pick for a job: stick-gatherer. She dropped them all in a heap in the center of the rock ring and then went over to the woodpile, searching for bigger pieces. She selected a few and dumped them on top of the twigs.

She wanted to have it lit and burning cheerily when Grant returned. If she had trouble getting it going, she could always use the camp stove for the hot dogs. Assuming she could hook it up. She stooped to examine it. Hmm. Didn't look too hard.

The tent, on the other hand…

She stared at the massive amounts of overlapping metal poles that she'd dumped out of the tent bag and onto the ground. The tent itself had tumbled out, too. Its material was lighter than canvas, maybe nylon or something similar, and it was dark green.

She stretched it out on the lawn.

It was enormous. Maybe fifteen feet across. Whoa.

The diagram she'd studied on the kitchen table showed it came together in a hexagon shape. It had little mesh windows, a big zipper door with a flap thingy you could prop up in front of it like an awning, and cool LED lights in the ceiling.

But wait.

Nell hunted around on the ground and lifted up some poles.

Next, she peeked under the bedroll.

The instructions. Where were they?

• • •

When he reached the stream, Grant slapped his forehead. He'd been so intent on his interactions with Nell he'd forgotten his cooler. That infuriating woman. He could not let her get the best of him. He'd never drive her off successfully then. If she got him so twisted up in knots that he accidentally confirmed what he knew she suspected, she'd just dig in her heels and stay.

And this was *his* cabin. His domain. He owned it. At least, until yesterday. Now he wasn't sure who was getting the best of whom in this tug-of-war contest. He was certain about who was going to arise victorious, though. Him. He was a man with a plan. All he had to do was continue acting on it—without Nell's interference with her coyly playing along like she was so cool with everything. Seriously. She'd never survive today.

He returned to the cabin as stealthily as he could

and stole through its front door. The kitchen had been neatened up except for the large frying pan he'd used for the fish. That sat soaking in the sink. He spied Nell through the glass panel in the back door sitting on the bedroll. She kept picking up different tent poles and staring at them before setting them back down.

Grant chuckled.

She'll never figure that out.

He spotted the unfolded instructions on the kitchen table.

Especially without the instructions.

He shook his head, wondering if he should take them to her, then decided no. This venture was all on her. She'd been so sure she could do this, but he was pretty sure she couldn't. Jordan had assured him this was the most wicked-difficult tent they had. It would probably be a challenge even for Grant to put it up, especially single-handed.

He picked up his cooler, but then his gaze snagged on that pesky frying pan in the sink. Maybe it hadn't been exactly fair of him to leave her *all* the dishes, even if he had cooked. That stainless steel frying pan took extra care anyway. For having such a basic kitchen, he'd made a big splurge on fancy cookware. You needed a special cleaning powder to get off any sediment caused by cooking.

He set down his cooler, unable to resist the urge to peek at the pot that Nell had washed and dried and left on the counter. It wasn't dirty, but it didn't gleam like it could. Not Nell's fault by any means. He hadn't told her about his high-end pots and pans. He hadn't wanted to, either, lest she judge him for being precious about his cookware. He sighed and walked to the kitchen sink, staring down at that frying pan.

It would only take him a couple of minutes to clean it. He'd give the pot a quick scouring, too. Then he'd leave everything where it was, and Nell would believe that messy old frying pan had soaked itself into pristine condition. He'd save his cookware and help Nell out without her knowing it.

The back door popped open, and Grant froze where he was at the sink. The water was running, and his hands halted in the frying pan mid-scrub.

She called out in surprise. "You're back!"

"Yeah, I…" He shrugged. "Forgot my cooler."

"What are you doing?"

"I was just, um—" He shut off the tap.

She walked over to where he stood. "Washing the frying pan?"

"No."

"Grant." She gawked at him. "You're up to your wrists in soap suds—holding a sponge."

He cast a look at the frying pan and dropped the sponge. "Oh yeah." He winced because she'd caught him red-handed—again.

"So you, what?" She cocked her head. "Came back to do the dishes? I thought you felt that was *my* job."

His shoulders sank. "Maybe that wasn't fair."

"Ooh. Having an attack of conscience?"

"No." He fiercely met her gaze. "Are you?"

She set a hand on her hip. "Not in the least."

Lovely. Just like her. He groused and turned the water back on, rinsing the frying pan thoroughly—inside and out. "I didn't come back to do the dishes, if you must know," he said without looking at her. "I came back for my cooler, like I told you."

She stared at it where it sat on the floor beside the table. "It's over there."

"Right. Yes, it is." He licked his lips. "The only thing is, I saw this frying pan, and then I remembered I forgot to tell you it's an All-Clad."

Her eyebrows arched. "What's an All-Clad?"

His face burned hot. "A type of cookware that requires special care."

"Really? I never knew you were a foodie."

"I'm not a *foodie*, Nell. I just know what I like."

"And what do you like?"

"Things made to last." He reached for a dish towel, but she grabbed it first.

"I'll dry."

He snagged the dish towel by its edge. "Oh no, you won't. I've got this."

She tugged back harder on her end, yanking him toward her. "And I said *I* did."

Grant set the wet frying pan down on the counter. "Let me have the towel, Nell."

Her eyes flashed defiantly. "No."

She was one infuriating woman. But that infuriating part also made her a little sexy. "Why not?"

"Because you said the dishes were my job."

He scowled at her. "Well, maybe I've changed my mind."

"Why's that, Grant? You can't possibly be feeling guilty?"

"Guilty? Me?" He scoffed and tugged at the dish towel, but she tugged back. He gave her credit for being a lot stronger than she looked.

"Yes, you." Her eyes flashed. "For every little thing you've put me through."

Grant's jaw clenched. "What about the *big things* you've put me through?"

She shook out her hair. "I have no idea what you're talking about."

"Nell." The word was a growl. "Give me that dish towel."

She stubbornly set her chin. "Make me."

"All right." He pulled the dish towel toward him in one smooth move, and she scooted across the kitchen floor, trying to hang on to it with both hands. But he was bigger and stronger than she was, and she nearly slid into him.

"Stop that!" she charged.

He raised the dish towel above his head, trying to shake it free from her grasp, but the bullheaded woman clung to it with all her might. She had both arms extended, rising up on her tiptoes and gritting her teeth. "Grant!" Suddenly she was right in front of him, breathing hard. "Let. Go." *Yank*. "Of that. Towel." *Yank. Yank*. Each time she yanked, she bounced on her feet, moving closer and closer to him until—

Her gorgeous face was just below his with her incredible golden-brown eyes big and wide.

Grant's pulse pounded.

Then she licked those sensuous lips, and warmth flooded his body.

It took *everything he had* not to forget about that dish towel and tug her luscious body up against his, taking her in his arms.

Wrong. Wrong. Wrong.

What was he thinking?

He let go of the dish towel, and she dropped back on her heels. "Whew!" She set her chin in a smug way, but her forehead glistened with moisture, and her cheeks were flushed. "Thanks."

She began buffing and buffing that frying pan so hard it shone. Her eyes were locked on his as her hair tumbled into her face and those sweet, sweet freckles became swept up in a ruby red blush that grew wider and wider, encompassing her whole face. Maybe she was thinking what he was. About the unbearable chemical attraction that crackled and sizzled between them every time they got too close.

He had to stop this.

"Thank you for doing such a great drying job." He went to his cooler and picked it up, needing to get out of there. That moment with Nell had been too dangerously combustible. He'd nearly forgotten himself and lost his head.

"No problem." Her voice was breathy. She latched onto a door handle, like she needed to hang on to something. "This goes"—she asked, still panting a bit—"in here?"

"Nell."

"Huh?"

He resisted a grin, liking that he'd had that effect on her. "That's the refrigerator."

She glanced over her shoulder, and the color drained from her face. "Right."

He pointed to the cabinet where the cookware went, and she put the frying pan away.

Grant hovered in the doorway. "So, I guess I'll see you later?"

"Later." She caught her breath. "Yeah."

"So." He swallowed hard. "Good luck with that tent, then."

"Thanks." She beamed at him. "Happy fishing!"

What had just happened between them? Current still hummed through his body like an electric rain pouring down from a thunder-and-lightning-torn-up sky. He could not keep doing this, risk experiencing an attraction with Nell. He needed to put all thoughts of the two of them being together completely out of his mind. But that was very hard to do with so many antagonizing, infuriating, and—yes, darn it—*enticing* memories of his interactions with her swirling around in his head. Fishing generally helped him forget about everything else. This time, though, he wasn't sure it would be enough.

• • •

What seemed like hours later, Nell sat cross-legged on the sleeping bag almost in tears. She'd gotten the poles all mixed up when she'd laid them out on the grass trying to organize them. Now she wasn't sure which ones were A, B, or C. The D, E, and F parts were even more elusive, since those were the shorter rods and there were a gazillion of them.

At least focusing on the tent had helped keep her mind off of what had happened in the kitchen. When she'd fought over that dish towel with Grant, she'd nearly lost her mind with desire for the guy, even though she knew that was so wrong. She didn't want Grant any longer. She didn't even *like* him. Much less want to go getting all physical with the—okay,

okay—incredibly hot and in-some-small-ways still attractive man.

Her heart fluttered at the memory of his kisses on the sofa on Saturday night. He'd been so caring and tender at the time. They'd been in such a different place. Totally and happily falling in love. She'd been foolish to believe so many wonderful things about him. Trusting and naive to a fault.

She never would have pegged Grant for a guy who would grow so coldhearted and calculating, orchestrating a really horrible way to dump her by having her dump him.

She hoped he was enjoying himself immensely.

Because she was *not*.

She dug her hand into the potato chip bag and pulled out a bunch more chips, shoving them into her mouth. This tent was worse than a thousand-piece puzzle. Much worse. It was like that 3D puzzle Misty had gotten as a present last Christmas. The one of the Majestic, Maine, lighthouse with tons of blue waves and brown sand, then more blue sky above that. All this brain work had made her hungry, but the junk food hadn't helped her come up with any solutions, either.

She had the nineteen stakes at least. She'd recognized those almost immediately. There was a small rubber mallet in the tent bag, and she'd used that to drive the stakes into the ground, approximately where she gauged they would go with the tent laid out. That was before she'd read on the instructions that she was supposed to do that part last. Didn't matter. Fact was, she still had no clue how to put the stupid tent up or get inside it.

Don't freak.

You can do this.

You're especially going to do this because Grant thinks you can't.

She'd wielded a log splitter of all things. Putting up a tent should be child's play compared to that. In truth, kids put up tents all the time. Nell used to do that with her sisters in their bedrooms by stretching out sheets and blankets across the furniture. The issue before her seemed a little more complex, though. Maybe if she crept in through the front flap and lifted it up with her hands above her shoulders, she could get a clue how this whole thing fit together?

She slunk through its opening, and the weight of the tent sagged against her back. She held her arms up overhead and pushed with her hands—way up. There were the LED lights in the ceiling—sweet!— but they weren't switched on. And oh! Interesting. Here were the pockets into which she could insert some of those poles, maybe. She just didn't know which pockets went with which poles, or which poles connected, or how. It would have been nice to have things color coded. Could someone *please* tell her why nobody'd thought of that?

Hang on. Maybe she should figure out first which of the poles fit together?

She could do all that on the ground as a dry run, then bring the poles in here.

Okay. She had a plan. This was worth a shot.

Forty minutes and two YouTube video tutorials later, she'd finally done it. Yay! She'd put up the tent. It looked beautiful, too, with that awning up above its front door. She held the small remote for the LED lights inside and couldn't wait to try them out. Grant was going to flip when he returned. She'd not only beaten him at his own game, they now had a pretty amazing intact tent. All she had to do was start the campfire.

She slipped into the tent and turned on the lights using the remote, and well, it was almost magical in there. Then something scary happened, breaking the spell.

A shadow moved outside the tent, and Nell's heart lurched.

It couldn't be Grant. It was still too early, wasn't it?

She told herself to be still and not breathe.

No, that was hard—and made her lightheaded.

She had to breathe a little.

She sucked in a breath, and the hulking image loomed closer.

Okay, not good. Her pulse pounded. *Not good at all.*

Something shuffled in the grass, and Nell bit her lip.

She'd heard there was wildlife in these mountains. All kinds. Including people-eating bears. But the bears only attacked when they were really hungry and the people were careless.

Nell's heart stuttered.

What did bears consider careless? Probably people like her, who'd left potato chips out as bait. Or maybe as bear appetizers.

If she'd been smart, she would have had that pocketknife of Grant's on hand. But no, she was dumb. Which meant that she was extra tasty, because she was basically available.

Free lunch!

Or. *Dinner!*

Linner?

She felt faint.

It turned toward her, probably smelling her in the tent. Inwardly, she groaned. Of course, she'd used *strawberry* shampoo, and bears loved berries. Everyone knew that.

She decided to run and scream. Really loudly. Because seriously, by staying in here, she was making herself into the inside part of a tent sandwich. The meaty part. It was probably too much to hope the bear was a pescatarian or only into plant-based. This was *all Grant's fault.*

The monster raised a grisly paw and reached for the tent flap, and her hair stood on end, her pulse racing. Fight-or-flight time!

She shoved her arms out in front of her, shielding her face with her hands, and rocketed forward, screeching like a wild woman. *Noooo. Don't eat me…* "Arghhh!"

Wham! She rammed straight into the beast, and it caught her in its arms.

CHAPTER NINETEEN

"Nell?" Grant peered down at her ashen face. "Are you all right?" He steadied her shoulders in his hands, and her knees shook.

"Gr—Grant, oh!" She blew out a breath. "It's you."

"Who did you think it was?" He chuckled. "A great big ol' bear?"

"That is *so* not funny." She straightened her posture and smoothed back her hair. "But, uh. Yeah? Maybe?"

He felt bad for making her panic. Poor thing. She really was not a natural in the outdoors. She'd probably be ready to go home at any minute, which was all well and good. He didn't need another moment between them like they'd experienced in the kitchen with that dish towel, or like yesterday's waterplay with the hose. He'd never be able to get her out of his head—or out from under his skin—then.

"I'm sorry I startled you." He stared at the erected tent. "But wow, look at you! You did all this?"

She gave him a shaky yet proud smile. "I did."

He studied their surroundings, noting she'd made other accomplishments. "I see you got the bedroll done, and the sleeping bag, too."

His eyebrows arched at the fire ring. "And the campfire is set up and ready to go. Very good." Which was a lie. It looked more like she'd deposited a willy-nilly supply of sticks in a heap rather than intentionally laying a fire, but that didn't matter in the scheme of things.

She seemed to notice that he'd showered and changed. "How long have you been back?"

"About fifteen minutes. Why?"

"I didn't hear or see you return."

"That's because I left my gear on the front porch and came in that way." He'd had his nose glued to the bathroom window for most of that time, sneakily watching her get that tent up. He couldn't believe she'd done it. He'd never met a more determined woman. Nell Delaney did not give up. He gazed at her ankle. "How's it feeling? Still doing better?"

"Yeah, thanks." She hesitated a beat. "Which is why I probably won't need to stay up here much longer."

Yes. He sensed a breakup coming. *Finally*.

He frowned for her benefit. "You're probably right." He shook his head at the tent. Even though she'd gotten it up, the effort had to have been exhausting. "I get that this has been a lot for you."

"Oh no." Her eyebrows shot up. "It's not about that. What I meant was, since I'm doing better now, I no longer need to rest up."

Grant rubbed the side of his neck, his guilt flaring up again. He was supposed to have been taking care of her, but he'd been vehemently attempting to get rid of her instead. "I'm sorry if that tent was a pain to set up. I get that it's harder than it looks. Some of those newer models can be tricky."

She grinned like she wanted to kill him. "Tricky indeed." He was finally wearing her down; he could sense it. Well, good. He was ready for this to be done.

He peeked inside the tent, deciding to play his final card. No way would she stay out here tonight all alone. Not after the way she'd reacted when thinking he was a bear. "Looks nice with those LED lights. You should be quite comfortable once you get settled."

"Settled? You mean we're sleeping out here?"

"Not we, Nell."

"Er." She bit her bottom lip. "Where will you be?"

"Staying toasty by the woodstove."

She blanched. "Are you serious?"

"I thought you wanted to practice?"

"Yes, but. What about you?"

"I don't need to practice." He winked. "I'm the camping expert." He leaned toward her and whispered, "Remember?"

She looked like she wanted to bite him. Then a hoot owl called, and she jumped. "Are you sure that it's safe out here?"

He gestured toward the woods. "The coyotes don't like the fire. Just be sure to keep it going."

She glanced around like she expected coyotes to stampede into the clearing at any moment. "Makes sense."

He scanned her face. "But if it's too much…" *Please say it's too much.*

She took a deep breath and swallowed. "No. I can try it." She licked her lips. "Try sleeping in the tent, and um…see how it goes. I'll just keep that fire burning!"

Now what was he going to say? Nothing seemed to dissuade her.

Her smile brightened. It was hard to tell if her grin was pretend or real. He voted for the former. "Hey. I can still fix those tofu hot dogs, if you'd like?" She motioned between the campfire and the camp stove. "Flame-roasted or grilled—which would you prefer?"

He couldn't believe this. The woman would *not* give up.

Fine. He was worried it might come to this. Which was one reason he'd left a little surprise for her in the cabin. Given how bullheaded she was being, it might help to heap on an extra layer of his newly inconsiderate nature.

"I'll tell you what," he said. "How about you let me work on this campfire while you cook those hot dogs inside?"

She scrunched up her nose. "On a regular stove? That's hardly camping."

Oh, she was good. "Yeah, but that'll make it easier for you to handle the side dishes."

"Which side dishes are those?"

He rubbed his chin. "There are some vegetarian baked beans in the cupboard. Would you mind heating those up?"

"Sure."

"You know what else I'd really love? Deviled eggs."

"Deviled eggs?" Her voice cracked at the end of the word. *Excellent.*

He had to bite back a grin. "Do you know how to make them?"

"I think so? I'm sure I can look up a recipe on my phone if things get too…complicated." She batted her eyelashes, and his heart thumped.

No, Grant. No.

"Great." By which he meant very much *not* great. He dug in his heels. "But try not to break the egg whites when you shell them. I really hate it when they get messy that way."

"No breaks. Got it."

She turned to go, but he stopped her. "Uh, Nell?"

"Yeah?"

"Do you think you could cook up some of those crispy tots from the freezer for something hot and crunchy?"

"Absolutely! Hot and crunchy sounds good!" she said with a huge grin.

Really? Why did she have to be so darn agreeable? And that grin…his stomach swooped in response. *Get it together, man. She's playing you.* He stared up at the sky and tried to think of something that'd be more of a pain to make. *Got it.* "You know what I haven't had in a while?"

"What's that?"

"A really good mac and cheese."

Her shoulders sank just a fraction. Good. "Homemade?"

"That would be awesome."

"Uh," she said. "You're talking the lactose-free kind?"

"I bought all the ingredients."

"Oh nice." She looked like she was keeping a mental tally of the menu. "Okay then, let me go—"

"Hon?"

She blew out a breath but kept her tone cheerful. "Yes?"

"I know you don't eat chocolate." He pressed his palms together. "But I've got this desperate craving."

"For?"

"Brownies." He shrugged sheepishly. "From scratch. You can use the cocoa powder."

She twirled a lock of her hair around one finger. "Aren't we having s'mores later?"

Darn it. She was right. "You probably think I'm being *unreasonable*."

"Unreasonable? No. I just think you're a big, strapping guy with a big, strapping appetite." She swung her arm through the air when she said that, and he was glad she wasn't standing closer. She might have slugged him. "Good thing you go on so many outdoor adventures to keep you fit," she teased. "Or we might have to rethink those brownies and s'mores on the same night." She winked, and his neck burned hot.

Wrong response. *Wrong. Wrong. Wrong.*

He cleared his throat. "I...tend to work up a big appetite when I'm fishing."

She grinned up at him. "And today the fishing was good?"

"Um, yep."

"Nice. Lots of them?"

"Yes, ma'am."

"Yum."

He just stood there, drowning in her sparkling eyes. He felt thrown off-balance. Like she'd taken the ball on this somehow and he'd fumbled.

He scratched his head. "You sure you got all

that? The side dishes, I mean."

"Think so." She began reciting. "Hot dogs, baked beans, crispy tots, mac and cheese, and brownies?"

He did a quick mental tally himself. "You're forgetting the deviled eggs," he said in lilting tones.

"Oops. Sorry." But she didn't really look sorry at all. She'd probably hoped he'd forgotten. "Well then," she said, bouncing off toward the cabin. "I'd better get busy!"

The moment she'd gone, remorse swamped him. Maybe he'd laid in on too thick. Asking her to make all that food? Seriously? He knew she was only following through because she was onto him. Still, it felt so wrong.

The goal had never been to make her *do* anything. She was supposed to cut and run the second she realized what a world-class chauvinist he was. Instead, he had a spotless cabin, a fresh pile of split wood, groceries he'd never eat, a huge tent set up in his yard, and what was about to be a spread of epic proportions.

He scrubbed his hand over his face. He was making such a mess of this. She was clearly going to beat him at his own game. Just like she'd creamed him playing Scrabble. During every conversation they'd had, she'd never backed down, had never admitted any fault. Instead, she'd worn him down by being gracious and giving, making him feel worse and worse about himself.

This was bad. He'd gone too far. He had to go in there and tell her that plain hot dogs would be all right. He grumbled, recalling the little surprise he'd left for her inside. That had been unfair of him, too.

Maybe he could apologize for thoughtlessly leaving a mess and pick it up before she stumbled across it.

· · ·

Nell walked in the cabin's back door, and she almost tripped.

She'd stepped on something near the kitchen table. What?

She looked down and picked it up.

Ew. It was one of Grant's socks. One of his... pretty grungy socks. She held it out in front of her with pinched fingers and dropped it back on the floor. Then she spied its mate near the stove.

Two socks and...there's his fleece jacket halfway to the sofa.

His dirty jeans were near the woodstove, wadded up around the ankles.

T-shirt by the bathroom door. Turned inside out.

What had he done? A striptease all the way to the shower?

She spotted his briefs on the bathroom floor, along with a damp towel. Yep. That's what he'd done all right, and she hadn't even been there to see it. At least that would have been some consolation.

Nell sighed, staring at the mess. He'd done all this just to vex her. He'd probably picked out the most difficult model tent he could find at his store, too. Now, he wanted her to sleep in it alone? He had to be banking on the fact that she wouldn't and would beg to be driven home first.

Not on your life, Grant.

Nell squared her shoulders. She was feeling

stronger every moment, and she would not be played by Grant. She stared at his damp towel on the floor, fighting the urge to pick it up. But no, she wouldn't do it. Wouldn't clean up any of his discarded clothing, either. Now, it was his turn.

"Uh…I'm sorry about the mess."

She spun around, spotting Grant on the threshold. He clutched his dirty clothing in his arms. He'd apparently crept in behind her, snagging his laundry off the floor, piece by piece. He shrugged, and his ears tinged pink. "I forgot that I'd left these lying around. Sorry."

"Forgot?"

"Well, no. Not exactly—forgot." He clucked his tongue. "It's more like I thought better of it."

"Of what, exactly? She cocked an eyebrow. "Being a pig?"

He winced. "Yeah. Maybe."

She folded her arms across her chest. Did he actually believe that pretending to be a slob would push her over the edge? After what she'd already endured in his game? Hardly.

"Grant Williams," she said sternly. "Don't think for a second that I don't know what you're up to."

He blinked. "I don't know what you mean by that, Nell."

"I'm talking about this!" She pointed at his bundle of soiled clothing. "*That*." She glared at the toilet. Next, she glanced out the bathroom window at the tent. "All of it." She scanned his eyes. "I'm starting to think you've been making these unreasonable demands as a way to get rid of me."

"Unreasonable?" His shoulders sank. "I thought

you liked—"

"Scrubbing floors and cleaning toilets?" She blew out a hard breath. "No."

He backed up a step. "I never said that you *had* to do any of those things."

She laughed, but her laugh had a bitter edge. "You certainly encouraged my *participation* in our very inequitable household duty split. Wasn't that why you handed me that toilet brush? As a gentle nudge?"

His whole face turned red, and he backed up farther. "I never thought you'd do it. Clean the bathroom. Chop wood. Any of it!"

She followed him. "No, you didn't. Did you?" The air hung heavy between them as she gazed up into his dark brown eyes. "You were hoping I'd leave first."

He set his chin. "And why, exactly, would I do that?"

Her heart pounded because he stood so close. "I don't know. Why don't you tell me?"

He stared at her long and hard. "Seems to me like you're the one with a confession."

What was he even talking about? Aidan? She wouldn't give him the satisfaction. Especially not when he'd obviously already figured that out. "I don't know what you mean." She and Grant had no future. Therefore, *her future* was none of *his* business.

His gaze blazed into hers. "Oh, but I think you do."

He was baiting her, trying to get her to say this was all her fault. But it wasn't. He was the one who'd set up this stupid battle of wills, not her. And, once he had, he'd been destined to lose, because she wasn't giving in. Ever. Not when she'd finally decided to stand up for herself instead of caving to whatever everyone else needed.

"You can try every trick in the book to push me away," she said. "But none of them are going to work."

He huffed. "Nell! Why are you being so pigheaded about this?"

"Why are *you*?" She scoffed. "One thing is for sure—you've given me plenty of reasons to walk, Grant. More than enough. But I'm not going anywhere until you say it's over."

A muscle in his jaw tensed. "That's *not* going to happen."

She locked his gaze. "Why not?"

"Because, sweetheart." He glowered at her. "Saying goodbye is going to be *your* job."

Her pulse pounded in her ears, and ire flooded through her. Forcing her to do his dirty work—again. She gritted her teeth and ground out the words. "Way to delegate, Grant."

. . .

Nell walked back into the kitchen and left Grant standing there feeling like the world's most colossal jerk. How did she always have the ability to turn things around and make him feel like the guilty party? Why wouldn't she call it quits? He hated what this was doing to both of them. Somehow, it had to stop. While he still stood by the fact that she was at fault here, maybe he could extend a bit of an olive branch, starting with him amending his ridiculous dinner requests.

He found her boiling eggs at the stove. "Nell," he said, his throat scratchy. He swallowed hard. "You don't need to cook all that food. That's actually what I came in the cabin to tell you. Just plain hot dogs will be fine. I'll even grill them myself over the campfire, if that will help."

She spoke without turning. "I don't mind cooking."

He wished she would look at him so he could read her expression. Her voice was blank. "Yeah, but it *is* an awful lot. I mean, maybe we can cut out a thing or two?"

"Like what? The eggs are boiled already." She still wouldn't look at him, and maybe he was lucky she was talking to him at all, after all his unreasonable demands. But what about her and her big secrets? About Aidan and that bet?

"Great," he said about the eggs being boiled. "We can save them for breakfast." Assuming she'd still be here. That only made him feel worse. He didn't want Nell's company under these conditions. Everything was all twisted up and felt so wrong. Like a battle he couldn't win, no matter which way it went.

He sighed and stared at the cocoa tin. A cheese grater sat beside it by a cutting board and a hunk of vegan cheese. He walked up to her, speaking softly. "Let's skip the brownies," he said morosely. "You won't eat them anyway."

She shot him a glance, but she'd set her mouth in a hard line, like she suspected another trick. "Okay," she said. "We'll skip the brownies."

He hated the wariness in her tone, knowing he'd put it there. "Same with the mac and cheese."

She shrugged and turned away. "Fine by me. Still want the baked beans and tots?"

"Sure," he said, because he knew those were easy. "I'll work on the campfire for the hot dogs." The mood had changed between them, settling into a quiet disillusionment. He'd give anything to bring back their fiery heat. Or even a smidgen of a smile. "Need any help in here?"

"No thanks," she said, finally turning to face him. "I'm all right."

Her eyes were flat, devoid of emotion, and it churned him up inside. She *was* all right. Of course she was. Nell was the solid sort of woman who would always land on her feet. And she pretty clearly wanted to land there without him. Frustration, and maybe a little hurt, burned through his chest as he headed for the back door. "I'll go work on that fire."

• • •

Grant threw another log on the fire. It crackled and caught, emitting short flames. It was one of the logs Nell had chopped during her wood-chopping frenzy, which only served to increase his frustration.

Their conversation inside hadn't gone well. Not only had she refused to own up to why she'd tried to trap him into a relationship, she'd refused to walk away. Apparently, for Nell, it was all about winning. What he couldn't understand was *why*. Why wouldn't she walk away? He had his reasons. What were hers?

His heart ached over the whole situation, but then his gut twisted, indignation rising to the surface once again. Her reasons didn't matter. None of this was worth it. Not the games, not the apologies, not how he was feeling—none of it. He trudged back toward the cabin, determined to have it out with her once and for all.

"Nell," he said when he entered the kitchen. "We need to talk."

She pulled the baked beans from the oven and set them on the stove top.

"You're right." She sighed. "We probably do."

He spread his hands out in front of him. "Why couldn't you just be honest with me?"

She stared past him and out the back door at the tent. "And why couldn't you resist sticking it to me, Grant? Hmm?"

He raked a hand through his hair. "Why didn't you just walk away?"

She stepped toward him. "Why didn't *you*?"

"This is *my* cabin."

"I'm not talking about that, and you know it. I'm talking about us."

He stared down into her eyes, breathing hard. "I'm not sure there is any us." His heart ached when he said it.

Her eyes glistened. "I thought we felt something for each other. That first night—"

"That was before. Before I knew about your bet—and Aidan." He frowned. "And that I'd been targeted as your last-minute groom."

She blanched. But she had to have figured it out at some point. Had to know that he knew. "Grant.

That's not how it was."

"Are you sure about that? Because your sisters sure seemed to think you'd gotten out of marrying that guy by winning me over."

All the guilt he'd expected to see earlier flooded her wide brown eyes. "I was going to tell you—about Aidan, the bet, everything."

"Oh yeah? When?"

Her chin trembled, but she held her ground. "On your birthday."

"Oh wow," he said sourly. "That's rich." He clapped his hands together. "Happy birthday to me."

She stood up straighter. "You have a lot of nerve being angry with me. Especially after pulling your ogre thing."

"Ogre thing?" he said, trying not to sound like one, but failing, he guessed. He wasn't the only bad guy here. She'd been playing her share in this. "You're the one who started this, Nell. Not me. If this was all about that bet, why didn't you tell me sooner?"

"I think you know why." Her eyes flashed angrily. "Because you—"

"Would have walked. Right." He set his chin. "What rational man wouldn't have?"

She balled her hands into fists and glared at him. "If you knew all along about the bet and Aidan, then you've been acting impossible on purpose—just to torture me."

"Oh sure," he said sarcastically. "Pin this on me."

Ice crystals formed in her gaze. "When were *you* going to talk, Grant? Why not confront me directly? Instead you did what? Designed a payback plan?"

He huffed. "You told everyone we were engaged, Nell. *Engaged*."

"No, I didn't!" She shut her eyes and groaned. "It was my texts. They got it all wrong."

Texts? What texts? He shook his head. That didn't matter. "Don't go blaming this on your sisters. They didn't think they were betraying you. They assumed I already knew. That you'd *told me*, like you should have. And anyway. Now, it's all over town." He scowled. "The McIntyres want to be added to the list."

"What list?" she asked weakly.

"For our wedding invitations."

She gaped at him. "Why didn't you correct them? The McIntyres? And my sisters?"

He ran a hand through his hair. "My family has a reputation in Majestic, and not necessarily a great one. The last thing I need to do is feed into that by dumping one of the town's sweethearts. That's why I had to get you to walk away from this. Not me."

"I didn't know." Her eyes brimmed with tears, but she was not going to gain his sympathy. Not when she'd blown his life—and heart—to smithereens.

He exhaled sharply. "For crying out loud, Nell. Trying to catch a husband in thirty days? Do you have any idea how that makes me feel? Any clue at all? Like easy game in hunting season!" He took one step closer and dove into her eyes. "I have news for you, Nell Delaney. Grant Williams can't be caught."

Her breathing went ragged, and so did his.

Emotion flickered in her eyes. Heat. Attraction. Devastation, too. Awareness of their impending goodbye. His heart beat furiously as she spilled her truth.

Her breath shuddered. "I didn't target you, Grant. Not like that. It was never like that. You weren't any kind of 'game,' and I wasn't trying to *catch* you."

"No? Then what?"

A few tears escaped her, and she wiped them back. "I wanted you to want me." Her eyes said *love me.* "For who I am."

An arrow shot straight through him, cleaving his soul in two because he believed her when she said it, with his whole heart. The crushing thing was, he *had* wanted her. He'd fallen so hard before fully understanding what she was doing. Playing him, using him, and that cut so deep. There'd be no coming back from that ever. No matter how badly he wished things were another way. Like when they were laughing together, or watching rainbows, or trading silly jokes or puns—or kissing like their two souls were fused as one. He'd never found a woman who suited him so well. Or so he'd believed.

Heat surged in his eyes. All that wasted potential. The relationship that might have been but that could never be anymore. Not after this.

"You might not believe it," she said, "but I am sorry, Grant. For everything."

Understanding coursed through him. Melancholy, too, because he knew that she meant it. But it was too late. He placed his hands on her cheeks and rasped softly, "I'm sorry, too."

Her voiced quivered. "I thought I could win this war. Could stand up for myself and what I want. But

I can see now it's a losing battle." She smiled through her tears. "So yeah, I guess you're right. I'm the one who started this. So. I need to end it." She released a shaky breath. "We're done."

They were two of a kind in the saddest sort of way. Headstrong to a fault. And now that fault had become a chasm—an insurmountable divide that neither one could get over.

His voice was husky when he said, "Yeah. I guess we are."

He scanned her eyes, searching for something, some earthly way to salvage this. But no. The fragile thing between them had broken into too many shards to be put back together. They were wrecked. That didn't mean they couldn't share one last good-bye.

Grant tugged Nell up against him, and she latched onto his shirt, pulling him nearer as he devoured her mouth with torrid hot kisses, singeing their souls with a bittersweet goodbye. She whimpered, and they deepened their ardor, clinging onto each other for dear life. But, even as his mouth burned hot and his heart caught fire, blazing like the brightest supernova, Grant knew this was no good.

He released her, panting hard.

Their ship had sunk, and there was no saving it anymore.

"Stay tonight," he said. "I'll drive you home tomorrow."

CHAPTER TWENTY

Nell stared at the campfire, barely tasting her food. She poked at her baked beans and tots, but everything tasted like cardboard. The hot dogs were the worst of all. But that hardly mattered.

After her fight with Grant, she felt anything but hungry. Guilt clawed at her soul over hoarding her secrets—the ones about Aidan and that bet. If she'd told him sooner, he might have walked, yeah. But maybe that was an outcome she should have been willing to accept.

"Thanks for making the dinner," he said, making an effort to be civil. "It's all really good."

"You're welcome." Those were the first two words she'd uttered since they'd come out here. It had grown colder, and they both wore their jackets over their sweaters.

"You don't really have to sleep out here in the tent if you don't want to. You can sleep in the bedroom. Or I can go ahead and drive you home tonight."

She set her plate down on her lap. She'd scarcely touched a bite.

"No, really. It's fine. We're both… What I mean is, it's dark and probably better for both of us if we go in the morning."

"The sleeping bag is graded for below-zero temperatures."

"Nice." She doubted very seriously she would

feel the cold. Every part of her body was numb, including her heart. A bag of marshmallows sat on the table between them. Graham crackers and chocolate bars, too. But they were never going to make those s'mores.

She swallowed past the burn in her throat.

Not tonight or any night.

"I don't think I want to eat anymore." She stood, holding her plate.

He exhaled and set his elbows on his knees. "Yeah, me neither."

Operation Ditch Me had totally failed, and now she was the one walking away. She couldn't have felt more terrible if she tried. The memory of Grant's goodbye kiss washed over her, making her want to weep so hard. But she wasn't going to do it. Even though her world was falling apart and her heart cleaving in two, she wasn't going to let Grant see her cry.

She walked into the cabin and set their plates in the sink while Grant stayed out by the campfire. She'd pack up her things so she'd be ready to go first thing in the morning. Then she'd turn in early so she wouldn't have to deal with Grant. Being around him now was just too hard. She should have known better than to devise her plan: Operation First Bride. What a joke that seemed like now. She guessed she would be the "first bride" in a way, since she'd be off to marry Aidan.

With Grant out of the picture, there was no other guy she'd want to pursue. She didn't have the heart. Better to wall that heart up and lock it away during those five long years she'd be married to Aidan.

Then maybe afterward she'd have a chance for true love again. Or not. Either way, she'd learned a lot during her time here with Grant. Apart from acquiring new skills, she'd become better at standing up for herself. She'd never been very good at that before. But she was now—and would be in the future, going forward.

She returned outside a few minutes later wearing her PJs under her jacket and carrying her pillow and a blanket. She also held her knitting project.

"I'm going to turn in now," she told Grant.

He frowned, worry creasing his brow. "Nell, really—you don't have to stay out here."

"You know what?" Her eyes felt moist. "I'd kind of prefer it."

He seemed to know what that meant. She'd rather take chances with bears and coyotes in her mind than spend one more minute in the cabin with him.

He handed her the camping lantern. "I'll leave the door unlocked in case you want to come back inside."

She stepped through the flap of the tent and turned, knowing she had to say it and that it was way past time. "Grant?"

"Yeah?"

Her heart throbbed painfully. "Thanks for taking care of me that first day. My ankle."

"I was glad to do it."

She stared wistfully in his eyes, wondering what might have been. He looked like he wished that he could know that, too. But there was no turning back on this road. Nell's exit was impending, and this was a one-way street.

"I'm sorry," she whispered. "Sorry for everything else. For not telling you sooner about Aidan and the bet, and that an engagement story leaked out…"

"Yeah," he said hoarsely. "I'm sorry too. We should have talked. I should have asked you what was going on." He shook his head. "But I didn't."

Her voice shook. "We're quite a pair."

"Yeah." He pursed his lips. "A mismatched one."

Heat prickled the back of her eyes, and Nell turned away before he could see her crying. "Good night, Grant," she said as she zipped up the tent.

"Night."

• • •

Nell tied off the knot on her knitting project and wiped back her tears.

There. She'd finished the hat. After all the love she'd put into it, believing she was going to give it to Grant, now she wasn't going to do that at all. This September seventh would be just like all the other years, and she'd sell this project on Etsy.

It had to be very late. She checked her phone.

It was nearly three a.m. Weirdly, the campfire outside her tent hadn't burned out.

She heard an eerie howling in the woods, and she shivered, snuggling down in her sleeping bag. Maybe she should go inside. Grant was probably sleeping soundly by now. At this point in the night, what would it matter anyhow? When she'd retreated here after dinner, it was because she'd needed that physical separation. She'd been hurting so badly she could barely stand to look Grant in the eye. They'd both been heartbroken, and with good cause. But he hadn't been half as upset with her as she'd been with herself. At least they'd both apologized and had made their peace in a gut-wrenching way.

She got up and unzipped her tent, then stood stock still.

Grant was there, sound asleep by the campfire, his head bowed against his chest as he sat in his folding chair covered with blankets. A stack of small logs sat beside him. He'd been tending the fire and keeping it going, watching over her all night long.

Hot tears streaked down her face.

She'd blown it with Grant and blown it big time. He looked so peaceful resting there, she decided not to wake him. So she zipped up the tent and crawled back into her sleeping bag, crying into her pillow.

She clutched her hands to her chest, every inch of her being aching, but she'd laid this all on herself. She'd decided to put herself before her sisters for the first time ever, and so everything had broken down. Nothing good came of self-interest and selfish desire. She should never have chased after Grant to begin with.

Aidan was the man she was destined to be with. She could do a world of good by marrying him, and in the end it wouldn't be too bad. They'd have their separate lives, and it would only last five years. Maybe they'd even be friends. She was the oldest so should accept responsibility for her family. She had to think of her dad, her mom, Charlotte, and Misty.

She was a great accountant, and that would come in handy in helping merge the family businesses together. The truth was that she and Aidan were the natural fit. Charlotte was intelligent and pretty. She could have so many choices. And Misty—Nell sighed—was the baby, her sweet, goofy little sister with so many talents she'd not yet explored. Plus, gobs of options for romance, too.

Nell's romantic options had pretty much dried up.

She'd thought she stood a chance with Grant, but no. That ship had sailed.

Or maybe, and much more tragically, it had never been in port to begin with.

CHAPTER TWENTY-ONE

When Nell woke up the next morning, the sun was high in the sky and burning brightly. The campfire had just been quenched, and gray smoke rose from its damp, chalky ash. The folding chairs had been put away. The collapsible table, too. She gathered her things from the tent and crossed through the backyard, fall breezes rippling through the trees.

It was odd to think she was going to miss this cabin, but in some strange way she was. She and Grant had had some good times here. She glanced at the hose caddy. And some really sexy ones. That passionate kiss last night had been their last one, but at least she had its memory to take with her and hold close in her heart.

During those long, lonely nights in England, she might think of Grant at his cabin, and that selfie of them by the waterfall would bring her some joy. Maybe after England, after Aidan, she'd find someone different, but Nell doubted he'd be nearly as great as Grant.

He probably wouldn't be a star Scrabble player, or a banterer, or half as handsome. It was doubtful he'd have Grant's unique combination of strength and caring. But that was water under the bridge. Looking back would only make things more painful. For now, she needed to move forward. She could relieve her sisters of their scramble to find husbands of their own by telling them she was going to marry

Aidan, and she was going to do that today.

Nell entered the kitchen and found Grant sitting at the table, his expression drawn. He had a mug of tea in front of him. He looked up when she came in. "Hey," he said miserably.

Her heart ached. "Hey."

He nodded toward the stove. The French press and a clean mug sat on the counter beside it. "Made coffee if you want it."

"Thanks," she said. "I'll just go put down my stuff." She noticed it was chillier in here than normal, and then she saw there was no fire in the woodstove. He'd probably let that burn down in preparation for their leaving, just like he'd doused the campfire.

She dumped her blanket and pillow on the bed. Her phone and Grant's knitted hat, too. Her heart twisted painfully. Maybe she should still give it to him anyway. No. That would be ridiculous. He clearly wouldn't want anything from her and would likely donate it to charity.

She was better off donating it herself. That seemed like a better option than selling her "Grant gift" this time. She had so much of her and him wrapped up in that hat, including her hopes for their now nonexistent future. Somehow, selling it didn't feel right. But donating, yeah. Maybe she could do that.

She returned to the kitchen, and Grant scraped back his chair, standing. "I'll go pack up the tent while you get your things together in here." His tone held a sense of mournful finality, and Nell got that she was never giving him that hat or any gift ever.

She blinked back the heat in her eyes, staying strong for herself and her sisters. For her parents and Bearberry Brews. "Okay, thanks." Then she went to shower and get dressed and finish packing up.

• • •

When Nell placed her packed bag by the front door, she noticed Grant's small daypack was there, along with another bag he'd picked up in town earlier. Some filled grocery bags were there, too. She peeked into one, seeing eggs and cheeses. They appeared to be perishables.

Then she remembered about the chicken parmigiana. She opened the fridge, seeing it was mostly empty, except for the casserole dish. She took that out and placed it on the counter before checking the freezer compartment. That held several foil-wrapped packages of frozen fish and loads of frozen vegetables. The ankle ice pack was there as well, but she decided to leave it, since that really didn't belong to her.

She stared at Charlotte's casserole dish, thinking she needed to wash it and return it to her. She didn't think she'd want any chicken parmigiana for a while. Not now that its memory was tied to being at this cabin. She decided to pack some up for Grant and searched his cupboards for a portable storage container. She could slip it in with his groceries for him to find later, and maybe he'd enjoy it, seeing as how there was no "Robby" anymore.

• • •

It was a long, quiet ride down the mountain. Grant drove them the shorter way, over the one-lane bridge, which had been repaired. Nell had her athletic bag by her feet on the floor and the chicken parmigiana casserole dish on her lap along with her purse. He saw the ends of two knitting needles poking out of it.

"Ever finish that hat?"

She avoided his eyes and stared out her window. "Yeah."

"Bet it looks great."

She shrugged, and Grant got that it was useless to make idle conversation. Well, what did he think? He didn't feel a ton like talking himself. So he focused his gaze back on the winding road. When they neared town, she pointed to a gravel road on the right-hand side. A tall green street sign read: Galloway Ridge.

"We turn here."

They drove through a patch of countryside, climbing a steep incline. A cute cottage sat near the top of the slope, fronting a cranberry bog overlooking the ocean. The one-story house had a covered front stoop crowded with plants and wicker furniture. Mixed foliage and underbrush hugged its perimeter. The landscaping had an unkempt look, almost like an English garden. The cottage was small, probably only one or two bedrooms.

"That your place?"

She nodded.

He dipped his head to peer out his windshield at the stunning views of the bog and the cliffs beyond it. Waves crashed and splattered against the jagged rocks below. "Great location."

"Yeah, thanks."

He parked in front of the cottage, and she opened her door.

"Nell." He touched her jacket sleeve, and she turned to him. "I am sorry. About everything."

"Yeah." She frowned, and her chin trembled a little. "Me, too."

She climbed from his SUV holding the casserole dish, then grabbed her purse and bag off the floor. "Bye, Grant."

"See ya."

She shut her door, and Grant hung his head, slumping against the wheel.

He looked up in time to see her enter her cottage and close the front door.

Well, that was that. He'd met his goal. He was a free man by his birthday.

Somehow, though, he didn't think he was going to feel like celebrating.

• • •

Nell waited to text her sisters until after communicating with Aidan.

Hey Aidan, it's Nell.

So guess what? It's me!

I'm your lucky bride.

He wrote back ten minutes later.

Very pleased. How soon can you get here?

She'd already checked the airlines, and the first available flight was on Thursday. She texted him the flight information, asking if that would work.

Brilliant, yes. I'll send a car to get you.

A car, of course.

Maybe it had been too much to hope that he'd want to meet her himself. But that was okay. At least he hadn't sounded disappointed that she was the one coming.

The sooner she married Aidan the better, so they could get this merger done with. There was no sense in putting Bearberry Brews and her parents' home at further risk by dragging this out until the last minute. What if something went wrong and the paperwork didn't go through in time? No. Much better safe than sorry.

She texted her sisters next.

I have news. Meet me at my cottage after work?

Misty answered immediately.

Yay! Are you married?

Nell's heart sank.

Not yet.

Charlotte joined in a few minutes later.

We'll be there! Can't wait to hear.

A short time later, her sisters arrived at her cottage.

"No, Nell. We can't let you do this." Charlotte began pacing around Nell's tiny living room. She held a full champagne flute. She and Misty had arrived with prosecco and both had popped it open the moment they walked in the door, shoving a skinny glass into Nell's hand and offering her hugs and congratulations.

Until she'd informed them directly that she was marrying Aidan.

"Maybe it's not up to you?" Nell sat on the old

piano bench matching the piano she'd inherited from her grandmother. None of the Delaneys played, but Nell was sentimental about family things, figuring someone in their lineage might take it up someday. She'd considered having the piano shipped to London, then decided it was best leaving it here. She could always rent her cottage out furnished.

Misty gawked at Nell from the futon. "You're not seriously going to hop on a plane?" Charlotte finally gave up on her pacing and sat beside Misty.

The more they protested, the more Nell decided that she'd made the right choice. She was doing this for them and the family. "I'm sure not *swimming* to London, and boats are too slow."

Charlotte huffed. "But Nell, what about your engagement to Grant?"

Nell pursed her lips. "There is no engagement, honestly."

Misty set her glass on Nell's coffee table. "What?"

Nell shook her head. "Never was."

Charlotte blinked. "What?"

"You guys just kind of assumed that, but I never... I mean, Grant didn't—"

Misty viewed her sadly. "No?"

Nell's lower lip trembled. "No."

Charlotte covered her mouth with her hand. "Oh, honey. What happened?"

"We had a big fight," Nell told them. "We broke up last night."

"Oh no." Misty's eyes went damp. "Is it final?"

Nell's shoulders sank. "About as final as things can get. He was really mad about everything, and the fact that I hadn't told him the truth about Aidan and the bet. He thinks that I used him." Her voice warbled. "There's no way to convince him that's not true."

Charlotte scooted over and patted the futon between her and Misty.

Nell dolefully stood and went and sat in the middle of her two sisters.

Charlotte sipped from her prosecco. "I don't believe there was nothing going on between you and Grant. When he came into Bearberry Brews to buy you breakfast, there were stars in his eyes."

"Yeah," Misty said. "He was definitely smitten then." She pulled a face. "That's when we slipped up about your engagement. Sorry. We had no idea it wasn't true."

"I don't believe Grant was faking being into you," Charlotte said. "When Misty and I saw you at his cabin, you looked like a real couple to me."

"All lovey-dovey-like." Misty's eyes glimmered. "And hey! What about that selfie by the rainbow? You can't tell us that you staged that."

"No. That was real." Nell steeled her emotions so she wouldn't crumble again. She'd done enough crying last night to last her a lifetime.

"So you see?" Charlotte said softly. "There's hope."

"No." Nell's tone grew weepy. "Not really."

"Aww, sweetie." Charlotte leaned in for a hug, and Misty hugged her, too, then Misty gasped.

"Uh-oh," she said, pulling back. "What about the McIntyres?"

Charlotte handed Nell a tissue, and she wiped her

damp cheeks. "What about them?"

"They've been telling everyone in town about your pending nuptials."

"Oh yeah." Nell sniffled. "Grant might have said something about that."

"It's not just them," Charlotte said. "The people at the wineshop asked if we needed to order any cases for the wedding."

"And, ugh." Misty grimaced. "I kind of ran into Karl, and he's offered to help cater." She slunk down in her seat. "I'm so sorry, Nell. I honestly thought it was for real, you and Grant."

"Yeah." Charlotte frowned. "Me too."

Nell's heart hammered painfully. Yep, she'd blown that one, but now was not the time to cry over spilled milk. Now was the time for moving forward. She drew in a cleansing breath and picked up her champagne. None of this would be happening if she hadn't let things get so out of control. While she hadn't known how far out of hand things would get, she hadn't helped matters, either, with her flirty hinting about Grant to her sisters. "Okay, well." She licked her lips. "We'll just have to squelch that rumor and put a new one in its place: the one about me marrying Aidan."

"Uh. But that's not a rumor," Charlotte said. "You're telling us that it's true."

Misty's eyebrows arched. "What will people think, Nell? You're engaged to a hometown guy the first minute and then off to marry someone in London the next?"

"I don't care what anyone in Majestic thinks," Nell said, but that wasn't true. She cared about

Grant's opinion. Her heart ached because she'd sunk so low in his estimation. And at this point in time there was no repairing that.

"So Mom and Dad?" She stared at her sisters, but she already knew the answer. "Did they know about…me and Grant?"

"Yeah," Misty said. "They heard all about it, from the McIntyres and the wineshop guy. After they pressured Charlotte and me, we had to tell them it was true. Because it was!" Her face fell. "As far as we knew."

"They're actually pretty excited about it," Charlotte said.

So that's what all those text messages were about. Both her mom and dad had been texting her frantically "checking in" and asking her to please call as soon as possible, but Nell hadn't had a minute in between everything else. Misty had to have told Mei-Lin. That was a given. She sighed. "I'm guessing Lucas knows, too."

Charlotte nodded. "Everyone knows, Nell."

"Well then, they're just going to have to 'unknow' things. Please do me a favor." She shot pleading glances at her sisters. "Help buy me some time? I'd rather this not get out until I'm already on that plane to London."

Charlotte wrapped her arm around Nell's shoulders. "You don't have to do this," she said firmly. "I'll go."

Misty wrapped her arm around Nell from the other side. "I'll go, too. You've been taking care of us for years. Let us take care of you."

Nell's heart broke, but she shielded her suffering

with sarcasm. "I don't think they allow polygamy in England."

Charlotte shoved her arm. "Oh you!"

"Ne-ell." Misty pushed her in the other direction, then latched onto her tight.

Charlotte hugged her, too. "You're sure about this?"

"Yes, very."

"So who's going to tell Aidan?" Misty asked.

"I already have."

Her sisters pulled out of their hug.

Charlotte stared at Nell. "And?"

"He's cool with it." Nell shrugged. "His car will get me from the airport on Thursday."

"Wait," Misty said. "He's not coming himself?"

Charlotte moaned. "*This* Thursday?"

Nell pursed her lips. "Yeah."

Misty and Charlotte glanced at each other, and then Charlotte said, "When are you going to tell Mom and Dad about this change in plans?"

Nell grimaced. "Guess it's gotta be sooner rather than later."

Misty held Nell's hand. "We'll help you."

"Yeah." Charlotte took Nell's hand on her other side. "We'll tell them together."

CHAPTER TWENTY-TWO

The next morning at Bearberry Brews, Nell and her sisters were waiting when their parents walked in. "Mom. Dad," Nell said nervously. "We need to talk."

"Is something going on, girls?" Their mom glanced around the room as Charlotte and Misty pushed two tables together. It was early still, with first sunlight streaming into the room. She smiled. "Something interesting?" She clearly was expecting happy news, and Nell hated breaking her heart. But maybe she'd be happy about Aidan, too? That marriage would benefit all of them.

"What is it, loves?" their dad asked, but his eyes were on Nell. They held that knowing twinkle, and Nell wanted to sink through the floor, because whatever he thought he knew was so, so wrong. He unwrapped his thick scarf—one of the many that Nell had knitted him—and sat at one of the tables when Misty pulled back a chair. Charlotte scooted another one back for their mom, and the five of them sat.

Nell twirled a lock of her hair around her finger, unsure of how to begin, so Charlotte started for her. "This is about Aidan."

"Aidan?" Their mom blinked.

"You mean this isn't about Grant?" their dad asked, flummoxed.

Lucas entered through the kitchen, then stopped.

The look on his face said he guessed he was inter-rupting a family meeting. "Oh, sorry." He started to back away, but Nell patted the table.

"No, Lucas," she said. "Come sit." He was so much a part of their group, he deserved to be in on this, too. Lucas cautiously crossed the room and came and sat beside Misty.

"What's going on?" He frowned. "Nobody's sick?"

Charlotte smiled to reassure him. "It's nothing like that."

Misty jutted her chin toward her oldest sister. "This is about Nell."

Lucas exhaled. "Oh. About you and Grant. Yeah! Congrat—"

Nell held up her hands. "Sorry, no. That's not happening."

Her parents' faces fell. "I'm afraid we don't un-derstand," her mom said. "Your dad and I heard. And we're so happ—"

Nell frowned. "I'm afraid that was wrong."

Her dad sank back in his chair. "But I saw him. With my own eyes. Now there was a young man in love."

"Your dad can spot them," their mom said. "From a million miles."

Lucas squirmed in his seat, and Nell found her-self wondering about something. His gaze was on Misty. Wait. The gray-eyed hottie couldn't possibly be crushing on her baby sister? She studied Misty's stance, but Misty was intent on their parents and the situation at hand. So maybe this attraction was one-sided. All in Lucas's head, and maybe in his heart?

He cleared his throat and asked, "So what's going on, then?"

Nell opened her mouth to speak, but not much came out. "I...I'm..."

"Nell's going to marry Aidan Strong," Misty supplied. She grinned broadly, trying to put a positive spin on it.

"Aidan?" The color drained from their mom's face.

Their dad steadied her arm, then stared at his daughters. "Wait. One. Minute."

"Dad—" Nell cut in. "I *want* to do this."

His blue eyes glimmered sadly. "My Nelly, no."

"When did this come about?" their mom asked.

The three girls hung their heads.

"We kind of made a bet," Nell murmured.

"What?" their dad said. "We couldn't hear you."

"A bet, Dad," Charlotte told him. "A wager."

"Yeah," Misty said. "About one of us marrying Aidan Strong."

Their dad brought a hand to his heart. "You can't be serious."

Their mom gasped. "This is about that marriage of convenience and the merger?"

Lucas dragged a hand down his face and stared up at the ceiling.

Nell nodded, and her mom's lips trembled.

"Oh honey, no. Please. I've thought and thought about that, and it's not worth it. Not for any of you girls. It was unconscionable of me to bring it up."

Their dad took their mom's hand. "I've forgiven your mom and Jane for their cockamamie idea, just like I'm willing to forgive all of you for that wager."

He viewed his daughters sternly. "Now, let's set this aside."

"I'm afraid that I can't." Nell reached into her purse and placed her boarding pass on the table.

"That says London." Their mom blanched. "I won't let you go."

"I'm thirty years old, Mom." She and Aidan had worked out the details by text last night. They would have a civil service wedding and sign the merger documents, then he would help Nell find a place in London. Afterward, she would fly back to Majestic to collect her things. It wouldn't be so bad, and he'd seemed nice enough in a British-sounding way.

"Well, I should have some say in this, too," her dad said. "I'm your father."

"I know you are, and I love you." Nell swallowed hard. "I love you both, and my sisters." She glanced at Lucas. "You, too, Lucas. But not like, you know."

"Yeah, yeah." He held up one hand.

"It's not only you that I love," Nell continued, "but this place, this café: Bearberry Brews. It's as much a home to all of us as the house on Mulberry Lane." She firmly set her jaw. "I'm not about to let us lose it. Not when I can stop that from happening by creating a much better financial future for everyone."

"But what about Grant?" Her dad took her hand. "You've loved him forever."

Hot tears sprang to her eyes. "You knew that?"

"Sweetheart." He squeezed her hand. "We've *all* known that. It's been no secret around here."

Nell's mouth went sandpaper dry, and she licked her lips. "I'm afraid that Grant's out of the picture.

He wants nothing to do with me anymore."

Her dad frowned. "I'm sorry."

"I'm sorry, too." Her mom scowled. "His loss."

"Thanks." Nell dabbed her eyes and sniffed, glad to have her family in her corner. They always had her back, which was why she needed to stand up for all of them now.

Her mom rubbed her arm. "This thing with Aidan, Nell. You don't need to do it. Your father's right. We Delaneys will find our way."

Nell shook her head. "It's already too late."

Her dad picked up the ticket. His brow furrowed. "This boarding pass says it's for tomorrow."

"Yeah." Her voice trembled. "I'm going to miss you guys." She broke down, and her mom hugged her. Her dad stood and did the same. Next, her sisters joined in, and Lucas awkwardly patted her shoulder.

"We'll FaceTime every day," Misty told her.

Charlotte nodded. "And text a ton."

"Your mom and I will come and visit," her dad said, and Nell sobbed harder, because that was as good as him giving her his blessing.

"If you don't like it, though," her mom said, "we'll want you on the next plane."

"Yeah," Lucas said. "Or we'll come and get you."

Nell drew in a deep breath, pulling herself together. It was good to know she had an escape hatch in case being paired up with Aidan became unbearable.

Somehow, though, she didn't think it would be.

"I'll text you," she promised them. "The minute I get there."

• • •

Grant poked at his chicken parmigiana, attempting to stir up his appetite, but he was anything but hungry. He'd found this container of leftovers when he'd unpacked his groceries yesterday after coming home from the cabin. Nell must have put it together for him and tucked it into one of the grocery bags. If he'd known about it, he would have thanked her, but it seemed awkward reaching out to her now.

"This is really good," Jordan said, sitting across from him. Wanting company for his misery, Grant had invited Jordan to dinner. He'd also had plenty of food to share.

"Yeah," Grant answered. "It is."

It had felt crowded at his little cabin with Nell there, but having her around had also made the place seem homier. He could still see her in his mind's eye, sitting on the sofa by the woodstove, knitting on that silly hat of hers. He'd never forget how beautiful she'd looked when he'd come back from fishing only to find her knitting by the fire. And she'd accomplished so much. Even chopped wood. Pretty amazing.

She was pretty amazing, or she was going to be for the right guy.

My domestic goddess, sure.

He sighed, thinking of their hike in the rain and that water fight behind the cabin. As long as he lived, he didn't think he'd ever forget that rainbow or the look on her face when she'd seen it. He'd never met anyone he'd had that much fun with, or that he'd been as attracted to, either. There'd been their teasing banter about the corny frozen vegetables and that fierce way she'd beaten him at Scrabble, and then their amazing make-out session on the couch.

When she'd hilariously made up those stories about her camping expertise and that phantom bat that had invaded his cabin, she'd been so cute and convincing he'd barely been able to resist laughing out loud and then hugging her. He'd gotten her back with his stories about being a pescatarian and his tall tale about Robby, but canny Nell had seen right through him. She was smart and determined, giving every task her top effort.

She'd been rightly proud of herself for wielding that log splitter *and* for putting up that impossible tent. Nell Delaney was an impressive woman, capable of pretty much anything she set her mind to. Including, very depressingly, getting rid of him.

"You can still reach out to her, you know," Jordan said.

Grant set down his fork. "There's still that bet about Aidan and London."

He frowned, wondering if she was already on a plane by now.

Jordan stared at him in surprise. "You don't think she's actually going to do it?"

Someone knocked at his door, which was unusual. Not many people came up this way after dark, only the occasional hiker or camper looking for his store, which was located at the top of his drive. His Alpine-style A-frame was set back a few hundred yards behind it in the woods. In the summer months, it was mostly concealed by the edge of the forest, but you could see telltale signs of his house from the main road once the leaves started to drop off the trees.

The open floorplan was simple, with a kitchen at one end and a dining area at the other. The section in the center housed living room furniture and looked out through a floor-to-ceiling window onto a deck and into the trees. He slept in a simple loft area upstairs that was only accessible by a built-in ladder.

"Who's that?" asked Jordan.

"No idea. I'll go and see."

Grant stood and went to the door, switching on the outdoor lights.

When he opened it, Nell stood on his steps.

"I'm sorry to surprise you." She shrugged with an adorable blush. "Maybe I should have texted first."

You could have knocked him over with a feather. "No, no. It's fine." He tried to gather his wits. "Want to come in?"

She shook her head and looked down at a package in her hands. "I can't stay. I just wanted to drop this off, so you have it for your birthday."

He saw that it was a midsize gift covered in colorful wrapping paper showcasing geometric cubes. It had a big blue bow on top.

His throat burned hot. "You didn't have to—"

"I know." She gave a dejected smile. "But I wanted to."

She handed it to him, and he accepted the package.

"You're a really great guy, Grant." Her golden-brown eyes sparkled, and for a moment he was lost in them. "You deserve to be happy."

His heart clenched. "So do you."

She nodded and backed down a step. His house sat up on stilts, so there were several of them. "Just do me a favor?"

His eyebrows rose.

"Don't open it until tomorrow."

He swallowed past the lump in his throat. "All right."

She drew in a breath and seemed to be gathering her nerve. "Grant," she said. "I really care about you. I always have. For a really long time—probably longer than you know. That's why I'm extra sad things didn't work out between us."

His heart pounded. He was extra sad, too.

"In any case." She turned to go. "I hope you have a really great birthday."

She reached the bottom of the stairs, and he called out to her. "Nell!"

She gazed up at him, her face bathed in the floodlights.

He wanted to say *don't go*, but he couldn't.

Because she was already on her way. He'd read it in her eyes.

He thought his heart had already broken, but now it was breaking again.

Nell Delaney was moving on without him.

"What will you do?"

"I have some plans."

"Involving Aidan?" The name was a bitter pill on his tongue.

She pursed her lips, but her expression said yes.

He tried to man up and be an adult about this. "Well, good. Good for you. I hope that you find your happiness, Nell."

"Thanks. You, too."

She started to pivot, but he stopped her again. "Nell." She peered over her shoulder. "Thanks for the chicken parmigiana. That was really kind of you. Please tell Charlotte it's delicious."

"I will." She shot him a cockeyed grin, but there was sorrow in her stare. "I'm glad there was no Robby."

She turned away and walked toward her car.

As she did, she lifted her right hand to wipe her cheek, and Grant suspected she was crying. He wanted to cry, too. Or scream or shout. Run after her. Something.

But instead, he took the present she'd given him and went back indoors.

"And?" Jordan asked because he'd heard their voices.

He slumped back down in his chair. "That was Nell."

"What did she want?"

Grant's gut twisted. "To say goodbye."

Jordan waited a while before commenting. After a pause, he said, "It's not over until it's over, Grant."

Grant pursed his lips. "Oh, I'm pretty sure that it's over."

"No chance?"

"Maybe if she'd given me a sign."

Jordan stared at the package he'd set on the table. "Looks like she brought you a present."

"Yeah, but I'm not supposed to open it until to-morrow."

"What if it's a sign?"

"I doubt that. It's probably more of a guilt gift."

Jordan frowned, thinking this over. After a while, his eyes glistened sadly.

"Then I'm sorry, man," he said. "I really am."

CHAPTER TWENTY-THREE

The next morning, Nell's family saw her off at the café. They'd all come in early for her send-off. Mei-Lin and Lucas, too.

"Here's a neck pillow for the plane," Charlotte said, handing her a gift bag.

Misty gave her a gift bag, too. "This is one of those eye masks, so you can sleep if you want to."

Nell hugged her sisters. "I love you both so much."

"We love you, too," Charlotte and Misty said.

Her mom handed her an envelope. "Your dad and I wanted you to have this little bit."

"Mom, no," she said. "You need that here."

Her dad gave her a fatherly grin. "You can pay us back shortly."

Lucas cleared his throat. "Here, this is for you." He gave her a flash drive.

"What's this?"

"I downloaded one of the playlists from Bearberry Brews," he said. "I thought it would remind you of home."

Nell hugged him, and Misty said, "Aww, Lucas. That's so sweet."

Charlotte folded her arms in front of her and observed Misty's completely oblivious gaze. "That was sweet, Lucas."

Mei-Lin stepped forward. "I have something for you, too." It was an envelope holding a gift card to an online store. "I wasn't sure what you'd need so thought maybe you could pick something out for yourself once you get there."

"Oh, Mei-Lin." Nell hugged her. "Thank you."

"Be sure to let us know about the wedding, now," her mom said.

"Right." Her dad nodded. "Civil or not, we'll all want to be there."

"All right," Nell said. "I'll let you know when the date is set." She stared at them uncertainly. "I don't know about the plane tickets, though, and how much they'll cost."

"I've already talked to Jane about that," her mom said. "She's bringing us over. All of us." She grinned around the room. "Lucas and Mei-Lin, too."

This made Nell feel a thousand times better, like reinforcements were coming in.

"Oh, that's awesome. How great."

Headlights poured into the café, and they turned toward the street.

Her heart thumped. This was really happening. She was going to England.

More importantly, she was going to save her family. Her "me time" would come. She believed that now. It hadn't been derailed—only delayed.

"I guess that's my car."

She peered out the front-facing windows, for a moment having the fleeting hope that Grant would be there. But he wasn't.

"Safe travels, love," her dad said with a hug.

Nell hugged each of them in turn again.

"Well." She picked up her bags. "I'm off to London."

• • •

Grant sat at his breakfast table before dawn, drinking his tea and staring at his one birthday gift from Nell. His small staff at his store often did something nice for his birthday, like bring in a cake or some cookies, but Grant hadn't gotten an actual present in years. When Susan and he had been on and off again, they'd typically been "off" during his birthday, which had suited him fine.

He was glad Susan was back with Paul and that they were building a life together. She'd known Paul first, and he'd always been her true love, Grant guessed. He considered the lofty ideal, the concept of a once-in-a-lifetime romance. Then he shook his head, remembering he'd foolishly believed he'd potentially found that with Nell.

And now, she was off to find that with Aidan.

Or would she?

It was hard to conceive of any man kissing Nell the way that he had, with his whole soul and being. He didn't enjoy thinking about it, either. What did this Aidan guy have that was so special? Billions of bucks? So what?

There were tons of rich folks in the world, but money didn't make a person.

Character did.

So, Aidan owned his own business? Well, Grant could claim that, too. Only Grant started his store — he didn't inherit it from his dad.

Did Aidan have a great sense of humor? Could he turn a phrase?

Probably not. It was doubtful.

Play Scrabble with Nell and make her laugh?

Grant doubted those things, too.

Could Aidan reach into his pocket and pull out a rainbow?

Grant hadn't *exactly* done that, but the smile on Nell's face had made him feel like he had.

Grant thumped the table with his palm, then reached for Nell's package, sliding it toward him. He didn't know why she'd brought him a gift, and he was conflicted over the fact that she had. Maybe it was a goodbye gift, a peace offering of sorts. Something to make up for the way she'd lied to him.

He pulled off the blue bow, recalling that he'd told Nell that blue was his favorite color. Had she remembered, or had this pretty ribbon just been the luck of the draw? He guessed he should be grateful she'd brought him a gift, but it was hard to be happy knowing she was flying off to marry somebody else.

He ripped back the paper and found a simple white box with a lid.

It looked like a shirt box from a department store.

He frowned. Maybe she'd gotten him a polo?

Why?

He pulled up the lid, and there was tissue inside. He had to pry it back to find what was underneath.

Wait.

Grant's heart thumped.

It was that hat.

He picked it up in his hands, and his fingers shook. But why would she...?

His mind had captured a snapshot of her saying

she was making it for somebody special.

Hang on.

All that time at his cabin, she'd been knitting this for him?

There was a note underneath. No. It was a business card from Nell's Etsy shop. He was impressed she was official enough to have one. She called her store "Nell's Knits," and there was a URL on the card. He flipped it over, and she'd written a note on the back in pen.

For Grant,
Happy Birthday!
Love,
Nell

He was stunned and touched.

But even more than that, his bruised heart felt like it was bleeding.

Why had she done this? What did it mean?

He grabbed his laptop from nearby and pulled up her site. She didn't have a ton for sale at the moment, but there was a string of reviews for items she'd made in the past. Wait. That was weird. Most of them she'd finished and sold in September, right around his birthday.

He stared down at his hat and then back at the screen, clicking through the different reviews with his mouse. All were five-star raves about quality and prompt delivery. She'd made three scarves, a few ties, a cardigan, a vest, a throw blanket, some mittens, a couple of hats... *Click. Click. Click.*

He picked up the hat, having a funny feeling about the former items in her store.

Nell had been the shy girl in high school. The bookworm. He'd barely know her at all until she signed up for his hike. Was it possible—or even probable—that she'd always felt something that went beyond platonic friendship for him? A secret crush? A longing?

A snippet of her conversation came back to him from yesterday evening.

"*I really care about you.*" she'd said. "*I always have. For a really long time—probably longer than you know.*"

Grant's world whipped into focus.

And then he knew.

This was that sign he'd told Jordan about. The one he'd been hoping for.

He had to see her.

Grant grabbed the hat and his jacket from his coat closet and then nabbed his wallet and keys, heading out the door. Then he raced down the steps and to his SUV.

Ten minutes later, he pounded on Nell's front door. It was still dark out, with the blanket of night gently lifting. If she was there, she should be up and getting ready for work. Her car was in the drive, but no lights shone inside her cottage. Grant huffed and dashed back to his SUV, his pulse racing. She couldn't have left town already. Maybe she was at the café.

When he got to Bearberry Brews, they'd not yet opened for the day.

"I'm sorry," Lucas said when he came in. "We're not— Oh. Hey."

Misty looked up from the register with wide hazel eyes. "You're wearing Nell's hat."

Charlotte came out of the kitchen. "Grant? What's going on?"

"Nell," he said, breathless. "Is she here?"

"No," Charlotte said. "I'm afraid you've missed her."

Grant clenched his fists. "Where?"

"The airport," Misty said.

"How long ago?"

Lucas answered. "About an hour."

Nell's parents approached him with rapid steps. Mrs. Delaney gasped. "You're here for Nell?"

Grant swallowed hard. "I've made a huge mistake."

Mr. Delaney walked toward Grant, pulling something from his pocket. It was Nell's flight itinerary. He handed it to Grant. "Go, go!"

Grant nodded, his heart pounding. "Thanks."

"Drive safely!" Mrs. Delaney called as he dashed out the door.

• • •

Nell rolled down her back seat window and leaned out of it. "Don't you think we should call for backup or something?" The sun had just peeked over the horizon, sending orange and purple hues across the sky.

Her driver crouched by her back tire, a lug wrench in his hands. "No, miss. I've got this."

He'd been saying that for the past twenty minutes, and she needed to get to the airport soon to check in on time. She stared at her phone, becoming more anxious by the minute. Fortunately, they'd only been on Route 1 when they'd had this flat tire, moving through slow fall beach traffic. They'd pulled off on a lonely stretch of road with towering ocean cliffs on their righthand side. The ocean crashed and churned below them.

Nell sighed and texted her sisters.

Flat tire. Ugh.

Hope I make my plane.

Seconds later, her phone dinged.

Message failed.

Lovely.

Okay, fine. Maybe she should document this to show Charlotte and Misty. They'd probably think it was funny. The many misfortunes of Nell.

She angled her camera out the window and snapped a pic of her driver holding a spare tire. "You're not going to post that?" he asked. "Lady, I've got kids."

What was that supposed to mean? That no one would take his service if they knew he'd had one random flat?

"It's fine," she said. "I'm just texting my sisters."

"Good." He got back to work. "Because I don't need any bad reviews. I need all the business I can get."

Nell shook her head and tapped her camera app. The driver pic loaded, but so did a few others next to it. Her heart seized up. Including the one of her and Grant by the waterfall.

Had he opened her gift yet? Would he be hating her—or loving her—right now for thinking of him? Whatever he thought, she hoped she hadn't made things worse. But, when she'd started packing for

London, she'd come across the hat and knew she had to do something. This was her last chance to tell Grant how she felt. How she had felt about him for the past fourteen years.

She slumped back against her seat and closed her eyes.

Happy birthday, Grant.

Then, she said in her heart the words she wished she'd said out loud.

I love you.

CHAPTER TWENTY-FOUR

By the time Grant reached the airport, he was frantic. Traffic had been gridlocked everywhere. He'd kept his eyes on the road and the other passengers, but since Nell had taken a car service it was impossible to know which vehicle she was riding in.

He pulled up to a spot in airport departures and put his SUV in park.

An airport cop tapped at his window. "Sorry, buddy. There's no parking here."

"But I just need to dash inside for a moment."

The cop shook his head. "Nope."

"Right." Grant put his SUV in drive and roared toward short-term parking. He'd texted Nell twice but hadn't heard back.

We need to talk.

And...

Coming to the airport!

He checked his watch. No.

Her plane was boarding soon.

• • •

Nell hustled into the airport, dragging her rolling suitcase behind her. She had her athletic bag slung over her shoulder. She scanned a monitor screen, identifying her gate, and then raced toward the escalator. She hurried up each moving step, her rolling bag thumping behind her as she squeezed past stationary travelers. "Oh. Sorry! Excuse me."

She was dressed for the outdoors and growing warm in the knit hat and scarf that she wore with her gloves and jacket, but there was no time to remove anything now. Her phone kept dinging in her purse, and she suspected that was her sisters responding to her photo of the flat tire. She'd read their texts and reply once she was safely seated on the plane.

She reached the top of the escalator and saw the security line for her section of gates stretching on for what seemed like miles. Great. She ran up to one of the security guards, waving her boarding pass and passport. "I'm boarding in ten minutes!"

He pointed to the priority line, which was only five passengers deep.

Nell nodded, huffing and puffing. "Thanks!"

• • •

Grant hustled his way through the crowded airport, turning sideways to squeeze between passengers carting large duffel bags, backpacks, and rolling suitcases with them. He followed directions to Nell's gate, racing up the escalator and scooting past those standing still.

There! Security!

His heart raced.

Nell.

She'd just gone through the metal detector.

He bounded in her direction. "Nell!" he called out as loud as he could. "Nell!" Still, his shouts were mostly drowned out by the hubbub of the airport.

Through the glass-wall protective barrier, he saw Nell grab her luggage and jacket off the conveyor belt. She wiggled into her boots, preparing to take off. No.

He bounded toward security and then veered off to a hallway section cordoned off by a rope. Nell was in the hallway hurrying toward her gate, her back to him.

Grant yelled with all the power and might in his lungs. "Nell Delaney!"

"Hey, you! Stop!" Three security guards were on him in an instant. Two had him around his chest and the third one patted him down.

"I'm sorry," Grant said hoarsely. "It's just my…" His heart sank. "Nell."

Then a miracle happened.

She stopped and pulled something out of her purse. It was her phone.

She looked down and stared at the screen. Next, she looked up and glanced around.

"I'm sorry," one of the guards said. "You'll need to come with us."

"Wait. Please," Grant said, pleading.

Nell turned on her heel, scanning the hallway.

"Nell!" he called again, and this time she saw him.

Her face lit up all pink and rosy. "Grant?" she yelled. "What are you doing here?"

The security guards released their grip.

"I…" He glanced at the guards and their stony gazes. "I had to see you! We need to talk!"

"Oh yeah?" she called back. "About what?"

Other people around them had started watching. Airport workers and passengers in the security line stopped chatting to watch the scene.

Grant's heart pounded harder than it ever had.

He really hadn't thought this through. He wasn't prepared.

"I need to ask you a question!"

"What question?"

Then he had an idea. "Will you go hiking with me?"

"Hiking?" Her shoulders sank, and the shoulders of all their onlookers did, too. This was clearly a disappointment to everybody. But not to Grant. He had a plan, and he needed to do this right.

"Yeah! Hiking."

Her eyebrows rose, making her look extra adorable in her cute knit hat. She stared at his head.

"You're wearing my hat."

"I know, and I love it! And…" He drew in a deep breath and released it. "I love you, Nell Delaney. More than a million rainbows!"

The crowd collectively sighed.

All eyes turned on Nell.

She bit her bottom lip and blushed.

"I love you, too," she finally said.

"Then don't get on that plane."

Nell broke into a grin, and people started clapping. Their cheers escalated as she raced toward him. The security guards stepped back and unhooked the rope, and Nell ran past it like a sprinter reaching the finish line. She dropped her rolling bag handle and leaped into Grant's arms.

He caught her, his heart full to exploding.
"I thought I'd almost lost you."
"You'll never lose me again."
Then, to his joy, she kissed him.
And the airport roared with delight.

CHAPTER TWENTY-FIVE

Nell turned to Grant when he pulled his SUV into a parking spot near the White Pines Overlook. "I had a feeling we might come here," she said with a sassy lilt. She covered her mouth in a yawn. "I just didn't think we'd come so early." A purple curtain hugged the earth, and it was not yet daybreak.

He chuckled, then said warmly, "The sunrise will be worth it."

She smiled at his handsome face. "Yeah. Can't wait to see. It will be a first for me."

"Watching a sunrise?"

"Watching one from up here." Her cheeks warmed. "With you." She glanced around at the darkened parking area, noting it was empty. "Doesn't look like we'll have much company."

He kissed the back of her hand and grinned. "No."

They both wore jackets and their knitted hats. It pleased Nell to no end that Grant loved his birthday present so much. It pleased her even more than he loved her. His arrival at the airport on Thursday had been so unexpected and amazing, and every day since had been like a dream.

They'd waited until today, Monday, for their hike, since Bearberry Brews was closed. In between Thursday and now, they'd spent tons of quality time together doing couple-y things, like going for a romantic dinner at Mariner's, where they'd both had lamb stew. Nell's parents had invited Grant and the whole family over for dinner, and her dad had fixed him shepherd's pie. Everyone loved Grant, and her sisters were overwhelmed with tears and happiness when Nell told them about his airport confession.

She'd cooked for Grant at her cottage, too, and they'd spent most of the weekend laughing and cuddling, and playing lots and lots of Scrabble. Grant absolutely kissed like a waterfall, and she adored kissing him and receiving his kisses. She probably couldn't be any happier, because she'd found her true love.

Nell had texted Aidan Thursday morning, and he'd been surprisingly cool about the change in plans. She told him she'd fallen in love, and he'd offered what had sounded like his sincere congratulations. So maybe Aidan Strong wasn't such a terrible person after all. Her parents and sisters had all been super supportive. None of them were upset with Nell for changing her mind. All the opposite—they claimed to be extra glad that she had.

Grant stepped from his SUV, and she exited the vehicle, too, zipping up her jacket. It was a little windy today, but this time she'd dressed much better for their hike. Grant had helped her pick out an ensemble from his store in her favorite color: green.

"Don't forget the rope!" she teased lightly.

He popped open his hatchback and winked. "On it. Although it's mostly for emergencies."

"Let's hope we don't have another one of those."

Grant settled his headlamp around his hat and switched it on. "We won't."

His headlamp cast bright light ahead of them,

illuminating the path. But dawn was breaking, so it was gradually growing lighter anyway.

Grant slipped on his daypack and slung his coiled rope over his shoulder. "Ready to get started?" His dark eyes sparkled, and Nell's heart skipped a happy beat.

He held out his hand, and she took it. "Yep."

"Great." He pulled her toward him and kissed her on the lips, and she tingled all over.

Then he firmly held her hand and they headed up the path together, with shadows weaving through the trees.

As they walked, they chatted about things. TV shows, movies, local events coming up. Different things they wanted to do together. One of those was camping. Grant joked that since she was so great at it, maybe she should put up the tent, but she countered that she'd definitely want his help with that.

She smiled, thinking of her and Grant camping out together, which could be romantic in that tent. "I did kind of like those LED lights."

"Oh yeah?"

"Yeah. I thought they had romantic possibilities." She wiggled her eyebrows at him, and he chortled.

"Domestic goddess and Greek god possibilities, you mean?"

She blushed, wishing she hadn't told him about her silly fantasies. Then again, maybe it was okay that she had. They were in love now, after all. "Well yeah. Like maybe kissing under the fake stars."

He kissed the back of her hand. "You're making me really like that tent."

She laughed.

They arrived at the summit before she knew it, and Grant paused behind her. "You going to need help going up?" She glanced at the rope and then at the sky, which was slowly opening up in orange and violet hues. In another short bit, the sun would start peeking over the ocean.

Her knees shook a little, and then she told herself she could do this.

"No, no. I'll be fine going up! It's just the coming down part that might be a little tricky."

"No worries. I'll help with that." He patted the rope. "We've got this if we need it."

He stayed beneath her to spot her as she made the short climb, and she arrived at her destination in no time. She grinned down at him, and he scrambled up to the top next.

Grant wrapped his arms around her waist from behind her as they gazed out at the spectacular view. They could see the ocean from here over the fall-colored treetops that were beginning to glisten red and gold in the blooming light. The scenery was breathtaking.

"It's beautiful," she said.

"Yeah."

He offered her some water from his daypack, and they both had a drink.

"Want a snack?"

Now that he'd mentioned it, she was a tiny bit hungry. "What have you got?"

"Trail mix."

That usually had chocolate in it, but she didn't want to be rude by picking the chocolate out. "Um. No thanks."

He grinned. "I also brought a blueberry scone."

Her heart fluttered. "You didn't?"

He dug a small container out of his pack and snapped it open. "For you."

She kissed his cheek. "You, Grant Williams, are the very best boyfriend any woman could have."

"Yeah, well. I don't want just any woman to have me," he teased.

Nell chuckled and contentedly nibbled on her treat as they both sat on a large rock.

He munched on his trail mix. "Any second now," he said, pointing toward the ocean. And then she saw it. The very top crescent of the rising sun, casting its magnificent glow across the water. Nell caught her breath. "It's so beautiful," she said. "We'll have to do this again."

"Look at you!" he ribbed. "Becoming such a nature girl."

She nudged him. "I'm learning."

"Yes, you are." His eyes twinkled. "Very well, too."

He reached into his daypack for something else, concealing it in his hands.

"Nell?"

"Yeah?"

"I wanted to ask you something."

"Okay." She glanced back at the sun, which had risen farther and now appeared to be halfway out of the sea. With the shimmering autumn leaves and rocky mountain slopes between them, the sight was knock-your-socks-off spectacular. Then she turned toward Grant, and an even more gorgeous sunrise was written in his eyes.

He gazed at her with wonder, hope, and adoration.

"I want you to know I ran this by your parents first. Charlotte and Misty, too. Oh. And Lucas. And Mei-Lin."

Nell's pulse stuttered, and then she saw what he had in his hand. It was a ring box. He opened it, exposing the most amazingly beautiful solitaire. Its diamond sparkled in the waxing sunlight.

Shock and joy shot through her.

"I never knew I could fall for a woman as hard as I have for you." He smiled softly. "But I did, and I never want to lose this feeling. I want us together forever, Nell, and not just as boyfriend and girlfriend, but as a whole lot more. So we can love each other, support each other, find rainbows together, and beat the daylights out of each other in Scrabble—"

Nell gasped, her hands covering her mouth and her heart brimming over.

"Nature girl," he said. "Will you be my bride?"

She grinned so big her cheeks hurt. "You know I will."

He chuckled with relief and desire. "Good." He placed the gorgeous ring on her finger, and it fit just right, thanks to tips, she supposed, he'd gotten from her sisters.

"So this is it, huh?" she asked giddily, wrapping her arms around his neck. "We're engaged? For real?"

"This is it." His warm voice rumbled. "For the rest of our days." He studied her adoringly. "There's just one little thing."

"Oh yeah? What's that?"

"In order to make things official, we might need to announce this in the *Seaside Daily*."

Nell chuckled, her spirit so light. "I'll get that done." She pulled him closer, preparing to give him the biggest, baddest kiss any domestic goddess could deliver. "This is the best outdoor adventure *ever*."

"Yeah." His eyes danced. "I'd say so, too."

They stole another peek at the ocean, where the sun had risen fully above the choppy white-tipped waves. Its glow filled the grenadine sky, and seagulls soared across the horizon.

Nell's whole heart became flooded with sunshine. She sighed. "I love you, Grant," she said, staring into his eyes.

His dark gaze glimmered. "I love you, too."

Then he kissed her on that mountaintop and swept her away.

EPILOGUE

Nell brought Grant some hot tea as he sat at the piano holding three-year old Lanie on his lap. He guided her chubby little fingers in the best rendition of "Chopsticks" Nell had ever heard. Grant grinned over his shoulder. "I think she's going to be our next maestro."

Nell set his tea mug on a coaster. "Great idea about bringing this piano to the cabin."

"Yeah." He laughed. "That way the neighbors won't complain."

"Ha-ha," she teased. "The neighbors are nothing but a bunch of old cranberries."

Nell hadn't known that Grant could play until he'd sat down at the piano in her cottage. He'd stunned her with a jaunty arrangement of the "Wedding March" the evening after he'd proposed. She'd asked him what else he could play, and she'd been amazed to learn almost everything. He was gifted enough to play by ear, a skill he'd apparently inherited from his mom.

He finished the piece with Lanie and shouted, "Yay!"

He clapped her baby hands together, and she copied him. "Yay!" She turned her sweet freckled face to Nell with a big smile.

"Excellent!" Nell clapped her hands. "Encore!"

Grant positioned them to play another song, then started "Mary Had a Little Lamb" with a ragtime beat. The cabin door burst open and eight-year-old Alexander rushed inside. With his blond hair and dark eyes, he was all Grant, only pint-sized.

"Mom! Dad! Come quick!"

Alexander had been outside gathering rocks for their gratitude garden. Nell and Grant had started one in the backyard of the cabin. They'd painted rocks honoring things they were grateful for, like special places, things, and people they loved, including all of Nell's family. Alexander had begun painting his own rocks, too. Lanie would get her chance when she was a little older.

Grant and Nell exchanged startled glances.

Had he found a snake or something dangerous?

Nell shot toward the door, and Grant followed, carrying Lanie.

"This way!" Alexander's expression was urgent as he coaxed them down the hill.

"Alexander," Nell said. "What is it? Where are we going?"

"You'll see." He gave her an excited grin, and then Nell knew she had nothing to fear. Whatever it was, it wasn't dangerous. Maybe he'd found something by the stream. A special rock or a burst of four-leaf clovers? As they moved along, Nell could hear the sound of the cascades growing louder and louder.

"Slow down, little buddy!" Grant called, traipsing after them.

Lanie giggled in his arms, enjoying the jiggly ride. "Giddyup, horsey!"

Alexander reached the clearing and pointed to the sky.

Nell clasped her hands to her heart.

A spectacular rainbow arched through the air high above the crest of the falls.

Red. Orange. Yellow. Green. Blue. Indigo. Violet.

Nell caught her breath. "Alexander, it's beautiful."

"Yout-if-ful," gurgled Lanie, and the others chuckled.

Nell's heart fluttered, and happiness blanketed her soul.

Grant held her hand. "Do you remember?"

She stared lovingly in his eyes. "I'll never forget." This had been the best ten years of her life, and they were only going to get better. She'd found her one true love, and together they'd built a wonderful home and family.

Alexander tugged at her free hand and glanced at the rainbow.

"Mom, Mom! Can I paint it?"

"For our gratitude garden?" Grant asked, clearly pleased with the idea.

Alexander nodded, and Nell and Grant grinned at each other.

She thumbed Alexander's nose. "Absolutely."

Lanie laid her head on her Daddy's shoulder, and Nell held Alexander's hand.

Then they all stared up at the heavens, knowing all was right with the world.

ACKNOWLEDGMENTS

I have many people to thank for bringing this book to fruition, chief among them my loving family. My husband, John; my children and stepchildren, Sally, Kelly, Kaitlin, Gordon, Karen, and Andrew; and my kids' partners, Tom, Zach, and Brian, have been steadfast in their encouragement of my work in being an author, cheering on new endeavors and patiently understanding the demands of looming deadlines. I can't thank them enough for their support.

A special shout-out to my son, Gordon, this go-round for his generous feedback on the camping, hiking, and wilderness first responder aspects in this plot. It's so great to have a world-class outdoor adventurer on my team! Also, huge hugs to my girls, Sally, Kelly, and Kaitlin, for showing me how fiercely loyal and bonded three sisters can be.

In crafting a story about sisters, I additionally benefited from having grown up with three sisters of my own, and thank Carmen, Ana María, and Victoria for their loving support, as well as the many happy memories.

I'd also like to thank my agent, Jill Marsal, for her unwavering faith in my abilities. Without her belief in me and kind endorsement, I never would have contracted this three-book series, which has been such a joy to write.

I owe a sincere debt of gratitude to my publisher, Liz Pelletier, for coming up with the concept for this trilogy and for her show of confidence in me as a writer for getting the job done. Liz has been an amazing publisher who continues to impress me with her ingenuity and professionalism in heading up Entangled Publishing in a forward-thinking way, working ever harder to improve opportunities for her authors. I am honored and humbled to be among them!

Thanks go out as well to my incredible editor, Heather Howland, for always pushing me further to deliver the very best stories, and to my entire team at Entangled, without whom you wouldn't be reading this book. To Heather Riccio, my Author Liaison, for cheerfully staying on top of publication and promotional efforts, while unfailingly keeping me posted. To Curtis Svehlak for tirelessly working as Production Editor in pulling everything together. To Riki Cleveland for her publicity acumen, and to Bree Archer for the fabulous cover! Associate Publisher Jessica Turner, Managing Editor Meredith Johnson, Editorial Director Stacy Abrams, and Royalty Director Katie Clapsadl have my eternal appreciation for their invaluable contributions as well.

Last but not least, I'd like to acknowledge the countless readers, bloggers, and reviewers who've picked up and enjoyed *First Bride to Fall*. I can't thank you enough for sharing this journey with the three Delaney sisters and me, and, in this book in particular, with my heroine Nell and hero Grant. You are the force that compels me each day to sit down at my computer and write. I treasure your loyalty and am so very grateful when you share your enthusiasm for my stories with others. Every happy ending I write is for you!

Warmly,
Ginny

The chance of a lifetime requires a leap of faith and… and only one dollar in this new contemporary romance.

it takes a
VILLA

USA TODAY BESTSELLING AUTHOR
KILBY BLADES

For the reasonable price of $1, Natalie Malone just bought herself an abandoned villa on the Amalfi Coast. With a detailed spreadsheet and an ancient key, she's arrived in Italy ready to renovate—and only six months to do it. Which seemed reasonable until architect Pictro Indelicato began critically watching her every move…

From the sweeping ocean views to the scent of the lemon trees, there's nothing Pietro loves more than his hometown. And after seeing too many botched jobs and garish design choices, he's done watching from the sidelines. As far as he's concerned, Natalie should quit before the project drains her entire bank account *and* her ridiculously sunny optimism.

With Natalie determined to move forward, the gorgeous architect reluctantly agrees to pitch in, giving her a real chance to succeed. But when the fine print on Natalie's contract is brought to light, she might have no choice but to leave her dream, and Pietro, behind.

Falling in love wasn't part of the fake marriage ruse in this new small-town romantic comedy.

accidentally PERFECT

MARISSA CLARKE

Workaholic Lillian Mahoney has given *everything* to her job. The hugely popular lifestyle show she helped create monopolizes her time, energy, creativity, and anything remotely resembling a life. But all it takes is the show's womanizing, egomaniac star throwing a massive hissy on live TV to utterly implode Lillian's career in a New York minute.

Now Lillian's hiding out in the gorgeous and completely unknown seaside village of Blink, Maine. Out of gas. A stolen wallet. A broken heel. And worse, she's somehow managed to completely piss off the town's resident hunk, Caleb Wright. She'll show that hot, grumpy single father *exactly* what she's made of.

But Blink isn't quite what Lillian expects—and neither is Caleb...or his feisty teen daughter she can't help but love. And while her entire life and career are in shreds, Lillian might just discover what happens when she gives her bad first impression a second chance...

From the bestselling author of the Angel Falls series, two enemies say "I do" in the first irresistible book about Blossom Glen.

the
SWEETHEART DEAL

MIRANDA LIASSON

Pastry chef Tessa Montgomery knows what everyone in the teeny town of Blossom Glen says about her. *Spinster. Ice Queen. Such a shame.* It's enough to make a woman bake her troubles away, dreaming of Parisian delicacies while she makes bread at her mother's struggling boulangerie. That is until Tessa's mortal enemy—deliciously handsome (if arrogant) chef Leo Castorini, who owns the restaurant next door—proposes a business plan...to get married.

Leo knows that the Castorinis and the Montgomerys hate each other, but a marriage might just force these stubborn families to work together and blend their businesses for success. The deal is simple: Tessa and Leo marry, live together for six months, and then go their separate ways. Easy peasy.

It's a sweetheart deal where everyone gets what they want—until feelings between the faux newlyweds start seriously complicating the mix. Have they discovered the perfect recipe for success...or is disaster on the way?

Sometimes the perfect arrangement can lead to something more, even when you least expect it.

CONSTANCE GILLAM

Rashida Howard has never been a one-night-stand kind of woman, but she has good reason for making an exception with Elliott after meeting him in a bar. Cliché? Yes. Utterly amazing? Absolutely. Regrets? None.

Elliott Quinn is a workaholic. The one night he decides to break his routine, he has an encounter with the woman of his dreams. But no matter how amazing they are together, work will always come first.

Both of their lives get turned upside down when they find themselves on opposite sides of an ongoing fight between Elliott's company and Rashida's community. Though their chemistry is undeniable, neither of them will risk their integrity…or their heart.

And just when they think they might have found a solution that benefits both sides, they uncover a secret that will change everything.

USA Today *bestselling author Ophelia London brings a sweet, heartfelt, and surprisingly funny take to the popular Amish romance canon.*

NEVER
an
AMISH
BRIDE

Everything changed for Esther Miller with the death of her beloved fiancé, Jacob. Even years later, she still struggles with her faith and purpose in the small, tight-knit Amish village of Honey Brook—especially now that her younger sister is getting married. All she wants is to trust in the Lord to help her find peace...but peace is the last thing she gets when Lucas, Jacob's wayward older brother, returns to town.

Lucas Brenneman has been harboring a secret for years—the real reason he never returned from Rumspringa and the truth behind his brother Jacob's death. Honey Brook still calls to him, but he knows his occupation as a physician's assistant must take precedence. With sweet and beautiful Esther he finds a comfort he's never known, and he feels like anything is possible...even forgiveness. But she was Jacob's bride-to-be first. And if she knew the truth, would she ever truly open her heart to him?

AMARA

an imprint of Entangled Publishing LLC